Quick Study

Maggie Barbieri

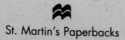
St. Martin's Paperbacks

For information address St. Martin's Press, 175 Fifth Avenue, New York, NY 10010.

Library of Congress Catalog Card Number: 2008028961

EAN: 978-0-312-37676-5

Printed in the United States of America

St. Martin's Press hardcover edition / December 2008
St. Martin's Paperbacks edition / November 2009

St. Martin's Paperbacks are published by St. Martin's Press, 175 Fifth Avenue, New York, NY 10010.

10 9 8 7 6 5 4 3 2 1

To Anna: Every day I give thanks for your big, giant brain and even bigger heart.

Acknowledgments

To Deborah Schneider—thank you for convincing me that ending the book "…and then they all died" wasn't really a crowd-pleaser.

To Cathy Gleason—thank you for your business sense and your ability to do math (which I appreciate around royalty-statement time, particularly). You're a left-brainer, I'm a right-brainer, yet we still manage to laugh at each other's jokes.

To Kelley Ragland—thank you, as always, for your wise counsel. And for convincing me that *The Da Vinci Code* wasn't an appropriate title for this book, despite my protestations to the contrary.

To Matt Martz—thank you for everything you do to help the publishing process go so smoothly for me and everyone else who is lucky to have you in their corner.

To my posse at NYU—Kathy, Juliet, Norma, Rosie, and Joanne—thank you for the laughter, the tears, and everything in between. You've seen it all—and it ain't pretty.

To Mom, Tricia, Dea Classic, Colleen, Alison, and Annie—thank you for the early reads on the manuscript and for laughing in all the right places.

To Jim, Dea, and Patrick—thank you for allowing me to lapse into temporary fugue states, for grinning and bearing successive servings of chicken nuggets and French fries for two solid weeks before manuscript submission, and for being my biggest fans. I am a lucky girl.

One

"I don't know who you are, but I love you!"

The voice was deep, rough, and heavily inflected with the accent of one of the outer boroughs, and it belonged to the guy sitting in back of me at Madison Square Garden, home of the New York Rangers, my favorite professional hockey team. And the comment, which had been directed at me, was all the more interesting because I was sitting beside my best friend, Max, who had slipped her one-hundred-pound frame into a slinky size-two black cocktail dress, her cleavage prominently and proudly displayed for all to see. She's tiny but she's got a great rack. It's a veritable "rack of ages." Nobody, and I mean nobody, had ever noticed me when Max was around. And we had twenty years of friendship to draw on proving this point.

I was not in a cocktail dress, having opted instead to wear my new Mark Messier jersey (he was number eleven and the sole reason for the Rangers' Stanley Cup win in 1994, thank you very much), a pair of jeans that I had purchased in the last millennium, and sneakers that had seen their fair share of painting projects. My hair was pulled back into a ponytail, I had a smear of ketchup on my cheek and now, after jumping up to take umbrage at a call, a glass of beer soaking my chest. I don't even like beer, but when in Rome . . . you know the rest. But apparently, when I yelled, "Shit, ref, you're killing us! That's a bullshit call!" after a bogus hooking penalty, I had forever pledged my troth to Bruno Spaghetti, as Max had dubbed him when we arrived, seat 4, row D, section 402.

He ran his hands through his spiky black hair and grabbed me in an embrace, his silver hoop earring brushing my cheek. Max, who had been standing for the better part of the last period and who thus had incurred the wrath of everyone behind her—many of whom had missed said bogus penalty because their only view was the back of her well-coiffed head—fell back into her seat, her cocktail dress riding up on her yoga-toned thighs. But Bruno didn't notice; he only had eyes for me. See, we were sitting way up high in Rangerland, a place that used to be called "the blue seats," in which only the hardest-core hockey fans sat. Now they're teal, which doesn't lend them the same menacing air. A gorgeous woman in a slinky black dress with spectacular boobs had nothing on a five-foot-ten college professor with a pot belly and beer breath who loved hockey and who could curse with the best of them.

It was my birthday and my boyfriend had given me the

jersey and the tickets. Crawford—Bobby to the rest of the world—is a detective in the New York City Police Department and was working overtime that night, hence my birthday date was Max. Crawford had stopped by school on his lunch break to wish me a happy birthday, appearing in my office doorway at around one; I was preparing for my next class, a two o'clock literature seminar, and was delighted to be distracted from the critical essay on *Finnegan's Wake* that was putting me to sleep. I'm a Joyce scholar, but even I recognize that obscure is not the same thing as exciting, and that makes my relationship with the subject of my doctoral dissertation tenuous at best. I love a challenge, though, and had spent the better part of my academic career trying to figure out if Joyce was laughing *with* us or *at* us. I was slowly coming to the conclusion that it was the latter.

I could tell that Crawford was excited by the items in the gift bag he was holding behind his back. He leaned over and gave me a peck on the cheek; although he is a seasoned detective and an all-around good guy, he gets really nervous around the nuns I work with at St. Thomas University, my employer. Whenever he visits me at school, he looks like he's on his way to detention, even though I'm sure he never did anything more scandalous than pass a note in class. He took the bag from behind his back and set it on my desk, settling himself into one of the chairs across from me, a self-satisfied smile on his handsome, Irish face.

I love the guy, but there's one thing that bugs me: every time he gives me an item of clothing, it's always extra-large. I'm extra-tall but not extra-fat, so this concerns me. Is this how he sees me? Or does he think women should wear tentlike clothing? I still haven't figured it out. I held his gift aloft and spread my arms wide to examine it, full width: a Messier jersey. Despite the size, I couldn't have asked for a better present.

"Crawford, I love it!" I said and came from around the desk. I kicked my office door closed so I could give him a proper thank-you, sitting on his lap and putting my arms around his neck. "Now the best present you could give me would be your undivided attention tonight," I said hopefully, although I guessed this wouldn't be the case.

He shook his head sadly. "I can't. I pulled an extra shift so I could go to Meaghan's basketball playoff Monday night." Meaghan is one of his twin daughters; she was banking on a basketball scholarship to get her through college. I had come to realize that basketball was like a religion in that family; what teenage girl would count former New York Knick Bill Bradley among her crushes if it wasn't? He reached into his jacket pocket and pulled out an envelope. "Here. These are for you, too."

The tickets were the icing on the cake, but I was extremely disappointed that another Friday night would go by and I wouldn't see him. A little slap and tickle in my office just wasn't cutting it anymore. The relationship, and Crawford himself, were everything I wanted but not in the amount that I had hoped for. I tried to be the good and understanding girlfriend, but I felt like Crawford's wife was the NYPD and I was the jealous mistress. And, in fact, for a very short while, I had been kind of a real mistress: unbeknownst to me, Crawford had been married when I first met him. But that's all in the past; she's almost married to husband number two and Crawford and I are still going strong, so things couldn't have worked out better for all concerned.

I had two choices for alterna-dates: my best friend, Max, or my other best friend, Father Kevin McManus. I called McManus first, but he had a Lenten reconciliation service to perform and penance to dispense, so he was out. He reminded me that I had a couple of sins to confess myself—premarital sex being the worst and most oft-committed of the lot—but I hung up before he could recount all of them in detail. I went to Plan B and invited Max. She arrived at the Garden right before the puck dropped, breathless and a little tipsy from a cocktail party that she had attended for a new show that her cable network was launching. She tottered toward me in four-inch heels and the aforementioned cocktail dress and I immediately got a sinking feeling. Max is not what you would call a responsible drinker. She holds her liquor less effectively than a dinghy with a hole in its bottom, which has resulted in more than one late-night, four-hour phone call to discuss the merits of kitten heels versus stilettos. I thought we might be in trouble. Once I got a whiff of her champagne-tinged breath, I was fairly confident.

Bruno Spaghetti noticed me the minute we arrived and commented on my Messier jersey. He was wearing a Steve Larmer jersey, a testament to his hockey knowledge and devotion. No Johnny-come-lately Jaromír Jágr jersey for him; he was a Ranger aficionado and wore a jersey that harkened back to the good old days when the Rangers actually made the playoffs and even won a few games. "Lady, you can curse with the best of them!" he yelled, grabbing me in another embrace.

He hadn't heard anything yet. And I was fairly certain I wasn't a lady. Dating a cop had increased my cursing lexicon tenfold. Although Crawford was a gentleman and didn't curse at all in my presence, two trips to police precincts had expanded my horizons. I broke my embrace with Bruno Spaghetti and sat back down, signaling the beer vendor; he ignored me. I considered asking Max to flash some leg so I could get some service.

The Garden erupted as the Rangers scored their first goal, despite the fact that one of their players was in the penalty box. I was excited but afraid of what kind of display of love this might elicit from Bruno, so I did the old excuse-me-pardon-me into the aisle.

"Bring me back a box of Sno-Caps," Max called after me, taking her cell phone from her very expensive purse. Max is a newlywed and calls her husband every twenty minutes or so. Her husband is also Crawford's partner, so I knew these periodic phone calls had become mildly annoying—at least to Crawford. Fred Wyatt, Max's husband, still appeared to be completely smitten with her, even indulging in baby talk when she called. He's about eight feet tall and a thousand pounds and looks like a serial killer, so the visual eluded me, but Crawford assured me that it was chilling.

"They don't have Sno-Caps out there," I said. I had been to the Garden enough times to know what resided in the candy displays. Row D turned its collective hostile gaze toward me.

Max considered this. "How about Jujubees?"

"I don't think they even make Jujubees anymore." I strained to get a look at what was happening on the ice.

Max stood, thinking on her feet. "OK, how about Milk Duds?" At that moment, the Rangers scored another goal.

"Lady, if you don't sit down, I am gonna shove a pretzel up your ass!" Bruno Spaghetti had brought a pal—Max had named him Shamus McBeerbong—and he wasn't quite as enamored with us as Bruno was.

"Max, sit down," I cautioned her. "I'll surprise you."

She clapped her hands together. "I love surprises!"

Shamus McBeerbong sighed. "Bring her back something that keeps her in her seat," he said to me, and then to her, "Sit down, you stupid broad!" The rest of row D nodded in agreement, despite seeming a little aghast at his choice of language.

Max turned to Shamus and gave him the hairy eyeball. "*You* sit down!" she said, at a loss for a truly snappy retort. For effect, she adjusted her breasts defiantly.

"Max, sit down," I called again, waiting to see if the section would turn on her. She sat, just in time for everyone to see a melee erupt on the ice.

Once it was clear Max wouldn't be eaten alive by rabid Ranger fans, I went out to search for her Milk Duds and to get myself another beer. I'm not the biggest beer drinker in the world, but they don't serve chardonnay or vodka martinis at the Garden, and what's a Ranger game without a little booze? The Garden is a giant labyrinth comprised of long, tiled hallways that wrap around the seating area. I wended my way down one hallway toward the snack bar and was deep into a decision regarding Gummi bears versus Gummi snakes for Max when I felt a tap on my shoulder and turned to find Jack McManus.

Jack McManus is the director of marketing for the Rangers and Kevin McManus's brother. He is also a man with whom I had played tonsil hockey not too many months before. At the time, Crawford and I had been on a "break" and I had stuck my little toe briefly into the dating pool. Don't think I hadn't been completely guilt-ridden about that ever since. But confessing about cheating on your then-married boyfriend with your priest's brother to your priest, who is also one of your best friends, is complicated. Jack is gorgeous and single; inexplicably, he was interested in me for a time. My face immediately went red when I saw him and I smoothed my hair back, pulling my ponytail tighter to my head, a gesture that wasn't going to improve my appearance any but it was worth a try.

"Jack!" I gave him a quick, loose embrace, memories of going to second base with him flooding my mind. "How are you?"

"I'm great," he said, flashing me a winning smile. "Kevin told me that you were here tonight and that you didn't have great seats, so I wanted to find you so that I could move you down."

Move me down. Three little words that, at the Garden, held so much import. Three little words that meant the difference between high-fiving Bruno Spaghetti and going out for an after-game cocktail with Ryan O'Stockbroker. I would have to tell Max, Bruno, and Shamus that we were leaving the upper tier. I had sat in Jack's seats before and they were practically on the ice. They were so close to the Rangers that once I had almost become part of a line change. I stammered a thank-you and told him to stay put while I gathered Max and the rest of our belongings. As I turned to go back to our seats, I spied Max walking gingerly toward me, trying desperately not to slip on the polished hallway floors.

"There she is now!" I said.

Jack took one look at Max and burst out laughing. "I thought Max would be a middle-aged bald guy."

"That happens a lot," I said. Max arrived at my side. "Jack, Max Rayfield. Max, meet Jack."

"You weren't kidding," Max said under her breath. "But he's way better than a poor man's George Clooney," my words coming back to haunt me. "He's the real deal. Real Clooney. *Ocean's 11* Clooney. Nephew of Rosemary Clooney. Clooney to the white courtesy phone. . . ."

Fortunately, the roar of the crowd and the acoustics of the hallway masked her commentary; Jack was none the wiser.

Max shook Jack's hand. I noticed my coat hanging over her arm. "We're leaving," she said. "Shamus wants to make me Mrs. McBeerbong."

I explained to her that we weren't leaving and that Jack wanted to move us to fifth row, center ice.

"Can you get a decent martini down there?" Max asked, her maiden voyage to the Garden not fulfilling her original expectations. Maybe I had lied a bit and said that you could get a good martini, and maybe I had told her our seats were better than they were. And maybe I had fudged the truth a bit by telling her that more than one woman would be in a cocktail dress. Now that we were moving down to the expensive seats, that part might actually be true, since most of the people who sat there were either corporate types or models trying to marry Rangers.

Jack assured her that he would get her a martini as soon as we were seated. He can do things like that. He took the coats from her arm and led us to the escalators, where we made the journey to the hundred-dollar seats and the land of chilled vodka, never-ending vendor service, and hockey players so close you could touch them. Which I made a mental note not to do.

We settled into our seats just as the first period ended. Jack took our drink and food orders but stayed rooted in the aisle next to our seats, watching the Rangers skate off the ice. I noticed him give a little wave to someone and the lights went down in the rink.

The Rangers' announcer came on the public address system just as a giant spotlight found me in my fifth-row seat. "Ladies and gentlemen! Please join the New York Rangers organization in wishing our number-one fan, Alison Bergeron, a happy birthday!"

Max turned to me, her eyes wide. The fans let out a giant roar, followed by thunderous applause.

I shielded my eyes, a motion I could see depicted on the Jumbotron that hung over center ice. I looked like a deer caught in the headlights—one with dried ketchup on her right cheek. I looked at Jack, stricken. He had a huge smile on his poor-man's-Clooney face as he leaned over to give me a hug.

The announcer continued over the deafening din. "And now, welcome our own John Amarante!"

John Amarante was the Rangers' longtime anthem singer. He appeared on the ice, as he usually does before games, but instead of singing the anthem, he broke out into a rousing rendition of "Happy Birthday."

Here's the thing: if the entire fan base at Madison Square Garden began singing to Max, she would have been thrilled. Not only that, she would have almost expected it, given her fabulousness. Me? I wanted to melt into the sticky, beer-stained floor. I had been in those seats once before, been viewed by every Ranger fan in the tristate area on my first date with Jack, and had borne the brunt of Crawford's ire for longer than I cared to recall. I prayed that the first period's highlights were being discussed and that my giant, petrified face wasn't being broadcast for all of New York to see. And that Crawford was out on the hunt for some kind of homicidal maniac whose antics would keep him busy for the next decade.

Max read my mind. "You better hope this isn't on TV," she said, fluffing her hair and, at the same time, exposing just enough of her spectacular breasts in case it was.

Jack bent down and pulled a bag out from under my chair. A microphone appeared in his hand and when Amarante stopped singing and the fans quieted down, he prepared to make some kind of presentation. He put the mic in front of his mouth. His lips were moving, but I had conveniently gone deaf, just hearing the voice inside my head telling me, "You are so screwed." When he saw that I had gone into some kind of fugue state, he opened the package and unfurled its contents.

It was a Mark Messier jersey, identical to the one I was wearing.

Except it was autographed by Mark Messier. To me. With love.

Max looked at me disdainfully. "You are so screwed."

Two

It took me a minute to realize that the knocking was at the door and not on my forehead.

A piece of advice? Never have two giant Madison Square Garden beers with a martini chaser. It's not a smart thing to do, and I consider myself a fairly smart individual.

I opened one sleep-encrusted eye and saw that the clock read eight-thirty. Trixie, my faithful companion (of the canine variety), was standing next to the bed, looking at me with a mournful expression on her face. That could only mean one thing: I would have to tread carefully until I discovered why she looked so mournful. Something told me that it would be wet and smell really, really bad.

The knocking continued, a polite but steady tap at the front door. I rolled out of bed and put on a fluffy terry cloth robe, one that would hide the fact that I had slept in nothing but underpants and the beautiful Messier jersey. I sincerely hoped that the knocking wasn't being perpetrated by Crawford, who would see that I had slept with Mark's signature close to my heart. That wouldn't make him happy.

I was midway down the stairs when it dawned on me who was at the door: I had hired someone to paint my dining room and he was due to start today. Thank God I had remembered to clean everything out of the room earlier in the week. When I threw open the door, the sunlight streamed into the hallway and hit me in the face. The painter looked as alarmed as I did hungover.

"Miss Bergeron? Am I too early?" he asked, two paintbrushes in one hand and a roller in the other.

I threw the door open wide. "No, Hernan. Come in." I stepped aside. "And please, call me Alison."

Hernan entered, another man at his side, carrying paint cans filled with primer. "This is my nephew, Jose. My sister's boy. I think you have met before?"

Yes, we'd met. Jose regarded me warily, just as you would someone who had sixty hours of community service to perform, which is where he, and Hernan, for that matter, knew me from—my community service job at the local soup kitchen. That's basically what you get when you have a run-in with state troopers, but I guarantee you, it was a giant misunderstanding. Yes, I was following my neighbor, who turned out to be a murderer; yes, I had flouted Crawford's advice and taken off in my own car down the Major Deegan Expressway in a speeding car chase in the rain after aforementioned murderer; and yes, I had ignored the state trooper's warning to exit the car slowly, carefully, and without reaching for my cell phone. The judge had been kind: serve sixty hours of community service and the whole affair would be expunged from my record. My permanent record. The one they warn you about in Catholic school. I found the easiest, most complementary-to-my-skill-set job that I could: serving dinner at a church in a town a bit north of my house to anyone who wanted to attend. I had met Hernan, his wife, Alba, his daughter, Amalia, and a host of other family members, including Jose, during my time there. After several weeks, I had found that you generally don't attend a free dinner week after week unless you really need to.

I don't know how word had gotten out that I was the community service server, but Jose seemed to know my story. He smiled hesitantly and stepped into the hallway with his uncle.

"The paint is in the dining room," I said, walking through the living room and into my small dining room. "It's from the Benjamin Moore Serenity Collection. It's called Tumbled Marble," I babbled, finally realizing that Hernan didn't care and Jose didn't seem to understand a whole lot of English. "It was either that or Morning Dawn. I finally settled on Tumbled Marble." I motioned to the two unopened paint cans on the floor when I saw that they couldn't give a rat's behind about how I had chosen the color. "And there they are. Did you bring drop cloths?"

Hernan put his hands on his hips and looked around the emptied room. "I have some in the car," he said. "This shouldn't take us too long. We'll get started right away." He turned to Jose and said something in Spanish that made Jose scurry from the dining room and out the front door.

"I can't thank you enough, Hernan. I've been putting this off for months. I'm really glad that you mentioned your business."

Hernan knelt in front of the paint cans and pulled a screwdriver from the pocket of his white painter's pants. "Jose and I do this on the side. During the week, I drive a cab." He mentioned a company I had never heard of and asked me if I knew it.

I shook my head. I didn't venture up to his town often—mostly just to serve dinner at the church and drive through on my way to points north—and I had no need for a cab, having my own car. "Does Jose work for them, too?"

"No," he said. He kept his eyes on the paint cans. "He does some construction work." Trixie wandered into the room and sniffed Hernan's shoes. He tensed slightly and I assured him that Trixie was a nice dog and that she wouldn't hurt him. I hoped she wouldn't prove me wrong and decide to take a hunk out of his leg.

"Does he work for a local company?" I asked. I knew that the Escalantes, by and large, were in the country illegally and I wondered how Jose could get work. I knew that a bunch of men gathered on some designated corners in the town every morning and performed odd jobs for homeowners and were often picked up by contractors looking for cheap labor. I suspected Jose fell into that category.

"Here and there," Hernan said. He fell silent and I realized that I had pushed the conversation as far as it would go.

"Coffee?" I asked as I went into the adjoining kitchen.

"No, thank you," he called after me.

I decided to make a full twelve cups in case he changed his mind and went about setting up the coffeepot. With the way my head was pounding, I considered drinking the whole twelve cups myself. When the drip finally stopped after what seemed like hours, I took the milk from the refrigerator and poured a generous helping in, turning the black coffee a lovely cocoa shade not too far from the color Hernan would be putting on the walls in the dining room.

Jose came back in through the front door and Trixie ran to meet him. He dropped the drop cloths and the extra paintbrushes in his hands and fell to his knees, allowing Trixie to lick his face. He was a young guy with a chubby baby face. Hernan had told me when I hired them that Jose was twenty-six, but he didn't look older than eighteen. Trixie liked him very much, but then again, she likes anyone who shows her any positive attention, so I wanted to tell him not to be too impressed by her display of affection. Trixie is a dog slut. She'll go to whomever she feels will show her the most affection and love. He rolled around on the floor with her for a few minutes until Hernan called him back to the dining room, and the painting commenced.

I asked Jose if he would like a coffee. Unlike his uncle, who was all about painting, Jose accepted a cup, laden with sugar and milk. He took a sip and smiled at me.

"You have a beautiful house," he said.

"*Gracias*," I said. I saw Hernan give him a look.

Jose took my thank-you to mean that I spoke Spanish, which I don't. He said something about my house that escaped my limited understanding. Hernan handed Jose a paintbrush and when his back was turned, Jose shot me a look followed by a smile that said *my uncle is all about work*. I took my cue and went back into the kitchen, where I mainlined coffee until I couldn't tolerate any more caffeine. I went upstairs to take a shower and get ready for the day.

I tried to enjoy the shower and not think about Crawford and his possible reaction to my birthday at the Garden the night before. Had he seen it? Had someone told him about it? I was obsessed with the whole situation and spent the entire shower going over the events of the night in my head. There was no use worrying about something that I had no control over, but that philosophy is more difficult to embody than one would think. By the time I had dried off, dressed, and pulled on my clogs, I was in a state of mild hysteria. I went back downstairs to forage in the refrigerator for the food that would comfort me enough to make me forget about thirty thousand people celebrating my birthday. Live. And televised.

When I got back downstairs, I was surprised to find that the first coat of paint was already on the walls and Jose and Hernan were standing and admiring their work.

Jose gave me a big smile and threw his arms out wide. "Whaddya think?" he asked.

I put my hands on my hips and looked at the biggest wall. "I like it," I said. "Great job." I went into the kitchen and pulled down another coffee cup. "Come on in here, Hernan, and have a cup of coffee. You have to wait for the first coat to dry anyway."

Hernan appeared to be deciding whether this idea was a good one. He finally relented and followed Jose, who was ready for another cup. I motioned toward the table. "Please, sit down." I rustled around in the refrigerator and cupboards and finally came up with some Oreos and prepackaged coffee cakes, which I unwrapped and put on a plate. Jose dug in and ate with gusto, while Hernan eyed the plate. "Come on, Hernan. It's not much, but coffee cake and Oreos go good with coffee," I said, putting an entire Oreo in my mouth.

He took a coffee cake reluctantly. "My daughter is bringing us lunch," he said by way of explanation.

I didn't know about him but I could eat an entire box of coffee cake and still have lunch, but I decided I didn't know him well enough to say, "What's your point?" I sat down at the table with my coffee, Trixie coming to my side, knowing that I was a messy eater and that her lunch was a few hours off.

"I like the color you picked," Hernan said in between bites of coffee cake and sips of coffee.

"Thanks. I'm hoping that it makes me serene."

He looked at me quizzically.

"The Serenity Collection? Make me serene?" I said and then, seeing that I wasn't getting anywhere, dropped it.

"It's very warm," he said.

I got up and opened the back door to let in some air.

"The color," he elaborated. "The color is very warm." He looked up at the ceiling, clearly uncomfortable with me and the situation. I decided to put him out of his misery and excuse myself.

"If you need me, I'll be in the office upstairs," I said, closing the back door. Jose smiled at me and finished off another coffee cake while Hernan just nodded. I headed up to my spare bedroom and settled in at my desk, a stack of essays waiting for me next to the computer. Before I started, I sent Max an e-mail. *"How are you feeling today?"*

Max's BlackBerry never leaves her side and her response was almost instantaneous. *"Great. You in trouble?"*

"I don't know."

"Bet you are."

"Thanks for the vote of confidence," I wrote back, deciding that she wasn't helping. I started in on the essays, getting through about half of them before I heard the doorbell ringing. I looked at the clock and realized that I had been working for close to three hours. The rumbling of my stomach indicated that it was time for another food break.

I live alone and have for over a year. So to have two sets of visitors on one Saturday—even if I had paid one set to come over and paint—was out of the ordinary. I hustled downstairs, hoping that it was Crawford, and hoping that it wasn't. I opened the door and found Amalia, Hernan's daughter, standing there, a grocery bag in her hand. "Hi, Mrs. Bergeron," she said. Amalia and I are very friendly, having chatted quite a bit during my stints at the Lord's Bounty, but I hadn't been able to convince her to call me by my first name.

I opened the door. "Come on in, Amalia." We exchanged a hug.

She bent down to pet Trixie. "This is Trixie?" Trixie's pretty famous around these parts.

"Yep."

Jose came out of the dining room and smiled at Amalia. "Lunch?" he asked.

The two of them bantered back and forth, more like brother and sister than cousins, supporting my theory that Jose was younger than Hernan let on. Amalia went into the kitchen and put the bag on the table. "Daddy, time to eat."

I had grown very fond of Amalia since I had started at the Lord's Bounty; she was a bright, funny girl who went to one of the local high schools and who had confided in me that she wanted to be a nurse. I kept that piece of information in the back of my brain because St. Thomas had one of the best nursing programs in the area. She always looked for me when she arrived so that she could bring me up to speed on what she had done the week before. I was following her soccer career with interest.

At the last dinner, she had told me that she wanted to meet Crawford to make sure he was "good enough" for me. If she only knew—at this point, Crawford was getting the raw end of the deal.

Something occurred to me. "How did you get here?" I asked her as I pulled sandwiches, salads, and drinks out of the bag.

She looked at me, surprised. "I drove."

"You what?" I asked.

"Drove." She made a motion like she was turning a steering wheel. "A car? Daddy and Jose came in Jose's car and I have my dad's cab," she said, making a face.

"Oh, god, I feel old, Amalia. I knew you were seventeen but it never occurred to me that you could drive around Westchester by yourself." I got some glasses from the cupboard and filled them with ice from the freezer. "Go look at the dining room and tell me what you think of that color."

She poked her head into the room, where her father was working on the window trim. "Oh, it's beautiful," she said. "Very soothing."

"That's what I was going for!" I said, delighted that someone finally got it. I pulled out a kitchen chair. "Are you staying?"

She shook her head, her long black hair swinging back and forth. "No. I have to go to work. I work at the Wendy's on Route 9 in Ossining." She crumpled up the bag that the food came in and asked me where the garbage can was.

I held out my hand. "Here. Give it to me." I pulled out the garbage drawer and pushed it down on top of the overflowing garbage. I listened while she, her father, and her cousin exchanged some words in Spanish. I couldn't catch what was being said, but it sounded like Jose wanted to leave with Amalia and Hernan wasn't happy about it. I tried to busy myself so it didn't appear that I was eavesdropping. Which I was.

Most of the words were unfamiliar but I heard "work," "lazy," and "trouble," which in combination didn't sound very promising for Jose. He bantered back and forth with Hernan, who grew increasingly agitated. The smile never left Jose's face, which I think made Hernan even angrier. Amalia looked nervously at both of them; she wasn't a stranger to this kind of discussion, that was clear. Finally, seeing that I was still in the kitchen and making every effort not to listen, Hernan stopped talking and, in Spanish, told Jose to do what he wanted. That much I understood.

Jose got his jacket out of the dining room and buttoned it up, ignoring Hernan's disdainful look. He reached in the pocket of the jacket and took out a small dictionary, which he handed to Amalia. "Here."

She gave him a disappointed smile. "Finally. I thought you only needed it for a day. It's been a week, Jose, and I needed that for my paper."

He smiled and shrugged, obviously used to getting by on his broad smile and not insignificant charm. Indeed, Amalia didn't seem all that upset as they chatted while walking to the front door.

"Will I see you both tonight?" I asked as I opened the front door for them.

Jose nodded enthusiastically while Amalia responded. "We'll both be there. What about you?"

"Oh, yes," I said. Without going into any details, I said, "You'll be seeing me for a long time." Which, I had decided, would be true regardless of how many community service hours I had left.

Amalia reached out and gave me a quick hug. "See you later."

I watched them go down the walk. "Thanks, Jose!" I called after him. He looked over his shoulder and gave me a big smile, and I was struck again by how young he looked.

Three

Nobody follows the rules better than I do.

So, a little more detail on my conviction and my community service hours. How did I end up at the Lord's Bounty? Well, it all stemmed from that run-in with those New York State Troopers in the fall. My lawyer, Jimmy Crawford, brother of my former boyfriend Detective Crawford—and yes, I'm jumping to conclusions—managed to get me out of my situation with a promise that I would be nice to animals, not speed or stalk my neighbors (long story), and generally be a good citizen. I thought

I could do all that and still be helpful to others, which is why I chose a program called the Lord's Bounty that was run out of a local church and whose participants served a Saturday night meal to the needy denizens of a town not far from me. It was perfect. It only took about two hours, it was close to my house, and I would be serving the meal rather than actually cooking it, which was a good thing for everyone concerned.

When I spoke to the guy who ran the program on the phone to sign up, he assured me that he was a volunteer firefighter, so even if I did help cook and burned the church down, he could get every company in a five-town radius to respond.

Funny.

So I can't cook. And apparently, I don't do laundry, either. Because when I opened my drawers to find something appropriate to wear to dole out chili or lasagna to the guests, all I could come up with was a lovely T-shirt that Max had given me that had a map of Idaho and the following witticism printed on it: IDAHO? NO, YOU DA HO. I pulled it on, covering it with a hoodie from my college I found buried in the back of my closet; no one would be the wiser.

The day had passed and I hadn't spoken to Crawford yet; I was getting concerned. His work schedule is crazy but he always calls, even if it is just to find out what I had for lunch. I had offered up several Hail Marys and a few Our Fathers that he hadn't watched the Rangers game. I was still in shock over hearing the entire Garden sing "Happy Birthday" to me and in awe of the Mark Messier jersey. On eBay those things go for a lot of money. Not that I would ever sell it. That jersey was staying in my possession for as long as I lived.

While Hernan finished up the trim downstairs, I went back up to my office and wrote Jack a thank-you note that expressed my gratitude for his thoughtfulness. I guess if Crawford did see the game and decided that I had betrayed him in a terrible fashion, I could always use Jack as my "rebound man," as Max likes to refer to guys you go to when your heart's been broken. I didn't want a rebound man. I wanted Crawford. But Jack had really shown him up, what with the autographed jersey and the Garden sing-a-long. If I were Crawford, I'd be really pissed off. I hoped that Crawford, being Irish American, didn't have the jealous, passionate, crazy streak of my French Canadian fore-fathers.

Hernan had left around two, which was perfect timing be-cause I had to leave a bit after three to get to the Lord's Bounty on time. He had cleaned up the dining room; all I had to do was vacuum the bits of dried paint that had fallen from the drop cloth after he had picked it up while trying desperately not to make a mess. He had offered to help me move the furni-ture back but I assured him that I would get Crawford to help me. I didn't go into my hope that I still had a Crawford, and Hernan left, content that my big, giant boyfriend would come to the rescue.

I had several Saturdays of community service under my belt and found that I was enjoying the work. The people who came to the meal were nice, for the most part, and I had actually grown close to a couple of them: Mrs. Dwyer, who was blind and came with her guide dog, Patty; Joey, a recent "guest of the state" who was the de facto leader of a table of ex-cons and who made sure everyone said grace before the meal and thank you before they left; and, of course, the extended Escalante family.

I grabbed my keys and gave the dog a kiss good-bye. "Don't eat any shoes while I'm gone, Trixie." I thought all my shoes were up too high for her to get to, but I always liked to give her a warning. I hadn't had her too long and I still had to remind myself to put things out of her grasp, so it was entirely possible that there was a pump or mule within chewing distance. She's a gorgeous dog and a wonderful companion, but she's sneaky. Fortunately, so am I. When I found a brown suede boot buried in my backyard, I knew she was a worthy adversary.

I drove down the driveway and pulled up in front of my neighbor's house. Once Jane had heard that I was doing good deeds for the community, she decided that it would be a good thing to have her teenage son Frankie join me. I wasn't sure he agreed, but he came along just like a dutiful son should. He was my go-to dog walker and adored Trixie, but he always regarded me warily. After all, what kind of kid wants to hang around a woman who's not his mom, much less do community service with her? I would have regarded me warily, too. I honked my horn and sang along to the radio as I waited for him to lope down the front walk.

He got into the car, his white-blond hair wet and slicked back. "Hi, Mrs. Bergerson."

Not my name, or my marital status, but I have given up. "Hi, Frankie." In my head and to Crawford, I refer to him as Accordion Boy, or AB for short, based on his kick-ass accordion playing, but I always use his name in his presence. His brother plays the bagpipes—that's Bagpipe Kid to you—so they are a veritable one-family Irish band. "I read in the paper that you had three three-pointers in last night's game," I said, in an effort to bond. In addition to playing the accordion, he also played something more mundane—basketball—for his all-boys' Catholic high school. Since I had met him, I had started following his career.

My high-five hand hung in the air, and I reluctantly dropped it after a few seconds.

He mumbled something that sounded like "mush only thin five thirty" and moved closer to the passenger's side door in what appeared to be an effort to get away from me. OK, I've got it. No talking.

I sang along with an old Duran Duran song on the radio. "*And I'm hungry like the wolf*," I sang, looking at Frankie out of the corner of my eye. See, I'm hip! I wanted to tell him, but I refrained. The kid was doing time with me and nothing was going to cheer him up.

He brightened momentarily. "Hey, I saw you on TV last night."

"Oh, that."

He readjusted his long legs. "It was your birthday, huh?" He paused for such a long time that I thought the conversation was officially over. No such luck. "Do they do that for everyone who turns fifty?"

Fifty? I smiled. I guess, to him, fifty was a conservative estimate. "I'm not fifty. And I have a friend who works for the Rangers."

Even in the dark, I could see the flush rise up from his collar to his hairline. "Sorry."

Fortunately the ride north to the Lord's Bounty didn't take very long and we were at the church in about fifteen minutes. It was freezing outside. I wondered how many people would venture out on such a cold night; never having allowed myself to feel a pang of true hunger, I couldn't put myself in their shoes.

Frankie and I went in through the kitchen door and were hit with the delicious smell of pot roast. I would have walked over hot coals to get to that pot roast, never mind make a trek in bitter cold weather. My mouth started to water and I had to remind myself that I had leftover Chinese food at home for my dinner. We said hello to my favorite cooking team: Kerry, a marathon-running mother of three and optometrist, and Rebecca, mother of two and a preschool teacher. These two made me look like a giant schlub; I had just me, my job, and my dog to deal with, yet I couldn't seem to organize a thought, never mind a meal for fifty people. I flashed on the IDAHO? T-shirt under my hoodie; neither Kerry nor Rebecca would be caught dead in it. They had brought two of their combined five children with them, teenage girls who were a few years younger than Frankie. The girls were slicing bread and putting butter on plates to set on the tables in the dining room.

"You remember Frankie?" I said, pulling an apron on over my head. Frankie had attended one other Saturday service with me, and Kerry and Rebecca had been cooking that night, too.

Frankie mumbled a greeting and shoved his hands deep into his pockets. The girls gave him a sideways glance and the giggling commenced, making him flee the kitchen. I called after him to make sure the tables were set and that each place had a plate, fork, and knife.

"Hey! I saw you on TV last night!" Kerry said, chopping up iceberg lettuce for the salad.

Doesn't anyone read anymore? Play board games? The NHL is always talking about declining ratings but, judging from my instant celebrity, it had nothing to fear.

I made chitchat with Kerry and Rebecca and waited for the guests to arrive. They started streaming in right before five o'clock, the cold not keeping the majority of our usuals away. I saw Mrs. Dwyer and Patty take their usual seats at the front of the hall; Joey and five of his cohorts from the halfway house; and finally, around five fifteen, Hernan and Alba, with Amalia and a couple of other people in tow. I noticed Frankie, usually not one to display any kind of energy off the basketball court, make a beeline for their table. Nothing like a good shot of hormones to put the kid into action. When he delivered their sodas he actually smiled, and I saw that he had two nice, straight rows of teeth. (I had begun to have my doubts that he had any teeth at all because he never opened his mouth wide enough for me to see them.)

The church hall was cavernous, with a peaked, beamed ceiling, wood wainscoting, and stained glass windows. Six tables that sat eight guests each were set up and covered with plastic tablecloths. A longer table at the front of the hall held sodas, water, and a big bowl of ice. A few steps led up to a room that was sectioned off by pocket doors, behind which were an array of desserts made by the older parishioners of the church in the next town up, which sponsored the dinner.

I said hello to Mrs. Dwyer and Patty, asking Mrs. Dwyer if she had enough food to last her the week. She had confided in me a few weeks earlier that her monthly checks weren't covering her grocery bill and she had started running out of food for herself at the end of the month. Patty, she assured me, always got enough food; she was Mrs. Dwyer's priority.

"Oh, Alison, thank you for asking. If you have an extra loaf of bread in the back, I'll take it. I just started running low," she said. Patty, who looked like Trixie's twin, gazed up at me, and I gave her one of the treats that I'd stashed in my pocket for my dog. I told Mrs. Dwyer that I would pack a bag of food for her from the pantry and that Frankie and I would drive her home. I knew that she walked to and from the church and while it wasn't a long walk, it was all uphill on the way home.

Joey got my attention as I walked by his table. "Hey, the guys and I saw you on television last night," he said, motioning to his dinner companions. Tiny, the ironically named hulking ex-convict to Joey's right, stared at his salad plate while a small smile played on his lips. Guess he had seen the game, too.

"Really?" I said. Why was I surprised? These guys had a curfew of six o'clock, so they watched every televised sporting event there was; with no women or other nighttime pursuits allowed them there wasn't much else to do.

"Yeah, I thought you looked pretty." He looked down at the table, a little embarrassed by that admission. "You still dating the cop?"

I hope so, I thought. "Yep."

"What did he think of you being on TV?"

He's used to it, I thought again, but kept it to myself. "Oh, he thought it was funny." Not. I decided to throw an extra Hail Mary onto my nightly prayer schedule to compensate for lying. I changed the subject and filled the table in on the menu for the night. "And chocolate pudding for dessert!" I said, with extra enthusiasm to make sure that we were off the topic of the Rangers game for good.

Joey and his crew broke out into applause. "We love chocolate pudding!" he exclaimed, high-fiving Tiny. I was a little perplexed by their enthusiasm for chocolate pudding, but, never having been denied life's simple pleasures behind bars for any length of time, I had nothing to compare their reaction to.

Frankie and I began serving the meals. By the time we had finished, there were thirty people in the room enjoying Rebecca's pot roast and mashed potatoes. Frankie lingered for a few minutes at the Escalantes' table, chatting with Amalia. Their family had been joined by another Ecuadorian family that I knew only slightly—a young woman, two young children, and an older woman. I moseyed over and sat down alongside Alba and Hernan. Hernan was still sporting some flecks of Tumbled Marble in his dark hair and a streak across one hand. He stood when I came over.

"Hi, Hernan, Alba," I said in greeting. I reached across the table and touched Amalia's shoulder. "My dining room looks great. Thanks for coming over today," I said.

"You're welcome," he said.

I looked at the other guests at the table. "Where's Jose?" I asked. '

Hernan looked down at his plate, most of his pot roast untouched. "I don't know," he said quietly.

I looked at Amalia, but she gave nothing away. She shrugged

slightly and averted her eyes, eventually going back to her conversation with Frankie.

I thought back to the conversation that had gone on in my house between Hernan and Jose, but not knowing much Spanish I had had no idea what had really been said. I sat for a few more minutes, and when it was clear that we had nothing else to say to one another, I moved on to the front of the room to spend a little more time with Mrs. Dwyer and Patty.

A few minutes later, I gave Frankie the high sign that we needed to start clearing the dishes. He was still hovering around the Escalantes' table, uninterested in cleaning up after the dinner. I stopped by Joey's table and announced the start of dessert. Rather than a joyous chorus singing the praises of chocolate pudding, the guys all got up abruptly and headed for the door.

"Gotta go," Joey said, pulling on his camouflage winter jacket.

"Wait!" I called after them. "We have tons of chocolate pudding!" I cried, but one by one, they gave me a wave and practically ran to the front door, which closed with a loud thud that reverberated throughout the hall as Junior, the last to leave, made his hasty exit.

I heard someone mutter "*policía*" and the scraping of chairs as they were pushed back from the tables. *Policía?* That was a new one at the Lord's Bounty.

I stood, facing the door, my hands on my hips, confused. "Wait," I called out weakly one last time and then turned back to their table to clean up the Styrofoam dinner dishes that they had left. I wondered what had happened to make them leave en masse without even saying good-bye.

It didn't take long for me to figure it out. As I collected their dirty dishes, I spied a tall, thin shape by the stairs that led to the dessert room out of the corner of my eye. It was Crawford. He was standing with his hands in his pockets, regarding me while I cleaned up. He was still in his work attire: blazer, white shirt, striped tie, and black trousers. And, of course, a huge gun sat in his shoulder holster. Even though I couldn't see it, the bulge near his blazer pocket made it clear. He had probably worked a twelve-hour shift, but the only indication of that were the bags under his eyes and the stubble that lined his jaw. He was as clean and pressed as he had been that morning. You could take the boy out of Catholic school but you couldn't take Catholic school out of the boy.

I straightened up and walked toward him, flashing what I hoped was my most dazzling smile. He remained stone-faced.

"Those your friends from Sing Sing?" he asked, motioning toward the front door. The room had gotten very quiet and even his normally low voice sounded loud and out of place in the large room.

"They don't live in Sing Sing anymore. It's a *halfway house*," I said, enunciating broadly to make sure he understood. I grabbed his arm. "Want to help me serve dessert?" I frog-marched him out of the dining hall and toward the back room. I passed Kerry on the way out of the dining room; she gave me a raised eyebrow and Crawford the once-over.

We got into the back room and Crawford looked over the desserts after pawing at me for a few minutes behind the refrigerator in the dessert room. I pushed him away. "This is a church, you know." I smoothed down my hoodie. "Want to see something?"

He was entranced by the desserts on the table. "Chocolate pudding and brownies? You guys really throw a great party."

I unzipped my hoodie and flashed him.

He did a classic double-take and broke out into a smile. "What did that say?"

"You read it right," I said, and grabbed a stack of plates.

"You da ho?" He laughed. "Where the heck did you get that?"

I raised an eyebrow. "Take a guess."

"Kevin?"

"Try again."

"Sister Mary?" He shoved a brownie into his mouth. "That has 'nun' written all over it."

I shook my head. "She only thinks I'm a ho. She would never come out and say it."

"The lovely Mrs. Rayfield-Wyatt?"

I nodded.

"She's quite the gift giver." He looked over the other desserts. "What else you got?"

"You should have been here for the pot roast. You missed it." I smacked him playfully on the shoulder. "Way to clear a room, Crawford." I tried to balance a couple of plates of dessert on my arm. "To what do I owe this honor?"

"I thought we'd have dinner when you're done here."

I considered that, and him. See, although he's the poor man's Clooney, Jack McManus has nothing on Crawford. Crawford is also classically handsome—tall, dark, and handsome, to be exact—but with just enough of that war-weary cop thing that I'm a sucker for. This is a guy who's seen some action, and not in some boardroom. That comes across, but not enough to make him as scary or unapproachable as say . . . Fred. I thought about his dinner offer. It seemed innocuous enough and I wondered if we would even dare to tread on the subject of the Rangers game. "OK," I said slowly, "but I have to drive Mrs. Dwyer home. You can take Frankie home and I'll meet you back at the house."

"Who?"

"Mrs. Dwyer. The blind lady with the dog."

He shook his head. "No. Frankie. Who's that?"

"Accordion Boy."

"Oh," he said, "I didn't know he had a name. Tell him to meet me by the front door."

I saw him eyeing the brownies again. "You can have one

more brownie. There aren't that many guests left after you scared them all off."

He grinned sheepishly; maybe I was off the hook. "Sorry about that." He picked up a brownie and took a bite, moaning a little when he tasted it. "You didn't make these," he stated. "They're good."

"That's not really fair, is it, Crawford?" I asked. The tension had kicked up a notch and I suspected that we were going to discuss *l'affaire Rangers* as soon as we got home.

He shrugged slightly. "We can talk about what's fair later." He took another bite of brownie and smiled. "And make sure you're wearing that shirt."

OK, so maybe he just came for the brownies, I thought, starting for the dining hall, the brownies and pudding on a tray. There were hardly any guests left, and those who were still there seemed anxious to leave. The Escalantes and the other people at their table had gone, which I thought was odd, because I hadn't had a chance to say good-bye to them. I bagged up some of the brownies and containers of pudding and handed them out as people left the room. I reminded Mrs. Dwyer that I would drive her home as soon as I cleaned up and went back to the kitchen to grab a couple of sponges.

Frankie was reclining against the counter, chatting with one of Kerry's daughters, who was elbow deep in hot, soapy water; the pot she was washing was almost as big as she was. She was fully engaged in her conversation with the boy, and, judging from the way she was regarding him, I suspected that eau de laconic teenager was her aphrodisiac, and Frankie had that in spades. I told Frankie that Bobby would drive him home.

"Who?" he asked.

A proper introduction was obviously in order but I didn't have time. "Mr. Bergerson."

Recognition dawned slowly on his face, and by the grimace

that replaced it, a vision of the previous fall and Crawford wrestling with our former neighbor on the grass behind my house—an event he had witnessed—came to his mind. "Oh, OK," he stammered.

No need to fear, I wanted to remind him. He's one of the good guys. I tousled his blond locks. "I'll see you during the week. Get going. He's by the front door."

Rebecca was wiping down the stove with a dish rag of questionable cleanliness. "You take off, too, Alison. The girls and I will break down. They need additional service hours for school so it would help if they did the cleanup."

"Thanks, Rebecca. I'll take Mrs. Dwyer and Patty home." I stripped off my apron and hung it on the back of the kitchen door, grabbing a loaf of bread and some canned peaches from the cupboard before heading out to the dining hall. They were both waiting for me at the table and I helped Mrs. Dwyer up and out the back door to the back parking lot.

"Alison, this is so nice of you," Mrs. Dwyer said as I settled her into the front seat of my car and strapped her in. Patty jumped into the backseat as if it was something she did every day. I opened the trunk, stowed the bag of food that I had assembled, and slammed it shut.

I turned and was startled to see Hernan standing behind me. My hand flew to my throat. "Oh, you scared me."

He held his hand out in a conciliatory gesture. "I'm so sorry," he said, shuffling from one foot to the other.

We stood in the dark, silent, each clearly waiting for the other to speak. Finally, I asked him if he needed a ride.

He shook his head. Still at a loss for words, he hemmed and hawed until he blurted out, "I need your help."

Four

By the time I arrived home, I was no closer to figuring out how to get Crawford's help with Hernan's situation than I had been when I left the Trinity Church parking lot.

Hernan's silence at dinner had been a function of his intense worry about Jose. The last time anyone had seen him was when Jose had left my house. He and Hernan had had another painting job that they were going to bid on that afternoon; Hernan had gone to the house to meet the potential client, but Jose had never shown up. Calls to his cell phone had gone unanswered, something that Hernan swore was the most telling indication that something was wrong: Jose had two cell phones on him at all times and could always be reached.

Two cell phones sounded suspicious to me, but I kept it to myself. The only reason you would carry two cell phones is if one was for personal use and one for business use. But Jose didn't seem to have a business.

Hernan was sick with worry by the time Jose didn't show up for the dinner. But the appearance of Crawford, whom Amalia had told Hernan was a cop, had convinced him that I could help him. I wasn't sure about that, but I figured I would give it a try. I was still chewing on the whole situation as I drove home.

It turned out not to matter how I was going to figure it out. When I got home, although I had been prepared to zig, Crawford had already zagged. He and Trixie were nowhere to be found, so I assumed they were off for a walk. Crawford had left the kitchen table set with forks, knives, plates, and wineglasses and had arranged several takeout containers of my favorite Chinese food in the center, right between two unlit candles. A chilled chardonnay, my favorite, stood in a ceramic holder next to a bouquet of flowers that he had put in a vase.

I had two theories: either he had seen the game and I wasn't in trouble, or he hadn't seen the game.

I went upstairs to wash the stench of thirty served and discarded meals off me and to change into something a little less comfortable, like my best push-up bra. Nothing's sexier than my almost Bs shoved into an underwire bra under a tight T-shirt. I discarded the Idaho shirt with a kick to the laundry basket in front of my closet. Although I had been at a loss for finding suitable community service wear prior to leaving the house, I did find a nice shirt (without any witty bon mots) that did my newly compressed breasts justice, revealing just enough décolletage to make me seem alluring. Or so I told myself. Let's face it—I wear contrite well, and I hoped that would help. I looked out the window of my bedroom to see if Crawford and Trixie were walking along the street, but it was dead out there. They had taken off for parts unknown and that was fine by me. I took a birdbath in the bathroom sink and tried to spruce up, knowing that I had some explaining to do.

I came downstairs a half hour later in the aforementioned push-up bra just as Crawford was returning with Trixie, who looked liked the most contented dog ever, having gone on a long walk.

"We met some new squirrels," Crawford said, hanging her leash on the hook by the back door. "That always makes her happy."

I bent down and paid proper homage to Trixie, who wouldn't allow me to eat my dinner in peace unless I had done so. When I was done, I paid proper homage to Crawford by planting a long, lingering kiss on his mouth. "I missed you."

He kissed me back. "I missed you, too." He took off his coat and his blazer and loosened his tie. He left on his shoulder holster, his gun attaining its usual third-wheel status.

"Going back to work?" I asked as I opened one after another container of Chinese food.

He shook his head. "Not if I can help it."

"Bad night?"

His face closed, a common occurrence when he doesn't want to think about work. "I don't want to talk about it."

I continued serving the food, sitting down across from him when I was done. He had poured me a healthy glass of wine, of which I took a giant sip. "This is delicious."

He held his glass up and tipped it gently against mine. "Happy birthday," he said quietly. "I love you."

This was certainly a change of pace. My last birthday had

been spent with Max, who, on the way to dinner, had had a very loud argument with a cab driver from Sierra Leone about the implications of reality television; the one before that had ended with my finding a pair of women's thong underpants attached to my foot when I turned over in bed. Suffice it to say, they weren't mine. And that little discovery had been the catalyst for my throwing my ex-husband—God rest his soul—out on his ass. Happy birthday to me! I looked at Crawford to see if I could detect any hostility below the surface but he looked calm, even happy. I decided to leave well enough alone.

He was using chopsticks to stab at a fried dumpling, staring at it for a while before popping it into his mouth. "How was the game?"

The jig was up. I looked down at my General Tso's chicken and considered what I would lead with. My engagement to Bruno Spaghetti? The bench-clearing fight in the second period? Max's inappropriate cocktail dress and spectacular boobs? I decided to throw the whole story at him; Father Kevin doesn't call me the Great Confessor for nothing. "I saw Jack McManus and he moved us down to the seats on center ice and the whole Garden sang "Happy Birthday" and I got a signed Mark Messier jersey." It was out of my mouth before I had a chance to really think the whole thing through. I stuck a piece of chicken in my mouth to avoid talking anymore.

Crawford studied another dumpling. "Really?" Before putting the dumpling in his mouth, he asked, "Did you have fun?"

If you call being besieged by stomach cramps and a cold sweat for most of the second and third periods, accompanied by the drunkest woman this side of the Hudson "fun," then yes, it was a laugh riot. "It was OK," I said weakly.

"Did you meet Mark Messier?"

I shook my head. "No. He only signed my shirt."

He sat back in his chair, tipping it back on its legs. He looked at me for a few moments. "What are you going to do with my shirt?"

"Wear it! Every chance I get! I may even wear it to school!" I said with an overabundance of gratitude and enthusiasm. I thought about what I might wear with an oversize hockey jersey but couldn't come up with anything.

He let his chair drop to the floor again and resumed his dumpling eating. "I'm sorry I couldn't go with you. Once Meaghan's basketball playoffs are over, things will get back to normal."

Normal for us wasn't like normal for other people but I let it drop. If we were returning to one night a week to be together he could take normal and shove it. I was getting depressed by how little we saw each other but since we were moving past the Ranger game, I figured now was not a good time to bring it up.

"You do know that everyone in the tristate area saw the game, right?" he said, laughing.

I let out a sigh of relief. "If one more person mentions it to me, I think I'll scream." I ate a dumpling. "And by the way, Frankie thinks I'm fifty."

"You didn't look a day over twelve on television."

"I'll take that as a compliment?" I said, not sure whether or not he was sincere.

"I had a flashback to you in braces and a Catholic school uniform. That's how terrified you looked," he said.

"I never had braces," I protested. But he had me on the uniform. I had worn one of those for twelve straight years, with no time off for good behavior.

We finished all of the Chinese food and I set about throwing out all the empty containers. I started on the dishes.

"Leave that stuff," he said, coming up behind me and wrapping his arms around me. His shoulder holster jabbed me in the hip.

"Can you get rid of that thing?" I asked, turning off the water in the sink.

We disengaged and he removed it, putting it on the counter. I pointed at his ankle. "And that one." He took off his small ankle revolver and put it next to the big gun in the holster. I told him to turn around. "And the handcuffs."

"I need those," he said, a smile starting on his lips.

"Trust me. You don't," I said, unclipping them myself and adding them to the weaponry on the counter. He put his arms around me and gave me a long kiss. "Let's go upstairs," I whispered.

He kissed me again. "You smell like pot roast."

"You're a little fragrant yourself," I said, taking his hand. "Where you been, Crawford? In a dank cellar?"

"Close," he said as we started up the stairs. "Down by the river." I started to ask him about it, but he put my hand over my mouth. "Don't." He started peeling off his clothes and leaving them behind as we got closer to my bedroom. By the time we got there, his shirt and undershirt were off and his pants were open.

I sat on the bed and took off my socks. "Well, I don't know what you were expecting, but I'm a little tired," I joked, waving my hand in the direction of his open pants.

"My ass, you're a little tired. I love a woman who smells like pot roast and I won't be denied," he said, coming over and pushing me back on the bed. He covered me with his long body and kissed me deeply. "And mashed potatoes." He stuck his nose into my hair. "And garlic." He pulled off my shirt. "Oh, and the push-up bra. My favorite. You're bringing out the heavy artillery."

I had to, I thought. I never thought that we would move past the Rangers game so quickly. The bra was agony and I was relieved when it finally came off. He reached around and put his hands under my ass.

"Are you wearing a thong, too?" he said, coming up for air and regarding me suspiciously.

"No. Just experiencing your garden-variety wedgie," I said, and discarded the offending underpants.

"You really pulled out all the stops," he said.

I flipped him over and lay on top of him. "Take your pants off and shut up."

A half hour later, he was close to sleep beside me and I was in control of the remote. I flipped around, deciding the right time to broach the subject of Hernan Escalante's missing nephew.

A snore escaped from his lips and I kissed him until he woke up. "I can't," he protested, half asleep. "Not enough time. I'm too old."

I bit my lip. "It's not that, Crawford. I have to talk to you about something. Something serious."

That got his attention. He bolted upright. "What?" He looked at me, wide awake.

I rarely talk about anything serious if I can help it, so the fact that I did now, coupled with my serious mien, had him a little worked up. It occurred to me that he might think it had something to do with me so I started talking.

I told him what Hernan had told me: Jose, who had been in my dining room that very morning, was a day laborer who had been going to the Bronx every day to work construction at the riverside site of a new luxury condominium complex. Although he had been due back home by one to go to the other painting job and then by five to go to the Lord's Bounty with the rest of the family, he had not returned, nor was he returning the messages that Hernan had left on his two cell phones.

Given the Escalantes' illegal status, they were hesitant to go to the police. Amalia knew about Crawford and knew that he was a cop; it was her idea to have her father ask me to get Crawford's help on the case, even though he was reluctant to involve the police in any way. "I told her that the chances were slim that you would be able to do anything because . . ."

He cut me off. "I'm pretty sure I know what happened to him."

If you've been missing, and Crawford knows what happened to you, it can't be good.

Five

"My vagina is not a filing cabinet!"

That got my attention. I was loading my dishwasher while talking to Max on the phone and had only been half listening until the subject had turned to the female genitalia and office supplies. My mind was on the wet, dead body of Jose Tomasso, who had been found the afternoon before by a fisherman who had been casting his line into the Hudson. He had been beaten, murdered, and left on the banks of the river, his body half in and half out of the water. Although he had had no identification on him when he had been found, Crawford knew almost immediately from my description that my missing Jose and his John Doe were one and the same.

It was Sunday morning and Crawford had just left, beating a hasty getaway so that he could get to Connecticut in time to see Meaghan's quarter-final game. He had called into the squad, told them what I had told him about Jose Tomasso, and made arrangements for the detectives on duty to go to the Escalantes' home in Ossining to find someone who could identify the body. When I thought about Hernan and his concern for his nephew, a lump grew in my throat.

"And my uterus does not function as a honing device!"

"It's *homing* device, Max. H-o-m-i-n-g," I spelled.

"Whatever!" she said, continuing with her train of thought. She was really on a tear and I had to stop and think about what we were talking about. Fred. Right. And how he doesn't know where anything is. Got it.

"Why do men think that estrogen acts as radar? Why?"

"I don't know, Max." I closed the dishwasher. "Listen, I have to talk to you about something. Did Fred mention anything about the case he and Crawford are working?"

She let out a snort. "He's been too busy looking for a fork for the last half hour. Why would he talk to me about work?"

I filled her in on the story of Jose Tomasso. "He was working on the luxury condo by Spuyten Duyvil. You know, not too far from school?"

"Yeah, I know it."

"Turns out Jose was working there as a day laborer. Can you even use illegals on a job like that?" I asked.

She snorted. "What do you think?"

I took that for a no.

She was silent for a moment. "That's weird. Why would they

use undocumented workers for that job? That's a Leon Kraecker building."

Max runs a cable television network and is accustomed to working with unions. I wasn't surprised that her first thought had been the issue of illegal workers at the job site. "It's actually a Richie Kraecker building," I said. "I did a little snooping online this morning."

She made a retching noise. "I thought we agreed never to say that name again?"

"Sorry. I just thought it was interesting that the whole job has been turned over to son of Kraecker. Wasn't he trying to make a name for himself in construction, away from daddy?"

"Yep. But for such a connected guy, he was as dumb as a box of rocks. I had my fun with him but I couldn't ever see him becoming big in construction. That's Leon's turf. I thought he was going to go back to Wall Street."

I took a glass from the cabinet and poured myself some water. "Not according to what I read. It's Richie's building and he's running the show, according to the *Wall Street Journal*."

"OK," she conceded. "But undocumented workers? I find it hard to believe that he would go that route. Leon prides himself on running a clean business and, in particular, on hiring union." She put something in her mouth before asking her next question. I hardly ever see Max eat anything, yet she's always chomping on something when we talk on the phone. "Why are you so involved in this? The guys'll figure it out."

I paused for a minute. Why *was* I so involved? I saw the Escalantes every Saturday for an hour; I liked them, talked to them, but, in all honesty, wasn't all that close to them. "I'm not sure, Max. I just feel like the police won't give it as much attention as they would if a Park Avenue society matron turned up dead."

"Don't let Crawford hear you say that," she warned. "Remember: the police, as you call them, are my husband and that big galoot you call a boyfriend. They don't discriminate."

She was right and I felt ashamed for letting my mind go there. "Right. Listen, let's have dinner this week. I'm free on Wednesday."

"I'll meet you at the Steak House at seven. How's that?"

"Sounds good." I twirled a length of phone cord around my index finger, looking out the window at the yard behind me.

I heard Fred's muffled voice in the background. "In the linen closet! That's where we keep extra rolls of toilet paper!" She exhaled loudly into the phone. "Hey, did Crawford ever mention a Melanie Moscowitz to you?"

I filed through the mountains of useless information in my brain. "No. Who's she?"

"The new Bronx ME. Fred mentioned something about her and I don't know," she said, pausing. "It just didn't sound kosher. He tried to sound casual about it. Like she just happened to turn up and he had no idea where she'd come from or that she'd been transferred. And you know how much Fred likes autopsies. They're like his favorite part of the job. So they'll be spending a lot of time together."

I didn't know why any of this mattered—Fred and Crawford worked with a bunch of different women and some of them were even attractive. It didn't bother me that Crawford worked alongside some beautiful women—was it supposed to? I smoothed my hair down and considered my belly, thinking about some of the uniformed cops in his squad; I made a mental checklist and began to compare myself to each one while Max nattered on about the Bronx ME. I felt one of my ears. Were my ears getting bigger? Was that a jowl forming on my jawline? Was I getting . . .

"Are you listening?" she asked when it was clear that I had

gone somewhere else. I snapped back to reality. "Anyway, I googled her but I got nothing. I hope she's not a knockout. What happened to the old ME? You know, that guy Fred said smelled like ass?"

"Don't know." Didn't care. Crawford and I have a don't ask, don't tell policy about his work. I couldn't have picked the old ME out of a lineup, ass smell notwithstanding. Max wasn't the jealous type; she's the type that other women get jealous of. "And what do you care if she's a knockout? It's not like they see her every day. Or that you're not a knockout in your own right."

"I know," she said. I wasn't sure which part of my statement she was agreeing to. If I knew Max, it was the knockout part. I heard Fred rumbling in the background. "I've gotta go. If Fred goes to work without wearing boxers tomorrow, Lieutenant Concannon's going to put him on desk duty."

I had no idea what she meant by that, but that wasn't unusual; a conversation with Max usually includes one or two non sequiturs. After she hung up, I stared at Trixie and tried to think about the case, although my mind kept wandering to Amazonian women in NYPD uniforms who could bust perps, shoot guns, and look gorgeous while doing so. . . .

My reverie was broken by the ringing phone. I looked at the caller ID and saw Kevin's number.

"You are in such big trouble," I said in place of a true greeting. We hadn't spoken since the Ranger game and I knew that he was responsible for Jack's involvement in my birthday celebration. Kevin's got this idea that I should date Jack and then eventually, if I knew Kevin's thought process, marry him. Although Jack is pretty handsome and I guess what you would call a "catch," I'm into Crawford big time and nothing's going to change that. I don't think.

He let out a sigh. "Well, I was calling to invite you to dinner, but if you're going to give me crap about the game, I guess you're not available."

My ears perked up. "No, I'm available for dinner, but just know that we'll have to spend a few minutes with you engaged in serious mea culpas."

"Whatever," he said, unimpressed by my anger. "Meet me at the Garden Path in an hour."

I looked at the clock. It was four o'clock.

"And before you say it," he interjected, knowing me all too well, "yes, it's the early-bird special."

I let out a derisive snort.

"You want to hang around with priests, honey, you gotta be prepared to roll like one."

So now Kevin was getting all hip-hop on me. What was the world coming to?

I was wearing jeans and a hooded sweatshirt, but the Garden Path is casual and so is Kevin, so I decided not to change. After taking Trixie for a quick walk, I grabbed my wallet and jumped in the car.

My plan was to stop by school to pick up a book that I had left on my desk and that I needed in order to work on some papers. But about ten minutes into my twenty-minute car ride I began formulating a new plan. I drove past the exit for the restaurant, which was a few blocks from St. Thomas, and continued south on the Henry Hudson Parkway. Near the southernmost part of Riverdale, I got off the parkway before I hit the bridge that would take me into Manhattan. I snaked my way through the streets until I got as close to the river as I could and hung a left onto the street where a sign greeted me: "Welcome to the home of the future! Welcome to Riviera Pointe . . . a Kraecker development."

Fancy. I always love when people Frenchify things by adding an *e*. Forevermore I would refer to this hideously appointed complex—and that was just judging by the stucco on the foundation—as Riviera *Pwant*. If they wanted French, I'd give them French.

I pulled onto a side street and parked my car, staring at the row of little houses that fronted the river, those that eventually would lose their view once Riviera Pointe was fully constructed. Houses that had stood in this location for probably close to a hundred years. Houses that sheltered old Bronx families that worked hard for their little pieces of land and space, for their panoramic views of the majestic Hudson.

These houses would drop in price once they were in the shadow of Riviera Pointe and Richie Kraecker executed his master plan of getting high rents into this working-class neighborhood, this accidental little jewel of a burg. I'm as much of a fan of free enterprise and capitalism as the next person—until it starts to affect the working class; then I turn into what Max refers to as a "leftist-commie-liberal-Sandinista."

I realized I had been sitting there staring at the houses for almost a half hour. I was in that dreamy place between fully awake and almost falling asleep so I didn't notice the man who had walked right up to my window. His knuckles connected with the tempered glass, and he rapped so hard that it sounded like the window was going to shatter.

I had slumped down in my seat, but I turned and noticed that he was banging on the glass with a giant Joliet College class ring. Class of '59. Joliet's the brother school to my school, and, yes, I had been to a party or two there during my time as a student at St. Thomas. So I was well acquainted with the design of the class rings. I turned the car on and hit the button to roll down the window. "Can I help you?"

Class of '59 was not happy and had a bit of an axe to grind. He had on horn-rimmed glasses and what looked like a letterman's jacket, replete with the Joliet blue and gold colors and white leather sleeves. Like the ring, it looked like he had owned it since the fifties. Based on the design, it appeared that he had lettered in wrestling. Seems Class of '59 also had an inferiority complex; what man approaching his seventies still wears his college letterman's jacket? "Do you live in this neighborhood?"

I tried to shake off my grogginess because this obviously wasn't a social call. What's the deal? Never seen a woman sleeping in her car before? "Uh, no."

"Well, you can't sleep in your car here."

No kidding. "I was just leaving."

He moved closer to me. "I'm serious. You can't sleep in your car here."

I saluted him, probably unwisely. "Got it, chief. No sleeping. I was just leaving."

"Do you think this is a joke?" he asked, peering in at me in the semidarkness. He was so close that the edge of his blue and gold Joliet scarf blew in and tickled my cheek.

"No." I sat up even straighter and attempted to put the car in drive. "Don't think it's a joke, don't know what your issue is, and just want to leave." I tried to put the window up but his hands were on the opening.

"Do you know how many people have come to this neighborhood because of this . . ." he sputtered a bit, trying to find the right word. He waved his hand in the direction of Riviera Pointe. ". . . monstrosity?"

"No idea. I'll be going now," I said, thinking that if he would take his other hand off the car door, I could roll up the window and leave without dismembering him.

"Hundreds. Maybe a thousand. It's a disgrace." He backed up a little bit and I started to roll up the window. "I've lived here all my life and now . . . this," he spat out and waved again toward Riviera Pointe. "I'll lose my view," I heard him say as the window rolled to its closed position.

I gave him a little wave as I pulled slowly away. When I looked in my rearview mirror, he was still standing there, getting smaller and smaller as I headed down the street and away from the job site. Hopefully, he would find someone to wrestle and get rid of that excess hostility and built-up aggression that was bubbling just beneath the surface. I headed north, back toward the restaurant, to meet Kevin.

Father McManus was seated at a table for four, holding a chardonnay in his hand. He looked up when I entered, giving me a wave and a smile. His "hi!" was a little too vibrant, too enthusiastic. It wasn't lost on me that he sucked down half of his wine and wiped a thin sheen of sweat off his upper lip as soon as I sat down.

I approached the table, noticing two busboys constructing a makeshift stage next to the kitchen door. I hooked my thumb toward them as I sat down. "What are they doing?" I was still a little off-kilter after my meeting with Joliet, class of '59, and I expected that the answer to my question would throw me further out of whack.

"Setting up the stage for karaoke night."

Dread started to take hold of me, in the form of icy tendrils making their way up through my muscles and grabbing hold. "What are we doing here on karaoke night?" I looked up as a waitress delivered a vodka martini with extra olives. "I didn't order this," I said.

A voice from behind me said, "But I did."

I turned and looked up at Jack McManus, his white teeth glinting intermittently in the reflection of the blinking strobe light. Kevin drained the rest of his chardonnay, the last one he would ever consume if I had anything to do about it.

Six

I sat in stunned silence; nursing my martini, surrounded by McManus brothers.

Kevin had invited not only Jack but another of his four brothers, Patrick—aka PJ, one of those initial names that years of teaching taught me belonged to bad seeds. He did not disappoint. Patrick, the youngest of the McManus clan, was a driver for Budweiser, a job that seemed completely suited to his skill set and strengths. When I told him I lived in Dobbs Ferry, he recited every bar within ten miles that carried the product he transported. Twenty years ago, this information might have excited me, but now I was just bored by recitations of beer-carrying establishments and their proximity to my house.

"Have you ever been to Sadie's?" he asked.

It was the first place I had ever shared a meal with Crawford. I nodded.

He slapped me on the shoulder. "They carry Bud there!" He got up from the table and went over to the karaoke area to pick out his song.

I thought that just about every restaurant or pub in the free world carried Bud, but he was so excited that I didn't want to burst his bubble. I took another sip of my drink, spearing an olive and shoving it into my mouth.

Jack regarded me from across the table. "Do you do karaoke?"

I raised an eyebrow in reply. "What do you think?"

"I was hoping we could do a duet."

I shot Kevin a look and muttered just softly enough so that nobody but him could hear me. "*Je vais te tuer.*" I am going to murder you.

Kevin speaks passable French and knew that this didn't mean "I love you." His eyes went wide behind his thick glasses. He pushed away from the table. "I think I'll take a look at the songbook, too."

A plate of hot wings arrived at the table, courtesy of Patrick. "Should I do 'SexyBack' or 'You Give Love a Bad Name'?" he called over. He was serious.

"'SexyBack,'" I called as I filled up my plate with wings. I looked around the restaurant, noting that almost every table had filled since I had arrived. I started cramming wings in my mouth so that I wouldn't have to talk to Jack.

"This wasn't my idea," he said, looking down at the table.

I shrugged.

"I told Kevin that you're obviously involved with someone else, but he isn't getting the hint." Jack took a swig from his bottle of beer. "I didn't even know you were going to be here until a few minutes ago. We've had this dinner on the calendar for a week."

"Just so you know," I said, wiping sticky orange residue from my fingers onto my paper napkin, "if my boyfriend gets wind of this, I'm telling him you're gay."

Jack took another swig of beer, which apparently went down the wrong pipe. He sprayed beer into his napkin and began coughing violently.

I put a hand on his back. "And if you die from coughing, even better. Then I don't have to endure any more of these set-ups." I sucked the meat off of another wing, throwing the denuded bones onto my plate. There was a time I had tried to impress Jack and make him think that I was a dainty flower, but those days had passed.

His coughing subsided and he regained his composure. "I get it," he said, hooking a thumb in Kevin's direction. "Just make sure you tell *him*."

Kevin took the stage, microphone in hand, and launched into his song: George Michael's "Faith." I looked at Jack. The mood broken by the ridiculousness of the situation, the two of us burst out laughing. "Good choice," I said and took another wing. Something occurred to me as I was wiping wing sauce off my mouth. "Hey, do you know Richie Kraecker?" Richie Kraecker was a hockey fan and had been photographed at more than one game with a reed-thin model on his beefy, and extremely hairy, arm. I was sure I had seen a photo of him in one of the gossip columns just a week earlier with one such woman, a six-footer in head-to-toe spandex and hair the color and texture of an igloo.

"It's Kray-ker," he corrected me.

"Whatever." I hailed the passing waitress and ordered another martini. "Extra olives!" I called after her. "Do you know him?" I asked him.

Jack didn't know me that well—just well enough to be suspicious of why I was interested. "Yeah, I know him. He's got a luxury box at the Garden. Why do you want to know?"

I looked at Jack, getting distracted for a moment by his Clooney looks. I realized, a moment too late, that I had been staring. "Oh. Well. I'm interested in the condo complex he's building. You know, down by Spuyten Duyvil?"

He nodded slowly.

"What?" He knew something and I wanted to know what it was.

He considered how much he wanted to tell me. "I've actually got an accepted offer on one of those condos." When he saw my face, he seemed to regret having told me.

"You mean you're leaving Long Island City?" I said, pretending to be surprised.

"You're a terrible liar," he said. Kevin had entered the bridge of the song and was singing the heck out of it, distracting both of us. He turned back to me when Kevin started dancing like the eighties' George Michael. "Yes, I'm leaving Long Island City." His eyes narrowed. "Why are you so interested in Richie Kraecker and Riviera Pointe?"

Pwant, I wanted to correct him, but didn't. "No reason."

"God, you are maybe the worst liar I've ever met."

I didn't want to go into the whole Jose Tomasso/soup kitchen/community service connection, so I gratefully accepted my new martini from the waitress and took a huge sip. "I'm interested in a condo?" I said weakly.

"You'll never leave Dobbs Ferry." He shook his head, taking a long swig of his beer. "What the hell do they teach you at St. Thomas anyway?"

"Well, they don't teach us how to lie, obviously." I grabbed another olive from my glass and ate it.

Kevin attempted a split which left him in a precarious

position at the edge of the stage. Patrick came to his rescue and brought him to his feet to thunderous applause. The opening strains of "SexyBack" began and Patrick began his portion of the show.

Jack shook his head sadly as he watched Patrick gyrate, not unlike Justin Timberlake, but not really like him either. Had I just arrived, I would have thought he was having a seizure. Jack looked back at me, something occurring to him. "Listen. Richie Kraecker is having a cocktail party for investors at a place not far from here next Wednesday night. Any interest?"

I thought about that for a moment. I wanted to meet Richie Kraecker and I also wanted to know why he had illegals working at the site. "I think I *would* like to go," I said.

Jack looked at me for a moment. "It's going to cost you."

More than you know, my friend, I thought, but pushed the image of Crawford's face out of my mind. I nodded. "OK. What are we talking about here?"

Jack pushed away from the table and approached the stage. He looked through the song book and after a few minutes, settled on a song. Patrick had taken off his shirt and was swinging it over his head, which was his big finale. Apparently, hoisting beer all day did a good job of developing one's abdominal six pack; you could bounce a quarter off Patrick's midsection. So far, we had the brother with the great teeth, the one with the great abs, and the one with a devotion to the almighty Lord. Quite a group. Jack wiggled a finger at me, beckoning me to come to the stage, which snapped me out of my fugue state. I finished my martini in one gulp and got up.

Patrick was writhing on the stage to the hooting and hollering of the crowd, especially the women. When the song finished, he jumped up and threw his arms in the air in a gesture of triumph. "Woo!"

Jack and I got on the stage. "What are we singing?" I asked. When I heard the opening notes of the song, my stomach dropped. A mic was thrust into my right hand while Jack grabbed my left.

"*Don't go breaking my heart . . .*" he sang.

I stood in silence while the crowd called out the next line.

Jack chimed in with his next line, looking expectantly at me.

I responded, my voice weak. My knees were knocking together as I looked out at the crowd and saw all of the smiling faces. A few bars later, I started to relax a bit and when Jack turned to face me, I sang to him instead of the drunk guy at the bar who had captured my attention and who seemed to be mesmerized by my lackluster performance.

We reached the chorus and the martini began to take effect.

Jack grabbed me around the waist and began to slow dance with me while singing the words to the song, which he knew by heart. I consulted the screen every now and again but realized that I knew the words, too. I stared at his teeth, wondering who his orthodontist might have been. That guy deserved the dental equivalent of an Academy Award.

Despite being completely into my performance, it was hard not to notice the two giant men who entered through the front door of the restaurant.

Especially when one was as handsome as Crawford.

Seven

The next morning, I went to school with a heavy heart. I didn't know what was worse: the look on Crawford's handsome face, or Fred's sad shake of his head as he saw me gyrating on the stage with a man who wasn't Crawford. I didn't know neanderthals were capable of judgment, but clearly, this was one upset caveman.

I didn't attempt any kind of explanation then or when I got home; I know screwed when I see it. I'm incapable of lying, but I'm not stupid.

I'm just horribly misguided. Yes, that's it.

Crawford had taken one look at me and walked out. I myself had left the stage after the performance and, after punching Kevin a few hundred times, the restaurant. Jack had offered to go after Crawford, but I reminded him that he had a huge gun on his hip and another concealed weapon on his ankle and that he was prone to violent outbursts. He thought better of his suggestion, chivalry dying a quick death on the karaoke stage of the Garden Path.

I entered the office area and said hello to Dottie Cruz, the office secretary and all-around busybody. I'll admit it: I looked like hell in a handbasket, and this fact didn't get by Dottie. She looked up at me, a vision in lavender and pink, eye shadow artfully applied to look like butterfly wings and buffeted by the longest false eyelashes I had ever seen.

"Hi, honey," she said, pushing her bagel aside to make room on the edge of her desk for my behind. She patted it with her hand, her nail tips making a tapping sound on the formica.

She's also insane. I wasn't putting my behind on the edge of her desk or anywhere near her. I looked down at her and grimaced. "Good morning, Dottie."

"What's the matter, sweetheart?" she asked. "You look down."

I've decided that I'm one of those people who, when not smiling broadly, always looks unhappy. The sides of my mouth just naturally turn down when I'm not smiling or lost in thought. If I had a nickel for every person who said "cheer up!" when I was just thinking about how to conjugate a French verb correctly, I'd be a rich lady. I plastered a big smile on my face. "Not down. Just thinking," I said. I decided to make her earn her pay, something I did occasionally if only to amuse myself. "You don't happen to remember when Flag Day falls this year, do you?"

She looked perplexed. "I don't," she admitted. "But I can find out." She turned to her computer.

I took the opportunity to scamper away and got to my office just as she was calling out, "June 14!" I thanked her and closed the door. I put my hand on my phone, thinking about my next move.

One good thing about having a boyfriend who's a cop is that someone always answers the phone at his job. After one ring, I heard, "Montoya. Fiftieth Detective Squad."

I knew of Carmen Montoya but had never met her. According to Crawford, she was a wife, mother, and excellent detective. Based on his physical description—one I always demanded of his female colleagues—which was probably kinder than reality, she was cursed with an enormous behind. I knew he wasn't an ass man, so I was cheered to learn that news. However, I wasn't a wife, mother, or excellent detective, so I was instantly intimidated when I heard her voice, big ass or not. "Hi, Detective Montoya. This is Alison Bergeron. Is Bobby Crawford in?"

She hesitated for a second longer than was necessary, in my opinion. "Uh, no he's not, Alison. Can I take a message?"

I thought for a second. "Yes. Tell him that I called and said 'to take it up with Kevin.'"

She read the message back to me. "That it?"

"That's it. Many thanks," I said, hanging up before she could ask any more probing detective questions. I stared at the phone and jumped when it rang a few seconds after I had hung up. It was Max.

"Guess where I'm going Wednesday night?"

Ah, Wednesday night. The night we were supposed to meet for dinner. The night on which I would continue my deception and go out with Jack McManus, a convenient foil for my sleuthing. "Listen, Max, I have to talk to you about that. . . ."

"Richie Kraecker's cocktail party for Riviera Pointe!" she hollered. "And I have a 'plus one'!"

I had no idea what that meant but I was happy to hear that we would be in the same place on Wednesday night, even if my date would not be the person it should have been. "I'm going, too," I said.

"I know!" she said, excited. "You're my 'plus one'!"

I took a deep breath. "I'm actually not."

Let the eating commence. She put a healthy portion of something in her mouth and then attempted to speak. "Huh?"

I took another deep breath. "Without going into too much detail, let's just say that Jack McManus invited me."

It was Max's turn to take a deep breath but it sounded more like she was suffocating. "What?"

I told her about karaoke night at the Garden Path, "Sexy-Back," and "Don't Go Breakin' My Heart." "The upshot is that Jack McManus knows Richie Kraecker and I need to meet him. Case closed."

She snorted. "Yeah, 'case closed' if you didn't have a boyfriend."

"It's business, Max. I'm trying to find out who killed Jose Tomasso and the only way I can do that is by getting inside Richie's head and business and finding out why he's got undocumented workers pouring his foundation." It sounded reasonable, but even I knew it was pretty thin.

"'Pouring his foundation'? Does that sound dirty to you or is it just me?" When I didn't answer, she continued, speaking slowly. "You are to get nowhere near those straight McManus teeth of his. Especially with your lips or tongue. Or any other naked body part for that matter."

I'm not that experienced in the bedroom, but even I got her drift.

"You understand me?"

"I'm not going to kiss him, Max. He understands what this is about. Actually, I think he's kind of interested in helping me figure this out." The digital clock on the phone ticked off to 9:45 and I pushed back from my desk. "I have class in fifteen minutes and I want to get ready." I really didn't want to talk about this anymore. I was prepared for class but I didn't tell Max that. "I gotta go. I'll see you on Wednesday?"

"You will."

"And you won't be weird?"

"Oh, I'll be weird," she said. "You can count on that."

"About Jack. Don't be weird about Jack."

"Oh, that. All right, I promise. No weirdness about Jack." She hung up.

I had a few minutes before class so I decided to do a little Web research on Richie Kraecker. When Max was dating him I didn't understand what she saw in him. I recalled that she had broken up with some guy prior to that and was looking at Richie as her "rebound man." Whatever. I only knew what I read about him and, from what I gathered, he was a guy who had coasted along on his father's construction empire coattails. Which was fine. Except if he was dating my best friend. For her, I expected someone of a little higher caliber.

I googled his name, and it all came rushing back to me. Of the couple hundred thousand hits that came from typing in Richie's name, number one? A photo of Max sitting on Richie's lap in a downtown club wearing the shortest, tightest leather dress I had ever seen. Suffice it to say it was the kind of dress that for me would require massive amounts of latex, never mind plastic surgery. But Max was ensconced on Richie's lap, no latex in site, looking gorgeous, as the two of them sipped champagne. I had forgotten about the picture, although once I saw it, I remembered having seen it in one of Dottie's gossip rags at the time. And feeling a weird combination of envy and shame. Just like a good Catholic girl should.

I knew the people that Crawford worked with, and more than one of them would be delighted to leave that picture on Fred's locker just to let him know that they knew what his wife had been up to prior to their marriage, even if he didn't. And if Fred was anything like most men, that wouldn't be such a good thing.

I gathered up my books, put the sight of Max sitting on that cretin's lap out of my brain, and took stock of my workday. It was Monday and I was teaching creative writing. I headed out of my office. Dottie looked up from her *New York Post* (tucked into the *Webster's New Abridged Dictionary*) and said, "Big plans for Flag Day?"

I stopped short. "Pardon?"

She smiled. "Flag Day? June 14? Big plans, huh?"

"Oh, that. Yes, it's a huge holiday in Canada. I'll probably celebrate it with my cousins," I lied.

She looked confused. "But don't they have a different flag?"

"Right," I said, looking at my watch. I had two minutes to get to class, two floors above the floor I was on. "Canadians love all things American. Old Glory is huge up there," I said. I smiled, throwing my arms out to illustrate just how much Canadians love the American flag. She was clearly dubious but she bought it, and that allowed me to get off the floor and up to my class.

I got to the fifth floor and turned the corner toward my classroom, running smack into Kevin, who wasn't where he was supposed to be at that hour. I had never seen him on a classroom floor during actual classes, which indicated to me that he was there for one reason: to find me. I gave him a hard stare. "There are no words to describe just how pissed I am with you," I hissed. A couple of students were clustered outside the classroom door, and the last thing they needed to witness was a contretemps between their professor and the college chaplain. That would set tongues a-waggin' for sure. Especially when just last year said college professor had endured a very public cuckolding at the hands of her late ex-husband. Some might conclude that a priest was just what the love doctor had ordered.

He stared back at me, his eyes wide behind his Coke-bottle lenses. "Sorry?" he said, more of a question than a sincere apology.

I grabbed his arm and pulled him into an alcove between two classrooms. "I don't know what it is that you can't understand about my situation with Crawford, but we are very happy and very much together."

"Which is why you're going on a date to a black-tie affair with my brother on Wednesday night?" he asked, going all patronizing man of the cloth on me.

I sputtered for a minute. "That's about a case!" I protested.

"A case?" he asked. "Last time I checked, you were an English professor, not an investigator."

I looked at my watch. In another five minutes, one intrepid creative writing student who had been conscientious enough to read the school catalog would discover that if I didn't show up, the class was within its rights to leave the classroom and not be charged a cut for the day. I gave Kevin a sad head shake and started to move away from him.

"I want in," he said, just as I turned the corner.

I stopped and turned back around. "What?"

"I want in," he repeated.

"You want in on what?"

"The case. I want in on the case." He took in my shaking head and frown and continued. "I speak Spanish. Fluently. And my collar gets me in places and gets people talking faster than you can say 'extreme unction.'"

My books, housed in my messenger bag and hanging on my shoulder, were getting heavy. I had one minute to get to class before the students bailed. "I'll think about it," I said.

That seemed to placate him and he drifted off, back to where he was supposed to be: upstairs in his office, next to the chapel.

But as I jogged down the hall, my book bag jostling against my hip, I thought about his request and came to a conclusion.

He could come in very handy indeed.

Eight

We were now approaching seventy-two hours since the karaoke incident and the last time I had seen or heard from Crawford. Even someone who lacks as much common sense as I do could conclude that that wasn't a good sign. Tonight was my not-a-date with Jack "we're just friends" McManus, and the only reason I was nervous was because I knew that if Crawford got wind of things, it would be the final nail in our relationship coffin.

But part of me still believed that I was doing a good deed.

Helping move things along in the investigation and finding out what had happened to Jose were my main motivations, and I was convinced that my altruism could only help, not hinder. I'm not stupid enough to think that the NYPD would agree with me and that there was no way that I could get in the way.

I tried not to think about the not-a-date or the fact that I was poking my nose into a situation where it didn't belong as I gussied myself up, throwing an Asian-inspired red raw-silk dress over my head and slipping my feet into matching sling-backs. I wasn't dressing to impress; just trying to look halfway decent at an event that would boast the crème of New York society. In the Bronx. In the middle of the week. Heck, I would take what I could get.

I had done a little research on Richie Kraecker. OK, maybe "research" is too strong a term. I actually called Max and picked her brain. I learned that Richie didn't like onions, drank Veuve Cliquot by the case, and was "dynamite in the sack." (I didn't need to know any of that, really; none of it shed any light on the case.) I also learned that although he came off as a bit of a buffoon, he had gone to business school at Wharton, where he had specialized in finance. Not bad. But not great if you considered that one of the business buildings on campus was called Kraecker Hall. Max had dated him three years earlier. She had moved on and married; he was still single and dated what seemed like a different model every week. This week, according to Page Six in Dottie's *New York Post*—which I surreptitiously read while she was ostensibly researching the origins and upcoming dates of Boxing Day for me—that model's name was Morag Moragna.

I'm not kidding.

As I brushed some mascara onto my eyelashes, the phone rang; my hand slipped, and I stabbed myself in the iris. "Good god!" I screamed, cupping my palm over my eye, which was tearing ferociously. I picked my way across the room and with my good eye, saw Crawford's cell phone number illuminated on my caller ID. Karma is a vengeful whore, I decided. I took a deep breath and put on my best casual voice. "Hello?"

"Hi," he said.

"Oh, hi!" I said. He knew I had caller ID, so he knew that I knew that it was he on the phone. The faux surprise in my voice was wasted on him. "How are you?" I found a used tissue next to the phone on my nightstand and dabbed at my eye.

"What are you up to?"

"I'm getting ready." I bit the inside of my mouth trying to decide exactly how much to tell him. I decided to focus on about fifty percent of the truth. "I'm going to a black-tie event."

"Yeah?" He sounded surprised.

"With Max."

"Really?"

"Yep." I pulled the tissue away from my eye and blinked a few times, deciding that the worst was over.

"Something for *Crime TV*?" he asked, coming to the logical conclusion that it had to do with the cable network that Max ran.

"Not exactly," I said. When he didn't respond, I came to the conclusion that he was waiting for me to elaborate. "Uh, it's for Riviera Pointe. It's a Richie Kraecker party." Again, no response, which triggered my diarrhea of the mouth. "To launch the condo thing. You know, the one down by the river. Riviera Pointe . . ."

He interrupted me. "I know where it is, Alison. And you know that I know where it is." I heard a loud exhale of breath. "Just so you know, I'll be there, too."

I got that watery feeling in my abdomen that precedes intestinal distress. "Yeah?" I said, sitting down on the bed and crossing my legs, which were going up and down in a nervous jig.

"Well, I'll be outside. Fred and I have to sit on the location just to see what's going on." He chuckled but it wasn't a merriment-filled sound. "You won't see me on your way in, but I'll see you."

I laughed nervously. "So, after that, when will you see me again?"

"Probably on your way out of the restaurant," he said, without a hint of irony. Crawford's never ironic and hardly ever sarcastic.

"And after that?"

He paused a moment and I felt the blood in my veins run cold. It was time for the brush-off, I suspected. "Well, that depends on how well-behaved you are tonight," he said, cryptically.

Not for the first time, I thought, I am so screwed. My eyes filled with tears, and this time they were real, not mascara wand induced.

I hung up and threw a lipstick into my tiny purse, giving myself a disgusted look in the mirror over the dresser. You're sleuthing, I told myself. He'll forgive you when you solve the case. But even I couldn't convince myself.

Jack had sent a car service for me and a shiny black town car was idling at the curb when I went downstairs. I had to admit, it was better than riding around in Crawford's cruiser, but I would never tell him that. I looked out the window as we sailed down the Saw Mill River Parkway and thought about what I had undertaken. So Hernan and Jose had painted my dining room. I'd paid them to. That wasn't enough to make me get so involved, and even though I had grown somewhat closer to Amalia, in reality, I knew nothing about the family. Was my wanting to get to the bottom of this tragic death sincere in its intent? Or was I desperately trying to be in the life of the boyfriend I never saw? Was I just bored? I didn't know. But I did know that if I was able to contribute to finding out who killed this innocent man, I would feel better.

By the time I had gotten to the restaurant, close to Riviera Pointe, I had convinced myself that I was going to butt out of the situation. I would enjoy the champagne and hors d'oeuvre at the party, bid good-bye for a final time to Jack, and be on my way. Hopefully, Jack had heeded my suggestion to meet him inside the restaurant and not outside, which would mean that Crawford wouldn't be any the wiser as to who had sent that shiny black town car for me.

I got out of the car on a block adjacent to Broadway to go into the restaurant and looked around for Crawford's puke-brown cruiser, but as I suspected, it was nowhere to be found. Crawford knows a thing or two about surveillance, and I had a feeling that he and Fred were lurking in the shadows somewhere, drinking lukewarm coffee and bantering back and forth about the people entering the restaurant.

Max and I had debated the merits of the party being at a restaurant in the Bronx; Max; whose marketing/publicity genius had launched her career at *Crime TV*, thought it was an exceptionally good idea. She explained it to me. "See, he's trying to get in good with the people in the neighborhood. If he launches the place at a local restaurant, everybody's happy. And it gives potential condo buyers a feel for the area." She paused. "And it's cheaper than having it in Manhattan."

I chewed on that for a while. It wasn't a very complicated or sophisticated plan for engendering good will. I guessed that she was right, but the Bronx? Since I spent almost every waking hour in this neighborhood, I was kind of disappointed that I was attending a black-tie affair not twenty blocks from St. Thomas. I stood on the sidewalk and, when I was sure that everyone had entered the restaurant, I faced Broadway, where I suspected Crawford was parked. I pulled up the hem of my dress and went into a spastic bump and grind for his benefit.

"What are you doing?"

I turned and came face-to-face with Jack, who looked resplendent in his very traditional tux and bowtie. I flushed deep red.

"Do you always dance before entering a restaurant?"

I coughed and cleared my throat. "Uh, no." I held out my hand to assure Crawford and his long-distance camera lens of my intentions toward this gorgeous man. "Nice to see you, Jack."

He took in my dress and shoes. "You look lovely." He took me by the elbow and steered me toward the restaurant door. "And your boyfriend is across the street in a puke-brown cruiser. He's sitting next to a guy who looks like a caveman."

"That's his partner. And my best friend's husband," I said and walked through the door.

I had never been to the River Garden Restaurant and I was pleasantly surprised to see that it was quite elegant. Jack stopped and began talking to another tuxedo-clad man and I used that as an excuse to move around the room to try to catch a glimpse of Max. I spied her across the room, heading in from the garden at the rear of the restaurant, a backless black dress hanging off her bony shoulders. She was deep in conversation with an eight-foot-tall woman—Morag, I presumed—who was wearing what appeared to be a Kleenex and high heels.

I was totally out of my league.

Max spied me across the restaurant and shouted my name. I had the good sense not to shout back, and that is what makes us completely different. She sashayed my way with the giant woman and introduced her as Morag, Richie's girlfriend.

Morag took my hand in what felt like a Vulcan death grip. Was that really necessary? I grimaced and managed to extricate my throbbing appendage and tell her how nice it was to meet her. She looked me up and down and then looked at Jack, who had sauntered up behind me and put his hand on my shoulder. When she looked back at me, her cold, dead, blue fish eyes said, "what is *she* doing with *him*?" I held her gaze, though, and smiled. If she thought he was a winner, she should get a load of Crawford.

"So, Morag," I started, determined to make something approaching polite conversation, "what do you do?"

She waved a skeletal arm, dripping with diamond-encrusted bangles, dismissively. "Oh, this and that."

Max jumped in. "Morag is doing some consulting at Riviera Pointe."

I was bored already. Is there a more boring word—or profession—than "consulting"? What does that even mean? "Really? What kind of consulting?"

"I help Richie with his accounting," she said and took a glass of champagne off a tray held aloft by a passing waiter. "Just to make sure he's not getting ripped off."

Richie getting ripped off? That was a good one. What about the people who actually bought his condos? From what I gathered, they were the ones who should be concerned. I smiled again. "You must be a great help to him."

"I am," she said and I could almost see a film of boredom cover her eyes. She looked over my head and around the room to see who else she could find to talk to. "Oh, I see . . ." she started, and realizing that she couldn't come up with somebody's name fast enough to get away, continued, ". . . somebody I know. Enjoy the party," she said, moving away in a cloud of expensive perfume.

Max waved her hand in front of her face and coughed loudly. "It's like she took a bath in that crap."

Jack turned around from the person with whom he had been

conversing and greeted Max with a two-cheeked kiss. Kind of continental for a guy from Long Island City, but I held my tongue.

"I'm ravenous," Max said and looked around for the buffet. "Coming?"

"No," I said, taking Jack's arm. "I want to say hello to Mr. Kraecker."

"Suit yourself," she said, "I'm going to look for a pig in a blanket." She started off and then turned back around. "Who isn't Richie Kraecker."

It didn't take me long to spot Richie, holding court at the end of the bar. He was exactly as he appeared in the newspapers—except way shorter. He had slicked-back hair and a jowly face that sat atop the thickest neck I had ever seen. As we got closer, he spotted Jack and called for him.

"And this is Jack McManus, director of publicity for the Rangers," he said to the crowd gathered around him. He grabbed Jack in a bear hug and did that back-slapping embrace that jocular men are fond of. "And the first owner of a gorgeous condo at Riviera Pointe."

"Good to see you, Richie," Jack said, breaking away. "This is Alison Bergeron."

I held out my hand, only to find it crushed in the firmest handshake I had ever encountered. That was two for the evening. I had sustained a knife injury to that hand earlier in the year and the scar tissue that crossed the palm was tender and slightly painful. I winced and fought the urge to cry out in agony as Richie pumped my hand up and down.

"Nice to meet you," I said through gritted teeth.

"Alison's interested in . . ." Jack started, turning to look at me with a bemused look in his eyes, ". . . what is it that you're interested in, Alison?"

I pulled my hand out of Richie's and held his gaze. "A condo. I'm interested in a condo in your beautiful building."

Richie broke out into a wide grin. "You'll love it. Ten stories of luxury condos, an Olympic-size pool, full state-of-the-art health club! And the most fantastic views of the Hudson anywhere on the waterfront. I'll put you in touch with one of our sales reps." He looked at Jack. "And if you're a friend of the big guy here, you know you'll get the best deal I can make," he said, laughing.

The crowd around Richie, full-fledged sycophants one and all, laughed on cue.

"How far along are you in the process?" I asked.

"Foundation is poured, so actual construction will start any day." He took a swig from the martini sitting on the bar next to him.

"Everything going well?" I asked, all faux sincerity. I tried to slouch a little bit so that I didn't look like Queen of the Amazon while standing over him in my three-inch heels.

"Fantastic." He took another long swallow from his drink.

Jack squeezed my elbow. "Why don't we . . ."

"I heard something about . . ." I barely had it out when he interrupted me.

"Accident," Richie said and finished his drink. He motioned to the bartender for a new one. "It was an accident. Can I get you a drink?"

"Vodka martini, three olives," I said, still looking into his eyes. It had already been pretty well-established by the local papers that Jose had been murdered and that the NYPD had an entire team of homicide cops on the case, but apparently Richie had a story and he was sticking to it. It was an improbable story, but Richie's version of events, nonetheless. I guess I couldn't blame him: nothing like a murder at your job site to make the place undesirable to just about everyone.

"Grey Goose OK?" he asked, his eyes going up to my hair-line.

"Perfect." I smiled. "I heard something about . . ."

"I said it was an accident."

". . . the possibility of an electronic floor plan that I could access?" I said. Jack's grip on my elbow got tighter and I shook him loose.

Richie exhaled a little bit and looked like if he could have put us in a time machine and gone back about thirty seconds, he would have. He returned to blowhard building tycoon. "Of course! Madeleine," he said, turning to a blowsy blonde on his right, "give Ms. . . ."

"Bergeron," I said. A martini was handed to me and I took a hearty sip.

". . . Bergeron a card, would you?"

Madeleine pulled a card out of a binder she was holding and handed it to me. She tapped an acrylic nail on the Web site address. "Here you are? And if you have any questions, please feel free to call me anytime, day or night?" Oh, she was one of those, I thought. A questioner. A person whose every sentence ends with a question mark.

I thanked her. I didn't think I'd have any questions that would occur to me in the middle of the night but if I did, I would definitely call her immediately.

Before I could tell Richie what a pleasure it was to have met him, Jack had steered me into the middle of the restaurant, as far away as we could get from Kraecker. "What are you doing?" he asked.

"What do you mean?"

"What was that?" he asked. He grabbed a glass of cham-pagne off of a tray floating by on the outstretched hand of a waiter and downed it one gulp. "I didn't actually think you were going to do that. Kevin said you were hard-headed . . .

but . . . that . . ." He sputtered a little bit and handed his glass off to another waiter who handed him another glass of champagne. That one disappeared down his gullet just as quickly as the first.

"I told you why I was coming."

He looked at a spot over my head. "I know you did." He let out a big breath and deflated a little bit. "Maybe this wasn't such a good idea."

I drained my martini glass and set it on a tall cocktail table. "Maybe you're right," I agreed. "Thanks for the invite. Now, where did you say my boyfriend was parked?"

With a full set of directions as to Crawford's whereabouts, I left the restaurant and headed back down the street toward Broadway, tottering unsteadily on my high heels. I spotted Crawford's car across Broadway and calculated that I would have to cross four lanes of traffic to get to him. But then I calculated that it was worth the risk.

A woman in a cocktail dress, flimsy wrap, and high heels walking across Broadway wasn't a common sight, and I have to admit I did get a few catcalls. Car horns blared at me as I made my way across the first two lanes of traffic, followed by the second two lanes after a brief wait on the median for the light to change. As I got closer, I could see Crawford's face in the passenger's side car window and, despite the anger that initially passed across his face, my unsteady gait, accompanied by the last catcall—"Can I have an order of fries with that shake!?"—made him burst out laughing. I finally made it to the back door of the cruiser and hopped into the scummy backseat. Fred was sound asleep in the driver's seat, snoring loudly.

"Hey, I've never been in the backseat of the cruiser," I said.

"It's not a cruiser," Crawford droned from the front seat. The entire first three months of our relationship had centered on the definition of "cruiser" and he was clearly tired of that conversation. "Can I join you?" he asked, turning around. "We could make out."

I didn't respond, figuring I would get business out of the way. "Jack McManus doesn't have the stomach for amateur sleuthing." I closed the back door with a loud thunk. "And Richie Kraecker's got something to hide."

Nine

The phone was nestled between my head and the pillow and Max was blathering on about the party the night before. I tried to stay coherent.

"That is some set of teeth on your date," Max said. "I didn't notice that at the hockey game."

Probably because you were three sheets to the wind, as my beloved father used to say.

She continued. "And here's what I learned about Morag Moragna."

I looked at the clock and saw that it was six thirty in the morning. Chances are Max hadn't been to bed yet from the night before. Morag wasn't really my concern but Max seemed to feel compelled to tell me everything she knew, and I was happy to listen—as long as I could listen while in my bed, my head buried in Trixie's neck.

I had gotten home nice and early, all dressed up with no place to go. After I had reported everything I had surmised from my meeting with Richie, Crawford left Fred standing on the corner while he dropped me off at the train station.

"You're not a detective, you know," were his last words to me. I suspected we would have a long talk about a few other things when we had the chance; we made our usual promise for a Sunday night date, which was only a few days hence. I had given him a long kiss and jumped out of the car when I heard the train whistle blaring a few feet down the tracks.

Max was still talking, even though I didn't care one iota about Morag Moragna. I asked her why she did.

"I made a mistake with Richie and I am fascinated to find out why another gorgeous, successful woman would make the same mistake."

So, no self-esteem problems there. And to think I had been worried about her, given her jealousy of some autopsy lady.

Max continued. "She's a supermodel, but we already knew that. And she was on the 2004 Swiss Olympic team."

Of course she was.

When I didn't reply, she continued. "When she told me that, I immediately thought *skier* because of her build, but it turns out I was only half right. She was one of those goofy biathletes—you know, those ones who cross-country ski, stop, and then shoot at things?"

I didn't think that the people who trained to be biathletes considered their sport "goofy," but that was a discussion for another time. I couldn't walk and chew gum at the same time so anybody who could ski *and* shoot while remaining upright was OK in my book.

"Isn't that interesting?"

I had drifted off to sleep again but was jolted awake by Max's "Hello!" in my ear.

"Yes. Interesting." I yawned loudly.

"Anyway, she feels the same way about that troll, Richie. He's got short-man complex, so he feels like he has to overcompensate by being really controlling in all business dealings, yet, shall we say, extremely *attentive* in bed."

Hell, there had to be a reason he was able to date women like Max and Morag and keep them on the line for any amount of time. "Attentiveness" in bed was not something to be taken for granted, I had learned. My late ex-husband had apparently been very attentive, but to a bunch of other women.

"So I saw you talking to Richie. What did he have to say?"

"Can we talk about this later?" I shifted. Trixie jumped off the bed, knocking my alarm clock to the floor and pulling half the comforter with her. I was awake now. "I'll call you when I get to school." And before she had a chance to hang up on me, which is how our phone calls usually ended, I hung up on her.

Trixie stared at me expectantly. I knew what that meant. I rolled over with a groan and propelled myself out of bed. Trixie bounded out of the room and down the stairs; I knew that by the time I was dressed and had made it down to the kitchen, she would be waiting by the back door with her leash in her mouth. That was a trick that either Frankie or his brother Brendan had taught her and that never ceased to amaze me. I couldn't train her to stay in the yard, which on the learning scale had to fall below the leash-in-the-mouth trick.

Although we usually went out the back, I decided to throw caution to the wind and take her out the front door. I had gone to bed at ten, so I had a little spring in my step after a good night's sleep, during which I had dreamed that Jack McManus had been sent to Finland permanently to scout local hockey teams for new talent for the Rangers. We had shared a chaste kiss on the tarmac before he boarded Icelandair and set off to the land of the midnight sun. Or was that Greenland? Anyway, in my dreams, he was gone and I was beyond finding myself in any further compromising positions.

I headed down the front walk in the semidarkness, clad in my pajama pants, a St. Thomas hooded sweatshirt, and Ugg boots, figuring the only people who would see me would be those speeding by on their way to the train station. As usual, my radar for these sorts of things was way off, and as I crossed the street I encountered my neighbor, Jane, and her son Frankie. Frankie looked miserable, carrying the heaviest book bag I had ever seen, a pair of giant sneakers tied to the loop at the top of the bag. His flannel plaid tie with the insignia of his school embossed on it was half-tied, and his shirt was unbuttoned, exposing a crisp white undershirt.

I gulped. I'm a sucker for a clean white undershirt. That's not to say that I was preparing to hit on a teenager; the undershirt reminded me of Crawford, who has about four thousand in his possession. An image of Crawford, clad only in an undershirt and his gun belt, flashed through my mind, and I flushed deep red.

Jane, as always, was smiling and didn't seem to notice my hot flash. "Good morning, Alison!" She turned to Frankie, who was wrestling his book bag into the backseat of their Subaru. "Say good morning to Mrs. Bergerson, Frankie." Jane has this thing about Frankie calling me "Mrs." even though I had told both of them that it wasn't necessary; however, neither of them knew that they had my surname wrong and it had gone on so long that I was embarrassed to tell them.

"Grudemornmizbergerson," he mumbled.

I nodded in his direction. "Hey, Frankie." Trixie sat by my side, and Frankie came over to give her a hug. "You're up early."

Jane smiled. "I was going to say the same thing to you."

I pointed at Trixie. "Nature calls."

"Frankie has an early practice this morning," she said, opening her car door. "Playoffs are coming up." She tossed her purse onto the seat. "But he still has time to go to the Lord's Bounty on Saturday night."

The morning chill had started to seep into my pajama pants. "Great. I'll pick him up at our usual time."

Frankie mumbled something to Jane and realization dawned on her face. "Oh, right!" She pulled her blond hair into a ponytail and tied it with an elastic band. "Frankie's with his dad in Peekskill this weekend, so Greg will drop him off at the church and pick him up."

Oh, so that's why I never saw a man around. I'm a little dense.

Jane fiddled with her hair a bit more, and I studied her face in the dawning light, noticing for the first time how attractive she was, dressed for work in a suit with a smattering of makeup on her youthful face. Self-consciousness started to creep into my thoughts and I pushed it aside; I decided that not every chance encounter was an opportunity for me to feel bad about myself or the fact that I was seven feet tall when compared to this petite, fine-boned woman.

Frankie mumbled something to Jane and she translated. "We have to go." Before she got into the car, she turned back to me. "Would you like to come over for dinner some night? It's just me and Frankie now that Brendan's away at school, but you can bring someone, if you'd like."

"I would really like that," I said and flashed on Crawford's face. I doubted I'd be able to drag him away from the Fiftieth for a night out, but I had another thought, and even though I didn't know this woman from Adam, I believed that Plan B was genius. It involved my divorced neighbor and one Jack McManus and to me seemed foolproof. "Actually, I would like to bring a friend," I said.

"Great!" She hopped into the front seat. "I'll call you later and we'll set something up."

I watched until they were safely down the street and then let Trixie, who had been pulling insistently at the leash, deposit a big, giant load on their front yard that nearly exceeded, in mass and weight, the *New York Times* plastic bag that I had brought along just for that occasion. I scooped it up and held it an arm's length from my body as I trudged back to the house.

I figured that since I was up, I would head off to school. Maybe an early arrival would get Sister Mary, my boss, off my back about, well, just about everything she is constantly on my back about.

My first class wasn't until twelve ten, so everybody I encountered on my way into my office was beyond surprised to see me at eight thirty. Dottie looked up from her *Us Weekly* and let out a long whistle. "D'ja sleep here?" she asked in her thick-as-pea-soup Bronx accent. I gave her what I thought was a disdainful look, but she just peered back at me through all her lavender eye shadow wonder.

"No," I said. "Do I have any messages?"

She shook her helmet of hair back and forth. "No. But Father Kevin's been looking for you half the morning."

Considering morning had just broken, I wasn't sure what that meant, but it sounded urgent. Eight o'clock mass would be ending shortly, so I headed up to the chapel floor and stepped into the back of the vast room and watched as Kevin went through the motions of putting away the hosts, water, and wine from mass and said the final blessings. The pews held a smattering of old nuns, but nary a student. Poor Kevin. Ministering to the drunk and promiscuous and a couple of octogenarian nuns—it seemed a stern punishment for a young priest who couldn't get along with the cardinal, but it was the punishment meted out nonetheless.

I couldn't tell if he saw me standing at the back of the long aisle, but when he raced out of the sacristy after changing back into his regular clothes—which today consisted of traditional black priest garb and a Roman collar—and hustled down the aisle toward me, I knew that he had.

"Hey, you almost knocked over Sister Anselm," I said, giving him a quick hug.

He watched as the old nuns who frequented the daily morning mass filed silently out of the chapel and gave a solemn nod to each and every one, exchanging a few words with one or two of the sisters. They clearly revered him, even though he was a good forty years younger than the youngest nun there. Sister Alphonse—there since I was a student and aptly nicknamed "the Fonz"—patted him on the head as she walked past, a good six inches taller than the vertically challenged Kevin. When the last one bade him farewell, he grabbed my arm. "I have an idea."

He pulled me into the back pew and told me what he had in mind. The next thing I knew, we were in his Honda Civic, heading south on the avenue and winding our way through the labyrinthine streets of the neighborhood and down to the river. Kevin drives twenty miles an hour on a good day, but it was a little drizzly so it took about ten minutes longer to get there than it would have normally. He's also the worst parallel parker I've ever seen, so after failing at several tries to get into a parking space that could have held three Honda Civics, I wrested the steering wheel from him and angled my way in, leaving him standing on the curb looking perturbed.

We were parked exactly where I had parked a few days earlier when I had stopped by the condo site. Unlike that day, the construction area was bustling with activity. My usual attire consists of a skirt, cardigan, and moderately high heels. Fortunately, I had worn a pair of dark wool slacks and my trusty Dansko clogs instead—perfect for picking around the debris that littered the area. I stepped over a large piece of wood and followed Kevin over to the site. There were enough people that nobody noticed a tall woman with a head full of frizzy hair blowing in the breeze and a myopic priest.

Kevin asked me what my friend's name was as well as the name of the dead man. "Escalante," I said. "Hernan is the uncle and Jose Tomasso is the deceased. Jose's his sister's kid."

Kevin walked over to a group of men working with cement and spoke a few words in Spanish that sounded suspiciously like Spanglish to me. I pulled Kevin aside. "I thought you said you spoke Spanish," I whispered. I knew that Kevin had done some work in rural Mexico when he was first ordained and I had taken his proclamation of fluency seriously.

He shrugged. "I guess I'm a little rusty."

Being fluent in a romance language myself, I caught a few words, yet nothing made sense. Finally, a man who spoke broken English on par with Kevin's broken Spanish stepped away from the group and approached Kevin. This ought to be interesting, I thought. He was holding a large mallet, which he tapped against his side as he spoke to Kevin. Kevin asked him if he knew Jose Tomasso. I didn't hear his response because out of the corner of my eye, I spotted Hernan walking with a group of men. I hurried down the hill and called his name.

I detected a slight hitch in his step; he had heard me. But he kept walking. I finally reached him, avoiding a suspended and swinging batch of two-by-fours, and tapped him on the shoulder.

He turned and stared at me like he didn't know me. He said a few words to the men he was with while holding my gaze and they scattered.

"Hernan, what are you doing here?"

"You shouldn't be here. I've got it under control," he said.

What had happened to the cab driving and the odd painting job? By the looks of it, he had apparently joined the ranks of the day laborers who routinely left their towns and villages to work for a cut rate at the homes of residents and at the job sites of companies who flouted union rules. "*You* shouldn't be here," I said. "Do you want to jeopardize the investigation or be in danger yourself?" I asked.

He sighed, defeated and angry. "The police won't help. Jose was just another illegal."

I shook my head. "That's not true. Crawford is one of the investigating officers. I promise you. He'll help." I took Hernan's rough hand in my own. "He's a good guy, Hernan. And there's a lot of publicity surrounding this case. They won't let it drop."

Hernan dropped my hand. "I haven't seen anyone around here asking questions about the case. No one," he spat out. "You tell me how that helps us find Jose's killer." He closed his eyes. "Tell me."

I thought about that and about Crawford sitting outside of the restaurant last night. I didn't know enough about police work to figure out what they were doing there, but I had to believe they were doing something. I knew that they were "sitting on" Richie, as Crawford described it, which to me meant that they were working a specific angle. I told Hernan that.

"That means nothing to me." He started to walk away. "Don't come back here again," he said over his shoulder.

I stood for a moment and watched him walk away. The Hernan that I knew from the Lord's Bounty, a quiet, humble man, had been replaced by this angry, surly individual. But I didn't have time to think about it because a voice from behind me called, "Hey, lady! Watch out!" and I turned to see a cement truck barreling down the hill. I moved out of the way, twisting my ankle in a ditch. After the truck rumbled past, I started back up the hill and found Kevin waiting by the car for me.

"You look shaken," he said, popping the locks on the Civic.

"I am," I admitted. I rubbed my sore ankle.

We got into the car. "Well, I don't know if I learned anything besides what we already knew: Richie Kraecker cuts corners by having illegals do some of the preliminary work, like foundations." He put his hands on the steering wheel. "And someone makes sure that they get illegal green cards." He turned and looked at me, his eyes wide. "That's not good, right?"

"Who told you that?" I asked, amazed.

"I can't say. I promised."

I was stunned that he got all of that in five minutes from a group of non-English-speaking workers. But he was right: the collar opened up a lot of doors.

And, obviously, a lot of mouths.

Ten

"The foreman at Riviera Pointe told me that a tall woman and a priest were nosing around the job site this morning," Crawford said.

I wedged the phone between my ear and neck. "Really?"

"Any idea of who that might be?"

"Not a clue," I said with all the innocence I could muster.

"No ideas?"

I tried to sound like I was thinking hard. "No." I knew he wasn't stupid; how many tall women—or even garden-variety average-height women—pal around with priests? Not too many. I heard a knock at the door and was grateful for the interruption. "Hold on. Someone's at the door."

I ran down the hallway and peered through the side window at the front door. Trixie hovered by the living room, growling. I opened the door.

Crawford was standing there, a tight smile on his lips, his cell phone still pressed to his ear. "Are you sure that you've never seen a tall woman with a priest?"

I shook my head. "Nope."

"The foreman said she was cute."

I blushed a little bit. "He did?"

"But you don't know who it is, so I guess we'll never know," he trailed off, walking into the kitchen. He spied the two pots on the stove. "Cooking?"

"Sort of," I said. I can boil water and open up a prepared tub of pesto. I crossed my fingers behind my back. "Can you stay for dinner?"

"That depends," he said, taking off his blazer and loosening his tie. "Is anybody else going to be here?"

I was confused. "Anybody else?"

He raised his eyebrows. "You know what I'm talking about."

I thought for a moment, the realization finally dawning on me. "About that . . . let me explain," I said. I thought I had done a good enough job of explaining the night before, but this was one angry former altar boy. He had seemed fine when we had parted, but the intervening hours had obviously changed his attitude for the worse.

He held up a hand, stopping me in midsentence. "I don't want to hear another word about him."

"I only went to the cocktail party because I wanted . . ."

"Did you hear me?" he asked, his face reddening. "Not another word. I don't want to hear his name, the name 'McManus,' anything about Rangers tickets. As a matter of fact," he said, his voice getting higher and coming dangerously close to cracking, "I don't want to hear about the Rangers period!"

I was silent for a moment. "Well, that's going to be kind of hard. They are in a playoff race," I said quietly.

He stared me down. "I'm not kidding, Alison."

I tried hard to keep the tears that were pressing at the back of my eyes right where they were. Didn't he get that I was trying to help him? That I was trying to help my friend—who, in reality, was only kind of my friend—Hernan? My motives were purely altruistic, although I had to admit that they didn't look quite so pure if you put them all together. I was going to start explaining with how I had been bamboozled by Kevin, first on the night he invited me to dinner, and then on the day we went to the job site. Then I was going to explain how I only went to Richie Kraecker's cocktail party to get more information. But looking at Crawford—who usually looked at me with a reverence that I've only seen him reserve for his daughters—and seeing how he was giving me a look a perp might get during an interrogation, I held my tongue. I nodded. "Do you want pasta?" My voice was a little shaky, and I swallowed hard.

"Do you have a beer?" he asked testily.

I motioned to the refrigerator. "You know I do," I said.

"Do you want a glass of wine?" he asked, pulling open the door to the refrigerator.

I motioned to the half-full glass of red wine sitting on the counter next to the stove. "I have one."

He pulled out a kitchen chair with such force that it slammed into the wall behind it; he sat down heavily. I had thought that when he first walked in he was in a good mood, but apparently, I was sadly mistaken.

I stirred the pasta in the pot, silently, holding back tears. I pulled the lid off the pesto, struggling with the protective sheet of plastic that covered the top of the container. I finally pulled it off, pulling the container toward me, and flattening it against my chest. Pesto streamed down into the front of my T-shirt. Trixie, smelling a food disaster, bounded into the kitchen and jumped up on me, putting her paws on my shoulders and licking the front of my chest.

I responded by bursting into tears.

"I guess we're not having pesto," Crawford said, getting up and handing me a paper towel.

"I guess not," I said angrily, as if it were his fault. I flung the now-empty container into the sink and pushed Trixie off. I stormed past Crawford and went upstairs to change.

Crawford called up the stairs after me. "Put on some clean clothes and I'll take you out to dinner."

"Put on some clean clothes and I'll take you to dinner," I mimicked in my Crawford voice. "Like that's going to help." I stripped off my pesto-covered T-shirt, managing to streak my hair with green bits of basil and pine nuts. "Would that be before or after you take me to task for helping you with *your* case?" I said to my reflection.

"I can hear you," he called up.

"You're supposed to!" I called down, pulling off my jeans and socks. I decided that a long shower would be the only thing that would improve my mood and calm me enough to sit across from Crawford at dinner. After all, I'm a realist at heart—I was hungry, there was nothing to eat except for the plain, half-cooked pasta on the stove and the pesto in my hair, and the two of us had to get back on track, romantically speaking. "I'm taking a shower," I called from behind my closed bedroom door. "Walk Trixie." I waited a beat. "Please."

A shower was exactly what I needed. After spending longer than necessary washing my hair and loading up on scented shower gel to erase any lingering olive oil or basil smells, I emerged feeling happier, calmer, and ready to face Crawford. I came down the stairs a few minutes later in a nice suede skirt and a turtleneck. I stood on the bottom step and watched Crawford come back in from his walk with Trixie.

"Let's start over," I said.

He considered that for a minute. "OK."

"Give me a kiss, Crawford," I said. Standing on the bottom step in my black, high-heeled boots made us about the same height. He came over and I put my arms around his neck and gave him a long kiss.

"Don't go breakin' my heart," he said.

I chuckled. "I couldn't if I tried."

"I'm not kidding," he said, and a glimmer of insecurity flashed across his face.

That didn't deserve a response so I suggested a place for dinner. "How about Sadie's?" I asked. "It's quiet and I have a lot to tell you."

Sadie's was the site of our first unofficial date—Crawford had shown up at my house in the midst of a murder investigation ostensibly to ask me some questions. I didn't know him, he still considered me something of a suspect, and we were extremely cautious around each other. But somewhere between a perfectly prepared vodka martini and the rice pilaf, I found myself transfixed by this seemingly wonderful man who, as it turned out, came with a ton of baggage. Since that time, we had dumped the baggage (namely: his wife), smoothed out some of the kinks, and embarked on a romantic journey that had had its share of bumps in the road. And would continue to, thanks to me.

I resisted the urge to tell him that this was on the list of restaurants to which Patrick McManus delivered his precious cargo of Budweiser.

We were seated at a table in the back, in a dark corner.

Crawford made a show of trying to read his menu in the dark. "Just order the burger," I said after asking the waitress to bring me a vodka martini with extra olives. Crawford went with his usual beer.

He drained half the bottle when it arrived. "So, what do you have to tell me?"

I took a deep breath. "Well, you were right about the identity of the tall woman and the priest at the job site today."

Crawford smirked. "They don't call me Detective Hot Pants for nothing," he said, repeating one of my favorite lines to me. He took another sip of his beer. "And it was *so* hard to figure out."

"Anyway," I said, giving him the you're-not-funny look, "Kevin and I went down there and found out that, one, Richie Kraecker is definitely using undocumented workers, two, someone's giving them illegal green cards, and, three, I will never go out with Jack McManus again," I said, slipping in that last part almost under my breath.

He wrapped his hands around his cold beer bottle and thought about what I had said. He wisely chose to ignore the Jack McManus reference and focused on the other parts of my account. "How did you find out about the illegal green cards?"

I resisted the urge to sing out, "I know more than the police do!" "Kevin managed to get it out of one of the workers. Probably threatened him with eternal damnation. Hispanic Catholics, for the most part, take that stuff more seriously than French Canadians, I've found."

He nodded and then signaled the waitress for another beer. "Tell Kevin that that was his last visit to Riviera Pointe."

You tell him, I thought, but I nodded obediently instead.

"What else did you find out?" he asked.

I told him about running into Hernan and how he had behaved. Neither seemed to surprise him.

"Hernan needs to go back to driving a cab," he said. "Or painting houses." He pulled a pad of paper out of his jacket pocket. "Give me a description of him."

"Why?"

He jotted a note down. "Because if you conveniently forget to tell him, I can find him and tell him myself." He went back a few pages in his notebook. "I didn't question him in relation to the case. Moran did. So I don't know what he looks like."

"He's about forty-fivish, about five foot five, short brown hair."

Crawford stopped writing. "You just described about ninety percent of the workers at the job site."

"What do you want me to say? That's what he looks like," I protested. "Listen, I'll tell him when I see him: no more day laboring at Riviera Pointe. I won't forget, conveniently or otherwise."

The waitress dropped off his beer. Crawford looked down at the table. "And you're sure about that other thing?" he asked, not looking at me.

It took me a minute. "Oh, that. Yes. Promise." I crossed my heart and said a silent farewell to Jack McManus, his limitless supply of hockey tickets, and, lastly, his amazing orthodonture.

"And promise me you'll leave the sleuthing to me."

I grimaced. "Do I have to?" I whined. I had developed quite a love of sleuthing; I think it had happened when I had been jammed between the toilet and vanity in my late ex-husband's bathroom, my pants around my ankles. I had found a sex tape, quite accidentally, but the fact that I had found it at all—taped to the back of the toilet tank—after the entire Fiftieth Precinct had been through the apartment, convinced me that I was just the most excellent sleuth this side of Nancy Drew.

He nodded, his mouth turned down in a frown. "You have to."

I nodded slowly.

"If for nothing else, so that I can keep my job. If my girlfriend keeps turning up in places related to my cases, it won't be good for me, Alison." He looked at me. "Got it?"

I sighed. "Got it." I was only sort of lying but I did my best to convince him of my sincerity by giving him my version of a brilliant smile.

Crawford drove me home after dinner. We pulled up in front of my house, where we proceeded to make out in his car for a while before I got out. Sunday, our usual make-out day, was a few days away, and I needed my Crawford fix. I was standing on my front walk, pulling my skirt out of my underpants, when I spied Jane, waving to me from her front yard. I smoothed my hair down and adjusted my turtleneck.

"Alison! Hey!" she called.

"Oh, hi, Jane," I said, as if I had just spotted her in the previous nanosecond. It was dark, but the streetlights illuminated her enough so that I could see that she was wearing a Stepinac High School sweatshirt.

She trotted across the street and stopped when she got to me. "How are you?" she asked, not at all out of breath from her jog.

"I'm great. You?" I asked. I was more out of breath than she was and I had been standing still—but I had been sort of upside down, and that severely limits your ability to breathe.

"I just wanted to pin you down for a dinner date. Are you free Saturday night after the Lord's Bounty? Maybe around seven?" she asked. "Brendan's coming home for his break and I know he would love to see you. I managed to switch weekends with the boys' dad so that they could be around on Saturday night."

I hesitated. I didn't know if I could pull off my plan, the one that involved her and my very single friend, Jack McManus. "Can I get back to you?" I asked. "I want to bring a friend but I need to check with him first."

"Oh, darn," she said. "Was it the friend who just dropped you off? I didn't want to ambush you while you were sitting in the car."

I didn't want to tell her what we were really doing in the car since it didn't involve "sitting" at all, so I kept my mouth shut. Because of me, each of her kids had seen a dead body before his eighteenth birthday, so I was surprised she would even stand near me, never mind talk to me.

"So, get back to me, OK?" she said, noting my silence and impending fugue state. "It'll be casual."

"Great. I'll call my friend now," I said.

I am a genius, I thought.

I went into the house and greeted Trixie, who did odor reconnaissance on my boots, deciding that there was something on the toe of the right one that was worth licking. I shook her off and pulled my cell phone out of my pocketbook; Jack's number was in the previously dialed listing. The phone rang for a few seconds before a very tentative-sounding Jack picked up the phone. Boy, he really didn't have a stomach for sleuthing if just the sight of my name on his caller ID made him sound like this. "Hey, Jack, it's Alison."

"Uh, hi, Alison."

"I'll cut to the chase: a neighbor invited me over for dinner on Saturday night and I was wondering if you'd like to join me?" It was at that moment that it occurred to me that I sounded like I was asking him out on a date. Which I wasn't. "And her boys love hockey. Are you around? I know they'd love to meet someone who's involved with the Rangers."

He hesitated a moment, presumably to think about how he

was going to handle this. I jumped in. "I know the Rangers are playing an afternoon game. Maybe you could come over afterwards?"

He stuttered a little before finally saying, "OK."

"OK?"

"Sure. Fine."

Way to sound enthusiastic. He would be much happier once he found out that a lovely, attractive, single woman was the mother of the two boys. At least that's what I told myself.

It was only eight thirty but I was tired, and, with a full day of teaching waiting for me the following day, I decided that it was time to walk Trixie for the final time before turning in. I put her on her leash and took her outside into the chilly night air. I trudged down the street in my boots, proving Crawford's claim that I never wore the appropriate shoes for the task at hand. The toes of each boot had become uncomfortably tight and I whispered to Trixie to finish up so I could go into the house and put on my slippers.

"Come on, Trix. Please," I begged. Her impassive eyes stared back at me, reminding me that she didn't understand a word I had said besides her name. "It's cold, honey. Let's go." I tugged at her leash.

I heard the slow progress of a car behind me, its tires turning on the asphalt. I didn't pay it much heed; my concern was getting my dog to understand that her biological functions were of the utmost priority. Trixie stopped and turned, staring at the car down the road. A low growl started in her throat, then turned into a loud bark.

It was then that I heard the screech of tires as the car picked up speed.

The house we were standing in front of had a low retaining wall, a little patch of grass between it and the street. It was there that I was trying to coax Trixie into doing what we had come outside to do. She dragged me toward the low wall, keeping an eye on the speeding car and barking at me.

I turned and looked at the car, now speeding toward us, its headlights bathing us in an unnatural glow. I finally realized that the car was heading toward me and I dove over the retaining wall, Trixie close on my heels. The car drove up onto the patch of grass on which we were formerly standing, glanced off the retaining wall, and sped off down the street. I crouched behind the wall until I was sure that the car wasn't coming back.

A light came on inside the house, a few feet behind me and the dog. The front door flew open and one of my neighbors, a man I didn't recognize, stood on the front step in the shortest bathrobe I had ever seen. I got up so that I didn't get a look from my crouch at anything I didn't want to see.

"Get your dog off my front lawn!" he said.

I stood up on shaking legs, noticing that my skirt was torn. "That car tried to hit me!" I protested.

"I don't care if aliens were trying to kidnap you and take you back to their mother ship," he said. "Get that freaking dog off my front lawn!"

"I'm fine, by the way!" I said, and climbed back over the retaining wall; Trixie leaped gracefully onto the other side. Once there, she proceeded to do what we had come out to do. And then some.

"You'd better pick that up!" he warned, starting down the steps toward me.

I waved a blue *New York Times* home delivery plastic bag his way. "I've got it covered. Not to worry," I said, anger replacing fear. I picked up Trixie's deposit and started off down the street, not realizing until I had taken about ten steps that I had left the heel of my right boot on Cranky McCrankypants's front lawn. I hobbled back to my house, adrenaline coursing through my veins.

Once inside the house, I assessed the damage. My skirt was torn, my boot was wrecked, and I had a scrape on my hand that didn't look like it required any immediate medical attention. I looked at Trixie. "Do you think that was an accident, Trix?"

The dog responded by barking enthusiastically.

"My thoughts exactly."

Eleven

I made a few phone calls when I arrived at work on Friday: the first to Jane to accept the dinner date for the following evening; the second to Kevin to tell him that we were in big trouble with Crawford; and the third to Crawford. Fortunately, he was at the precinct and available when I called.

I was feeling very guilty about the whole Jack McManus thing and wanted to be upfront with Crawford about it. It was actually Kevin's idea to come clean, which I thought was very mature, given that he was constantly thrusting Jack in my face.

This wasn't a date, I would explain, it was a setup: I was going to set up my very attractive neighbor with my very attractive friend Jack, who carried an enormous torch for me. Or so I told myself when I was feeling bad, like when I donned a pair of pants that made my butt look huge. I'm not sure what the reality of the situation was, but he had found me attractive and desirable enough to take out more than once. Crawford would understand, I thought, once I explained the whole thing.

Nevertheless, I thought I would lead with the whole speeding car thing. I figured that concern for my well-being would trump any anger at my breaking my promise never to see Jack again.

"Fiftieth Precinct. Detective Squad. Detective Crawford speaking. How can I help you?"

Wow, that's a mouthful. That litany would have taken me a year to memorize. I cleared my throat. "Hiya, Crawford."

He sounded surprised and more than a little pleased, always a good sign. "Hi there."

I went into my dramatic retelling of the story of the speeding car, my jump over the retaining wall, and the indignation I felt when my neighbor showed no regard for my safety. I assured him that in spite of everything, I had only a scrape as evidence of what had happened.

"Can you believe that?" I asked.

"Which part?"

"About my neighbor?"

He made a noise that didn't give me any indication how he felt. "Did you get a plate number?"

"There was no time. It happened so fast."

"And you're sure you're OK?" he asked.

"I'm fine. Trixie's fine. I'm just not sure if this was a drunk-driving incident or someone was really aiming for me."

He was silent for a minute. "I'll call the detectives in Dobbs Ferry PD and just give them a heads-up."

I rolled my eyes. I'm sure they would be thrilled to hear from Crawford and to hear that he was calling about me. They probably had a dart board with my picture on it at which they regularly threw sharp objects. I had given them more than my fair share of trouble over the past year. "If you think that's necessary."

"Necessary? It's essential, Alison. I don't know what kind of trouble you might be in now, but suffice it to say that I don't think this was a random thing." He sighed audibly. "So, let's review. No more visits to Rivieria Pointe, no going near Richie Kraecker. Go to school, go home, take a cooking class . . ."

"Hey! What's that supposed to mean?"

"It means keep your nose clean. Stay out of trouble. People won't aim their cars at you then. Or maybe they will but it won't be because you've ruffled any feathers in the construction community." He was running out of patience; that was obvious. "Listen, I have to run, but I have to ask you something."

I was still smarting over the cooking comment, but I let it go. "Shoot."

"The girls really want to meet you and I was hoping that you would go to dinner with us tomorrow night." He paused. "I know that it's a big step. . . ."

I swiveled around in my desk chair and stared out the big window in my office. "Well, I'm not sure that I can."

"Oh," he said, a little hurt. "You have plans?"

I knew it was a big deal for me to meet the girls but I expected more than a day's notice to prepare for such an event. "I do."

He was silent, waiting for me to explain.

"Before you get mad, let me just explain that I'm performing a public service."

He snorted. "Yes, when I think of public service, I think of you."

I ignored that. "I'm having dinner at Jane Farnsworth's."

"No idea who that is."

"Accordion Boy and Bagpipe Kid's mother."

"Oh."

"Anyway, she invited me over and said I could invite a friend. She's divorced and she's a doll, just adorable, really. So, I thought that I would invite Jack because he's single, too, and then it won't be uncomfortable when we're together . . ." I babbled, hoping to persuade him of my good intentions.

He started laughing. "You're going to fix up Jack McManus with a woman you've had two conversations with."

Well, when he said it like that, it didn't sound like a great idea. "I know it's not a perfect plan."

"Not a perfect plan?" he asked. "It's about as imperfect a plan as I could think of."

"Well, I already invited him so it's too late."

"I've got to see this. What time is it happening?"

"You can't come. You're not invited." Smooth, Alison.

"Oh," he said. He hadn't considered that. "You know what? I've got to run. I'll talk to you later." He hung up.

I wasn't exactly sure what his mood had been at the end of the conversation, but I was left with that sick feeling I get when I've really screwed things up. I was going to have to have the push-up bra surgically applied to my torso so that I was ready for the make-up sex that was hopefully going to take place once I pulled off this setup.

I swiveled back in my chair and faced my desk, my head in my hands. I heard movement outside my door and realized it was time to teach my first class of the day, a freshman composition course for struggling students that sucked the life out of me every time I taught it. It started at ten fifty, met three times a week, and lasted the requisite one hour, which was about all I could take.

Sometimes I wondered why I had gotten into teaching in the first place, and then I would read an essay of such beauty and remarkable clarity that I would regret ever questioning myself. I didn't think I would be moved to tears on this day with this particular class, but you never know.

I steeled myself for the inevitable onslaught of illegible and incomprehensible five-paragraph argument essays that I would encounter, but before I could enter the classroom, I ran into Kevin.

"Lunch?" he asked.

"After I teach this class, yes," I said. "But it has to be on campus because I have a one ten class, too."

He looked at me closely. "You OK?"

I bit my lip, trying to stifle the sob that was stuck at the back of my throat. "I guess."

He grabbed my hand. "We'll talk later," he said gently. "Go teach."

I went into the stuffy classroom, the one with a window up so high it was unreachable, and tossed my messenger bag on the desk. I scanned the crowd for anyone over six feet and saw that the usual duo of basketball center Calvin Marks and small forward Jessie Mindeiro had chosen not to attend class and that the window would therefore remain closed. "Five-paragraph essays," I commanded, and held out my hand.

Fifty minutes later, I had come no closer to explaining the term "ad hominem" as it related to Diana Morgan's argument that the mayor's congestion pricing plan would hurt New Yorkers, not help them. "Diana, you can't call the mayor a 'sniveling mound of flesh.' Do you understand why?" I asked. "Though I do applaud your accurate use of the word 'sniveling.'"

The other fifteen students in the class laughed. I looked up at the clock and saw that we had five minutes left. "So, let's review: no arguments against the person. Your premise must support your conclusion. I'm talking to you, Diana. And if the premise is true, the conclusion is likely true." I clapped my hands together dramatically. "And you are dismissed."

The students got up and exited the classroom as quickly as they possibly could, a few giving me good wishes for a nice weekend. I pulled my papers together and shoved them into my bag, turning to erase the board. The door swung open as I got to the words "ad hominem."

Crawford took a seat at the front of the classroom. "So, what about this premise? My girlfriend persists in going out with another man. Jack McManus is another man. Therefore, my girlfriend is going out with Jack McManus."

I sat down at the desk. "That premise is true in execution but not true in fact. Or as it relates to me."

Crawford folded his hands in front of him. He looked oversized and out of place at the small desk, much like my basketball player students did when they chose to attend class. "How do you figure that?"

"Crawford, I'm not interested in Jack. I went to the Kraecker party because I wanted to snoop around. I now know that that wasn't a smart thing to do." I looked down. "And out of some misguided attempt to help someone not be quite so lonely anymore, I decided to take him to Jane's tomorrow night. Plain and simple."

"How do you know she's lonely?" he asked. "You didn't even know her last name until about two weeks ago. And you still can't remember her sons' names. *Your* argument is faulty."

Good point. "I'm just assuming that she's lonely."

"And when we assume, what happens?" he asked. He didn't expect a response because he got up from the desk and stood over me. "I've decided on a new tack."

I looked up. "And what's that?"

He smiled, not unkindly. "My new motto is 'if you can't beat 'em, join 'em.' Meaghan, Erin, and I will be joining you at Jane's tomorrow night." I started to protest but he held up a hand. "Figure it out. Tell them you have extra guests and invite them to your house." He started for the door. "Or cancel it altogether. It's on you. We'll be coming to your house at seven, so whether we go to Jane's for dinner or we stay at your place, it's up to you to handle it."

"This is so not fair!" I cried, but the sound of his footfalls were already echoing in the empty hallway.

Kevin showed up at the door a few minutes later and took in my distraught face. "Did I just see . . . ?" he asked, hooking a thumb toward the hallway.

I nodded.

"He seemed like he was in a big hurry," he reported. He pulled at his collar, the priest version of Rodney Dangerfield.

"You could say that," I said. I pulled the strap of my bag over my shoulder; a thought occurred to me. "What are you doing tomorrow night, Kev?" I asked sweetly.

Twelve

My first thought when I awoke the next day was: must get boot heel back from Cranky McCrankypants.

I had an action-packed day in front of me, starting with Jose Tomasso's funeral at ten o'clock and ending with the mega–dinner party that I was now throwing. Jane Farnsworth had been exceedingly gracious about the change in plans and was looking forward to having dinner at my house, or so she said. I'm glad she was excited; I had no bloody idea what I was going to make and how I was going to make it, considering I had to serve at the Lord's Bounty in between the funeral and the dinner party. I wasn't even dealing with the fact that I would be meeting Crawford's daughters for the first time, something that normally would have sent me into an emotional tailspin. Given the events of the day, there was no time to get my panties in a bunch about that one. I rolled out of bed at eight, figuring that an early start was absolutely necessary if I was going to get everything done. I decided to look through the local paper when I got back from the boot heel reconnaissance mission to find out what their suggestion would be for feeding ten people in the easiest, most impressive way possible.

I took Trixie out and gave her a quick walk up and down the street, doing my best to do the "stern owner" routine. If dogs had the capability to laugh, she would have been roaring at me. We made sure to avoid Chez McCrankypants and went down the other half of the street, where she had tremendous success in completing the task at hand. Actually, she was a little too successful; I was beginning to wonder if her food was to blame.

After depositing her back at the house, I crept down the other half of the street to see if I could find my boot heel, which, as luck would have it, was not on the McCrankypants lawn but in an area that would be designated public property by any judge in the land: next to the sewer. I picked it up and hurried back to the street, muttering, "Don't know you. Don't like you. Never will." I was back at my house before being seen by anyone on the block.

When I got back home, I laid the broken heel on the counter and considered it for a moment. I decided that no good ever came from my wearing high heels. To wit: once I was wearing a gorgeous pair of black suede pumps and got shot by an old schoolmate of mine who also happened to be the head of a New York crime family. Another day, I was wearing the only pair of Manolo Blahniks I owned (courtesy of Max) when I was kidnapped by aforementioned schoolmate, who was quick to note my expensive choice of footwear. Leave it to a woman to acknowledge spectacular footwear even as she considered blowing your brains out. I concluded that these incidents proved that I was not a high-heel wearer but a sneaker or clog wearer. If I was going to be in that much danger all the time, I had to wear sensible shoes. Once I got through the funeral, to which I had to wear something at least a little fancy, it was back to my trusty Danskos. I could run, jump, swim, and do just about everything in those shoes.

The only thing in my refrigerator was a leftover container of takeout shrimp scampi that heated up very nicely in the microwave and a six-pack of iced coffee. I put both on the counter alongside my local newspaper and proceeded to scarf down the scampi, roasted garlic chunks and all. It did occur to me that I might be especially fragrant later in the day, but I threw caution to the wind and ingested more garlic than I probably should have. I washed it down with an iced coffee as I read through the paper and skimmed the restaurant section to see if anyone boasted a kitchen that could prepare a gourmet dinner for ten or so. As luck would have it, there was a place in town that fit the bill and was actually open at that early hour: Tony's Delicatessen. My heart sank.

Tony's my deli man and, interestingly, a sixty-something-year-old guy who thinks I'm the hottest thing this side of sopressata. I know how that sounds, but it's true. I don't know what it is, but he practically molests me every time I enter the place, which, until recently, had been frequently. Over the years, and particularly after my divorce, he had really stepped up his attempts to hold hands and kiss me. So out of concern for his feelings and my own, I stopped going there.

Yes, I knew there were other places in Dobbs Ferry to go for what I needed, but none were open and I was pressed for time.

I showered and dressed quickly in a black suit and heels and headed to the center of town to order the food for dinner, steeling myself for the onslaught of affection I would receive from Tony.

Tony was uncharacteristically quiet when I entered the store, the jangling bell over the door signaling my arrival. He turned around and regarded me with a look that was a cross between longing and disappointment.

"Hi, Tony," I said as nonchalantly as I could, pretending that I had been there every day since my last visit over the winter.

"Alison. Hello," he said guardedly.

I approached the counter and pulled a takeout menu from the holder next to the cash register. "Tony, I need dinner for a dozen or so people for tonight. Can you help me with that?" I skimmed the menu. "I'd like a tray of chicken francese, a tray of lasagna, a green salad, and garlic bread. Can you do that?"

He looked nervously toward the kitchen. "I'll have to ask Lucia."

I shrugged internally. Go ahead, I thought. I wasn't sure why he was so nervous and I didn't even know who Lucia was—it had always seemed that Tony's was a one-man operation—but I leaned against the counter and watched as he marched slowly toward the kitchen. A few words were exchanged in Italian, only one or two familiar to me. After a few seconds of silence, I heard the sound of pots and pans being thrown and more Italian, but this time it was accompanied by an ear-piercing howl. I crumpled the menu in my hand and tensed. Tony came out of the kitchen five minutes later, looking chagrined.

He stood in front of me, the counter separating us. "Yes," he said, nodding, "we should be able to do that for you."

I looked toward the kitchen and then back at Tony. "Are you sure?" I asked.

He pulled a notepad from his apron pocket and a pencil

from behind his ear. "Yes," he said again. "What time would you like to pick it up?"

"Tell-a her-a we close at seex!" the disembodied voice screamed from the kitchen.

"How's five forty-five?" I asked, mentally calculating how long it would take me to drive from the Lord's Bounty back to Tony's. I figured I would have to ditch my community service responsibility a full half hour before it was over in order to make all this work and prayed that there would be enough other people serving to make up for my absence. "And can I pick it up hot?"

Tony scratched a few words on the pad, careful not to catch my eye. Clearly, he knew that the woman in the back was crazy and he didn't need my acknowledgment of that fact. "Of course." He calculated the total and looked up. "That will be eighty-three dollars."

I pulled out my checkbook. "A check OK?"

"For you, of course," he said, and a small smile appeared. His hand crept across the counter and touched mine. I pulled back and began writing.

Another pan made its way across the kitchen in the back, creating a thunderous racket. I looked at Tony and he shrugged apologetically. I pulled the check out of the folder and quickly settled the bill without having to endure any further chitchat or public displays of affection. I fled the store, wondering just what in the hell was going on in there.

I headed north on Route 9 toward Croton-on-Hudson, where the Escalantes and Jose worshipped, according to the obituary that I had read in the paper. The funeral was being held at a church in the town just north of where the Lord's Bounty was held and I found it easily, maneuvering into a spot not far from Crawford's cruiser. It had never occurred to me that he would be there, so concerned was I with my broken boot heel and ordering dinner, but it made sense. One of the first times I had seen him he had been at the funeral of a former student of mine, where seeing him sing Catholic hymns in his solemn, Crawford-like fashion had immediately endeared him to me.

I got out of the car and picked my way across the uneven pavement of the sidewalk outside the church, praying that I wouldn't get my heel stuck in a broken piece of macadam and take a tumble. A face plant was the last thing I needed today after having run the Tony/Lucia gauntlet. Walking with my head down presented other challenges, though, and I looked up when I hit a solid mass of flesh.

"Fred. Hi!" I said.

He was standing a few feet from the front door of the church studying a sign adjacent to the stone building that read: READING THE BIBLE PREVENTS TRUTH DECAY. His brow was furrowed and his lips were moving. After a few moments during which he ignored me and the fact that my face had been in his chest a few minutes earlier, he broke out into a smile. He shook his head. " 'Truth decay,' " he said, continuing to shake his head, chuckling. He turned and looked at me, seemingly noticing me for the first time. "Oh, Alison. Hi," he said distractedly. He bent down and gave me an awkward hug. "What are you doing here?" he asked.

I tried to remain casual about the whole thing, looking around his girth to see if I spied Crawford. He was about a half block down the street, talking to a short, dark-haired woman with the most impressive *tuchis* I had ever seen. Carmen Montoya, I thought. He had not done that backside justice in his description. Packed into black dress pants, it looked like she was smuggling a basketball into the funeral.

"Huh?" I said, suddenly aware that Fred was waiting for a response from me.

"You. Here. Why?" he asked in his usual caveman speak.

"Oh, that. Well, I'm friends with the Escalantes," I said, continuing to stare at Crawford and Carmen.

Fred raised an eyebrow. "You are?"

I nodded, returning my attention to him. "Yes. I met them at the Lord's Bounty. You know, that place where I serve meals every Saturday night?"

He continued to look down at me.

"What? I can't be friends with them?"

He pulled a picture out of his pocket. "Who's this then?"

I studied it. "Jose Tomasso." His picture had been all over the papers so I would have had to have been on another planet not to know who he was and what he looked like.

He shook his head. "Not him," he said impatiently. "The woman."

She was of indeterminate age and ethnic origin and standing beside Jose in the photo. I took a guess. "His wife?"

Fred gave me a disdainful look and I knew that I had guessed wrong. "Good friend you are."

"Well who is it, then?" I asked.

He crossed his arms over his massive chest. "You don't know, I'm not telling." He sniffed the air in a manner not unlike that of my golden retriever. "What did you have for breakfast? Smells like shrimp scampi."

"Good guess," I said.

"Trying to ward off vampires?"

"Funny."

"Seriously, dude, lay off the garlic in the A.M. The smell's giving me a headache." He started off down the street, heading in the direction of Crawford and the woman with the spectacular rump.

"Oh, thanks." Wonderful suggestion, albeit a little too late to do anything about. I rustled around in my purse to see if I could come up with a breath mint but found only a dirty packet of Alka-Seltzer, a tube of Dramamine caplets, and a cough drop covered in lint, which I stuck in my mouth. Surely the scent of Mentholyptus would cover the garlic.

Fred caught up with Crawford and Carmen, all of them assiduously ignoring me as I passed within ten feet of them before entering the church. So that's how we're going to play it, I thought, as I threw Crawford a withering glance. I took a seat on the right side of the church a few rows from the back. The church was small—about twenty pews on either side of the aisle, which were rapidly filling up with a diverse group of people, some Hispanic, some not. I got the sense, watching the people take their seats, that this was a close-knit community and that a lot of people had come out of respect for the Escalantes and not because they were especially close to them. I saw Kerry and Rebecca take seats on the other side of the church and recognized a few of the other servers from the Lord's Bounty scattered throughout as well.

Crawford, Fred, and Carmen pushed in next to me, forcing me to sit between them and the people on my right. Carmen held her hand out to me, her long, gold nails glancing over my palm as we shook.

"Carmen Montoya," she said by way of introduction.

"Alison Bergeron."

"Pleasure," she whispered.

I leaned across Crawford and Carmen and tapped Fred on his tree trunk thigh. "Hey, what are you doing tonight?" I asked, sotto voce.

He shrugged. "Ask the little woman."

In Max's case, "little woman" was truly an apt description and I knew that Fred meant it as such. He would never use the term as a derogatory way of describing his wife. In his mind, she was little. And a woman. Ergo, she was a little woman. "Well, if you're not doing anything, come to dinner at seven."

He shrugged again.

I took that as a yes. I looked at Carmen. "You're welcome to come, too."

She patted my hand, which was resting on Crawford's leg. "Oh, honey, you don't want us. Trust me." She pulled the front of her shirt down, the buttons of which were straining across her chest. "I've got four kids and they're not housebroken."

Good to know. Thanks for the warning.

Crawford, seated next to me, leaned over and whispered in my ear. I got a whiff of his Crawford scent: freshly laundered clothes. My stomach did a little flip.

"I didn't expect to see you here," he said.

"Well, then you're not as astute as you might think."

He pulled back and gave me a tight smile. "I'm pretty astute."

I raised my eyebrows. "You think so, huh?"

"I'm astute enough to know that you had something with garlic for breakfast. A garlic croissant, maybe?" He leaned in closer. "This is a nice surprise," he said and slid his hand around my waist.

I jumped slightly as his fingers tickled my midsection, jostling the old lady sitting next to me. She glared at me. "Sorry," I said. I turned to Crawford, who was purposely staring straight ahead. "Stop it," I whispered, but the admonition only resulted in him pulling me closer. "I mean it," I said, trying to pull away. I lost my balance and tumbled into the old lady again. She was not amused. The organist started playing and Crawford straightened up, eyes on the altar, to my relief.

Over the sounds of the grand organ situated to the right of the altar, I could hear voices in the church vestibule behind me. I turned and was incredibly surprised to see Richie Kraecker entering with the skeletal Morag Moragna hanging off his arm, wearing a pillbox hat with a film of lace covering her eyes.

Oh, for god's sake, I thought, that's a little dramatic, isn't it?

I turned to Crawford, throwing my head toward the back of the church. "Hey, Detective Hot Pants. Were you astute enough to anticipate *that*?"

Thirteen

The mood at the Lord's Bounty that night was solemn. The table that the Escalantes usually sat at remained empty; the rest of the guests assembled at the other tables, it seemed, out of respect for Hernan and his clan. Nobody spoke of Jose's death outright, but the mood was somber and people chatted to themselves in whispered tones. I handed out the salads, and then the main meals, in silence. Even the kitchen staff, a team of women from a local Korean church who were always good for a few laughs, prepared the food in complete silence.

The funeral had been a lovely celebration of Jose's life—but as expected, extremely sad. I had even caught Carmen Montoya, a woman who dealt with homicide on a daily basis, tearing up at the pastor's sermon.

I had managed to snag a few moments with Amalia outside the church to express my sympathies. We had hugged for several minutes before Hernan came to her side and quietly asked her to join her family again. Hernan and I didn't speak but the sadness in his eyes spoke volumes. He had taken in his sister's son and had to bring him home to bury; there were no words to take away that pain.

I had parted with Crawford in front of the church. "I'll see you later," he had said, giving me a quick peck, heading off to trail behind Richie Kraecker, whose appearance had brought out a couple of photographers and reporters from the area newspapers. When Crawford and I parted, Richie was giving a statement to the *Daily News*, protesting that while Jose was a hard worker with a clean record, Richie had had no idea that he was an illegal alien. He then made a big show of taking out his wallet and promising to support the extended Escalante/Tomasso family. I wondered if it had occurred to him that they would be back in Ecuador before spring turned into summer. Maybe instead of giving them money, he could use his extensive clout to get them real, not manufactured, green cards.

I shook off my melancholy. I made a stop at Joey's table and even he, usually extremely chatty, had nothing to say. I stood for a few minutes taking in the depressed bunch of men sitting at the table and, when I figured out that they weren't in the mood to chat, moved on.

Mrs. Dwyer and Patty were at their usual spot. "Hello, Alison dear," she said. I leaned down and Patty gave me her paw.

"Hi, Mrs. Dwyer."

"Sad night." That was an understatement.

"It is." I picked up her empty plate and bent down to let Patty lick up the extra gravy on it.

"Jose seemed like a nice boy."

"You knew Jose?" I asked, surprised.

She nodded. "Of course. Everyone knew Jose. He didn't live here but he spent a lot of time at Hernan and Alba's, and they live next door to me. He grew up with them. Did you know that?"

I didn't. But I pulled up a chair and sat beside Mrs. Dwyer. Patty rested her head in my lap. "What else did you know about Jose?"

"He was a wonderful artist."

When I didn't say anything, and it was clear that she knew that I was wondering how she knew that, she elaborated. "Hernan told me. Jose wanted to be an artist. But life was hard for him here." She dropped her voice. "Because of the situation."

"Situation?" I asked.

"You know, the whole illegal thing."

Of course I knew about that. I waited for her to go on and I didn't have to wait long.

"They all desperately want green cards but it's not like the old days. It takes a long time to get one of those." She patted her dog's head. "Jose was the only one who had one. So he seemed to do OK with work. I always wondered how he got one when Hernan and Alba couldn't." She shrugged.

Me, too. Obviously Jose had been the recipient of one of the green cards handed out by Richie and his crew at Riviera Pointe. I decided not to press her anymore because the dining room was emptying out and I could see that the woman she came with—a cranky lady named Mrs. Jessups—was itching to leave. I gave Mrs. Dwyer a quick hug and looked at the clock, realizing with alarm that I had ten minutes to make a fifteen-minute trip to Tony's in Dobbs Ferry before he closed the store.

I bid a hasty farewell to the ladies in the kitchen and booked out to the parking lot.

I got into the car and started it up, only noticing after I'd been sitting there a few seconds that there was a note on the windshield. With one leg out the car door I reached around, grabbing it from under the windshield wiper.

"Mined your own bizness."

Bad spelling aside, it certainly had an ominous ring. Mind my own business? Who would take the time to follow me here and put that note under my windshield wiper? Was it someone who attended the meal? I went through the list. Although the prison guys certainly fell into the "most likely" category, none of them struck me as sinister; they were right out of *The Gang Who Couldn't Shoot Straight.* I mentally went through the room and couldn't come up with anyone else. I thought that maybe someone had approached one of the teenage boys outside the church and asked him to do it. That was a possibility. I looked around, simultaneously locking my doors. I shoved the note into my coat pocket and peeled out of the parking lot, not sure whether to be more scared of the note, its author, or the fact that I had less than five minutes to get to Tony's.

I touched the note in my pocket every now and again as I made my way south on Route 9. I thought about giving it to Crawford but figured it would just amount to a whole heap of trouble for Joey and Tiny and their crew, and I didn't want that for them. At the next red light, I took the note and balled it up, shoving it down into the space between the seat and the console.

I got to Tony's at five minutes to six and said a prayer that Lucia had gone home for the day or crawled back under her rock. Maybe a house had fallen on her and I could scurry off with her ruby slippers. Tony was cashing out the register when I entered, out of breath and sweaty. He turned and, unlike when I had been in earlier, gave me a big smile. Yep, she was gone, or at least very busy in the kitchen.

"Hello, *mi amore*," Tony said, and I knew that I was in for it. After my work at the Lord's Bounty, I didn't have the energy to fend him off, but fend him off I had to if I was going to get out of there before Lucia fried me in hot oil. It was kind of like the Italian version of *Sweeney Todd*.

My food was in three long trays, with the bread wrapped in tinfoil on top of them. I assessed the situation and determined that I couldn't carry it all to the car myself in one trip; if Tony helped me, at least his hands would be occupied and he wouldn't be able to feel me up. "Thanks, Tony. Can you give me a hand with this?" I asked.

"Of course!" he said, closing the register. "A girl like you can't carry all of that by herself."

Well, yes, I probably could, I was tempted to say, but I decided to go with the damsel in distress routine so I could get back to my house as quickly as possible. I had a lot to do and not a lot of time in which to do it.

"Just give me a minute, my love," Tony said, disappearing into the back of the deli.

The cacophony of pots and pans being thrown to and fro in the kitchen started quickly and violently and shocked me into action. I heard Tony protesting that he was just friends with me and that I was in love with another man and would never be his. He cried that I wasn't even his type. Could have fooled me. And what did that mean anyway?

I didn't have time to think about it because a pan hit the stainless steel sink in the kitchen and clattered to the floor. I felt a cold sheen of sweat break out on my brow and I grabbed the bread and the top tray of food from the counter, all I could handle in my maiden trip to the car. I hustled out, deposited the first batch of food in the trunk, and headed back in to get the rest.

"Just-a friends? Just-a friends?" The sound of the disembodied voice carried out to the front of the store.

I grabbed the rest of the food and stumbled toward the front door, cursing the jangling bell that announced my comings and goings. I prayed that Lucia would stay in the back and just let me take my food in peace. A pot whizzed by my head and hit the glass in the door, creating a spider web pattern, but not shattering the glass.

"Holy shit!" I said and kicked the door open with my foot, the sauce from the chicken francese leaking out the side of the container and running down the front of my sweatshirt. The heat seeped through the fabric and down to my bra, burning my boobs in the process. That'll leave a mark, I thought.

I should have cooked. This was just so not worth it.

I peeled out of the parking spot in front of the store and headed home, pulling the sweatshirt away from my skin, trying to minimize the damage that would be incurred by the hot sauce. I got home in record time, making a couple of trips to and from the car to transport the food, and finally stripping my sweatshirt off and throwing it into Trixie's bed.

"Here, Trix. Make love to this. There's chicken sauce all over it." I stood in the kitchen in my bra and jeans. The dog leapt into the bed and began to wrestle with the sweatshirt, finding all of the good drippings and licking them with a gusto normally reserved for the wet food that I treat her to occasionally.

I opened the refrigerator and took out a bottle of chardonnay. If I was going to make it through this evening, I needed wine, and lots of it. Before pouring myself a generous glassful, I took a swig directly from the bottle.

I leaned against the kitchen counter holding the wine bottle, the only sounds in the room coming from Trixie's dog bed as she fondled my sweatshirt. I closed my eyes and took a deep breath, enjoying the quiet of my house. I swirled some chardonnay around on my tongue, holding the oaky wine in my mouth.

"Alison?"

I spit out the wine, choking on the thimbleful that didn't come out with the rest of the expectoration. The bottle shook in my hand as the sound of Crawford's voice and his footfalls in my front hallway got closer. He was in the kitchen before I had a chance to respond, his daughters on either side of him, their eyes wide.

What's the matter? I wanted to ask. You've never seen a woman in a bra and jeans drinking wine out of the bottle?

"Is this a bad time?" he asked, taking in my attire, or lack thereof.

I crossed my arms over my chest. "You could say that."

He spoke to the girls, who appeared to have turned to stone. "Hey, go into the living room, please? I'll be right there." They beat a hasty exit and Crawford burst out laughing. "Is this how you dress when I'm not around? If so, I'm moving in."

I rolled my eyes. "Ever heard of knocking?"

He looked sheepish. "Sorry about that."

"I need a shower. Do you think you could express my regret at this unfortunate situation and tell them that we'll have a do-over in about twenty minutes?"

He leaned in and sniffed my chest. "Sure. You smell good. Is that chicken francese?"

"Yep. Do me a favor? Put the food in the oven at three-fifty."

"Lids or no lids?"

I had no idea. "Pick one." I headed off down the hallway and scurried up the steps to my bedroom, my heart still racing from the various shocks I had endured since leaving the Lord's

Bounty. I sat on the edge of the bed and took off my sneakers. The phone began ringing; I picked it up and put it between my ear and neck as I struggled to get my gym socks off. "Hello?"

"Ms. Bergeron? Madeleine Cranston from Riviera Pointe calling?"

Who? "Yes. Uh, hi, Madeleine." I went through my mental database trying to figure out who this was and why she was calling me. And why everything she said sounded like a question. A picture of a busty blonde popped into my head and I remembered meeting her at the party the Wednesday before.

"I wanted to follow up with you about your request for more information on the condos?"

Oh, right. The fake interest in buying a condo coming home to roost. "Thanks for calling, Madeleine. I'm afraid this isn't the best time . . ."

"I won't take too much of your time? I was wondering if we could make a date for you to come down to the sales office so we could talk about your needs?"

Now, that was a great idea. I needed to talk to someone about my needs. They ranged from the fact that I needed love, support, and encouragement on a daily basis to a need for a compliment or two on my hair. I decided to play it straight and threw out a suggestion that we meet on Monday afternoon.

"Let me look at my planner?" She paused as she consulted her schedule. "Yes, that should work? Two thirty?" she asked.

"Sounds great. Where's the office?"

"Right next to the construction site?"

Didn't she know? Didn't she work there? What was with all of the questions? I repeated what she said to make sure that it was indeed next to the construction site. I jotted a note down on a Post-it on the nightstand.

And now I had even less time than before to get ready. And I was a mess. I took an abbreviated shower, hoping that the garlic emanating from my pores would be washed away, along with the scent of chicken francese and any odors from dinner at the Lord's Bounty. Tonight wasn't a banner night for the cooking team—undercooked ziti, bland tomato sauce, and frozen meatballs. But everybody seemed hungry enough and every last morsel had been consumed.

I put on a pair of my nicer jeans, an oxford shirt, and my clogs. I was beyond wanting or needing to impress this crowd. Jane and Frankie had seen me walking the dog in my pajamas, and now Crawford's daughters had seen me in a bra and jeans. When you've been seen half-naked by a number of your guests there really isn't any point in upping the fashion quotient, is there?

I had spoken to Max, aka the "little woman," and confirmed that she and Fred could come to dinner as well. I didn't want to rely on Fred to convey the invitation; he wasn't entirely trust-worthy in that regard. Meeting Crawford's daughters, introduc-ing Jane to Jack, hosting dinner for eleven people—I needed reinforcements. And Max was my security blanket. Even if the evening went down in flames, I could count on Max to extin-guish the fire. I hoped. She was kind of a loose cannon.

I flew down the stairs and did a spectacular pose in the en-trance to the living room, arms in the air. I got a better look at Crawford: turtleneck, new jeans, loafers without socks. He looked like a model in the *International Male* catalog, wearing clothes I had never seen before. He smiled, and one of his daughters let out a hearty laugh at my pose. The other—whom I dubbed Sad Eyes but who seemed to be more an Always-in-a-Bad-Mood Eyes—looked at me like I was crazy. Get used to it, sister. You ain't seen nothin' yet.

I held out my hand. "Hi, I'm Alison."

The tall one, who looked like Crawford and who had a ready smile, introduced herself as Meaghan and Sad Eyes identified herself, through her father, as Erin. She was as tiny as Meaghan was statuesque and as quiet as the other one was gregarious.

I told them to come into the kitchen so I could get them drinks, which I had stocked up on between the funeral and the Lord's Bounty. I opened the refrigerator, which was filled to the brim with different kinds of soda, cider, and beer. "Help yourselves. I have to see what your father did with the food."

Crawford held his hands up in surrender. "I did exactly what you asked."

Max and Fred came through the back door as I was digging through the lasagna to see how hot it was. Max was in skinny jeans, black suede ballerina flats, and a tight black turtleneck, looking like Audrey Hepburn in *Charade*. I, on the other hand, in my jeans and oxford, looked like George Kennedy in *Charade*," minus the fedora. Max and I air kissed and Fred grunted a greeting, something along the lines of "me like lasagna."

Erin came to life at the sight of Max. "Hi. I'm Erin," she said, all happy and animated. She and Max embraced.

Hmmm. I'd have to see if they had skinny jeans in the big and tall girls' shop. Clearly, they were a way to this teen's heart.

Kevin and Jack were next to arrive, letting themselves in through the front door. Kevin was rocking his full priest regalia for some unknown reason, and Jack was in jeans and a turtleneck, holding a big bag marked "Rangers" that was filled to the brim with hockey loot. I braced myself for his meeting with Crawford, who emerged from the kitchen with a big smile on his face and his arms extended.

"Father," he said, embracing Kevin. "Good to see you. And you must be Jack."

I was blinded momentarily by Jack's teeth but did happen to notice a very firm handshake between the two of them; it had the whisper of a pissing contest, but when they released, nobody appeared to have any crushed fingers or hand bones.

I did see Jack drop his hand to the side of his thigh and flex his fingers a few times, however; Crawford had apparently employed his own version of the Vulcan death grip just so Jack would know who was in charge. I asked Jack if I could take the bag he was holding.

"You? No." He smiled. "The stuff in this bag wouldn't make it past the hallway if you got a whiff of what was inside." He reached in and pulled out a Mylar-wrapped wine bottle. "But you can take this."

I took the bottle from him and pulled off the Mylar sleeve. It was a 1998 Bordeaux. "Very nice. Thank you," I said.

"You like merlot, if I recall?" he said.

Crawford put his arm around my shoulders and gave me a little squeeze that was not at all affectionate and every bit proprietary. "Oh, she loves merlot. But not as much as a good old martini." He leaned over and kissed the top of my head, further underscoring the fact that I had no idea whom he had become between leaving the kitchen and entering the hallway. He had only kissed my head one other time and that had convinced me that we were breaking up. "Speaking of which, would you like me to make you one, honey?" His smile was stiff and fake.

"Sure," I said, cocking my head slightly. Honey? Who are you? I wanted to ask, but refrained. I took Kevin's black coat and threw it over the banister. "And what would you two like? Kevin, your usual chardonnay?"

"That would be lovely," he said. "Can I do anything to help?"

You could take off that collar and stop acting like an extra from *Father Flanagan of Boys Town*, I thought, but I asked him instead to bring everyone into the living room while I futzed around in the kitchen, pretending to cook.

I was finally alone in the hallway, the majority of my guests corralled in the kitchen, when the doorbell rang. Their seemingly happy voices carried into the hallway and I was pleased that everyone was having a good time. I walked to the front door and could see in the sidelight that it was Jane and her boys, with a couple of other people standing behind them. Frankie had been dropped off and picked up by his father from the Lord's Bounty, and, as usual, the kid and I had exchanged nary a word during our time serving. I hadn't seen Brendan since he had left for Notre Dame in the fall and was happy to see him. I opened the door and smiled, ready to embrace my former dog walker and a young man whom I had called Bagpipe Kid at one time.

Next to Frankie was Amalia. She came in and wrapped her arms around me. "Frankie invited me," she whispered in my ear. "I hope it's OK that I came."

I stepped out of her embrace and held her at arm's length, my hands on her shoulders. "I couldn't be happier that you're here. How are you holding up today?"

She shrugged slightly and gave me a sad smile. "I'm OK. I'm just happy to be here."

I hugged her again. "I am, too." I looked at Frankie over the top of her head and mouthed "good idea."

He blushed bright red and dropped his eyes to the floor.

The rest of the guests were milling about and I turned to greet Jane, who was standing off to the side with a woman I had never met.

"Hi," Jane said, unwrapping a silk scarf from around her neck. She was her usual put-together self in a pair of wool pants and a cashmere sweater, her blond hair pulled back into a ponytail. "Sorry we're late." She turned to the woman on her right, a tall gal with short hair and tortoiseshell glasses. "Alison, this is my partner, Kathy. Kathy, Alison Bergeron."

I shook Kathy's hand, a half-smile frozen on my face.

In back of me, I heard Max's signature guffaw reverberate in the hallway.

Fourteen

"Well, I didn't see that coming," I whispered to Max, the two of us in the kitchen, supposedly getting dinner ready. What we were really doing was standing nose to nose behind the counter taking stock of the fact that I had completely misread Jane's situation. How was I going to cover up the fact that Jack was there as a setup, which any third-grader could have figured out from the makeup of the guest list, which consisted of priest/friend, boyfriend, boyfriend's kids, best friend, best friend's husband, single white male with no seeming connection to anyone except priest/friend . . . and the list ends there? I made a loud sound as I banged the oven closed and leaned against the counter, taking a healthy slug of my wine. The martini that Crawford had made me was long gone.

Max doesn't whisper. Ever. I was sure her voice was carrying into the living room, two rooms away. "What do I know? I thought JC Chasez would be the breakout star of 'N Sync."

I had no idea what she was talking about and gave her a puzzled look.

"Justin Timberlake? Hello? 'SexyBack'?" she said as if I should know what she meant. For emphasis, she knocked her knuckles against my skull.

"Ow," I said, rubbing the spot where her bony little fingers had made contact with skull. "What does Justin Timberlake have to do with this situation?" And to clarify in case she still didn't understand why I didn't understand Justin's relationship to Jane's sexual orientation, I continued, "What does that have to do with the fact that Jane is gay?" I dropped my voice so that she could barely hear me.

"I'm just saying," she said, pausing dramatically, "you never know."

I folded my arms across my chest. "To think that I put my relationship with Crawford on the line to fix this woman up with Jack McManus. What's wrong with me?"

Max studied me. "What's wrong with *you*? We don't have enough time to delve into that one. What's wrong with tonight is that you screwed it up. Big time. But everyone will eventually get over it." She bent over and touched her toes, limbering up for what, I don't know. "In any event, you have to feed the people in the living room, including my husband, who gets very cranky when he gets hungry." She opened the refrigerator and pulled out another beer. "I'll fend him off with this."

I was left alone in the kitchen, figuring I had a few more

minutes to hang out there before it became obvious that I was avoiding everyone. Jane's partner, Kathy, was very nice and had thanked me for inviting her to come along to the dinner party. I acted like it was every day that my neighbor, whom I hoped I could fix up with my priest's handsome brother, came out to me at a dinner party I had no business having. The boys, Brendan and Frankie, were their usual silent selves, still regarding me with fear and suspicion after some collective experiences we had had involving dead bodies and knife-wielding maniacs. Who could blame them? They did thaw a bit when they discovered that there were two attractive teenage girls in the living room, but they also took note of aforementioned girls' giant father and his occupation almost immediately. Nothing like having a cop father around to throw a wet blanket on the raging fire of teenage hormones. I knew that Crawford was a big softie, but they didn't. And maybe that was a good thing.

I thought about Kathy and Jane again. I'm a moron, I thought, and not for the first time that week. It probably wouldn't be the last time, either.

Amalia came into the kitchen, interrupting my mental self-flagellation. "Do you need any help?" She stood at the counter opposite from me and leaned across.

"No, I've got it," I said. "It's all catered so it's not that much work." I grabbed a towel from the refrigerator handle and wiped my hands. "I don't do much cooking. That's why I'm glad they gave me serving duties at Lord's Bounty."

She smiled slightly. "We didn't feel like going tonight."

"Of course you didn't," I said. I leaned against the counter, across from her. "But I'm glad you came tonight. Are you feeling up to being with so many people?"

"It's better than being in my house. If I have to look at one more casserole of chicken and rice I'm going to puke," she said, sticking a finger down her throat.

"Yeah, what's with the after-funeral casserole? Does every culture have that?" I asked, trying to lighten both of our moods.

She nodded. "Seems like it. When Frankie called after he got home from the Lord's Bounty, I jumped at the chance to come here. It's been kind of a downer being at my house."

I nodded.

Her eyes welled up. "Did that sound bad?"

I shook my head. "No. Just honest. It must be very hard on your family."

"Jose was an idiot," she said, angrily and uncharacteristically. I had never heard her say anything disparaging about anyone, let alone a family member.

I flinched a little bit and she noticed, immediately backtracking. "I didn't mean that. He was just always in trouble."

"With the police?" I asked.

She shook her head. "Maybe. I don't know. All I know is that he and my father fought constantly about what he was doing. He was always looking for the fast cash."

Drugs, I thought immediately, and felt ashamed. I guess there were other ways to make quick cash, but I didn't know of any.

She gave me a look that indicated that she knew what I was thinking. "I don't know. I'm not sure. It's not like he didn't have the opportunity to get into that. I think it was something else, but I never did find out." She reached into the pocket of her jeans. "All I have is this." She pulled out a worn piece of paper and handed it to me. It was a lined sheet of notebook paper with names, addresses, and dollar amounts, all written in neat rows. "I don't know what it is, but Jose left it in my dictionary. You know, the one he gave me when we were here?"

Jane came into the kitchen, and Amalia immediately fell silent. "Can I give you a hand with anything?" she asked. She put an arm around Amalia's shoulders and squeezed.

I ran my hand nervously through my hair, which in the heat of the kitchen, had grown in volume. "Oh, no. Thanks, Jane."

Amalia excused herself and ducked out of the room. I put the folded piece of paper into my back pocket.

Jane smiled at me, her expression kind. "You didn't know?"

I burst out laughing. "Not a clue."

"I'm sorry," she said, leaning on the counter that separated us. "I really haven't been the best neighbor to you. We really should know each other better by now."

"What do you have to apologize for?" I asked, taking a wineglass from the cabinet and pouring some wine into it. "Wine?"

"Absolutely," she said eagerly. She took a small sip. "Jack seems lovely, though."

"Is it that obvious?"

She shook her head. "Just look at your guest list."

I held up a hand. "Stop. I've already been through this."

"I do have a single and straight sister who's adorable, though."

I laughed again and threw my hands up. "I'm out. No more setups." The oven timer, which I had finally figured out could be set and would let me know when my dinner was ready, rang. "All of this has just highlighted for me how little I know about you, though. Let's have dinner one night." I put on an oven mitt. "And it's on me. It's the least I can do."

She clinked her glass against mine, which was sitting on the counter. "It's a deal." She sniffed the air in the kitchen. "The food smells delicious. You must have been cooking all day."

I snorted. "Me? Not a chance. I brought it in. From Tony's. You know the place right in town?"

"Oh, yes," she said, seriously, her tone fraught with meaning.

I looked at her and raised an eyebrow. "What?"

"It's nothing," she said and took a sip of her wine. "It's just that Tony got a little too familiar with me, if you know what I mean?"

"Familiar how?"

She laughed, embarrassed. "You know. Trying to hold my hand, always telling me he loved me, stuff like that. Calling me *mi amore*. He even tried to kiss me once." She took the lid off of the tray of food that I had set on the counter, steam rising from the chicken and filling the space between us. "It's stupid, but it made me uncomfortable, so I stopped going there."

My mouth fell open. "He did? You did?"

She nodded. "He makes great food, though." She stirred the chicken with a spoon I handed her and ladled sauce over the cutlets. "I heard he got remarried, though, so maybe I can safely go back there."

Not a chance, I thought. No wonder Lucia, the new wife, was so incensed. They were married and he was still up to his old tricks. She wanted to inherit the Boar's Head franchise and nothing was going to stand in her way. I didn't know whether to be happy, sad, humiliated, or relieved that I wasn't the only woman in town being mashed on by the horny deli owner. I pulled out another tray of food and set it beside the chicken. "He hits on me, too," I said. "But I'm just too damned lazy to find another deli."

Jane started laughing. "Not going there has made things a bit inconvenient. Not being able to drop in there after getting off the train to pick up dinner is a drag."

I cut up some bread and put it into a basket. I heard Fred roar from the living room, "Are we ever going to eat or what?" and knew that I had to get the food out.

"What do you do?" I asked, pulling forks and knives out of the cutlery drawer. Hungry cavemen make me nervous. I knew it was just a matter of time before he came into the kitchen and made his displeasure known.

"I'm an architect." She started folding paper napkins into triangles. "I work for a local firm so I can be home relatively early every night."

I thought about that for a moment. "Do you know anything about New York City building codes and the like?" I asked as nonchalantly as I could.

She looked at me, curious. "Of course. Why do you want to know?"

I considered how much I could tell her and then figured— we've come this far, we might as well go all the way. "I'm interested in what's going on at Riviera Pointe."

"Oh, you mean Richie Kraecker and his less-than-stellar buildings?" she said. When I looked surprised that she knew, she explained. "I used to work for Kraecker's biggest competitor before I started locally. You know Donovan Corcoran?"

Of course I did. Their signs hung all over the city. I nodded.

"I used to bid jobs against Kraecker all the time. But when you have half the city building inspectors in your hip pocket, it's kind of hard to compete."

I dropped the knife that I was using to cut the bread and it clattered to the floor. Max was absolutely right: you just never know.

Fifteen

The evening ended well enough. After I served dinner, I was able to spend some time with Crawford's daughters, making a good enough impression to get even Erin to smile a few times. Crawford had told me once that she thought I was the catalyst for her parents' divorce, despite the fact that they had been separated for six years prior to their union ending for good. Although he had done everything to convince her otherwise, she was still holding on to hope that they would get back together. But now, with her mother getting married in the summer to a fellow divorcé with, alarmingly, four children under the age of ten and having seen that I wasn't the Wicked Witch of the West, she was starting to thaw. Meaghan, on the other hand, was fine with everything. She had made her peace with her family's situation long ago, according to Crawford. And she had been working on Erin to see things as they really were between her parents: over.

So Erin had smiled a few times. It was a start. It was, at the very least, détente.

Jane and I agreed to have dinner on Wednesday. I knew that Crawford probably wouldn't be able to make it, and she said that Kathy probably wouldn't be able to make it either; we agreed that if we waited for our significant others to rearrange their schedules, it would probably be a long time before we could plan anything. Kathy was an attorney at a white-shoe law firm in New York and worked very long hours, so Jane's and my situations with regard to our love lives were pretty similar. And Jane's being an architect was an added plus. I thought about all the questions I wanted to ask her about building construction, unions, and developers, and specifically what else she had heard about Richie Kraecker and his business practices. She could come in very handy indeed.

All in all, the night had been a success. Jack had handed out his cache of Rangers' merchandise, delighting Frankie, Brendan, Meaghan—and me—no end. I had been the recipient of a signed puck from the team's high-scoring center, which now had a prominent place on my desk at school. Crawford, finally seeing for himself that I had absolutely no interest in Jack besides his connection to my favorite hockey team, had thawed a little himself and had ceased acting like RoboBoyfriend.

I taught my morning classes and prepared for my meeting with Madeleine Cranston at Riviera Pointe. I wanted to see how far I could go before having to commit to anything or—gasp—show my financial records. I had played it a little fast and loose with the credit card lately, buying some clothes that were a bit out of my league financially. But what the hell? You only live once. And I wasn't about to live that life in Payless shoes and a faux shearling coat from Kmart. Especially now that I was divorced and only had myself to think about.

I pulled my emergency lipstick out of the top of my desk drawer. If any day called for lipstick, today was it. I applied, smacked my lips together, and moved the mirror around to see how much of my hair I could see. As usual, it was a mess. I did my usual time-saving trick of patting it down with my hands because I didn't keep an emergency brush or comb in my desk.

I took one last look at my reflection. Good enough. Madeleine Cranston, with her awe-inspiring décolletage and blond beehive of hair, had nothing on me.

Well, actually, that wasn't really true, but I needed a little boost of self-confidence if I was going to lie my way into Riviera Pointe. I don't know what I was expecting to accomplish but I figured it was worth a try.

I arrived at Madeleine Cranston's office, housed in a glass-enclosed sales building a few blocks from the actual construction site. I sat in a very well-appointed lobby, casually flipping through a sales brochure that was given to me by a reed-thin, long-legged young woman in a fashionable print wrap dress. I looked at her, immediately felt bad about my own cardigan/skirt combo (a sure bet every morning for me), and began to study the sales brochure as if there would be a test on it in a few minutes. I realized then that I had no idea what I was going to talk to Madeleine about. Did I really think I could wing it? Regardless of what I thought, the time was now: she was click-clacking across the marble floor toward me, a huge smile on her elaborately painted face. Between the face and the giant hair, it seemed as if the *Dynasty* look had returned and I hadn't been alerted: the twin set and the herringbone skirt that I was wearing harkened back to *Murder, She Wrote*.

I stood. "Hello, Madeleine!" I said with extra cheer.

"Ms. Bergeron? Hi?" she asked in that annoying, questioning way of hers. She extended a well-manicured hand. We shook.

"Thank you for calling me the other night," I said. "And please, call me Alison."

"And what is it that I can help you with?" Her smile held in place as if glued there.

I had no flipping idea. "Uh, I was thinking that it may be time to downsize since my . . ." I hesitated, wondering how I had concocted this lie so quickly and why I was giving her personal details about myself, ". . . divorce . . . well, actually he's dead . . . but that was after . . ." I took a deep breath and focused. "I was thinking that Riviera Pointe would be the perfect place for me since I teach at St. Thomas." There. That was easy.

She gave me a knowing glance that said, Yes, who would want to live in a house where a dead body had been found? Because unless she had been living under a rock, everybody knew that my ex, Ray, had been found in my kitchen missing his hands and feet. But she didn't let the gruesomeness of that detail cloud her thoughts. She clapped her hands together, the sound reverberating in the giant, marble-filled room. "Excellent!" It was the first time I had heard her punctuate a sentence with something other than a question mark. She leaned in and whispered conspiratorially. "And it will bring you that much closer to that delicious new man of yours?"

Crawford? I looked at her. Judging from the way she was practically drooling over the memory of said delicious man, and the fact that I didn't think she had met Crawford, I concluded that it was Jack to whom she was referring; that and the fact that she was tapping a pencil against her teeth. I remembered that he was moving into Riviera Pointe as soon as Phase I, as the brochure called the first condos to be built, was done. It took me a few seconds to make the connection. "Right! Delicious man," I said, sounding like an idiot. I wasn't supposed to talk about Jack in that way, but I had to keep the charade going.

She shuddered a little bit and I got concerned. When she closed her eyes and sighed, I knew she was thinking about Jack. Obviously, she was as turned on by good oral hygiene and symmetrical Chiclet teeth as I was. She came to again and was back to business. "Well, shall we go into my office?" As I followed her across the marble, she instructed the receptionist to hold her calls. Wow, she really meant business. She was going to be really pissed if she ever found out that this was one big hoax.

I took note of the fact that Richie's office was right next to hers. As is often the case with temporary structures like sales offices, and, I supposed, everything built by Richie Kraecker and company, the walls were paper thin, and I could hear him bellowing inside his office.

I took a seat across from her reproduction Louis XIV desk and crossed my legs. Behind her head was a spectacular view of the Hudson, a view that I see every day of my life as I walk around campus thanks to St. Thomas's location, but it never gets old. She riffled through some paperwork on her desk, finally looking up at me. "So, what are we interested in? A two-bedroom? Three?"

"Um . . ."

"Let's talk figures? Maybe that will help? Our standard two-bedrooms start at nine fifty and our river views start at a million two." There was no question in her voice as she dropped that little gem of information. I nearly gagged. She leaned onto her desk and folded her hands as if she had just told me that I had gotten an A in algebra. I buy generic cereal because the real stuff costs too much. Spend a million two on a property? Highly unlikely.

I resisted the urge to show her how shocked I was at those prices. When you considered the fact that Richie was paying most of his workers about a dollar an hour, it really was akin to highway robbery. I looked at her, my eyes dropping to the mountainous cleavage that had presented itself when she bent forward. "Two bedroom," I managed to get out.

"Excellent!" She pulled out a brochure that had a floor plan. My brain doesn't work in the way that allows floor plans to make any kind of sense to me; I have never been able to look at a floor plan and decipher what exactly the finished product might look like. I stared at it as if that weren't the case, oohing and aahing at all of the fabulous appointments a two-bedroom Colonnade model might contain. By the time she had finished her pitch, I was almost ready to pull out my checkbook and give her a deposit. The apartment sounded fantastic. One problem: I had a dollar thirty in my checking account. Max hadn't been over to balance my checkbook in months and I had written myself into a giant financial hole. I did have forty-seven bucks in my wallet, though; I wondered if that would be enough. "So, what do you think?" she asked, looking at me expectantly.

"It sounds great!" I said.

"So, how should we proceed? Would you like to write a check for the deposit? Of course, we'll need to do a credit check but that won't take too long?" She looked at me some more and I stared back. I wasn't expecting this part. I wasn't expecting the hard close so early in the process. And believe me, I knew about the hard close. I had once agreed to use an inferior textbook just because the publisher's rep had bullied me into buying it for my class, moving from the hard sell to the hard close in about thirty seconds flat. My head was still spinning and I still couldn't figure out how to use the damned book with a class of freshmen.

I started to backpedal. "Well, I'm not sure. Maybe a different arrangement might be better for me. I'm not sure," I repeated, chewing on my thumbnail in faux contemplation.

"Then maybe our Majestic might be right for you?" she asked, describing the other apartment in vivid detail. Yes, I did like this one better, if only for the extra walk-in closet that would hold all the clothes that I had held on to since 1978; my poncho from spring break in Cancun would fit fabulously on one of the built-in hooks. She pulled open a filing cabinet drawer next to her desk and looked for a brochure. "I'm sorry? I don't have a Majestic brochure here? Let me go out to Daphne's desk and see if she has one?" She got up, and leaving a cloud of Opium in her wake, sashayed out of the office and down the hallway.

I jumped out of my chair and put my ear to the shared wall between her office and Richie's but I couldn't hear a thing. That's because he was standing right behind me. "Well, look who it is," he said, clucking his tongue. "Boy, you're everywhere, aren't you?"

I spun around so fast that my hip caught the edge of Madeleine's credenza, over which I had been leaning to listen into Richie's office. I sucked in my breath, surprised at how much it hurt. "Like a bad penny, I guess," I said, chuckling nervously. I put my hand to my hip, trying to make it look like I was affecting a nonchalant stance. I squinted to hold back the stinging tears that had sprung to my eyes.

"You could say that again," he said, making his way into the office. "Whatcha doin'?" He put his hands into the pockets of his khakis. I guess he had adopted a "business casual" policy for himself but no one else in the sales offices, judging from the amount of makeup, perfume, and designer clothing that was on display there.

"Oh. That," I said, pointing at the wall. "Checking out your paint colors. Is that from the Benjamin Moore Serenity collection?" I asked, getting up close to the wall again. "Tumbled Marble, maybe? Or Naked Dawn?"

"Morning Dew," he said.

"Hmm," I said, surveying my surroundings like I really cared.

"So, you never answered my question," he said, pulling up to his full five feet five inches. "Whatcha doin'?" he asked casually. He hitched his pants up a little, his hands still in his pockets. Try as I might, I couldn't imagine this man being "attentive" in bed. Nor did I want to.

"Buying an apartment," I said, far too quickly and with much too much confidence and assurance. I really hoped that I wouldn't have to buy an apartment because there was no way I could afford a studio, much less the two bedroom with the great closet that Madeleine thought I was interested in. I'm a buy-high, sell-low kind of person and hadn't accrued that much equity in my two-bedroom Cape.

He regarded me warily. "Really?" He shifted slightly from one foot to the other. "Which one?"

"Oh, I'm not sure. Maybe the Colonnade, but the Majestic sounds lovely, too," I said. Shit, shit, shit. I thought about the amount of money in my checking account and tried to imagine it multiplied by a hundred thousand or so. The jig was going to be up sooner rather than later.

"Really?"

I nodded enthusiastically. "Really!"

He continued to look at me. "Tell Madeleine to give you a good deal."

If a good deal constituted ninety percent less than market

value or the equivalent of a dollar thirty, we had a sale. "I will. Thank you, Richie."

Daphne, the wrap dress–wearing receptionist, came to the office door. "Mr. Kraecker?"

Richie turned and I swear, gave her the once-over. You dog. Wasn't the drop-dead-gorgeous biathlete enough? "Yes, Daphne?"

"A Detective Crawford here to see you?"

The jig was definitely up.

Sixteen

I managed to escape the sales office of Riviera Pointe without writing a check and without seeing Crawford. I had remained in Madeleine's office, ostensibly considering the merits of both the Colonnade and the Majestic and making a great show of my indecision. I could hear Richie talking to Crawford in the office next door and when it sounded like they had settled into their conversation, I thanked Madeleine for her time and beat a hasty exit, promising to call her as soon as I made a decision.

She gave me a cheery, "See you soon?" as I made my way through the sales office to the front door, passing the lovely Daphne's desk on the way out.

As I trudged back to my car, I felt kind of bad for wasting her time. I hadn't really learned anything, other than that Richie was going to make a tremendous amount of money from this complex, he overcharged for his condos, he was still short, and he liked to surround himself with beautiful women. I didn't know—as Max had reported—whether or not he still hated onions and drank Veuve Clicquot champagne. I got back to my car and noticed a piece of paper fluttering under the driver's side windshield wiper.

I pulled it out and read it, recognizing Crawford's cop scrawl:

I could charge you with obstruction of justice. C.

I sighed in annoyance. No, you couldn't. You could charge me with wearing a hideously matched twinset and herringbone skirt, or with having the worst hair on the planet, or for lying to a seemingly nice salesperson, or for any other number of reasons. But I hadn't obstructed anything. I had merely gotten up the hopes of a saleswoman who thought she was looking at a big, fat commission when all she was really looking at was a big, fat liar. With bad taste.

I had just gotten into the car, which was facing the front door of the sales office, when Crawford emerged. He looked up at the sky and turned his face to the sun. After that, he spent a few seconds looking at the Hudson River, a sight he didn't get to see too much being as most of the crime he investigated took place farther inland in the Bronx. I crouched down in the front seat of the car, hoping that he wouldn't see me. He knew I was there, but hopefully, he would think I was still inside.

No such luck.

He's nothing if not pathologically observant. He sauntered

over to the car and knocked lightly on the window. His muffled voice came through the tempered glass. "I can see you."

"I can see you, too," I said.

He sighed and shoved his hands into his overcoat pockets. "How are we going to play this?"

I opened the car door and got out. "Where's Fred?"

"Don't change the subject."

"We're not going to play this any way," I said, leaning against the car and folding my arms across my chest.

"I thought you were going to stay out of this," he said.

"I lied."

He was obviously abashed at my honesty. "Yeah, you did," he snorted.

"I also might be looking for an apartment," I said defensively.

He nodded, pursing his lips. "Oh, really?"

"Yep. I think the Majestic has just what I'm looking for in condo luxury," I said, reciting what I had read in the brochure.

"Does it have enough room for all of the clothes that you've held on to since high school?"

"Sure does," I said. I didn't think he'd noticed. I must have forgotten about the pathologically observant part.

He turned his head and looked back out at the river. He spoke slowly. "Stay away from here. Stay away from Richie. Please. I'm begging you." He put his hands together in a prayerful way and bowed at the waist slightly.

I remained silent. I wasn't going to lie anymore. I was going to keep nosing around until I found out something useful to help my friends.

"Well, as long as we've got that clear." He knew that it was a hopeless case. "If you get killed, I'm not going to be able to help you."

The old scare tactic. I wasn't going to get killed. I was going to take a bath on a new two-bedroom condo I didn't want or need, but I was not going to lose my life over it. "Good to know."

He was quiet for a few more minutes, enjoying the view, if not the company. "You want to have dinner tomorrow night?" he asked, taking a new angle on an old argument.

I was surprised. "Sure." I opened the car door. "That is, if I'm still alive." I gave him a smile and closed the door, leaving him staring after me as I drove away.

I drove back to school and parked in my usual spot in front of the men's dorm. I took the back stairs into the building, checking out my office through the huge windows that faced the stairs. Everything looked to be just as I left it, which was to say, a mess.

Dottie was doing a Sudoku puzzle when I entered the office area. I had managed to avoid her earlier in the day so this was the first time she saw me. She looked up and whistled. "Where are you coming from all dolled up?"

That sealed it. This outfit was going into the trash.

"I was at a meeting off campus," I said.

She looked at me, expecting more information. There was none forthcoming.

"You know what, Dottie? I could use a little help getting some information about the Vietnamese holiday of Tet. Do you think you could help?"

She snapped to attention. "Of course! I'll let you know what I find out."

"Great," I said, and continued to my office. She called after me and I turned around.

"I forgot to tell you. Sister Mary was looking for you."

That couldn't be good. She only looked for me if she needed to take me to the woodshed. "Thanks." I turned and headed back out to the stairs, going up one flight to Sister Mary's office.

She was sitting behind her immaculately clean and empty desk, writing longhand in a notebook. Her whole look was steely, down to her short, gray coif. She looked up at me and, as usual, didn't smile or greet me, instead just telling me to come in and sit down.

I did as I was told. "How are you, Sister?"

"I'm fine. I wish the same could be said for Sister Louise."

I looked at her, waiting for elaboration.

"Sister Louise has had a terrible thing happen to her. She is devastated."

Sister Louise was a professor in the nursing department and I didn't know her except to say hello. I couldn't imagine what horrible event had befallen her, so I waited for Mary to fill in the details.

"Her car was stolen. It was a 1990 Chevrolet," Mary said, rather reverentially, but who could blame her? Nuns had to take a vow of poverty and a 1990 Chevrolet was worth its weight in gold.

I breathed a sigh of relief. I didn't know why I had been summoned to my boss's office to get this news but I was happy Louise hadn't been murdered or that she hadn't jumped in front of a train. Mary had a flair for the dramatic, so I wasn't surprised that it was something as mundane as having had her car stolen. In the Bronx. Where cars often get stolen. As a matter of fact, my own car had been stolen just the year before. I wondered if Louise's car was recovered if a dead body would be in the trunk.

Bet not. Only I have that kind of luck.

"I know that you are involved with Detective Crawford. It would be beneficial to have personal attention on this matter."

Now I got it. We needed a Crawford intervention. The squad

at the Five-Oh apparently hadn't sent out a team of investigators to look for Louise's nearly twenty-year-old car and now Mary wanted me to pull out the big guns. Crawford would be overjoyed to hear this.

I tried to phrase my response carefully so as not to incur her ire. "Crawford is extremely busy, Sister."

She stared back at me. "The car is yellow."

Of course it was. "But I'll see what I can do," I said, defeated. I got up. "Is that all?"

"Yes, that's all. But Alison, I can't impress upon you how critical this situation is. Louise is *devastated*," she said again. "It was a complete violation." She looked down at her desk, our conversation over. "*Tempus fugit*, dear."

I got it. She was devastated. What would she do without her Chevrolet? Instead of relaying my thoughts to Mary, I nodded subserviently and backed out of the office, shaking my head as I walked down the hallway to the stairs. I ran into Kevin outside the chapel. The smell of the chapel, so familiar to me after all these years on campus, wafted out, a combination of lemon oil, incense, and flowers.

"Did you hear about Sister Louise's stolen Chevrolet?" I asked sarcastically, trying to bring the proper drama to the retelling of the story. It's not that I wasn't upset that Sister Louise had had this misfortune befall her, it's just that I was sure the police had done all that they wanted to do on a case that I was also sure they would consider of little importance.

Kevin rolled his eyes. After looking around to make sure nobody was in earshot, he said, "That's all the nuns have been talking about. That car is nearly twenty years old. She'll do better on insurance if they don't find it."

"Yeah, well now Sister Mary wants the entire Fiftieth Precinct on patrol looking for it and wants me to get Crawford to make that happen." I continued toward the stairs, Kevin following me.

"Louise is a good egg," Kevin said, reminding me of his good nature. He had dropped the sarcasm and was thinking about this poor, middle-aged nun and her current transportation problems. "Do you think Crawford will help?"

I stopped just short of the landing. "Not sure. He was taught by nuns so he has a healthy regard for—and fear of—them. But he's got a lot on his plate right now. The Tomasso case is still open." I stepped aside as a trio of students raced by me to get to the stairs and, probably, their next class. "Gotta go, Kevin. I have office hours in five minutes."

When I returned to the office floor, Dottie handed me a thick packet of information on the Vietnamese holiday of Tet, with a summarizing cover sheet, written in her hand. Thumbing through the sheaf of papers, and feigning interest, it occurred to me that perhaps I had misjudged Dottie. Instead of being chronically lazy, perhaps she was just bored and needed a purpose. I looked at her. "This is great, Dottie. I can't believe you got all this information yourself in such a short amount of time."

"Glad I could help," she said, turning back to her Sudoku puzzle. "Sometimes you just have to do things yourself, you know? Just to stay sharp?" She etched a number into one of the little boxes on the page. "That's what I always tell Charlie."

I cocked my head to the side. Coming from Dottie, that was profoundly accurate. I gave my Sister Louise situation a little thought.

Dottie's boyfriend was a fireplug of a man named Charlie Moriarty. Dottie and Charlie had set out on a rather passionate love affair after meeting the previous spring. Charlie, as luck would have it, was a beat cop in Crawford's precinct and an all-around decent guy. I looked at Dottie, and thought about her advice. Sometimes you just have to do things yourself.

"Hey, Dottie," I started. "Want in on something really interesting?"

Her tattooed-on eyebrows rose a few centimeters, her curiosity piqued.

I laid out the details. When her day ended at four o'clock, she was out the door in a flash.

Seventeen

I stretched the black lace thong between my fingers and determined that despite the fact that my butt wasn't that big, there was no way this thing was going to fit.

I was having dinner with Crawford, which I hoped would lead to a spirited game of I'll show you mine if you show me yours. But I wasn't going to be wearing this gift from Max. I stretched it as wide as it would go. No, there was no way I was wearing this. It was back to the Jockey for Her panties and jogbra—the push-up was in the wash—that had served me well thus far.

I didn't know where Crawford and I would go for dinner, but if history was any indication, it would probably have "steak" in its name. Trying to pair the day's fashion choice with several hours of teaching followed by dinner was easy. I threw on a pair of wool pants, a black turtleneck, and a blazer, topping the whole thing off with a pair of black boots. I had no one to impress today—Madeleine Cranston was not on the agenda—so the day called for neat but professional. I thought I had accomplished both.

Until I got a look at my hair.

The situation was reaching crisis proportions and I needed to do something about it. My late mother had been a stunning woman with sleek, thick, black hair, which she normally wore in a chignon. She had impeccable taste and was elegant to a fault. I, however, took after the Bergeron cheese farmers: short of waist, pot-bellied, and long-legged, with the frizziest hair I've ever seen. I was never sure, as a child, if the concept of conditioner had ever reached the outer boundaries of Baie-Saint-Paul or if my forebears just eschewed it. My father was mostly bald as far back as I can remember, but old photo albums reveal the frizz that resided atop the head of all Bergerons. Sometimes I caught my mother looking at me out of the corner of her eye and knew exactly what she was thinking: "Where did she come from?"

I know! I wanted to scream. With a mother who resembled Cyd Charisse and a father who looked like Gene Wilder, why, oh why, had things turned out the way they had in the genetic lottery? But despite being follically challenged, the Bergerons were a smart bunch, spreading their cheese empire far through Canada. Put that in your vintage Dior coat and smoke it, Mom.

I put some styling gel in my hair and combed it straight back until it was flat. I took a hair band and tied it into a low ponytail, deciding to just let it go at that. If I stared at myself too long, it was trouble. I gave myself one last look in the mirror behind my door and called it a day, focusing instead on the things I could control, like my pants and sweater.

I said good-bye to Trixie and headed to school. It was gorgeous outside and after a dreadful winter, both on the weather and personal fronts, there was a hint of spring in the air. A light breeze threatened to undo my plastered-to-my-head ponytail and I rushed to the car before any stray hairs came loose. It was still crisp but the sun warmed my face as I walked across the backyard to my garage.

I drove down the Saw Mill River Parkway, about a twenty-minute drive during rush hour, and took the exit for St. Thomas. I was on campus less than five minutes later, parking my car in its usual spot at the men's dorm. I got out and yanked my beat-up leather messenger bag from the passenger side of the car and pulled it across the gear shift, normally a successful extraction routine. The bag opened and papers flew out, some landing in the car and some into the parking lot. The light breeze that I had enjoyed when leaving the house had kicked up into a sustained gust and I watched as my freshman composition papers blew across the lot and sailed toward the cemetery on the other side.

I left the stuff that was in the car right where it was and darted across the small parking lot toward the cemetery, thankful that I had worn low-heeled boots and could sprint after the errant papers. The parking lot also serves as a one-way exit for other parts of the campus but is rarely used; most students who use one of the several student lots exit later in the day. That early, most people were where they needed to be. So, like an idiot, I didn't look where I was going, single-minded in my task of getting the papers before they were strewn about the cemetery and stuck to the graves of long-passed nuns.

Out of the corner of my eye, I spied a yellow car making its way up the hill and toward the parking lot exit. Figuring I had a few seconds before the car reached me, I went for broke.

Bad idea.

The car, a Chevy Cavalier, grazed my left buttock and sent me flying onto the hill at the base of the cemetery. I heard the driver's side headlight burst at the impact, and glass went flying. I lay on the grass, stunned, a little sore, but, fortunately, atop most of the papers that had gone asunder when I exited my own vehicle. The carefully constructed ponytail of the morning was a goner.

I stared up into the sun and a tiny bonnet-headed nun appeared over me. "Oh, dear!" she exclaimed, kneeling beside me. "Dear, are you hurt?"

Two things worked in my favor. One, I was hit by a slow-driving nun so the damage to my ass would be minimal, and, two, said nun was a nurse. I stared up into the concerned face of Sister Louise, owner of the 1990 Chevrolet that had presumably been stolen. I sat up and put my hand to my left buttock. "Wow. That hurts."

She pushed me gently back onto the grass. "Stay down, dear. I'll have Sister Magella call 911." Sister Magella stood by the dented Cavalier, her own bonnet askew, her hands together in a worried prayer. She pulled a very sophisticated iPhone out from underneath her wimple and started to make a call. My cell phone has an antenna and is nearly the size of a man's shoe but this nun—who had presumably taken a vow of poverty— had an iPhone. Go figure.

I held up a hand. "Anything but that." The last thing I needed was anybody affiliated with the 911 system reporting this embarrassing turn of events to Crawford. I would put my own spin on it tonight over martinis, making it suitably hilarious. That is, if my butt wasn't swollen to the size of a watermelon and hilarity was still called for. I sat up again. "You're a nurse, right?"

Sister Louise stared down at me, her brow furrowed in worry. "I'm actually a nurse practitioner."

Oh, that's a relief, I thought. "I thought your car was missing, Sister?" I took in the group of students who had gathered at the base of the hill and gave them a little wave.

She smiled, forgetting about our little collision for a moment. "It was recovered!" she exclaimed. "Praise the Lord!"

Magella chimed in. "God is great!"

That was fast. I had put Dottie and Charlie on the case a little less than sixteen hours earlier. I knelt and picked up the papers, eventually standing on shaky legs. Sister Louise held my elbow and helped me down the hill. Sister Magella, who found a few loose papers herself, handed me a crinkled batch of essays. "These must be yours, dear."

"Yes, Sister. Thank you." I turned to Louise. "I'm sorry, Sister. I should have looked before I . . ."

". . . leaped?" she asked, smiling beatifically.

I nodded. "Yes. Leaped." I took in the dent on the driver's side and the headlight. "Sorry about the headlight."

She nodded enthusiastically. "I'll get an estimate and give you the bill." See, nuns are like that. Blameless. Innocent. Irreproachable. Above suspicion. Let's face it: I hadn't been running that fast or dead on into the path of the car. Yet, I would be handed a bill for roughly two hundred dollars to fix the oldest car in the Bronx. This day wasn't off to a good start.

"So, where did they find your car?" I asked, presuming that the police had something to do with it.

Magella got into the passenger side and slammed the door; Louise was about to do the same when I asked my question. She paused, her hand on the handle of the driver's side door. "It's the oddest thing. Dottie and her man friend, Charlie, were having dinner over by Mercy Hospital and saw my car parked on the street." She waited a beat. "It's actually more funny than odd. Apparently, I forgot where I parked the car and it was exactly where I'd left it!" She chuckled as if this was the funniest thing she had ever heard. She asked me one more time if I was OK and when she was confident that I wouldn't die from internal bleeding, she took off, burning rubber out of the parking lot.

Funny. And for this, I was supposed to have Crawford log overtime? I shook my head, laughing insincerely the whole time.

I was muttering as I collected all the papers and shoved them into my bag, the intense pain emanating from my backside coloring my mood. I slammed my car door, my ass throbbing to a salsa beat. I mimicked Sister Louise as I stepped gingerly up the back steps so as not to put too much pressure on my left leg. " 'It's the funniest thing!' " I said, laughing sarcastically. The few students I passed looked at me like I was insane. "If I can't have sex with my boyfriend because my ass hurts, lady, we'll have something very serious to talk about." I opened the back door, went in, and slammed it shut.

Dottie was at her desk when I entered, clearly waiting for me with the news. "Didja hear?" she asked. It was obvious that she was talking about the retrieval of the car, given her self-satisfied expression.

I stopped her in her tracks. "Yes, I did. Thank you. But Sister just hit me with the previously missing 1990 Chevrolet and I'm not happy, to say the least."

Dottie's eyes got wide. "You OK, doll?"

I rubbed my ass. "I'm fine. But she lost the car? It wasn't stolen?"

Dottie nodded. "Exactly. I asked her where she parked it and Charlie and I went over there to see if we could find anything having to do with the car being stolen and," she paused, throwing her arms wide, "there it was. Funny, huh?"

Not funny. Why didn't anybody understand that? Maybe it was just the pain talking and I would find it funny in a few days, but right now, I was not amused. "Hilarious."

"Do you want an ice pack for you bum?" Dottie asked helpfully.

I gave her a hard stare. "No, I do not want an ice pack for my bum," I said, slowly. I softened when I saw her hurt expression. "I'm sorry, Dottie. This just really hurts."

She opened her top desk drawer and rummaged around, coming out with a prescription bottle. She dropped her voice a few decibels. "Do you want a Vicodin?" she asked, shaking the bottle.

Yes, I want a Vicodin! I wanted to scream. I had had a very loving relationship with Vicodin, but we had broken up. I love, love, love Vicodin. I had only had it once, after a gunshot wound, but it had been great; it had been so great that I had flushed the remaining eighteen tablets down the toilet for fear of getting strung out on the stuff. I completely understood how people got addicted to it; it had made me incredibly high, but in a good way. In an "I can function and everything is great!" way. I looked at the prescription bottle. "No," I said firmly. "I'll take some Advil. And maybe a Midol." I went down to my office and closed the door.

It was an hour or so later that I heard Sister Mary's voice in the main office area, and I slid down in my chair hoping I could hide from her. I listened carefully and found that she was praising Dottie for her hard work in finding Sister Louise's car. At least she was giving credit where credit was due. I hoped she would deliver her thanks and then take off for her office, but no such luck. A few moments later, there was a knock at my door.

You don't just tell Sister Mary to come in; she considers that rude. So, I hoisted myself out from behind my desk and hobbled to the door, rubbing my sore buttock along the way. I opened the door and was stunned to see the chubby-cheeked Richie Kraecker standing in front of me.

I did a classic double take. "Richie? What are you doing here?"

"Is that any way to greet an old friend?" he asked.

We're not old friends, I wanted to remind him, but instead I gave him one of those half-smiles that doesn't go all the way up to your eyes. I stepped aside as he pushed his way into my office, taking a seat across from my desk. He turned and looked at the floor-to-ceiling book shelves that lined one wall and whistled. "You read all of those books?" he asked.

"Most of them," I lied.

He smirked. "Liar."

I did another double take. "What?"

"I bet you've read all of them," he said. "You're just too embarrassed to say." He turned back around and folded his hands on his lap, one ankle resting on the opposite knee.

We sat in silence for a few minutes. "What can I help you with, Richie?"

"Have you decided which condo you'd like to buy?" He smiled, revealing a smile that was not even close to that of Jack McManus. If I had Kraecker-type money, and if I were Richie, the first thing I would do is get all new teeth. His were small and crooked and a few were discolored.

I stammered a bit. "Well, I'm not sure . . . you never know . . ."

He waited.

"Probably the Majestic," I finally said, as definitively as I could being as that was a complete lie.

He nodded slowly. "The Majestic," he repeated.

"Probably."

"Probably," he repeated again.

"Yes." My hairline, under my ponytail, got a little damp.

He rubbed his chin with his hand. "That's interesting."

"How so?"

"Your boyfriend, Mr. McManus, had no idea that you were interested in moving."

"That's because he's not my boyfriend." Boy, way to sound like you're in junior high, Alison.

He leaned forward and stared at me. I looked at a spot over his head and focused on the spine of my classic edition of *The Elements of Style*, a book that Richie had surely never read. "What's your game? What are you doing?" He paused dramatically. "What's your angle?"

I felt like I was watching a bad film noir from the forties, what with this dialogue. "I have no game, Richie. I want to buy an apartment. Plain and simple." I held his gaze. My ass was killing me but I didn't want to grimace, lest he think that he had the upper hand. In reality, it was Sister Louise who had the upper hand; I was hurt, her headlight was broken, and I was footing the bill.

He leaned back, unsatisfied, clearly seeing that he wasn't going to be able to get me to budge on my story. "OK. We'll play it that way." He stood. "But if I find out that you've wasted Madeleine's time, or that you're poking around the site any more, I will make things very unpleasant for you."

I stood, keeping the desk between us. "Is that a threat?" I asked, narrowing my eyes in an attempt to intimidate him.

"No," he said, his hand on the doorknob. "It's a promise."

And . . . scene. After he left, I rolled my eyes. Couldn't he come up with a more original exit line? I was left more annoyed than frightened by Richie's visit and more convinced than ever that he had something to hide.

Eighteen

"Boy, have I had a day."

I was sitting in a cozy booth in a restaurant on City Island, one of my favorite spots in the city. Crawford had surprised me by taking me to a seafood restaurant, something I never would have hoped for given that it was still technically winter and most of the restaurants on the Island were closed until spring was in its final days. I snuggled in next to him, happy that I was with him and that he had found one that was open.

When he picked me up, I told him I had a lot to tell him, but he made me promise that I wouldn't launch into the details until he had had his first beer. Seeing as he didn't have a to-go cup in the car, I figured that meant until we were seated in the restaurant.

He leaned in and gave me a long kiss, his mouth tasting slightly like salt and peanuts, salted peanuts being his food of choice for when he was stuck in the car all day without any hope of getting real food.

"Were you sitting on somebody today?" I asked, proud that I remembered police vernacular for a stakeout. "You taste like peanuts."

He pulled back, surprised. "You're getting good."

I shrugged. "You're rubbing off on me."

He looked like he was going to take the conversation in a dirty direction, something about rubbing and me, but the waitress appeared with the appetizers we had ordered. I waited until he had eaten some of his Caprese salad before commencing with my story; I stole a few glances at his salad, which looked way more appetizing than mine. He dropped his fork somewhere around "sore ass."

"She hit you with her *car*?" he asked. Most boyfriends would be incredulous at this news but he was merely confirming that it was the car, and not Sister Louise, that had hit me. I must have confused my subjects in the retelling.

I nodded, my mouth full of baby greens and blue cheese dressing. "Can you believe it?" I asked, putting a napkin to my mouth to catch anything that could potentially fall out onto my lap.

"You obviously weren't hurt or that would be the first thing I would have heard about."

"Wait till you see my ass," I said, rolling my eyes. Throughout the day, periodic checks confirmed that my left butt cheek would be Technicolor before the day ended.

"Been waiting all day," he said. He shook his head and returned to his salad. "Is that it?"

"Isn't that enough?"

"Well, you implied that there was more." He finished his beer and signaled the waitress for another one. Then, seeing my half-drunk martini, pointed to my glass, too. The waitress gave him a dazzling smile. Yes, he's gorgeous. Got it. Now go get my martini. Hop to, serving wench.

"Richie Kraecker came by my office."

He frowned. "Continue."

"He said that if I had wasted Madeleine Cranston's time . . ." I said, and then seeing his confused look, elaborated, ". . . the sales rep? That he would be angry or make me pay or make things 'unpleasant,'" I said, finally remembering his exact words. I was still thinking about his dingy teeth.

He forked a piece of mozzarella cheese into his mouth and chewed thoughtfully. "So, you think Richie Kraecker can succeed where I have failed?"

"What do you mean?"

"Are you frightened enough to stay away from the site and from the sales office?"

"No," I said.

"Well, do you feel bad about getting up a sales rep's hopes for a commission on roughly one million dollars?" he asked, thanking the waitress when she dropped off our drinks. I gave her a scowl, just for good measure.

"Sort of."

"Then that should be enough." He downed a third of his beer. "Because you clearly don't have any fear of getting hurt. Or worse."

"You think Richie's going to kill me?" I asked and burst out laughing. I couldn't see it, but the thought made me nervous nonetheless.

"I'm going to say it one last time," he said, even though I knew what he was going to say and that it wouldn't be the last time. "Stay away from Richie Kraecker, Riviera Pointe, and anybody affiliated with it. I've got a large enough caseload without having to tail you and make sure you're OK." He cut the salad on his plate. "Now let's talk about something else." He handed me a piece of basil. "Basil?"

I opened my mouth and he dropped it in. "Oh!" I said, rummaging around in my messenger bag. I had made a copy of the list Amalia had given me and put it in my desk drawer; I rooted around for the original now, trying to unearth it from the mess of papers in my bag. I finally found it, pulled it out, and held it aloft. "I don't know what this is or what it even means, but I think you should have it."

Crawford looked at it. "What is this? Looks like a bookie's list."

"I don't know. Amalia gave it to me. She thinks it belonged to Jose."

He studied it for a few minutes. "Thank you, I guess?" he said, not sure what he was looking at. I was glad it wasn't only me who had no idea what it was. He folded it and put it in his shirt pocket. "I'd have it dusted for prints, but . . ." he looked at me pointedly, ". . . I'm guessing that you and Amalia had your mitts all over it?"

"And now you," I said.

He laughed. "Good point. Really, thank you. I'll bring it in and we'll see what we can figure out."

Dinner was pleasant and it was nice to spend time with him during the week. We went over the dinner the Saturday before and he confirmed my impression that after the initial awkwardness, the night had gone off without a hitch. Though he did relate that Fred didn't think one cake and a tray of brownies was enough dessert for the number of people assembled. I told him to tell Fred that I would take that under advisement. When we finished, I asked him if he was coming over. He looked conflicted. "I can't."

"Dang."

"I have to take Bea to the doctor in the morning," he said, referring to his aunt. She lived below him in the brownstone that he had lived in all his life.

"Anything wrong?" I asked, concerned. I had met Bea—well, let's say that Bea and I had a "shared experience" involving kidnapping—and liked her very much. We even spoke every few weeks, just to catch up.

He got a look on his face that told me that he didn't want to go into it.

"Are you taking her to the lady-parts doctor?" I asked, gently poking him in the ribs.

He nodded and grimaced. "She's having some kind of minor procedure but my mother made me promise that I would drive her there and back." He put his hand over my mouth as I started to ask what kind of procedure it was. "And no, I don't know what it is. All I know is that what she has isn't life threatening and that she should be fine."

I held up a hand. "Say no more." I slid out of the booth. "I'm disappointed but this sore ass might make the mood less than romantic, so it's for the best."

I had left my car at school in its usual spot and he drove me back there. He pulled up alongside my navy Volvo sedan, his headlights illuminating the whole car. He moaned.

"What's the matter?" I said, but he was already out of the car.

I got out and stood next to him and followed his sight line to the four deflated tires on the car. "Now do you understand why you need to stay out of this?" He walked around to the front of the car and snatched something from under one of the windshield wipers. "*Mined your own bizness,*" it read.

My eyes were wide—more from the fact that this was the second misspelled note that I had gotten than from the message itself. I thought guiltily about the first one—the one that I had never shown Crawford—still wedged deep between the seat and the gear shift in the car—and prayed that he didn't decide to do a full search of my vehicle. "Do you think Richie had something to do with this?" I asked, trying to sound as innocent as I could.

"Richie or one of those goons who works at the site," he said, pulling a pad out of his pocket and jotting down a few notes. After walking around the car to confirm that every tire had been slashed (they had), he came back to his car. "I'll drive you home and tomorrow I'll make sure that a tow truck comes and brings this to your garage. Or your dealer. Whichever you prefer."

I told him to bring it to my local service station, a place that I had been going to for the last ten years and felt comfortable patronizing. We got back in the car and headed to my house. It was getting late and I knew that Crawford had put in more than a full day's work, so I felt guilty that he had to drive me home and then turn around and go back to Manhattan after that.

"Do you want to just drop me at the train station?" I asked, knowing full well what the answer would be.

"Yes, Alison, I'm going to drop you at the train station at ten thirty at night, down by the river, and let you wait for the next local to come by." He pulled out of the campus parking lot and onto the sparsely populated avenue, wending his way down toward Broadway. He softened a bit as we pulled up at a light next to the park. "Thank you for offering, though."

We were both tired so our ride to Dobbs Ferry was pretty quiet. The town was pretty much closed up for the night. We passed the grocery store, the only store in town that stayed open until midnight, and made our way along Route 9 until we hit the road that would take us to my street. As we got closer to the house, I buttoned my coat and picked up my briefcase and purse.

"Tell Bea I'll be thinking about her tomorrow," I said as he pulled the car up in front of my house.

He threw the car into park and turned to say goodnight. He started to lean in to give me a kiss but got distracted, pulling back and looking over my shoulder.

"Who's that?" he asked, pointing to a huddled figure on my front steps.

I turned but couldn't make out the identity of the person in the dark. "Don't know," I said, putting my hand on the door handle.

Crawford put a hand on my knee. "Don't. Stay here," he said, taking the gun off his ankle and putting it into his right pants pocket. He got out of the car and approached the person, who stood up and came toward him. As the person got closer to Crawford, I could see that it was Amalia Escalante. I wondered what she was doing out at this hour on a school night. I got a sick feeling in my stomach.

I got out of the car and hurried toward her. She was nearly hysterical. Crawford had his arm around her shoulders.

"What's wrong?" I asked.

She let out a wrenching sob. "It's my father. He's gone."

Nineteen

The next morning, Crawford was working on Hernan's disappearance while I was speeding down Park Avenue in Crawford's car on my way to an outpost of Lenox Hill Hospital with a very mellow, and extremely grateful, Bea MacDonald, which gave me the opportunity to think about the events of the previous night.

When I had encountered Amalia on the front lawn the night before and heard her news, I didn't know how to react. It was good that Crawford had been there; he had had a very calming effect on her. I imagined that's what he was like at the scene of a murder: cool, measured, focused, and respectful. He went into cop mode immediately, getting all the information he needed to contact the police in her town to get the ball rolling and to add to his investigation of Jose's death. She revealed that her father hadn't been home for two days. Amalia had asked some of the other day laborers whom she knew went to work with him, but none could remember having seen him after Monday afternoon. She and her mother hadn't gone to the police because doing so scared them more than Hernan's disappearance.

Crawford had taken Amalia to the police station in her town to register the missing persons' report—Hernan had been gone long enough to ensure that this was now an actual missing persons' case.

I had pushed Amalia's long black hair from her face and held her cheeks in my hand. I asked her how she had gotten to my house, hoping that she had taken the train and not done something stupid, like driven in her current hysterical state, or worse, hitchhiked along Route 9. She confirmed that she had taken the train.

"I didn't know what to do," she had sobbed.

I had taken her in my arms. "It's OK." I'd held her until her sobs tapered off to sniffles. "We'll figure this out," I'd said, even though I suspected that the conclusion to this story might not be a happy one. I looked at Crawford over her head and when our eyes met, I could tell that he was thinking the same thing.

Crawford had driven Amalia home and then spent the night at my house. After he accepted my offer to drive Bea to the doctor in the morning, an offer he couldn't refuse, I had to drop him off at work. The only way to make that happen was for him to give me his car for the day. Crawford, after years of experience, kept a change of clothes in his locker at work; not being able to go home and change was a common occurrence in his line of work.

Sister Mary was uncharacteristically generous in her acceptance of my "sick" day, offering to moderate the two classes that I had to teach that Wednesday.

"I can't thank you enough, dear, for taking me to my 'appointment,'" Bea said, euphemistically, using air quotes in case I didn't get the veiled meaning. I still didn't know what Bea was going to the doctor for and I didn't ask. All I know is that Crawford seemed relieved to have a disappearance to investigate rather than sit in the waiting room of a gynecologist, which is where I assumed we were going. "This whole situation with your friends is very unpleasant, isn't it?" she asked, taking a mint out of her pocketbook and popping it in her mouth; she dumped one in my hand, too.

I told Bea what had happened, starting with Jose's murder and ending with Amalia's visit the night before. She clucked her tongue sympathetically. "I read about the young guy's murder. I really hope your friend hasn't gotten himself into the same mess," she said, looking out the window at the traffic going by on the city streets.

I continued down Park Avenue. Bea had asked me to drop her at a location on Seventy-seventh Street and to either double-park or drive around until I found a spot on the street; she didn't want to pay the exorbitant parking lot fees and she didn't want me paying them either. I gave her my cell phone number so she could call me when she was finished with her mysterious procedure. After I dropped her off, I found the closest parking garage I could and made my peace with the twenty-dollar-an-hour charge to park. There was no way I was going to double-park and sit in the car or drive around until she was done.

I found a coffee shop not far from the office where I'd left Bea and sat at the counter, getting caught up on the news of the day from a paper that was left on the stool next to mine. I was about midway through my coffee and the gossip pages when my cell phone rang. I threw two dollars on the counter and went outside to busy Lexington Avenue to take the call.

Max was in the midst of eating what sounded like a bubble wrap appetizer when I answered. "Fred wants to move."

"Move? Move where?" I asked.

"Anywhere but where we currently live," she said.

Fred had moved into Max's Tribeca condo when they married. All the stuff in the apartment was Max's; Fred had arrived with a duffel bag of giant clothing, a case of pretzels, two cans of Spaghet-tiOs, and not much else. "Did he say why?" From my point of view, Fred had made out quite well on that deal. He had lived in a one-bedroom walk-up in a not-so-gentrified section of Hell's Kitchen before marrying Max.

"Oh, something about me having sex with other men in the apartment," she said breezily.

My heart skipped a beat and it took me a second to compose myself. "Max, are you cheating on Fred?"

She snorted derisively. "No!" She ate some more bubble wrap. "The men *before*," she clarified.

"Well, you did entertain a few men in the apartment. He has a point," I said.

"I love my apartment!" she wailed.

I thought for a moment. "Why don't you start with a new bed? Maybe that will placate him."

She squealed with delight. "You're a genius! Of course. That makes total sense." She chewed some more. "He's been on this whole 'we can't have any secrets' kick. So I told him every-thing."

I moaned. "Everything?"

"Well, almost everything. I left out the threesome from '92."

I moaned again.

"Kidding!" She snorted.

"Thank god." I walked around on the street distractedly.

"Where are you? You sound like you're outside."

"Seventy-seventh and Lex."

"What are you doing there? Aren't you supposed to be at school?"

I moved to the interior of the sidewalk and looked into the window of a bookstore, ostensibly to see what they offered but, if we're going to be totally honest, to see if my skirt looked too tight. It didn't, although it was quite wrinkled. "I had to take Crawford's Aunt Bea to the doctor for some kind of secret procedure."

Max was silent for a moment. "Getting her tubes tied?"

"She's sixty-three, Max. I don't think that's necessary anymore."

"Boob job?"

"Don't know."

"Bikini wax? Brow lift? Chin implant?" she continued.

My response was loud enough to get the attention of a Time Warner Cable technician parked in his truck on the street. "I don't know!" I yelled. "What difference does it make?" I looked at my watch. It was now almost forty-five minutes since I had dropped Bea off and I didn't want to tie up my phone. I never had learned how to access call waiting on my cell. "Listen, I've got to go. She said that she would only be a half hour or so."

"OK. I'll let you know when I can go bed shopping."

I wanted to remind her that she really needed to take her husband on that expedition but figured I wouldn't get into it on the street. I changed the subject. "Hey, Max, if I needed to borrow, say, half a million dollars or so, could you lend it to me?" I asked, still convinced that I was going to end up with an apartment in Riviera Pointe, if only to save face.

She didn't hesitate. "Sure. It would take me a day or so to get that kind of scratch together, but I could do it."

She's a bubblehead, but she's always there in the clutch. I moved away from the bookstore, preparing to terminate the call.

"Hold on," Max said. I heard the sound of a television in the background. Because she runs a cable television network, she's the only person I know who's allowed to watch TV all day long. She's got three TVs in her office and often downloads programs to her phone, too. "Oh, that's interesting," she said, starting to chew again.

"What's interesting?" I said. Focus, Max! I wanted to yell.

"Hmmm," she said.

"I've gotta go, Max. If you've got something to tell me . . ."

She interrupted me. "They found a body at Riviera Pointe."

Twenty

I ran down Seventy-seventh Street to the building where I had dropped off Bea. I scanned the names of the doctors on the outside of the building, trying to figure out where she was. There was one Dr. Patel, the proctologist; Dr. Singh, the gynecologist; Dr. Patel, again, the plastic surgeon; and, leaving our brothers to the east, Dr. Pelligrini, the acupuncturist. I had no blessed idea which one of those she would be seeing and paced nervously back and forth until she emerged a few minutes later, pulling her down coat tight around her despite the fact that it was in the fifties and unseasonably warm.

She was surprised to see me. "Alison! I thought I'd have to call you." She hugged her purse close to her chest. "All finished."

"Bea, do you mind if I drop you off?" She and I had discussed the possibility of having lunch after her appointment. "I just spoke with Max and she told me that a body has been found at Riviera Pointe. I want to get up there as soon as possible," I said, as we started down the street together.

She hurried to keep up with me, her short legs working overtime. I cut my speed in half. "Do you think it's your friend?" she asked solemnly.

I nodded. "I'm hoping not, but I can't imagine who else it could be." We crossed Park Avenue again, a street divided by a median. Bea's short gait got us to the middle of the street but we had to wait for the light to change again. She was huffing and puffing after the brief jog we took and I asked her if she was feeling all right.

"I'm fine. Tell my nephew that." She peered out from around me, pulling back just as a yellow cab went whizzing by. "There's nothing wrong with me, Alison. I see an acupuncturist every couple of weeks for my arthritis. I've been a little stiff lately so I didn't feel like taking the subway. I was going to take a cab but when I told Kathleen about it, she insisted Bobby take me." She looked up at me, her eyes invisible behind her tinted glasses. "Have you met Bobby's mother?"

"Not yet."

"Well, she's a giant blabbermouth. Usually, I'm happy to listen to all the family gossip, but when it's about me . . ." She drifted off. "Well, let's just say I like to keep it to myself."

"You don't think she'd be so understanding about acupuncture?" I asked as I took Bea by the elbow and steered her across Park Avenue.

Bea laughed and shook her head. "This is a woman who prides herself on never having taken an aspirin for a headache." She laughed again. "Why would she need to take an aspirin? She's what I call a 'carrier.' She gives *other* people headaches."

And as a future mother-in-law prospect, that made Kathleen Crawford less than desirable. I was definitely getting ahead of myself but it was food for thought.

We made it safely across the street and walked to the parking garage, tucked in between two townhouses. We walked down the sloped driveway and to the office area where I handed the parking attendant my ticket. I held up a hand as Bea rustled around in her purse. "I've got it," I said, pushing Bea's hand away absentmindedly. I was still chewing on the fact that Crawford's mother sounded like a piece of work and that I still had to face my first meeting with her. "I'm glad to hear that you're going to an acupuncturist. When you didn't tell Bobby what you were going to do today, I was worried," I admitted.

"No need to worry, dear. All's well," she said as the attendant drove up in the car. Bea settled into the passenger's seat and turned to me. "When you find out what's going on up at Riviera Pointe, will you let me know? I'm worried about your friend."

"Deal," I said.

Traffic was light and I dropped her off fifteen minutes later, merging onto the West Side Highway within minutes. I sped up the highway and exited on Broadway, making my way down to the Riviera Pointe site, which was more than its usual hubbub of activity. There were emergency vehicles everywhere, their lights revolving, and I counted six police cars. I spotted Crawford's unmarked car and knew that many of the other cars parked at odd angles around the area were probably other police-issue vehicles. I spotted a news van from one of the local television stations with a handsome Ken doll come to life fixing his hair in the side-view mirror, a handheld mic hanging by his side.

A group of people had gathered at the edge of the scene, a couple of them straining at the yellow police tape that ringed the area. Work had been shut down and the workers—whose number approached sixty or so—were milling around, their tones hushed as they tried to discern what had happened.

I looked at the throng of people who were assembled near the police tape and recognized Class of '59, the guy who had accosted me the first time I had visited the site. He strained against the police tape trying to get the best look he could. He was staring impassively yet intently at what was going on and exchanged a few words with the young uniformed cop trying to keep the crowd behind the tape.

I got as close to the tape as I could, making my way through the people, who stood three-deep. I looked for Crawford or Fred but I didn't see either one of them. I found myself next to Class of '59; I prayed that he had forgotten me and asked him if he knew what had happened. He was his usual antsy self, shifting from one foot to the other as he watched the scene unfold at the job site.

He attempted a nonchalant shrug that wasn't so nonchalant in reality. "No clue. I just want to see how long this will close down the site for."

Well, that's self-absorption brought to a new height, I thought.

"I heard that they found a body," I said.

"If that's what it takes to get this job shut down, then it's OK by me."

I stared at him, amazed. "Really?"

"Yes. I'm going to lose my view, you know."

Yes, I'd heard that somewhere before. I stared at him for a few more minutes but he was so involved in watching the events unfolding before him that he didn't even realize it.

Behind me, I heard a commotion and turned just in time to see Richie Kraecker and Morag Moragna emerging from a black town car. Richie was in a suit but still looked like a troll; despite the weather, Morag was in an ankle-length fur coat that must have cost close to two thousand chinchillas their lives. The Ken doll reporter spotted him and ran toward him with his camera man in tow.

"Mr. Kraecker!" he called.

Richie turned toward him and, seeing the news logo on the guy's mic, straightened up and adjusted his tie. The group in which I was standing turned in unison to watch the interview take place, but as I was now at the back of the pack, I didn't have a view of what was happening. I turned around and watched the activity taking place in the section of the building closest to the river.

I spied Crawford making his way up the dust-covered road that led down to the river, his jacket off, rubber gloves on his hands. Even though the weather was still mild, there were two dark stains under his arms and down the front of his shirt, indicating the amount of effort that he had put into whatever he had been doing. He was lost in his thoughts as he trudged up the hill, only looking up at me when I called his name. I broke from the pack and ran along the length of the tape, away from where Richie was being interviewed to a place where there were no gawkers.

"What are you doing here?" he asked, by way of greeting.

"Max told me that a body had been found here." I cupped a hand over my eyes to block out the bright sun.

Before I had a chance to ask him who it was, the medical examiner, a short redhead in scrubs, a mask hanging on her chest, called out to him. "Crawford, OK to move her?" she asked.

"Her?" I said. Now that was an unexpected development. I didn't know whether to be relieved that it wasn't a male or to be concerned about the victim's identity.

Crawford looked at me and nodded. "Go ahead, Mel," he said. "Fred's done, too." He looked back at me, his face sad.

I got a sinking feeling that even though the body didn't belong to Hernan, finding out who it was was going to be a shock. I turned and got a look at Richie, who was gesticulating wildly at the reporter, the cameraman getting every flail of his short arms on tape.

He looked at a spot over my shoulder, his preferred view when he was delivering bad news. "It's Madeleine Cranston."

Twenty-One

Even the sight of a giant cheeseburger sitting next to a stack of French fries couldn't get me out of the doldrums.

Jane Farnsworth and I were sitting in a pub not far from where we lived, a place that she frequented with the boys and that she suggested we try for our dinner date. It was kind of a hole in the wall but boasted exceptional hot wings and hamburgers. Jane swore that once I had one of the burgers I would never eat one anywhere else. And surprisingly, it had great wine by the glass; the owner was a woman around our age who couldn't abide by bad house wine and offered pretty good selections. I took a sip of the house merlot and told Jane that the owner had done a good job.

"She'll be happy to hear that," Jane said, pouring a mound of ketchup onto her burger and digging in. For a small woman, she could really pack it away. "You don't seem like yourself. Are you still upset about what happened today?"

I looked up at the television over the bar and saw that the news was on; in a few minutes, I was sure they'd be going to Richie's unscheduled press conference at Riviera Pointe and the sight they'd shown repeatedly throughout the day: a body bag on a stretcher, Madeleine Cranston's bludgeoned and lifeless body inside. I returned my attention to Jane and answered her question. "I'm very upset. I didn't even know Madeleine," I said, keeping to myself my condo-buying ruse, "but from the few times I met her, she seemed very nice."

Jane shook her head sadly. "What a terrible way to be killed, too," she said. She closed her eyes at the thought.

I hadn't learned anything from Crawford, but the reporters who had swarmed the scene reported more than I would ever want to know about how Madeleine Cranston had died. "Blunt force trauma" had been thrown about quite a bit, which was a nice way of saying that her head had been bashed in. I gave a little shudder just thinking about it.

"That job site has really been afflicted by bad luck," Jane said.

"That's an understatement." I mulled this over for a minute, my mind going to Hernan and his disappearance. Madeleine's death didn't guarantee that Hernan was still alive, but it left the door open to that possibility. That was that. After dinner with Jane, I was going to come up with a plan to find out where he was. "Do you know who the inspector is on that site?" I asked.

She shook her head. "But I can find out," she said. "Will that help?"

"I don't know," I said, dejected. "I guess. Maybe."

Jane put her burger down and looked at me. "What's bugging you, Alison?"

I decided to lay my cards on the table. "There's something going on down there and I don't know what it is." I told her about Hernan and how Kevin and I had been to the site and what we'd learned. Her eyes grew wide. "At this point, though, I'm not sure where to begin. We've got allegations of shoddy construction, undocumented workers, two murders, and the distribution of illegal green cards. *Allegedly*," I stressed.

"And Bobby knows all about this?" she asked, shocked by what I'd told her.

"I told him everything but I'm not sure how much he knew already." I pushed my plate away and brought my wineglass closer, running my fingers up and down the stem. "I should probably just stay out of it," I said. "I should just leave it to Crawford and everybody else on the case."

Jane let out a little laugh. "Alison, you know as well as I do that that's never going to happen." She put the remainder of her burger in her mouth and started on her fries.

I dug into my jacket pocket and pulled out the copy of the list that Amalia had given me when she had come to my house for dinner. "Take a look at this, would you?"

Jane scanned the list. "What's this?"

"I'm not sure." I moved a fry around on my plate. "I'm thinking it's a list of inspectors who are on the take from Richie, but I'm not sure." I studied her face to see if she was coming up with anything. "Do you think that Jose was keeping a list of inspectors on the take?"

"None of the names looks familiar, but that's not to say that they're not inspectors," she said. "I don't know that many people since I started working in Westchester." She handed the list back to me. "But let's make me a copy of this and I'll see what I can find out."

I got home an hour or so later, having made a quick stop at a Kinko's. I was grateful to be back on familiar turf. I had been too preoccupied during dinner to really enjoy it, and, although I wanted Jane's help, I was loathe to drag her into this. I touched the piece of paper in my pocket as I approached the front door and thought back to my slashed tires and the note to "*mined my own bizness.*" Obviously, I was getting close to something, but what?

And most importantly, where was Hernan?

I mulled that over as I trudged up the steps to my front door, still in a black mood from the previous few days. I was greeted by Trixie's smiling face and the sexiest kiss this side of a Danielle Steele novel. And for once, it wasn't from my dog.

"Twice in one week, Crawford?" I asked after breaking our embrace. "To what do I owe this honor?" I hadn't noticed his police-issue Crown Vic out front and surmised that he must have pulled up the driveway.

He held my face in his hands. "I missed you," he said and kissed me again. "Where were you?" he whispered. What was it about the dark that made people lower their voices? "I've been waiting for you for two hours and you weren't answering your cell."

That's because my cell is on the bathroom sink, I thought. I decided to go with the least descriptive answer I could so as not to break the mood. "I was out."

"Out where?"

"Out with Jane," I said. I stripped off my coat and let it fall to the ground. "And before your mind wanders to some girl-on-girl action, there wasn't any." I took his hand. "Let's go upstairs."

"I'd do something romantic like pick you up and carry you up there, but my sciatica is acting up," he said. Even in the dimly lit hallway, I could tell that he was smiling.

"I wouldn't want you to strain anything," I said, kissing him again. My butt was still killing me, so between that and his aches and pains, we made quite a duo.

"Actually, it kind of hurts," he said, pulling my shirt out of my pants.

I rolled my eyes. "I can only guess where." We started up the stairs.

"I could show you," he said.

"I bet you could," I said and flicked the light on in my bedroom. It was exactly as I'd left it: messy, with the bed unmade and strewn with clothes. I had had a hard time getting dressed that morning.

Crawford stood in the doorway and put his hands on his hips. He kicked a pair of shoes out of the way. "Has this place been ransacked or is this how you left it?"

I grabbed his hand and pulled him onto the bed. "Just like I left it. Now shut up and kiss me."

Crawford's sciatica mysteriously disappeared. I fancied myself something of a faith healer: all it took was a laying on of hands and he was all better.

A half hour later, I untangled myself from the sheets and lay spread-eagle on the bed, sweaty and exhausted. "You have any thoughts on who killed Madeleine?" I asked, my mind still on Riviera Pointe.

I heard Crawford sigh in the dark and it wasn't the sigh of a sexually sated man—although I took it for granted that he was one. "Do we have to talk about that now?"

"No. We could talk about it in two hours after you've fallen into a deep sleep. Then you *really* won't want to talk about it."

He rolled over and put his arm around me. "Well, we're going to question everyone she's spoken to in the last forty-eight hours, for starters."

And that could be me, I thought.

"And everyone she's dealt with in a sales capacity."

Me, again. But I was sure that Crawford would make it so I wouldn't be dragged into this.

"So, let me know your schedule so we can get you down to the precinct or so Carmen and Moran can stop by your office." He rolled onto his back again. "Obviously, my questioning you would be a conflict of interest."

I sat up. "You're not serious?"

He chuckled. "As a heart attack."

"I'm going to be questioned in relation to this?"

"Yep."

I lay back down. "Do I need a lawyer?"

"I don't know. Do you?"

Considering my lawyer was Crawford's brother, the conflict of interest had just gotten more complicated. And more conflicted.

Crawford reached over me and turned on the light next to my side of the bed. I could see that he was smiling. "Relax. It's just procedure. Carmen knows you had nothing to do with this. But you and Madeleine might have talked about something that will give us a clue as to who did this."

I relaxed a little bit. "Do you have any ideas at all?"

"Not a clue." He rolled out of the bed and pulled on his pants. "So, if you think of anything, let me know."

"Our conversation ranged from which fake apartment did I want to which other fake apartment did I want. Nothing more."

He sat back down on the bed and prepared to put his shoes on.

"How's your sciatica?" I asked.

He contemplated that. "It still hurts a little bit."

"Do you think you need more massage?" I asked.

"I think I might."

I pulled him back down on the bed. "You won't need your shoes for that. Trust me."

Twenty-Two

Just like a year earlier, when my car had been stolen, I was taking the train to work. I had returned Crawford's car to him the day before and was awaiting the return of my own car, which would have four new tires when I got it back. But because of an "extreme backup" they wouldn't be able to get my car back to me until early the following week, leaving me to trudge back and forth from the Dobbs Ferry train station and the station near school. By the time I got to school that morning, I was cranky and tired.

Crawford had stayed almost the whole night, leaving at five in the morning. Because of the strenuous activity that we had engaged in during the night, I didn't want him to go to work without having breakfast, so I heated up some leftover chicken francese and pasta from the party over the weekend and sent him off full, albeit a little green around the gills. He admitted that he wasn't used to having copious amounts of garlic so early in the morning and by the time he was done eating, he was a little queasy. He even passed on a cup of coffee, opting instead for a glass of seltzer.

Good thing I was so amazing in bed; my skills in the kitchen certainly weren't going to keep him around.

He looked exhausted, but despite my desire to see him again that night, I told him to go home as early as possible and get some sleep. I had a full day of teaching and didn't know if I would be up to another night with him. The man was wearing me out.

But in the best way possible.

I arrived at my office promptly at nine and bid good morning to Dottie, who was engrossed in the daily jumble from the local paper. She was painstakingly circling letters that corresponded to the puzzle clues and barely acknowledged me, so intent was she on finding the right answers. I decided to leave her to the business at hand and went straight to my office to get started on the day.

My phone was ringing as I inserted the key in the lock and I fumbled for a few seconds with the doorknob before getting in. I threw my bag onto the guest chair that fronted the bookcase and grabbed the phone a half ring before it went to voice mail. It was Max.

"So, Madeleine Cranston," she said, mid-conversation even though I had just picked up.

"I know. Isn't it awful?" I asked, moving around my desk and falling into the wheeled desk chair behind it. The force of my body propelled the chair backward and I careered into the file cabinet next to my desk, a framed picture of Mark Messier falling on me. I grabbed the top of my head.

"You OK?" Max asked.

I groaned. "Yes," I said. "Did Fred tell you about Madeleine?"

"First thing when he got home. And you know he never talks. I think he was in shock."

"Crawford, too. You never expect something like that, but with Hernan going missing, I'm sure they assumed it was him."

She was quiet for a moment. "Did Crawford say anything about the medical examiner?"

"Are you still on that?" I asked. This was getting old already and it was only the second time that she had brought it up. Was I this whiny? Wait—I didn't want an answer to that question.

"No," she protested weakly. "Not really."

"Because I saw her and she's just a short lady with red hair. She's no Morag Moragna," I said dramatically. "And she's really no Maxine Rayfield."

"Oh, but who is?" Max said, laughing softly. I could tell that a nerve had been touched but I still couldn't figure out why. Fred worshipped Max and anyone could see that. "Really? Is she fat?"

"Fat? Obese! I think she has a hump on her back, too." I waited a minute, thinking about whether to ask her what this all stemmed from. If Fred had a thing for this woman, I certainly couldn't see it. He had a gorgeous, successful wife whom he had waited a long time for. What would make him risk it all for a short redhead in scrubs?

Max returned to the subject of the case. "They said the cause of death was blunt force trauma," she said. "The old hard object to the cranium. That's gotta hurt."

"I'll say," I agreed. "The weird thing is that she was found in her car. Did you see that in the paper?"

"I did."

"I wonder what that's about." I would have loved to get Crawford's thoughts on that but I knew that none would be forthcoming. "Who would want to kill her? Any ideas?"

"What do you think? You're pretty good at this stuff. You must have some idea."

I thought for a moment. "Not a clue. But guess who has to go down to the Fiftieth Precinct for questioning?" I asked, not giving her the opportunity to venture a guess. "Me!"

"How come?" she asked, digging into what sounded like a plate of ball bearings.

"Oh, I went down there the other day and pretended I was interested in buying an apartment because I wanted to snoop around."

"Now that's a really smart thing to do. Way to go, Nancy Drew." She ate some more ball bearings. "Who's questioning you? Not Hot Pants, I presume?"

"No," I said, rubbing the top of my head some more. I rolled the chair closer to my desk, careful to avoid the broken glass on the floor from the framed photo. "Carmen Montoya. Or maybe Arthur Moran."

"She of the giant derriere? He of the tight polyester pants?"

"Yes. And yes."

"Take my advice," Max said, soberly. I listened carefully, thinking that she had some kind of sage advice for me. Why don't I ever learn? "Make sure you leave the room first. You don't want her getting wedged in the doorway and holding you hostage until they grease her up and get her unstuck." She let out a huge guffaw, really impressed with the image and her own sense of humor. Or lack thereof.

"Will do," I said, not realizing that she had already hung up on me. I laughed sarcastically to myself. Why was nobody concerned that I had to be questioned by the police but me? Even the police didn't seem too concerned—Montoya or Moran hadn't been waiting for me at my office or even left me a voice mail.

I turned my attention to my e-mail and began to answer the twenty or so students and colleagues who had sent me messages on a variety of topics, including what kind of cheese was appropriate for the English Honor Society meeting that would be held later in the week. I was the default cheese chooser, given my heritage and known relation to half of the cheese makers in Canada. I kept it simple: a wheel of Brie and some kind of hard cheese. I really hoped that Sister Mary didn't take that to mean Velveeta.

I launched into a virtuoso performance, sotto voce, of a conversation about Velveeta between me and Sister Mary. I do a wicked Sister Mary impression but I'm really the only one who appreciates it. Kevin would, but he's just too damned kind and holy. Crawford would, but Sister Mary scares the bejesus out of him so I'm not allowed to say her name around him, let alone mimic her thick Irish brogue and love of arcane Latin phrases. And Max had been a math major and had never crossed paths with Sister Mary during her time at St. Thomas. So I was left to crack myself up with the sound of my own voice querying, "Quid pro Velveeta? Carpe Velveeta, my dear?" I asked solemnly, then turning to my favorite. "Veni, vidi, Velveeta, Alison?"

Not befitting her usual custom, Sister Mary knocked and entered simultaneously, catching me mid-Latin. I spun around and faced her, my face turning a deep red. "Sister! Hello!"

She stood in the doorway for a few seconds regarding me, her hand on the knob. I couldn't discern the look on her face; she always looks pissed off and today was no different. After a few seconds, she revealed her intent. "By 'hard' cheese, do you mean something in the Parmigiano-Reggiano family or something in the cheddar family?" she asked, her tone neutral.

My voice had left me so I cleared my throat. "Either."

She nodded slowly. "Are you sure?"

"Yes. But cheddar is much less expensive so that might be a good choice."

"And a crowd-pleaser," she said in a monotone, narrowing her eyes. Her miraculous medal, a round gold circle with the Virgin Mary emblazoned in the center, caught the sunlight from my giant windows, nearly blinding me. Serves me right, I thought. Blinded by the holiest woman who ever lived.

"And a crowd-pleaser," I repeated. I smiled broadly.

"Thank you, dear." She exited, pulling the door closed behind her but not before giving me a withering look.

I put my hand to my heart, which was thudding in my chest. What is wrong with you? I asked myself. I didn't have an answer. I remembered the broken glass on the floor behind my desk and busied myself cleaning it up, hoping that the previous thirty seconds would vanish into thin air and I could begin the day again.

A second knock at the door startled me and I narrowly missed hitting my head again on the underside of my desk. Two possible hematomas in one day; that was a record, even for me. I couldn't say that I didn't deserve them, given my less than Christian behavior toward my saintly, albeit kind of cranky, boss. I went to the door, my hand on top of my still-throbbing head.

"This day is getting better and better," I muttered when I laid eyes on Detectives Carmen Montoya and Arthur Moran.

He hitched his pants up by his belt and gave me a smirk. "Not happy to see us, Dr. Bergeron?"

"I'm sorry," I said, holding the door open wide. "Please come in."

Carmen sashayed in and took a gander at the floor-to-ceiling windows that took up one side of my office. "Nice view," she said.

Actually, it's not that nice a view. It looks onto the back steps of the building and beyond that, the nuns' cemetery. But I was done being contrary, so I smiled, nodded, and made a little sound in agreement.

She settled into one of the chairs across from my desk while Moran stood sentry at the door to the office, which he had closed. I wanted to tell him that I wasn't going anywhere, but Crawford once told me that he's a little trigger happy so I didn't want to give him any reason to fill me full of slugs. He rested his hand lightly on the gun on his hip and I got a little queasy.

Carmen smiled. "Now." She pulled a little notebook and pen out of her leather bag and held them on her lap. "Let's talk about your relationship with Madeleine Cranston."

I held up a hand. "No relationship. Let's be clear about that."

She wrote in her notebook "*no relationship.*" Or so I assumed. It could have been a notation on my stupidity for even speaking to Madeleine Cranston and mucking up their investigation. "Well, what would you call it?"

I thought that over. Moran fidgeted by the doorway and I looked at him again, watching his hand caress the gun. I looked back at Carmen. "Can I be honest?"

Her dark eyes narrowed and I realized she was smiling. "Please."

I took a deep breath. "Well, you know that I know . . . well, you know that I know Mr. Escalante," I stuttered. I took another deep breath. "I wanted to help the Escalante family, so I thought I would snoop around Riviera Pointe a little bit to see what I could find out about Jose Tomasso's murder."

Carmen waited a beat before asking, "And?"

I don't know how her backside was doing, but mine was falling asleep in my uncomfortable desk chair. I blurted out the next part, more than a little embarrassed by the confession. "So I pretended I wanted to buy an apartment so that I could talk to Madeleine Cranston and visit the sales office I know it was a stupid thing to do but I couldn't help myself do you know how expensive those apartments are?"

She kept looking at me but she had stopped smiling. "You pretended that you wanted to buy an apartment so you went to the sales office?" she asked, looking over at Moran, who had gone into some kind of fugue state at my admission. Montoya looked at me for a good two to three minutes before she could speak again. "And what were you going to tell her when it came time to make a commitment?"

"I hadn't thought that far ahead." My voice sounded small. Nothing like a confident and assertive woman with a real excuse to sleuth to make me feel like a giant moron. I had to admit: she was much better at making me feel guilty than Crawford. You don't learn that stuff in school, yet she was a professional. Must have been the mom gene.

I looked down at my desk. The good thing was that my head didn't hurt anymore.

"You know you were one of the last people to see Madeleine Cranston alive?" Moran asked. I could tell by the way that Montoya looked at him that she had had a few more questions to ask me before they got to that little tidbit. He looked down, a little shamefaced.

That couldn't be good. "What about Richie?" I asked. In my mind, all roads led to Richie.

"What about him?"

"What did he say?" I asked.

Montoya was losing patience with me and it was apparent. "About what?" she asked.

About killing her? I thought, but I kept that to myself. "About all this?"

Moran leaned on my desk with both hands and got in my face. "He said that he's very sorry. Now, what about you?"

"I'm sorry, too," I said. Jeez, wasn't that obvious? I wheeled a few inches back from Moran's sweaty face. I was glad that I wasn't the only perspiring person in the room. The mood had suddenly gotten very tense and I wasn't sure why. I resisted the urge to break the tension by asking Montoya if she considered cheddar cheese a crowd-pleaser and/or a hard cheese.

Montoya stared at me for a few more minutes. In those moments, I could see that she had decided that I didn't warrant their time and while she was disgusted that I had mucked around in their case, wasted the dead woman's time, and made a general nuisance of myself, I really was quite innocuous, not to mention innocent. And an idiot. It was all there, written on her face. She smiled and stood. "We may have more questions for you so we may contact you in the coming days," she said, holding out her hand to me to shake. "I'll be in touch."

Moran stormed out. These two needed to watch more television to see how to behave. One of them was supposed to be the good cop, the other the bad cop. Even Crawford and Fred knew that.

I watched Montoya make her way through the office area, mesmerized by her behind. That was one amazing set of hindquarters. The ringing phone in my office finally brought me back to consciousness and I rushed in to pick it up before it went to voice mail.

Crawford. "I just wanted to give you a heads-up," he started.

"They just left."

"Oh."

I waited a few seconds and when he didn't say anything else, I erupted. "Don't you want to know how it went?!" I shouted.

"Sure," he said calmly.

"Not good!"

"They think you did it?"

"No! They think I'm a moron who's not good enough for you!"

"That's what they said?"

"They didn't have to. It was written all over their faces." I put an arm on my desk and laid my head on top of it.

"Do you even care what they think?"

"Yes," I said, and then relented. "No!" I took in a gulp of air. "Sort of."

He was silent. "I've got to go," he said finally. "I'll call you later. Love you."

I hate being questioned by the cops and my mood was sour. "I love you, too," I said, my heart not in it.

"Gee, thanks," he said, and hung up.

That didn't go well. I turned back to my computer in the hopes of cleaning out some of my e-mail before going to class. I opened my browser, and my home page, that of our local newspaper, flashed on the screen; a full-size picture of Madeleine Cranston stared back at me.

I read the headline and got a little queasier.

Never in a million years would I have pegged Madeleine Cranston for an undercover FBI agent.

Twenty-Three

If I had been smart, I would have gone home, gotten into bed, and tried to wipe that day completely from my mind.

But I'm not that smart.

I'm not such an idiot that I don't understand that Crawford has to keep certain things from me. But the fact that he had known all along that Madeleine Cranston was an FBI agent, yet had chosen not to tell me, made me irate.

As the day wore on, it became apparent to me that my little bit of sales subterfuge had put me in a much more compromising position than I had at first realized—the Feds would now look at me as a "person of interest." Maybe I was blowing this out of proportion, or maybe not. The fact remained that Crawford could have given me a heads-up and had chosen not to.

By mid afternoon I had a bee in my bonnet, which, when I think back on it, was probably related to the lump on the top of my head that had left me with a raging headache. Combined with my being questioned by the police, being caught mimicking my boss, and breaking my favorite Mark Messier picture, it all added up to my being in a very sour mood.

I don't get irate very often. I usually hover somewhere between paranoid and mildly hysterical. I reserve irate for about once a year and I usually end up really screwing things up. But from year to year I forget the results of my flights of ire and eventually launch into another fit without thinking.

Which is exactly what I did at the end of the day.

I finished teaching my classes at three and left campus, despite the work that I had been planning to do to make sure everything was set for the English Honor Society meeting the following week. The cheese was ordered—really, what else needed to happen?

Crawford's precinct is not that far from St. Thomas but the neighborhood is a world away from the rarefied air that the denizens of the university breathe. Things start to get a little more urban as you make your way south of campus. I drove to the precinct—having borrowed Kevin's car—and found a spot across the street, where I deposited my last quarter in the parking meter. That quarter gave me twenty minutes to find Crawford, lay into him, and get back to the car.

I didn't really expect to find him there, but as luck would have it, he was coming out the front door of the precinct with Carmen and Fred, the three of them laughing at something Fred had said. Since Fred usually doesn't speak, I couldn't even imagine what he could have said that would have led to the hilarity that had the three of them nearly doubled over. I felt the temperature of my blood go up a few more degrees. There's nothing that makes me angrier than seeing happy people when I'm in a bad mood.

"Hey!" I called out as I crossed the street. They stopped in their tracks and saw me jogging across the street toward them, against the light.

"Alison?" Crawford said, the smile leaving his face. He knew this wasn't a social call.

I walked up to them, a little out of breath. I really need to get more exercise. I inhaled a few times to catch my breath. "What are you doing?" I asked.

Crawford looked at Fred and Carmen as if that would explain it. "We're working," he said. He gave me a look that said, "Not that it's any of your business."

Fred scowled. "We're going out to do a canvass. Wanna help?"

Carmen melted off back toward the precinct door, mumbling something about having forgotten her wallet.

"When were you going to tell me about Madeleine Cranston?" I asked once she was inside.

Crawford slumped a little bit. "I couldn't tell you. You had to find out just like everyone else," he said, his tone much like that of a kindergarten teacher.

"Did it ever occur to you that I might be a little distressed to learn that I was going to be questioned in the death of an undercover FBI agent?"

"We don't think you had anything to do with this," Crawford said.

"*You* don't," I said, "but the Feds might. Did you ever think of that?"

"Of course I did," he said. "That's why Montoya and Moran came to see you. They wanted to vet you before the Feds come in." He gave a nod to a trio of uniformed cops going into the precinct.

Fred decided, ill-advisedly, to push my buttons some more. "Are we done here? We've got work to do," he said as he started off.

I wished he'd go back to not talking. "And you. What are you doing to find Jose's killer? Or Hernan? Huh?"

Fred turned and fixed me with a steely glare. He pointed at me. "That's enough." He took a step toward me. "That's not even our case. He's a missing person."

I snorted. "Yeah, you're doing nothing. That's what I thought."

"You are totally out of line," Crawford said, his voice measured.

Although I hadn't used up my allotted twenty parking meter minutes, I thought it was best to leave. I had gotten in practically the last word and that was good enough for me. I turned my back and stood at the corner, waiting for the light to change, the two of them still behind me. I waited to feel Crawford's hand on my shoulder but I never did, so I walked across the street and back to my car, the sobs trapped in my throat.

OK, so that wasn't the best idea I had ever had. But emotion had won out and I had gotten my point across. Though that didn't make me feel any better about what I had done.

I got into the car and stared straight ahead. One thing that I hadn't considered while my anger got the best of me: Why did the Feds have an agent at Riviera Pointe? What was Madeleine investigating? Was it related to the green cards and Richie's half-assed construction practices? Did that sort of thing really bring out the FBI? I started the car and maneuvered out of the space, confused as to where this would all lead.

When I got home about an hour later after sitting in the worst traffic I had ever encountered on the Saw Mill Parkway, I was in an even fouler mood; had it not been for that fact, I surely would have seen the government-issue sedan parked in front of my house, which I noticed only after I pulled in and was confronted by two men standing on my front steps.

They introduced themselves as federal agents.

Unlike my friends from the Fiftieth Precinct, the Feds don't stand on ceremony, nor are they all that polite. Agent Goldenberg, a balding gentleman of about fifty in a neat blue suit, was civil, but not overly friendly. Agent Abreu, his younger, buffer, and much more handsome partner, was silent, not even cracking a smile when Trixie commenced her ass-sniffing routine when we entered the house.

"Trixie! Down!" I called and pulled her by the collar toward the kitchen. "I'm sorry . . ." I hesitated, unsure of what to call them, ". . . agents?" I questioned. Gentlemen? G-men? Men who are here to throw me in federal prison? My voice trailed off as we stood in uneasy silence in the hallway.

Agent Goldenberg broke the silence. "Is there somewhere where we could talk?"

I thought the hallway was as good a place as any, but Agent Goldenberg was staring into the living room, apparently thinking that would be a better place for interrogation. We went in, me taking the chair in the corner and the two of them settling into the sofa.

We went through my visit to Madeleine Cranston, but this time I left out the part where I was only pretending to buy a condo. That seemed to throw everyone off and leave them with a negative impression of me, so I decided to lie just a little bit to save face.

"As you can see, this place is a little small for my needs, so I thought a condo at Riviera Pointe would be the next logical step for me." I looked at Agent Abreu, who looked back at me blankly. "And I hate to mow!" I added for good measure. "And snow! I hate shoveling," I said. "Boy, do I hate shoveling. Not as much as mowing. Well, maybe as much." I finally shut my mouth and clasped my hands together between my knees. "I don't really like going outside at all."

Agent Goldenberg nodded slowly. "Got it."

It occurred to me that offering my sympathies might be in order. "I'm very sorry about Agent Cranston," I said. "She was very nice."

They both nodded, and Agent Goldenberg thanked me for my concern. "Now back to your visit to Riviera Pointe." He looked at me through small round glasses. "To buy an apartment," he added, for good measure. "Did you observe anything . . ." he paused, looking for the right word, ". . . I don't know, unusual? Interesting?"

I didn't think he wanted my thoughts on Richie's funky teeth, so I shook my head and told him that everything seemed perfectly appropriate and normal for a sales office.

I was surprised when Agent Abreu stood and Goldenberg followed suit. "OK, then," he said. "That's all we need for now. We may be back."

"We may be back," Abreu echoed in a very husky, throaty, and *mucho* sexy voice. I got to thinking about Agent Abreu in a totally inappropriate way, given the circumstances of our meeting, and felt my face flush.

"Thank you for coming," I said, unnecessarily. Only if I had added, "And don't forget your favor on the way out!" would I have sounded more ridiculous.

Agent Goldenberg gave me another look, decided that yep, I was an idiot, and bid me farewell.

As soon as I shut the front door, I burst into tears.

Twenty-Four

The Feds were looking at me, and Crawford was most certainly pissed. As Max would say, I looked to be in "big-ass trouble."

And just to confirm that was the case, Max called at eight the next morning to give me what for.

Her speech was slow and deliberate, which was very un-Max-like, so I knew I was in deep trouble. "Did you ask my husband what he was doing to find Jose Tomasso's killer? And did you ask him in front of his precinct? And two other detectives?"

"Just one other detective. Carmen had already gone inside."

Details, details. Maybe it would throw her off the scent. I hadn't gotten a lot of sleep the night before, and I was standing at the kitchen counter drinking coffee. I let her rant for a few seconds before I interrupted her. "I feel bad enough as it is, Max, so let's just let it go, OK?"

"Oh, we are not going to let it go," she said and proceeded to rant some more. I didn't know where she was but she was really screaming, so I hoped she was in the confines of her office and not out in public. She ran out of breath about three minutes into her evisceration of me and paused to get some more oxygen.

"Are you done?" I asked.

"For now," she said.

"I screwed up, Max. I'm sorry. I'm going to call Fred today to tell him I'm sorry."

"Fine," she said.

"Good."

She waited a moment and I could tell she was getting agitated again. "One thing I don't get," she said.

"What's that?"

"Why do you even care?"

I was confused. "About what?"

"About them. The Escalantes. Are you really that close to these people that you would risk your relationship with Crawford, not to mention your life, to find out who killed this guy? Why are you so invested?"

I thought for a moment. "Because I like them. And there haven't been any breaks in the case."

"Well, there probably would be if you kept your nose out of it," she said.

I ignored that remark. "I like these people, Max. I never thought community service would be like this. I figured I would just go, log my hours, and go home. But once Jose's body was found and Hernan went missing, I realized that I was more invested than I thought." I took a sip of coffee and looked at Trixie, who was looking up at me with her usual mix of ardor and admiration. "I don't know how it happened but it did."

"It happened because you are you."

"You are very wise, young grasshopper." I leaned down and ruffled the clump of fur under Trixie's neck.

"I wish I could be more like you."

"Well, here's a start. Help me out at the Lord's Bounty tomorrow night."

She chewed on that for a minute. "Are there cute guys there?"

"Uh, no."

"Is the food good?"

"Depends on who's cooking."

"I'll think about it."

That was good enough for me. "Are we still friends?" I asked, hoping that I already knew the answer.

"Of course!" she exclaimed, surprised that not being friends was a possibility. "I'm not sure how you're going to make up with Mr. Wyatt, but that's your problem."

"I'll figure it out."

"Oh, guess what!" she said suddenly, off topic. "I'm having dinner with Morag tonight."

"You are?" I said.

"Yeah. She called me and asked me to dinner. I must have mentioned to her at the cocktail party that I might be interested in an apartment," she paused dramatically, "for real, not like some people I know. Fred's still been ragging on me about the apartment's *history*," she said more dramatically. "I'm sure he has some kind of history, but I don't care about it. That's why they call it history," she said.

I waved my hands in front of the phone as if to say, "And? Hurry up."

"Anyway, she said she told Richie and he asked her to meet

with me to get the process started. She's bringing brochures on the different apartments so I can look at them and bring them home to Fred."

"Really?" I asked. The whole thing sounded very unorthodox but I wondered if Richie had deputized her, so to speak, in the wake of Madeleine's untimely demise.

"Yeah. Fred's still on this total honesty kick, which, frankly, is a giant bore, but I'm humoring him. And he doesn't like living downtown. So we may get a place at Riviera Pointe and keep the Tribeca place in case I ever need to get away from him for a couple of hours."

A two-thousand-square-foot apartment was a bit more than she needed for a little time to herself, but I didn't remind her of that. She had more money than I would see in two lifetimes on my professor's salary. Fred couldn't afford either place on his salary but god bless her, she was trying to keep him happy.

She hung up, her work done for the day, before I could comment on the multitude of strange turns of events.

I had a lot of penance to do, but figured I would start with Sister Mary. I would go to school early, teach my classes, make specific as opposed to general recommendations regarding cheese, and try to get back in her good graces.

Before I left for work, I got the unexpected and welcome news from the service station that my car was ready. I walked into town to get it, begrudgingly paying for damage that for once I had not inflicted myself. After that I drove to school, careful not to exceed the speed limit, as I often did, on the Henry Hudson Parkway. Crawford was mad at me, as was half his squad, so trying to talk my way out of a ticket was out of the question. I pulled into St. Thomas thinking that the thirty-five minutes it took me to get there clearly didn't represent my best time, but content that I had arrived without incurring further points on my license. It was an eminently good start to the day.

I wouldn't exactly say that I had a spring in my step, but I was feeling better than I had when I left the house. One look at the gorgeous riverfront campus starting to exhibit the first signs of spring and I was almost able to forget that my life was going down the toilet. I parked the car in my usual spot at the men's dorm and got out of the car, careful to make sure there were no yellow Chevy Cavaliers in my path, and started down the back stairs to my office.

I have one of the most unusual offices on campus. It's only about one hundred square feet in size, and its floor-to-ceiling windows look out on the back side of the building. Which means that I can see everybody coming in and out of the building during the day—and if I'm coming into the building, I can see if someone is sitting in there. I started down the stairs and, when the sunlight reflecting off the windows refracted, I could see two figures in my office standing at the windows and looking out at the back steps. Agent Goldenberg was one.

And Agent Abreu was the other. At that moment, a dream from the night before came back to me and I stumbled a little bit on the stairs, my heart pumping a little faster than it should have, given the amount of exercise in which I was engaged. I regained my footing, thinking that Agent Abreu looked way better in the tighty-whities and gun belt of my dream than in the black suit he was currently wearing.

Agent Goldenberg winced when he saw me stumble and then gave me a thumbs-up at my recovery. I gave him a little wave and the international sign for "I'll be there in a minute," an index finger in the air. He looked very excited to see me.

Dottie was waiting for me, a bit agitated. "OK, so there are two guys in your office and one of them looks like a Latino Omar Sharif," she said, breathlessly.

"I know," I said in a stage whisper. "How long have they been here?"

"What time is it?" she asked, holding up her wrists to show me that she wasn't wearing a watch.

Well, if she wasn't wearing a watch, what difference would it make what time they came in? I looked at my watch anyway. "Eight forty-eight."

"I don't know. I don't have a watch. Maybe fifteen minutes?" she said.

Great at finding cars, sucky at doing anything that required using her brain. "Thanks," I said and did the walk of shame toward my office. This had to be some kind of record. I had been teaching here for close to ten years and I seemed to be the only professor who had ever been visited by one member of law enforcement, never mind six. And now we were crossing jurisdictional boundaries. Four of the six had been from our local precinct at least. Now, we were into federal government territory.

I opened the door to my office and Agent Goldenberg turned from the window. "Great view," he said.

"Sure. If you like cemeteries," I said, throwing my bag into the little space between my desk and the filing cabinet.

Agent Abreu looked at me with his usual blank expression.

"So, you weren't looking for a new apartment," Agent Goldenberg said, a little chagrined. He chuckled slightly even as he grimaced. He was like a federal agent from central casting in a Woody Allen movie.

I sat in my desk chair, rolling slightly and hearing glass from the frame I had broken the day before crunch under its wheels. "You got me," I said, and held up my hands.

Agent Goldenberg looked a little stunned. "We've 'got you'?"

"Yep. You got me. I didn't want to buy an apartment. But being as Madeleine Cranston wasn't a saleswoman, I don't feel so bad anymore," I said, rolling closer to my desk and over some more glass. "Well, I do still feel bad about her death, but not about lying about an apartment." I folded my hands on top of a load of midterm exams. "How did you know?"

Agent Abreu finally spoke. "You've got a dollar thirty-nine in your checking account."

Despite the fact that he had possibly the sexiest voice I had ever heard, I bristled a bit. And truth be told, it was actually a dollar thirty. "How do you know that?" I thought and then asked out loud.

"We're not fooling around here, Dr. Bergeron," Agent Goldenberg said.

So he doesn't like witty insouciance. Got it. "You don't honestly think I had anything to do with this, do you?"

Agent Abreu was shaking his head in the negative as Goldenberg decided to go all bad cop on me. He slammed his fist on my desk. "Listen, lady. Jokey joke time is over. Yes, we think you had something to do with it. Would we be here otherwise?"

I felt like I was in an episode of *Starsky and Hutch* all of a sudden. And although I was stunned at Goldenberg's outburst and was trying desperately to hold his gaze, I managed to sneak a look at Abreu, who had the traces of a smile starting on his face. Outrage didn't become Agent Goldenberg but if he wanted to try it on for a few seconds, who was I to deny him? I looked at him, still leaning over my desk, still panting slightly from his performance.

"'Listen, lady'?" I asked and stood, giving Goldenberg the benefit of my six feet in heels. "I am not a lady, but I still don't appreciate you yelling at me in my office."

He backed up a few inches, obviously accustomed to being yelled at. An image of Agent Goldenberg at home, being henpecked by a woman in curlers and a housecoat, popped into my mind, and I suppressed a giggle—an outrageously inappropriate response to a very serious situation, my stock in trade.

"I've told you everything I know. Agent Cranston was probably the best actress I've ever met. I was convinced that she was a sales rep for Riviera Pointe. She was very good at sales, too. And to answer the sixty-four-thousand-dollar question," I said, pausing dramatically, "I did not kill her." I sat down again. "But I would love to know who did. And I would love to know what she was doing posing as a sales rep at a sleazy Kraecker project."

"Kray-ker," Agent Abreu said.

Goldenberg moved around his larger partner and opened the door. "Oh, and one more thing." He paused and stared me down. I held his gaze. His tough act fitted him about as well as his Men's Wearhouse suit. "Where's your friend Hernan?"

I was about to protest that he wasn't my friend but being as that was my only excuse for being knee-deep in this whole thing, I decided that wasn't a smart tack to take. "I don't know."

"If you hear from him, you know what to do, right?"

"I do." It wasn't the first time I had heard this admonition.

"We may be back," he said, obviously dejected at having lost control of the interview and by the fact that he believed that I didn't know where Hernan was.

"I'll be here," I said breezily and watched them walk down through the common area. One of my colleagues, Sister Marguerite, gave Agent Abreu the once-over and when she caught me watching her, gave me a look that said, "Yes, I'm celibate but I'm not dead." I rolled over to the door and kicked it shut.

My phone rang and although I was afraid to pick it up, things going the way they were, I did.

"Hi, Alison. It's Jack."

"Jack! Hi," I said. "How's everything?" If I had had to venture a guess as to who might be on the other end, Jack was the last person I would have imagined. I tried to sound like I hadn't just been interviewed by two federal agents. "The Rangers are going into the playoffs looking good. You must be happy."

"Well, that's why I'm calling," he said.

My heart skipped a beat. Anytime the Rangers, playoffs, and Jack were used in the same sentence, it could only mean one thing: free tickets.

"Yes?" I said, expectant and very, very hopeful.

"I've got two tickets for the last game of the season before the All-Star break. They're going to have an old-timers reunion from the '94 team." He paused for effect. "Mark Messier will be there."

"Shut up!" I screamed into the phone. I wheeled back from my desk and into the back wall, glass crunching under the wheels.

"So, if Bobby can get the night off and you want the tickets, they're yours." He gave me the date of the game. "Come early and I'll see if I can get you into the pre-game cocktail party."

I riffled through my day planner, still on a day from the previous week. The game was a week hence, on a Thursday. I did some quick calculations in my head (off two days, working three, one double . . .) and ascertained that Crawford was off that night. But was a week enough to make him forget about what had happened the day before? It had to be. "We'll take them!" I said.

"Great. I'll send them to you overnight mail. How's that?" he asked.

"Thank you, Jack. You have no idea what this means to me."

"Oh, I think I do," he said, chuckling.

I hung up and clapped my hands together. "Thank you, Jack McManus. Oh, publicity man with gorgeous teeth." I stood and gathered my books for my first class.

Little did Jack know that he had just paved the way for a miraculous make-up session with Crawford.

No man in his right mind could stay mad at a woman with two hard-to-get hockey tickets in her possession.

Right?

Twenty-Five

Amalia had been on my mind a lot since she had shown up at my house. I knew she already had a mother, but everything about her situation made me want to take her under my wing and set her on a different path, one that involved citizenship, college, and a nursing degree that would guarantee her a job in any one of the city hospitals.

Then I thought about what was housed under my proverbial wing, the foibles that I was usually engaged in, and decided that she was doing just fine under her own mother's wing.

In light of the fact that Hernan's had not been the body found at Riviera Pointe, I thought it would be a good idea to check in with her. I knew that we had all had the same thought once we found out the body was Madeleine Cranston's: where the hell was Hernan? I had taken her number the night she had come to my house and I was glad that I had it. I waited until the school day was over, both for her and me, and rang her cell phone.

I asked if she wanted to go for coffee or a snack somewhere and she suggested a little Colombian coffee shop close to the church where we attended the Lord's Bounty. I found the coffee shop easily and went inside, nearly fainting from the rich, wonderful scent of coffee, pastries, and sugar, a trifecta of delicious smells. Amalia was already there, sitting at one of the brightly painted wooden tables, playing distractedly with a napkin.

"Hi, there," I said, putting my bag on the chair across from her. "I have to get some coffee. What can I get you?"

She shook her head. "Nothing."

I think every culture has one thing in common and that is the belief that food can solve a world of ills; French Canadians are no different, although, in my case, cheese was offered before anything else. I decided to go with a combination of sweet and savory for my visit with the heartsick Amalia. I approached the counter and got two coffees, a meat pie, two coconut-covered donuts, and a piece of flan. The woman behind the counter put everything on a tray and I carried it back to the table. The amount of food made Amalia smile a little bit and that made me feel better.

"Coconut donut? Coffee? Flan?" I said, and waved my hand over the tray like a culinary Vanna White.

She took a coffee and a donut, picking off the coconut. "Thanks."

I opened my coffee and scooped a little steamed milk foam

onto my stirrer. I licked it off. "Any word from your father?" I asked.

Her eyes filled with tears and she shook her head. She continued picking coconut off of her donut, finally breaking off a little piece and putting it in her mouth, more to stem the tide of tears than out of any desire to eat.

"Where are the police on this?" I asked.

"I don't know," she said, shrugging. She bowed her head, her black hair falling forward and covering her face. "I'm not sure how much time they're going to spend on a missing illegal alien."

I couldn't disagree. I ate the meat pie and started in on the flan. "Have you or your mother spoken to anyone working the case?"

"No."

"Do you want me to?" I asked. I didn't know what I could do, but I figured it was worth a shot.

"Would you do that for us?" she asked.

"I would." I knew that the police department was around the corner but I figured it would be better if I enlisted Crawford in this. "I'll ask Crawford to make the call," I said, hoping against hope that he was still talking to me and that he was invested enough in the case—and frankly, in me—to do me this solid, as Fred would call it.

Amalia, whose long black hair had been covering her face, looked up and pushed her hair back out of the way. "Thank you."

"I can't promise anything, Amalia, but at least they'll talk to Crawford," I said. I didn't want to give her false hope, so I didn't say anything else. I reached across the table and gave her hand a little squeeze. "How's your mom?"

"Sad." She took a sip of her coffee. "And worried."

I was sure that was a vast understatement. I started to polish off the flan, offering Amalia the last piece before I shoved it into my mouth. "Do you need anything else?" I asked, knowing that without Hernan around to take care of them, they were only a day's pay away from being on the street.

She shrugged, noncommittal.

I took her hand again. "You have to promise me that if you need anything, you'll let me know." I could help them for a little while, if need be, but Max could pitch in for far longer and I knew she would. All I had to do was ask.

She shrugged again.

"You have to promise me," I said.

Amalia looked up again. "I promise," she said reluctantly. I knew that it pained her to do so but I hoped she would be true to her word.

We spent a few more minutes at the coffee shop talking about school and her course load. She had to take the SATs that Saturday and was trying to keep her anxiety about the test and her father at a reasonable level. I assured her that I was confident that she would do just fine on the test.

"Listen," I said, gathering up all of our garbage and throwing it into the trash can, "the next time you have a day off from school, come down to St. Thomas so you can look around. We've got a great nursing program, you know."

"I know that," she said. She stood up and put her backpack over one shoulder.

I brushed her hair off of her face and rested my hands on her shoulders. "I don't know when I'll see Crawford again, but I'll make sure he talks to the officer on the case. OK?"

Her brown eyes welled up with tears again and I felt my throat constrict. She fell into my chest and let out a strangled sob. I struggled to keep my composure—I was close to crying myself. I was used to falling to pieces and I had never been the one who had to be strong; it was a change of pace for me to comfort this young girl through her sorrow.

She broke away and pulled a tissue from her jeans. She blew her nose and composed herself. "Call me if you hear anything?"

I nodded. "And you do the same."

We went out onto the street and I gave her another hug before watching her walk down Main Street, passing the array of shops on her trek toward the river. I didn't know where she lived, but I did know that, unlike other towns, the closer you got to the river, the poorer the residents. The sun was setting and the gray gloom of dusk was inching its way up from the water, covering the streets. I watched Amalia until she turned the corner and I couldn't see her any longer, then walked back to my car dejectedly.

I felt powerless. I had been convinced that the body at Riviera Pointe would be Hernan's yet felt no measure of comfort in the fact that it wasn't. Where was he? And if he was alive, why wasn't he calling his family? He loved that girl; anyone who had spent a few seconds in their presence could see that. So, if he wasn't dead, where the hell was he?

I noticed that I had just two minutes left on the parking meter and that, curiously, I had left my doors unlocked in my haste to get to the coffee shop an hour earlier. The only thing of value in the car was my St. Thomas travel coffee mug, and I was certain I could get another should someone have had the audacity to steal it while I was eating flan. But the coffee mug was still there and the car was intact. I got in, locked the doors, and headed home.

I pulled into the driveway and got out of the car, hearing Trixie barking as I made my way across the backyard toward the kitchen door. I could tell that the sound was coming from the guest room, located at the back of the house. I called out to her and saw her jump up on the windowsill in the bedroom, barking furiously.

I had no idea what Trixie did all day while I was at school

but I was surprised that she spent any time at all in the guest room. It had a futon that was so narrow she couldn't fit on it comfortably and there were no loose shoes or sweatshirts for her to chew on; all the good stuff was in my room and I had started closing my bedroom door before I left.

I had slowly become "crazy dog lady"—that person who talks to her animal as if it had opposable thumbs and an intellect. I stopped in the backyard and looked up at the second-story window. "What are you doing in there, Trix?"

She responded the only way she knew how: she barked.

"Well, come out then," I said. "I'm home now." Yes, crazy dog lady is home now and can spend the entire evening talking to you, hoping that you'll answer.

I shook my head in wonder at her antics while pulling my key chain out of my messenger bag. I opened the kitchen door and stepped in, putting my bag on the counter and fiddling for the light switch.

A hand grabbed my wrist and pulled it away from the light switch. I let out a surprised yelp. Another hand clasped over my mouth, cutting off any sound I could possibly make.

Like water going down the drain, I felt the blood drain from my face and started to feel a little faint.

A voice, soft and accented, whispered in my ear. "Don't make a sound. I'm not going to hurt you."

Well, I couldn't count on that being true but I lied and nodded my head to indicate that I wouldn't make a sound even though I knew that, first chance I had, I was going to scream bloody murder. Whoever had his hand over my mouth was behind me and had something pointy pushed into my spine; he was also a head shorter than me, that much I could tell. The person shoved me further into the kitchen and pushed the back door shut. I heard Trixie set up a cacophonous howl in the guest room and the sound of her nails clicking on the hardwood floor over my head told me that she was pacing. The kitchen was dark; only the green glow of the clock on the stove illuminated the pitch black.

The hand slipped a bit and I felt a finger graze my lip. I bit down hard and felt bone collide with my front teeth. The owner of the hand emitted an anguished cry and let go.

I ran for the front door, the hallway looking like a funhouse corridor that was about eighty feet long when in actuality it was only about twelve feet from where I had been standing. I hit the edge of the carpet runner in the hallway and tripped, flying headfirst into the front door, my hands breaking my fall and cracking one of the sidelights. I landed, face-first, inches from freedom. I pushed up off of the ground and fiddled with the front door lock, my fingers shaking.

"Alison!"

I recognized the accent, if not the voice, and turned around from my crouch.

Hernan was standing in front of me, blood dripping from his injured hand, a plastic pasta spoon in the other.

Twenty-Six

I had a new lump on my head to go with the other self-inflicted lumps that I had acquired over the last several days. Hernan sat across from me at the kitchen table nursing his hand. Trixie lay at my feet, having been liberated from the guest room. I watched the kitchen towel around Hernan's finger bloom red just moments after I wrapped it and now it was close to becoming saturated. After having worked in a school with a respected nursing program for as long as I had, I could diagnose minor injuries with startling accuracy and knew that if I didn't get Hernan to a doctor for a tetanus shot and maybe stitches, he was going to be in a world of hurt in a very short amount of time.

"Let me see that hand again, Hernan," I said, taking the ice pack off my head.

He shook his head. "It will be fine."

I gave him the hairy eyeball and he reluctantly took off the kitchen towel that he had gingerly wrapped around it. I had done quite a job on his right index finger: he had a nice gash beneath the knuckle that was still bleeding and getting progressively more swollen. "We have to get that looked at." I ran my tongue across my teeth, the taste of finger still present. Maybe I needed a tetanus shot, too.

"I can't be seen," he reiterated. We had been through this already; he was on the run, he knew things that could get him killed, and he needed my help. Again. I was starting to feel like Crawford.

Trixie stirred at my feet at the sound of his voice and let out a low growl. She was still a little mad at him for locking her in the guest room, but I imagined she would thaw out over time.

I got up and got two glasses out of the cabinet, pulling a frost-covered bottle from the freezer and putting it on the table. I poured two shots and put one down in front of him. "Here. Drink this." I threw mine back and shuddered. "Now, what the hell is going on, Hernan?"

"How much do you know?" he asked.

"Well, from what I've heard, Richie is giving out fake green cards to . . ." I paused, not sure how to phrase it without insulting him, ". . . people like yourself. That way, he gets cheap labor but escapes scrutiny from officials. He also has a record of shoddy construction practices."

"That is just the least of it."

I raised an eyebrow. "There's more?"

"I don't have proof, but I think someone at Kraecker is bribing city building inspectors."

I wasn't completely surprised at this revelation but was more than taken aback that Hernan had found out about it.

He continued. "It's just like you thought. To build a . . ." he paused, searching for the right word to describe the monstrosity that Richie was erecting, "building that will pass an eyeball inspection but not be up to city code." He rubbed his good hand over his eyes. "He makes a lot of money in the process."

I'll say. The million-plus price tag on those apartments was pretty staggering. One million or so times thirty or forty apartments? I'm not that good at math but even I could figure that that was a lot of scratch, as Max called it. "Are you sure it's Richie who's behind this?" I asked.

He shook his head. "No. It could be any one of the foremen working at the job site. I was trying to find out who, but I was exposed."

"Exposed?"

"Someone found out I was Jose's uncle and that I used to be an engineer in Ecuador. They knew then that I was trying to find out what I shouldn't," he said, haltingly. "I left a few days ago and decided not to come back there. They are threatening my family. I had to disappear. I can't go home and put them in danger."

"Who's threatening your family?"

"One of the foremen. His name is David. He told me to get away from the site or he'd call INS. Or visit my family, he said." He wrapped his good hand around his finger. "But he is an idiot. I don't think he comes up with this on his own."

"What makes you say that?"

Hernan shrugged. "Just a . . . what's the word?"

"Hunch?"

"That's it. He takes orders from the big boss. Kraecker's manager."

"What's his name?" I asked.

"Not 'his.' Hers."

I raised an eyebrow. I knew what he was going to say before he opened his mouth.

"The big lady with the blond hair. Kraecker's girlfriend."

"Morag?"

He nodded and pointed at me. "That's her."

"Interesting." I tapped my fingers on the table, thinking. "Tell me about Jose, Hernan."

He looked down at his finger, studying the blood pattern on the towel. "What do you mean?"

"You know what I mean." I took a healthy swig of vodka. "I don't speak Spanish, but I sensed that there was something between the two of you the day you painted the dining room."

Hernan thought for a few seconds, probably about how much he was going to tell me.

"Listen, I ate your finger. We're way beyond being coy."

"Jose wanted to get rich without the work. I don't know what he was involved in, but he had something going on at Riviera Pointe," he said, clearly embarrassed by this revelation about his nephew.

"Like what?"

He shrugged. "I don't know. That's what I was trying to find out."

"Any ideas?" I asked.

His black eyes were filled with sorrow. "I don't know. I promised my sister I would take care of him and I failed her." He put his head on his arm. "He was ashamed that we went to the Lord's Bounty every week. He thought it was beneath us . . . beneath me. He knew me when I was doing well in Ecuador. He thought that I had given up." He lifted his head and looked me in the eye. "I haven't given up. I just want my daughter to do well. To have everything she needs. To have everything that I can't give her. A free meal and the groceries we take home every week gives me the opportunity to put money aside for her." He smiled sadly. "She wants to be a nurse," he said.

"I know."

"And I want her to be one, too. Like her mother."

"She'll be a very good nurse," I said. "I'll make sure that she can do that, Hernan." I prayed that Amalia had the grades to get her into St. Thomas and to remain there once she was in the program.

He reached down with his good hand and petted Trixie, who stared up at him. It was almost as if she knew how sad he was. She licked his fingers, having forgiven him for locking her up.

"Where was Jose going that day you were painting here?"

"I don't know."

Hernan was a bad liar. "Hernan . . ." I cajoled.

I could see the wheels turning in his head. "Down to the job site. To meet someone." Before I could ask anything else, he held up a hand. "I don't know anything else. But he was in trouble. He *was* trouble."

I looked at Trixie, who looked up at me with a mix of sadness and adoration on her face. "We have to get proof of what's going on, Hernan."

He pulled a worn piece of paper out of his pocket, dates, times, and names written in very small script on every line of the page. "This is all I have." He smoothed it out on the table. "Jose had started this list and I found it after he died."

I scanned the page. "Can I make a copy of this?" I asked. Nothing on the page made any sense to me, but I thought that it might be of value farther down the road. It was just like the list Amalia had given me—a bunch of meaningless names and figures unless we unlocked the secret of what it all meant.

He considered that for a moment and then realized he had no other recourse than to let me in. "Of course."

I ran up to the guest room and ran the sheet through my printer. The copy wasn't great but it was legible. I carefully folded the original and put it into an envelope, giving it back to Hernan when I returned to the kitchen. "I'll see what I can find out, Hernan."

We sat in silence, he sipping his vodka, wincing every now and again, obviously not accustomed to drinking hard liquor. He snuck a few glances at me, looking like he wasn't sure if I was going to bite him again. I poured myself another shot and sipped it slowly this time, knowing that I would have to drive him to get medical attention. The last thing I needed was a DUI to go along with the raft of other problems I had.

I fingered the copy of the paper that Hernan had given me and absentmindedly rubbed my head. "I need to think." Calling Crawford was out of the question. Although he probably knew more than he was letting on to me, this piece of paper could break things wide open if the names listed on it were those of building inspectors taking kickbacks from Richie. And giving him the paper would be tantamount to telling him that Hernan was alive, a fact that would put Amalia and her mother in jeopardy. But if the building inspector bribery tale was true, that explained what Madeleine was doing there. But what did it mean for Jose? And Hernan?

I looked at Hernan's injured hand, the blood from the towel dripping onto the table. I got another dish towel and we rewrapped the finger. I didn't relish the thought of going to the hospital with this man and having to explain to some crusty nurse why I had bitten him. I wracked my brain and suddenly, a light dawned. I reached behind me and grabbed the phone from the counter and dialed a number I knew by heart.

Less than hour later, I pulled up in front of the convent at St. Thomas, angling into a spot that wouldn't exist during the school day. Now that it was evening, the campus had emptied out and we were alone in the driveway, the lights from the building casting an ethereal glow over everything. I glanced over at one of the statues that flanked the stairs down to the great lawn and said a silent prayer for this proud, lovely man.

Hernan still looked hesitant but I assured him that we were safe. We went into the quiet foyer of the convent and waited at the bottom of the steps that led up to the sisters' residence. A few minutes later, a serene-looking nun in a bathrobe, a bandanna covering her head, descended the steps.

"Hi, Sister Louise," I said.

"Oh, hello, Alison dear." She landed on the bottom step, her slippered feet making no noise on the marble floor. "Is this your friend?"

I turned to Hernan. "Yes. Sister Louise Wisniewski, Hernan Escalante. Hernan, Sister Louise."

Hernan bowed his head slightly, unable to shake. "Nice to meet you, Sister."

Sister Louise took Hernan's right hand in hers and gently unwrapped the dish towel/tourniquet. Fortunately, the finger had stopped bleeding, which I took as a good sign. "Let me have a look at this." She let out a little air between her teeth. "How did this happen?"

Hernan looked at me. "I bit him," I said, catching Louise's startled look. I held up a hand. "It's a long story."

"I imagine it is," she said and rewrapped the hand in the dish towel. "Why don't we go upstairs to the sisters' infirmary so I can get a better look and decide what we want to do?" She took Hernan by the elbow and started up the stairs. "Good Lord, dear. Didn't your parents tell you to never bite anyone?" she muttered as she made her way up the steps. "And don't you have a boyfriend?" she added.

Whom I should be biting? Was that what she was implying? This incident would go a long way toward cementing my reputation as the campus pariah, that was for sure. They started up the stairs with Louise holding Hernan's elbow. She stopped midway up the flight.

"Oh, Alison, dear. I have the estimate on the broken headlight. I'll bring it down when I return."

Oh, good. I've been waiting for that! I thought. Not. I watched them go up the stairs and then settled onto the bottom step, pondering the current state of events. I took out the list and stared at it for a long time; the only thing that was consistent was the list of Hispanic names on it. I made a mental note to ask Jane how many Hispanic building inspectors were on the city's staff; maybe they had turned a blind eye to Richie's illegal hiring practices? I hadn't gotten any closer to figuring out which end was up when Hernan came back down the stairs, his finger wrapped professionally in a thick wad of clean white gauze. Sister Louise was behind him, gliding silently down the stairs. She landed on the second to last step, making us the same height.

"All better?" I asked.

Hernan tried to smile but it was pained. I suspected Louise had a heavy hand with the hypodermic by the way he rubbed his upper arm.

"I cleaned his finger and gave him a tetanus shot, so he should be fine. Fortunately, dear," she said pointedly, looking at me, "he only needed a few stitches. Had the wound been more extensive, he would have needed a hospital visit and I take it that that's not an option right now."

"You are correct, Sister." I started toward the door, Hernan behind me. "Thank you very much for your help."

"You're welcome, dear." She moved down the last two steps to the foyer. "One thing I need to know, however, is just where Mr. Escalante is sleeping tonight. From the little information he has given me, it's obvious that he has no home or can't go to his current residence, or he wouldn't be with you right now. Am I right?"

She's no dope, that Louise, despite the fact that she can't remember where she parks her car from time to time. She had done a stint in the missions in Latin America and she spoke fluent Spanish. She had probably interrogated Hernan—in Spanish—until he gave almost everything up. She was right; Hernan had nowhere to go but I hadn't gotten that far in my thought process. Getting him medical attention had been job one. I thought about taking him back to my house but staying with me wasn't an option; I was already knee-deep in this case and couldn't put myself in any more jeopardy. But I couldn't think of anywhere else I could stash him.

After a few minutes of looking up at the ceiling of the foyer and trying to think of a solution, one became crystal clear. I gave Louise a steely gaze and she looked like she knew exactly what I was going to say. Before she could protest, I reminded her of one thing: "You owe me, Louise."

Twenty-Seven

And that's the story of how one Hernan Escalante came to live in a convent.

Technically, Louise didn't owe me, she owed Dottie, but it was I who had come up with the brilliant plan to put Dottie and Charlie on the case of the missing Chevrolet. When I laid it out like that, and appealed to her sense of justice, charity, and good old Catholic guilt, she was a goner. Hernan was somewhat reluctant as well, but the promise of a bed and three hot meals a day was too good for him to resist after two days of living God knows where. Louise told me that she would stow him up on the sparsely populated fifth floor.

"The only other sister up there is Sister Catherine and she's legally blind," she said. "If you take the elevator and hold the number five, it won't stop at the other floors and you can sneak up there. Go to room ten." She thought for a moment. "I'll take you up the first time to show you how it's done."

I thought about the elaborate ruse and how quickly Louise had come up with it. She seemed extremely competent when it came to sneaking men into the convent but I didn't want to go there mentally. "See? Legally blind, Hernan. If you're quiet, she'll never know you're there," I said, trying to sell him on the idea that this was the best option for him at the moment. "Nobody will look for you in a convent, Hernan. You'll be safe."

He thought about it for a few minutes, looking down at his dirty work clothes. Almost imperceptibly, he finally nodded.

I clapped my hands together, the sound echoing in the high-ceilinged foyer. "Good. I'll come by tomorrow and bring you some clean clothes." I gave him a quick hug and then turned to Louise. "Thank you, Sister."

Hernan grabbed my arm. "Don't call my family yet."

That was the first thing I had planned to do when I got home. "Why not?"

"We have to figure this out. Just wait. I don't want them to be in any danger."

It went against my nature to hold off on calling them knowing how frantic they were, but I also felt like I had to respect Hernan's wishes. "OK. A couple of days. But then I'm calling them, Hernan. They're worried sick."

He loosened his grip on my arm. "Let's talk about it tomorrow. If you tell them, they'll want to come to get me or see me, and I can't risk it."

Sister Louise started up the stairs, Hernan behind her. She

turned and put her finger to her lips. "I'll take you to the elevator, Mr. Escalante, but you must be quiet." She pulled up the hem of her robe slightly so she wouldn't trip on the stairs. "I have some fresh fruit and crackers in my room and I'll bring them up in a minute."

As soon as they were out of sight, I went back out to my car and dialed the only lawyer I knew. He just happened to be Crawford's brother, but I didn't let that stop me. I needed some information on immigration law and wasn't sure if he could help me, but I figured it was worth a try. I left him a message instructing him to never mention to Crawford that I had made this call and to get in touch with me at his earliest convenience.

After leaving the message, I headed home. It was close to nine o'clock. I was exhausted and was looking forward to taking a hot shower, vigorously brushing my teeth (I still imagined that I could taste finger), and a long night of slumber.

When I pulled up to the house and saw the green Passat at the curb, I knew that all those things were out of the question. I pulled into the driveway and saw Crawford sitting on the patio on a plastic chair that was way too small for him, obviously enjoying the night air. He stood when he saw me.

"Where have you been?" he asked.

God, you're handsome, I thought. But I put that aside when I took in his impatient look. "And hello to you, too," I said, pulling my keys from my pocket. I stepped around the plastic chair on which he had been sitting and made my way to the back door, trying to avoid making eye contact with him.

"The sidelight on your front door is broken." He leaned in and gave me a chaste kiss on the cheek.

I opened the back door.

"And the screen in one of your dining room windows is ripped."

So that's how Hernan got in, I thought. We hadn't covered that in any of our conversations. "I'll have to get that fixed." I did a quick survey of the kitchen. There was a little streak of blood on one of the kitchen chairs; everything else looked pretty normal.

Except for the two vodka glasses that sat on the table. I kicked the chair under the table and attempted to seduce Crawford with my feminine wiles. I slid my fingers into the top of his pants and gave him a long kiss.

But he wasn't having any part of it. "Were you entertaining someone?" he asked, motioning to the two glasses, one empty, one with a little vodka in the bottom.

I hastily concocted a lie. "No. Yes. Just Jane." I laughed to cover my discomfort. "But I can guarantee you that I was not entertaining at all. Maybe slightly humorous, but not . . ."

He put his hand over my mouth. "Got it. Where were you?"

I took his hand off of my mouth and held it in mine. "School," I said. That wasn't a lie. "I had to drop something off." Again, not a lie.

He stared at me for a few minutes, deciding whether or not it was worth the trouble of pursuing the line of questioning.

"Wanna make out?" I asked.

"I thought you were mad at me."

"OK. Wanna have make-up sex?"

"I'll think about it." He pulled out the chair with the bloody streak on it and sat down. I prayed that the blood had dried and that he wouldn't end up with a blood stain on his ass. "I want to know why you thought it was OK to come down to the Fiftieth and give me and Carmen and Fred a hard time."

Good question. I didn't have an answer to that one. "Want a beer?"

"Sure." He watched me pull a couple of beers out of the re-frigerator. "Is that an apology?"

I handed him a beer and sat down on the other chair. "Yes. I'm sorry."

He took a long drag from the bottle. "I'm sorry, too." He pushed the two vodka glasses aside and grabbed a napkin from the holder on the table, putting it under his bottle to absorb the moisture. "But you know I couldn't tell you about Madeleine Cranston, right?"

I nodded. "I know that now. I was just angry, Crawford. I'm sorry." I got up and went over to his chair, falling onto his lap. I put my arms around his neck and kissed him deeply. I buried my head in his neck. "Am I forgiven?" I whispered.

He moaned a little bit. "You drive me crazy. And not in a good way." He reached around me and drained a little more of his beer. "What happened to the sidelight? And the screen?"

"The screen's been broken since last summer and I tripped in the hallway and broke the sidelight," I said, only some of that being true.

"Did you hurt yourself? Do you want some ice? And a pair of shoes you can actually walk in? Because you are . . ."

It was my turn to put my hand over his mouth to silence him. When it was clear that he was done talking, I kissed him some more, pulling away only when I heard the phone ring. I must have had other messages because the machine clicked on after two rings, well before I had a chance to grab the receiver. I heard Jimmy Crawford's staccato tenor come through loud and clear, as well as the sound of a screaming child in the background. "Hey, Alison, Jimmy Crawford. Got your message and I'm calling you back. I'll try your cell if I don't hear from you. I'm in the office tomorrow. You've got that number, right? And where's the fire, sister? Man, you sounded stressed. *Brooke, shut up! I'm on the phone! I'll get you juice in one minute!* Anyway, Alison, whatever you need, I'm your man. And if you see Detective Humorless, tell him I've got his new will and testament and

I'm really jacked that he's decided to leave the Passat to me. Yes, thank you very much. Just what I need. A car that has four cylinders and smells like Drakkar Noir. *Brooke, shut it*! *I'm on the phone*! I'll speak with you soon, Alison. Later."

I stared in horror at the phone and tried to avoid Crawford's gaze, just millimeters from my face. Right on cue, my cell phone started ringing and I suspected that Jimmy would leave an identical message on it but that his daughter Brooke would have escalated to the point of hysteria by the time he was done.

"I guess you'll want to tell me why my brother is calling you at nine o'clock on a Friday night," he said evenly.

"Can we have the make-up sex first?" I asked.

He shook his head.

I took a deep breath, my old fallback time killer. "Don't forget to pick up your new will."

"I won't."

"Funny thing. I need a will, too. So I called Jimmy. He's my lawyer, too, right?"

Crawford nodded slowly and shifted his legs, his indication that I was to get off his lap. "I've got to go."

"Wait!" I said, smoothing down my skirt, which had ridden up during our little make-out session. "I have to tell you something."

"You have a lot of things to tell me." He moved toward the back door and rested his hand on the doorknob, ready to leave. He was showing off his scare-the-perp face and wore it well.

"I've got tickets to the Rangers' season ender. Will you go with me? It's next Thursday."

There are a lot of things Crawford and I do not have in common: his job, the kids, and the Irish thing; the cheese, my teaching, and the French Canadian thing. But one thing we do have in common is a love for the New York Rangers. I saw his crusty façade fade as he considered my offer. "Is that the game where they're bringing back the '94 team?"

I nodded enthusiastically.

"Next Thursday?"

I nodded again. All this nodding was making the lump on my head throb.

I saw him doing some mental math in his head. "I think I can make it. Are these from your friend Jack?"

"They are," I confirmed. "But he specifically said that the tickets were for me and you. He said 'Bobby.' He used your name," I threw in for good measure.

He fiddled with the doorknob. "I think I can go. We can talk about the details later." He opened the door, letting in a blast of cold night air. "Tell my brother I said hi and 'screw you.'" He gave me what I assumed he thought was a parting kiss—a quick one on the lips that turned into a longer one and then into the make-up sex that I was hoping for. A few hours later, I walked him to the front door. I stood on my tiptoes and kissed him. "I'm glad you came over."

"Me, too," he whispered. He wrapped his arms around me. "So who are you going to leave the vast Bergeron fortune to?"

"What?" I had no idea what he was talking about.

"The will?"

"What will?" I asked. Wow—I've heard of don't drink and drive, but don't fornicate and think? That was a new one. I searched my brain to recover the thread of the conversation.

"Jimmy. My brother. The lawyer. The will," he said slowly.

"Oh, that!" I said. "Well, considering there is no vast Bergeron fortune, it should be pretty easy." I thought I had made a great recovery. "You'll get Trixie, obviously. And Max will get my shoes."

"Glad you've given it some thought," he said jokingly. He gave me one last kiss and left.

Trixie wandered down the hall, her tail hanging at half mast but wagging slightly. I let out a huge sigh of relief and studied her as I leaned against the back door. I was unsettled by the fact that I had lied outright to Crawford and she could sense it. She came over and licked my hand.

"How are you at fixing screens?" I asked her.

She gave me a little woof in response.

"Thought so. How about replacing glass?"

She remained silent.

"What do you think about lying to your boyfriend?" Although I had justified the lying, the subterfuge, and the omissions of crucial information, I still felt a wee bit guilty.

She started barking enthusiastically and jumped on me, her paws pinning me against the back door.

"Trixie, my girl, you are sleeping with me tonight," I said, and started up the stairs to my bedroom, my faithful friend, full of unconditional love for such a flawed master, right at my heels.

Twenty-Eight

"We have it on good authority, Ms. Bergeron, that there was a middle-aged Hispanic male in this neighborhood yesterday."

I looked at Agent Goldenberg through my sleep-encrusted eyes, the front screen door separating the two of us. It was seven thirty in the morning, on a Saturday, and I didn't appreciate being woken up by two blue-suited federal agents, as delicious as Agent Abreu looked at this early hour.

"And we have it on good authority that said Hispanic male was seen in your car yesterday evening."

I had no idea how he had gotten this information. I asked him who the "good authority" was.

"That, I cannot say," he said, rather dramatically and in such a way that I thought we were now in a production of Shakespeare in the Park.

It was probably Cranky McCrankypants, I thought. "Maybe the Hispanic male lives in the neighborhood," I said.

Agent Abreu smirked a little bit and spoke for maybe the second time since I had met him. "How many Hispanics you got around here, Ms. Bergeron?"

"Many," I said definitively. "Many," I repeated but not as forcefully as I intended. I crossed my arms over my chest.

Goldenberg went into *Starsky and Hutch* mode again and pounded on the frame of the screen door. "Face it, Bergeron. You're the closest thing to a Hispanic male this community has seen in a long time."

"Um, I think I resent that," I said, even though I wasn't quite sure what he meant. It sure sounded like something I should be offended by but I wasn't quite sure why.

"If you are harboring a fugitive, Ms. Bergeron, you could be in serious trouble," Goldenberg said.

"I understand that, Agent Goldenberg," I said, unlocking the screen door. "For all I know, the Hispanic male was Agent Abreu." Check. Mate.

Agent Abreu smirked. "I'm Portuguese."

Not to the naked eye, I thought. Any one of my neighbors would peg him for "Hispanic male #1" in a lineup. "You say to-may-to, I say to-mah-to," I said.

"What does that mean?" Goldenberg asked.

I shook my head. "I don't know. It's seven thirty in the morning. I don't know where your Hispanic male is. I don't even know *who* your Hispanic male is. Do you want to search my house?"

Goldenberg chewed on the inside of his mouth, considering the offer. After some deep thought and a quick conference with Agent Abreu, he decided that it wasn't necessary.

"OK, then. I'm going back to bed," I said, and slammed the door shut.

"We'll be back!" I heard Goldenberg's muffled voice from the other side of the door.

"I'll be here!" I called back.

"OK!"

"Good!" I called and traipsed back up to my bedroom. When I was sure they were gone, I climbed back into bed, calling Trixie to join me. The two of us, entwined, drifted off to sleep, until Trixie's bladder won out over canine-human connubial bliss and she licked my face until I awoke. I got out of bed for the second time that morning, shoved my feet into my fake Uggs, and wandered out into the bright morning sunshine, Trixie straining at her leash and pulling me along.

I let out a huge yawn and surveyed my surroundings. Even in my semiconscious state it dawned on me that Agents Goldenberg and Abreu might be in the vicinity. That might make things sticky. Especially since I had promised Hernan a change of clothes. I would never be able to get back into the convent with a bag of clothes if the two of them were skulking around.

Trixie did her business, looking back at me with a guilty expression as she unleashed a huge intestinal torrent close to, but not on, the McCrankypants's lawn. I had a bag in my bathrobe pocket and I did the best I could in terms of cleanup, praying that it would rain later.

"What the hell did you eat?" I asked, following her back up the block. I concocted a plan as we made our way up the street, one that would keep me in the house and under the watchful eyes of the FBI but that would also free Hernan from sleeping and living in one pair of dirty carpenter jeans and a soiled T-shirt.

Before I reached my house, Jane bolted out her front door, looking gorgeous as usual, and ran up to me. Trixie gave Jane the patented Trixie once-over, proclaimed her not smelly enough to continue, and lay in the street, looking up at the both of us with a mixture of boredom and contentedness, her limpid brown eyes darting back and forth between the two of us.

"I've called a couple of people about the names on that list and I've gotten nowhere." Jane pushed a blond lock out of her eyes. "They're not building inspectors, Alison."

That complicated things, but I wasn't surprised. "I know that list has something to do with the case but I just can't wrap my brain around what it is."

Jane stated what she thought might be an alternative. "Maybe it's just a list of Jose's poker buddies."

"Maybe." I thought back to Crawford's first guess: a bookie's list.

"It's the only thing I can think of. Why else would there be dollar amounts next to each name?"

I shrugged. "Don't know."

She started back towards the house, telling me that she had to take Frankie to basketball practice. "I'll talk to you later," she called back over her shoulder.

I looked down at Trixie, trying to sort this all out, but not coming up with anything. When we were back inside the house, I called Kevin.

"Hi," I said. "I hope I'm not waking you."

"Ever heard of eight o'clock Mass?" he asked.

"Uh, no."

"Well, I say an eight o'clock Mass every morning, so of course I'm up."

Ladies and gentlemen, Father McCrankypants! Must be the distant relative of Señor Cranky down the street. But since I needed his help, I decided not to point out his mood and instead told him that I would make an effort to get to Mass more often. This was obviously going to take a while so I pulled out a kitchen chair and settled in.

"Sister Alphonse said she saw a man on the fifth floor of the convent."

"Since when do you talk to the Fonz?" I asked. "Hasn't she declared this the year of the silent cloister?"

"Very funny. We don't call her the Fonz, by the way. Does the man on the fifth floor have anything to do with you?" he asked. "This has you written all over it."

I made some noises of protest but then had to relent. He wasn't stupid. If anyone was going to stow a man in the convent, it would be me. He wasn't wrong about that. "As a matter of fact, that man is a friend of mine."

He was silent.

"It's Hernan."

He let out a gasp. "He's alive?"

"He's alive and living in the convent. And I need you to help me," I said. I outlined my plan and gave him strict instructions to make sure that Hernan was safe, that nobody besides the Fonz knew that he was there, and that he stayed hidden. I gave him some vague sizes for pants, a shirt, and some socks and told him to go to the Galleria in White Plains and that I would reimburse him later for whatever he spent. I also told him to make sure that he wasn't being followed, knowing just the idea that he might be tailed would make his day.

Kevin's love of the caper won out over his anger that I hadn't told him about the latest developments. Once he had his marching orders, we hung up and I proceeded to get my life in order. I had to work the Lord's Bounty later that afternoon and had the usual Saturday errands to run to make sure that I was caught up for the week.

I wasn't sure when I would see Crawford again, but I had the hockey tickets in my possession and that was more of a lure than any make-up sex I could provide. I hoped I wasn't getting on Crawford's nerves, what with the sleuthing and general nosiness. When we had first met, I was a giant scaredy-cat who had gotten in over her head. Now that I was a woman with a mission and a plan, it seemed that he wasn't too thrilled. Or maybe it was just my imagination.

I was at a stage in my life where black was white and up was down. And the last thing I needed was some Max logic, but that's exactly what I got. She showed up at three o'clock, just as I had instructed, but in a terrible mood, and announced that she was ready for her afternoon of "Christian charity." I didn't know what kind of Christians she expected to encounter, but I did know that the belly-revealing tank top, black leggings, and velvet ballet flats were not exactly Lord's Bounty–wear.

"Why are you dressed like that for a night at the soup kitchen?" I asked.

"Watch this!" she said, and did a backbend in my hallway. She threw her feet over her head and executed a perfect back walk-over. "This outfit provides maximum flexibility."

Which you really don't need to serve people food, but I decided not to tell her. "That's great, Max," I said. "Fred must be very proud."

"Don't mention his name," she said, and I now knew to whom to attribute the bad mood. "We're not speaking."

I thought about whether I wanted to pursue it. "Anything you want to talk about?"

"Nope."

I reached into the closet and pulled out a sweater, a long,

crocheted number with a belt that would cover her to her knees. I handed it to her.

She held it in her hands as if it were one of Trixie's doody bags.

"It's a sweater. Put it on. You look like a streetwalker." I studied her. "Or one of those performers from Cirque du Soleil."

"A streetwalker? What is this, Victorian England?" She sniffed the cardigan. "And I love Cirque du Soleil," she pouted.

I pulled a St. Thomas sweatshirt from the closet and pulled it over my head. Trixie circled the two of us, getting the sense that she would be left alone for a period of time. "No. It's not Victorian England. But it is serving hungry people in a church. And I don't think they'll appreciate seeing your midriff. I don't even think it's sanitary to serve food with all of that skin showing." I bent down and gave Trixie a kiss. "And there're ex-cons there, Max. They shouldn't be seeing that," I said, waving my hand in the vicinity of her belly button.

"Oh, I bet those ex-cons will appreciate my midriff just fine," she said. "Some of those guys haven't seen a woman in ten to fifteen with time off for good behavior."

"Put on the cardigan."

"No," she said.

"I'm going to ask you nicely, darling, and then I'm going to get mad. Put on the cardigan," I said, getting a window into what it would be like to have a petulant child in my midst.

"This cardigan is the ugliest thing I've ever seen."

She was right about that, but that was irrelevant. My Aunt Monique had left it two summers ago, and she's a shortish crone who knows her way around milk fat and isn't particularly into fashion. I raised my voice, something I rarely do in Max's presence. "Put on the freaking cardigan, Max!" I was tired, I was hiding a middle-aged man in a convent, and I had two FBI agents on my tail. And we were going to be late. I wasn't in the mood for Max's antics.

She looked at me for a few moments, assessing how mad I really was. Relenting, she put on the cardigan, the sleeves covering her hands. "It doesn't fit," she whined. "And it smells like cheese."

I glared at her and she rolled up the sleeves. "Wear the sweater. It's cold outside."

We went out into the crisp air and got into my car. Frankie was waiting in front of his driveway and we stopped to let him get in. He folded himself into the backseat and attempted to melt into the upholstery. Max managed to twist herself within the confines of her seatbelt so that she was facing Frankie. She rested her chin on her hands, which gripped the headrest. "So, you're cute. Do you have a girlfriend?"

I changed the subject. "Is your mom home, Frankie? I need to talk to her about something."

"She's at Kathy's," he said. It was the clearest sentence I had ever heard him utter.

"So, a girlfriend? Have one?" Max asked.

I hit her backside with the back of my hand. "Sit down, Max. I'm going to get pulled over if the cops see you sitting like that."

She twisted around and fell heavily into her seat. "Just trying to make conversation." She contented herself with fiddling with my radio, making sure I would have to reprogram the tuner when I got back home if I ever wanted to listen to my stations again. She settled on the disco station and we endured an extended mix of "Love Machine," which seemed to go on forever.

"Will she be back tonight?" I asked after the song ended and we were treated to a more subdued selection.

Frankie grunted. I looked into the rearview mirror and saw him cross his arms tightly across his chest.

"I take it that's a yes?" Max said. "What is with teenage boys?" she asked, as if he weren't in the car or had no faculties whatsoever.

I swatted her again. "Enough." I changed the subject and asked her about her dinner with Morag.

She stuck her finger down her throat to indicate her displeasure. "Ugh. She's such a bore."

I slowed to a stop at a red light. "How so?"

"All she talks about is Richie, Richie, Richie. I really think the only reason she wanted to have dinner with me was to make sure that I was over Richie." She snorted. "Over Richie? Has she seen the man—capital M-A-N—who I'm married to? Why would I be interested in that troll Richie when I've got grade A, one-hundred-percent man-meat?"

I decided not to remind her that she was mad at said man-meat. I snuck a look in the rearview mirror; it looked like Frankie was trying to hang himself with the collar of his T-shirt, which was wound tightly around his index finger.

"And guess who picked up the tab?" she asked, answering before I had a chance to utter a word. "Me! Didn't she invite *me* to dinner?"

I agreed that this was in extremely bad taste, which seemed to appease her. "Was the food at least OK?"

"Oh, she took me to some Swiss place that reminded her of home. You would have loved it. It was cheese, cheese, and more cheese. Want some cheese with your cheese soup? How about our famous cheese martini? And here's our delicious cheese bread. And now," she said, throwing her arms out wide, "we will bring you our fabulous dessert cheese plate!" She gagged just thinking about it. "It was disgusting. No offense to your countrymen or whatever you call them. . . ."

"I think they're called my relatives. . . ."

"Whatever. But enough with the cheese. I'll be stopped up for a week after last night."

Frankie let out a little groan and I checked the rearview to make sure he wasn't hanging from the coat hook above the door.

"And she couldn't stop talking about how much money Richie stands to make at Riviera Pointe. That broad is obsessed with the almighty dollar." She shrugged. "I guess that's why she's so cheap. Probably got her First Communion money stuffed in her mattress."

We headed north on Route 9 and arrived at the church punctually about fifteen minutes later. We walked in the back door of the building and straight into the kitchen, where our nasal passages were assaulted with the smell of frying garlic. A troupe of large men—the "cooking firemen" that Rebecca and Kerry had mentioned to me once before—stood in conference in front of the commercial stove. Their attention was taken up with a giant vat of bubbling red sauce that looked like it was one good bubble away from exploding all over the ceiling.

I cleared my throat to get their attention. They turned in unison and regarded the three of us—a tall, unkempt woman; her spritely, sexy counterpart in an ill-fitting cardigan; and a sullen teenager with a red ring around his neck and a stretched-out T-shirt collar.

"Can we help you?" the biggest of them asked.

"I'm Alison. This is Max," I said, pointing to Max, who pirouetted in greeting. "And this is Frankie. We're your serving team."

The big one walked over and laughed heartily. "I'm Marian," he said, extending his hand.

"Well, you'd better be that big if you're gonna have a girl name," Max whispered under her breath.

"Oh, yes, Marian. We spoke on the phone," I said. Marian was the guy who had hooked me up with the program and I was forever in his debt. My community service hours were just whizzing by, thanks to Marian. I threw an elbow into Max's ribs and told Marian and his cooking team that we would commence setting up so that we would be ready for the guests when they arrived.

Max, as I suspected, was useless when it came to hauling out the tables, so Frankie and I humped eight tables out of the storage area and set them up, giving Max the job of putting out the paper plates and plastic wear. When five o'clock rolled around and the first guests appeared at the front door, we were in good shape, despite Max's propensity for losing focus.

Mrs. Dwyer arrived with Patty and took her usual spot at the front table. She greeted me without my identifying myself, which gave me pause. I wondered aloud how she did that. "You always smell like honeysuckle, dear," she said sweetly.

Instead of taking the compliment and leaving it at that, I had to ask. "I do?" I didn't wear perfume to the Lord's Bounty and honeysuckle is a pretty specific scent.

She looked at me, unseeing, for a few seconds and then came clean. "Well, no."

I waited for her explanation.

"You have very heavy footfalls, dear. I can always tell when you're coming my way." She half-smiled, a little chagrined at her brutal honesty. "The young man you bring with you is much lighter on his feet than you are."

Patty looked at me and yawned.

I didn't quite know how to respond, so I told her that I would go get her salad. Out of the corner of my eye, I saw Max settle in at the Sing Sing table and begin to hold court. Before I went back to the kitchen, I went over and pulled her up by the droopy cardigan.

"Hi, Joey," I said, nodding at the other guys at the table, including Tiny. There were six other men of varying ages and races, none of whose names I knew, all carefully staring down at their plates and not at Max, the human equivalent of a solar eclipse after you've been in the slammer for as long as some of them.

He held out a calloused hand. "Hi, Alison."

"I see you've met Max."

He nodded. "I have. She says that you're best friends."

"Since college." I looked around the room and saw that we had a full house—close to fifty. There was not an Escalante—or any of the people they usually attended with—in sight. Kerry and Rebecca had told me that the firemen usually cooked for a hundred or more despite the fact that the program hadn't had that many guests in over ten years, so I was sure that we would have enough food. I looked toward the door by the kitchen and saw Frankie balancing six plates of salad on his skinny arms, making his way gingerly toward the table closest to the front of the room; we were the only three servers tonight so Max and I needed to get into gear before the kid wore himself out. I pushed Max toward the kitchen. "Go help Frankie, Max. It's salad time."

Joey stood and I could see that he was wearing a clean and pressed oxford shirt over khaki pants; a soft, buttery-looking leather jacket hung on his thin frame. Rather formal attire for the Lord's Bounty. "May I say grace tonight?" he asked. He was serious today; our usual banter was nonexistent and the guys he ate with were a somber bunch.

"Of course you can," I said and gestured toward the front of the room. I walked ahead of him and called the room to attention. "Attention, please. Joey would like to lead us in prayer."

Joey draped his jacket over the back of his chair and approached the front of the room. He cleared his throat and folded his hands. "Dear Lord, thank you for this food and for Alison, Max, Frankie, and all the other people who made this meal possible. Forgive us our sins." He shuffled slightly and looked up at the beamed ceiling and the rotating fans that hung from the peak of the arch. "Bless our brother, Jose, and welcome him into your heavenly home."

I hadn't realized that Joey knew Jose and was surprised at his prayer. I had been there the week before and had led the group in grace, basically asking for the same blessings for Jose and his family. Joey seemed moved and continued with his benediction.

"We don't know why things happen, Lord. We don't know why people do bad things. But we know that you are forgiving. And that we will be forgiven." He took his eyes from the ceiling and regarded the other diners, who either had their heads bowed in prayer or were looking back at him, not sure what to make of this downer of a grace. "Forgive us," he said again before closing with, "amen."

"Amen!" Max called out before returning to the kitchen to pick up more salads.

"Thank you, Joey," I said and watched him shuffle back to his seat. One of the other guys at the table clapped him on the back. Joey looked down at the salad in front of him but didn't eat any of it.

What the heck had he been talking about? And why was he so emotional? Was he that close to Jose? That was the weirdest grace I had ever heard. I stood in between the two rows of tables, lost in thought. When I heard Max's cackle coming from behind me, I snapped to again, but not before I realized I had been staring at Joey the entire time. And he had been holding my gaze. I looked away quickly, not entirely comfortable with the grim set to his mouth or the serious expression in his eyes.

Even though Max turned out not to be any help at all—and sort of a hindrance, if I had to be completely honest—Frankie and I managed to get everyone served in record time. While the group was eating, we took a seat on the steps at the front of the room that led up to the storage area. I knew better than to try to engage him in conversation, so I was surprised when he started talking to me.

"Is that cop your boyfriend?"

I looked behind me to see whom he was talking to, shocked that he had actually asked me a question. "Uh, Crawford?"

"Yeah. The big guy."

"Sure. I guess you could call him that."

He shrugged, pulling at the neckline of his T-shirt again. "I wasn't sure what old people called each other when they were going out."

"I know what you mean," I said. "I feel kind of funny calling him my boyfriend, but that's the best description."

"Friend with benefits?" he suggested, smiling a little bit.

"Probably not," I said. "I think that's something you kids say, but I'm a bit old for that."

He stared out at the room, his hands hanging down between his legs. We were sitting so close to the ground that his knees came up almost to his chin. "Where's Amalia?"

"I don't know." I shifted to get comfortable. "Have you talked to her?" I wasn't sure how close the two of them were, but the fact that he asked about her made me think that they had some kind of relationship.

"A couple of days ago. She's worried about her dad." He looked at me and I could tell he was worried, too. "I hope he's OK."

I felt bad being part of the subterfuge that was keeping Hernan away from his family, but I also knew it was the only thing that was keeping him safe. And alive. If he had to live in a convent for a few days, and he believed he did to keep his family safe, and they had to think that he was still missing, then so be it. I had to respect his wishes, even if I didn't completely agree with them. "I bet this will all work out," I said. I could tell that he wanted to believe me but that he was dubious. I grabbed his hand and gave it a little squeeze. "Trust me."

He extricated his hand from mine and got up, going into the kitchen, I guess to get another shot of testosterone from the firemen. A few minutes later, he returned, his arms laden with plates of cookies.

I stood and peered out into the crowd, looking for Max. She was back at the convict table, laughing uproariously at something that one of the guys had said. I strode over to the table and gave the arm of her sweater a little tug. "Dessert time."

"I'll be back," she said and jumped up. We walked together to the kitchen. "This is hard work." She let out a breath that suggested she was exerting herself.

"How would you know?" I leaned into the takeout window and grabbed a bunch of dessert plates, a mixture of homemade and store-bought cookies on each. "All you've done is talk to the guys."

"And help serve salad!" she protested. She picked up one plate of cookies and sashayed back into the dining room, dropping it off at the first table and giving me a fake smile as I walked past her.

The rest of the service went smoothly and Frankie and I were breaking down the tables a full fifteen minutes before we normally would. Everyone seemed anxious to have their meal and leave and the firemen were more than happy to oblige. Preseason baseball had started and the firehouse had a satellite dish; once they were cleaned up, they were mostly out the door. Marian stayed behind and came into the dining room to see how Frankie and I were doing. Max lounged on the steps regarding the state of her French manicure.

"We're almost done, Marian," I said. "Get going."

He considered objecting for a moment but the siren song of

the firehouse, the satellite dish, and hot wings got the best of him. "The door locks behind you. So just let yourselves out through the kitchen."

I gave him a little salute. "Will do."

Max got up and stretched. "I need the ladies'."

Marian was on his way out. "The restroom?" he asked. "Right this way."

She followed him out of the dining room and down the hall. Frankie put the last metal folding chair in the holder and turned to me. "I think we're done."

"I think you're right," I said and began to turn off the lights. I heard the kitchen door slam as Marian left.

Max returned from the restroom and met us in the darkened hallway, tightening the belt of the cardigan sweater around her waist. "Ready?"

We exited the back door and heard the lock click behind us just as Marian said it would. We walked down the little alleyway to the parking lot, our trek illuminated by one spotlight attached to the top of the doorjamb. Max filled me in on her conversation with the guys from the halfway house.

"So, Tiny? He totally got the runaround. He spent twelve years in Sing Sing for knifing his girlfriend, which he didn't do. Do you believe that?"

I was only half listening, my attention taken up with finding my keys in the bottom of my bag. It wasn't the first time I had heard the story of Tiny's unjust incarceration. "Sure."

"And then Joey? He was a master forger, but he got totally railroaded, too."

My fingers met the metal of my keys, down deep in my pocketbook. "What?" I said, stopping in midstride.

"Joey. Got railroaded."

We ascended the steps to the parking lot and were a few feet from my car. "No. What did he do?"

"Tiny told me the whole story. Joey calls himself a master forger. I didn't realize that they had degrees in that line of work. I thought either you were a forger or you weren't. I didn't realize that you could achieve master status." She skipped across the parking lot and jumped onto the trunk of my car. "He did, like, social security cards, passports . . . stuff like that."

God. Sometimes she is really, really dense. A master forger? What did she think? He went to SUNY and got an advanced degree? I stopped searching for my keys and flashed on Jose's face. And the list that Hernan had given me. Frankie went around to the passenger's side and waited patiently while I stood in the middle of the lot, thinking about what she had just said.

Something clicked in my brain and all of a sudden, everything made sense. My fingers searched for my cell phone but my bag was so big and filled with so much stuff that I couldn't find it. "I have to call Crawford, Max. I think I know what happened to Jose." I dug deeper into my bag, rummaging around for the phone but still coming up short.

She looked at me blankly.

"Green cards, Max. Forgery. Jose and Joey were forging green cards and selling them to the guys at Kraecker's job site." I thought about the list that Hernan had given me; they weren't building inspectors, they were workers. Workers who needed to look legal.

"Ohh," she said slowly, the lights coming on. She looked at Frankie. "You see why we're friends? She's as sharp as they come."

Frankie grunted something and I couldn't tell if it was complimentary or not. He didn't seem quite as astounded as Max at my intellectual prowess.

"Max, is Fred working tonight, too?" I asked. "Max?"

Max didn't answer. And the look on Frankie's face, coupled with Max's alarmed visage, made me stop. She slid off the trunk and stopped.

I didn't have to turn around to know that we were in trouble.

Twenty-Nine

One thing I'll say for Max: she may be the fastest runner I've ever seen.

When she realized that Joey and Tiny were in the shadows just waiting for us to exit the church kitchen, she took off down the parking lot, a blur in black leggings and a lumpy cardigan.

"Tiny! Go get her!" Joey yelled to Tiny, who at close to three hundred pounds, had a better chance of catching the flu than the flash that was Max.

I looked at Frankie, his hand still on the car door, his face paler than usual. I mouthed "stay calm" to him and he gave me a little nod. This wasn't the first time we had been in trouble together and he had made it out alive before; I hoped he trusted me to get him out of this situation.

Joey came into view and I could see that he looked chagrined. "I'm sorry, Alison."

Sorry for what I didn't know. But if he was apologizing for something he was about to do, I started to feel the first tingle of fear nibbling at my extremities. "Why, Joey?"

He folded his arms across his chest. "I'm sorry for all this," he said, unfolding his arms and spreading them wide.

It still didn't make sense, and Tiny, whom I was beginning to suspect was developmentally challenged in some way, didn't offer any elaboration. He looked at me blankly, a few feet away from where I stood. He had made a half-hearted attempt to follow Max, but her speed, coupled with his girth and flat feet, had made him give up almost as soon as he had started.

"You figured it out, didn't you?" Joey asked, his right hand in the pocket of his leather jacket and pointing at me. The jacket, I thought, that was bought on the hard labor of green-card-needing illegal immigrants. I thought about Hernan and the plastic pasta spoon that he had stuck in my back to get me to be quiet but decided that I couldn't take a chance that Joey was holding the same utensil. Hernan wasn't an ex-con with some kind of grudge, but Joey was.

I shook my head, probably more vigorously than I intended. "No. I don't know anything."

Joey smiled. "Oh, you do. I know you do. I saw it on your face back there," he said, gesturing toward the church hall. "After grace. And then I heard it in your voice when you were coming up the stairs. And that Crawford you were talking about—he's your boyfriend, right?"

Oh, that again. "Sure," I said. I didn't want to get into the whole "what do you call the man you date when you're approaching middle-age?" thing again, so I just agreed with him.

"And he's a cop, right?"

I nodded slowly. That probably wasn't the best news to an out-on-parole ex-con like Joey.

He exhaled loudly. "I knew you'd figure it out."

I didn't know if I had figured it out, but I think I was getting hotter by the expression on Joey's face. I looked at him closely. I couldn't see any kind of weapon, but his right hand in his pocket, coupled with the pointy protrusion through the leather, made me reluctant to try anything or make any sudden moves. "Frankie, why don't you start for home?" I asked. "Catch that bus on Route 9."

"I can't let him do that," Joey said. Tiny nodded vigorously.

"He doesn't know anything, Joey." I shifted from one foot to the other. "Let him go home."

Frankie started to drift away from the car just as Joey advanced on him. Tiny grabbed me from behind and linked his arms through mine, rendering me useless except for my legs, which I used to kick backward at him. He finally threw me to the ground, landing on top of me, his almost three hundred pounds nearly smothering me.

I heard sneakers on pavement and assumed Frankie had taken off with Joey close behind him. I knew the kid could run; his speedy progress up and down the basketball court was often lauded in the local paper. I prayed that he'd had a good head start. My face was pressed against the pavement and I couldn't make out what was happening, but a few minutes later, I saw the soles of Joey's shoes. I didn't see Frankie's sneakers so I suspected that Joey had lost the foot race.

"Kid can run," he said, obviously a little awed by Frankie's speed.

"And he's running straight to the police station, Joey, so you have about three minutes to let me go."

Tiny hoisted me to my feet and I stood face-to-face with a man to whom I had given the benefit of the doubt. I now realized how stupid that had been.

Joey looked at me. "If that's the case, then I guess we'd better get going," he said evenly.

Although my instinct was to burst out crying I knew that wouldn't get me anywhere, so I decided to try to remain calm. "To where?"

"I have to think," he said. "I'm not sure."

"You know what, Joey?" I asked as I continued to struggle against Tiny's grip, "I don't know what you think I know, but if you let me go now, nobody gets hurt and you don't go back to jail." I was starting to get tired of fighting so I took a break from kicking Tiny. "But if you continue with this ridiculousness, you're going to be in big trouble." I figured this line of reasoning was worth articulating even if I knew that I didn't have a shot in hell of getting away from him with merely a sound argument in my arsenal.

Joey nodded almost imperceptibly at Tiny. "Give me your keys," Joey said.

I thought about it for a split second and then handed them over when Tiny released his grip, not sure what choice I had. Joey popped the trunk and motioned toward it with a shake of his head. "Get in."

I looked at him like he was crazy. "What?"

"Get in," he said softly, with just the slightest trace of menace. All of a sudden, the situation became all too real, and I realized that I wasn't getting out of this with any type of argument and that I couldn't count on Joey's good will toward me. Having a boyfriend who was a cop wasn't going to count in my favor either. This was a guy who had done hard time. And soft spot for me or not, he had done and seen things that I could only imagine.

I went over to the car and stood there, Tiny pushing me toward the open trunk. I implored Joey one last time. "End this now, Joey, and it's done. Over. I won't say a word," I lied. First chance I got, I was calling the police, his parole officer, and every other person in law enforcement I knew. I was even going to call Goldenberg and Abreu, and I hated them. "You've made a mistake but it doesn't have to get any worse." He continued to stare at me, his thick Brillo pad of hair blowing in the breeze and creating a soft cascade around a face that had been hardened by years of mistakes. He held his hand out to me and I saw that he wanted my purse. I saw his other hand in his jacket pocket pointed at my chest and handed it over.

I stood for a few more seconds, thinking that there must be a way out of this that I hadn't considered. But when I saw that I wasn't getting anywhere, and Tiny pushed me a little harder than he had the first time, I folded myself inside, trying not to cry. The trunk closed with a loud, ominous thunk. I lay in the darkness, hearing their muffled voices outside, surrounded by plastic grocery bags that I had meant to recycle and never had, an old pair of sneakers, and a twenty-five-pound bag of dog food that had never made it into the house. Boy, did that smell bad.

I started a running monologue in my head, more to keep myself from panicking than anything else: *When I get out of this I'm getting a car that doesn't have a trunk. No good has come from my having a trunk in the last year. I'm getting a sports car. Room for me and Trixie and nobody else. I'll put my groceries on the front seat. Maybe I won't even buy groceries. I'll get them delivered. Some places do that now, right? Maybe I'll even get a motorcycle so nobody can be found dead in the trunk of my car, I can't be kidnapped and put in the trunk of my car, and I never have to smell barbecue-flavored kibble for as long as I live. And I'm telling the judge that I'm done with community service. Nobody should have to fulfill the rest of their community service hours when they've been kidnapped by the people they're trying to help. It's just not fair. And I'm going to tell Crawford that I promise never to snoop around again or get involved in one of his cases because I love him so much that all I need is him. And Trixie. And I can be nice to his girls. And learn how to cook. . . .*

A sob caught in my throat as I flashed on his face.

The car sagged a bit as Tiny and Joey got in, or so I surmised after one of them started the car and backed out of the spot. I tried to focus on the number and types of turns we took after leaving the parking lot; after a few moments, it was clear to me where we were heading. I continued my novena to whomever would listen that Max had run like the wind straight to the police station or that she had called Crawford.

Because heading to the river in a stolen car with two ex-cons couldn't be good.

Thirty

I had been in the car far longer than I had ever thought I would last without losing my mind when I had imagined this situation in my head previously. Because who hasn't imagined the horror of being locked in the trunk of a car? I had, but I have a tendency to let my mind wander to bad places. It was more comfortable than I would have thought and would have been even more comfortable if I hadn't been lying on top of a ripped-open bag of Trixie's dog food, its tiny pellets boring into my back, even through my sweatshirt. I was surrounded by the stench of dog food. If I got out of this alive, I promised myself, I would never eat another piece of barbecued beef for as long as I lived. Or make Trixie eat this food.

No wonder she was having such difficulty when it came to digestion. Glad we solved that mystery.

I thought about my present situation as I lay in the car, which Joey and Tiny had stopped and vacated at least half an hour before. So, was this the plan? Kidnap me and leave me in deserted area to die in the trunk? I hoped I was in one of those areas where kids went to drink beer; from what I gathered from reading the local paper, the more deserted the area, the more kids were apt to congregate. But judging from the lack of noise outside, there was not a soul around.

My hands were free so I rolled onto my left side and pushed with my feet at the panel that separated the trunk from the backseat. But I was wedged in so tight because I'm built like a gazelle—OK, that's a lie, I'm more of a cross between a giraffe and a pot-bellied pig—and because of the largest package of dog food that a Costco card could buy—that I couldn't get any kind of momentum from thrusting and kicking. I succeeded in rocking the car back and forth so that if some kids did venture down to wherever I was with a six-pack of beer and a pocketful of pot, they would see a violently rocking, uninhabited car in what I presumed was a deserted parking lot. Maybe it would be enough to scare them straight.

I rolled over and tried, in the dark, to find the gizmo that locked the trunk. The pitch black was obviously a deterrent, so I rolled around as much as I could, laying my hands on whatever was in the trunk that could be used to either free me or hurt my kidnappers, whom I preferred not to think of by name. We were done. They were dead to me. I had served my last meal to both Tiny and Joey. I found a softball (no idea where that had come from or how it ended up in my trunk), which I stuffed under my shirt, thinking that if I had perfect aim—and I had no idea if I did—I could nail one of them in the head and run. I found a length of rope that I had used to tie the Christmas tree to the top of the car and stuffed it into one of my pants pockets. I didn't think I had the stomach to strangle anybody. I can't even pull the gizzards out of a Perdue oven-stuffer roaster without gagging. But if it came down to me or them, I was hoping I could choke the life out of someone.

My left foot was resting on something and I nudged it closer. When my hands rested on the ribbed handle of flashlight, I let out a sob of joy, which I quickly stifled when I heard muffled voices coming from outside.

I stuffed the flashlight, about a foot in length, into the front of my pants.

The voices got closer and I took inventory of the weapons I had amassed: the softball under my shirt, the rope in my pocket, and the flashlight down the front of my pants. I focused on Richard Dean Anderson, fellow Canadian and the actor who had played MacGyver on television when I was a kid: with a paper clip, piece of tape, and a can of baked beans, he could avert any crisis. I prayed in the names of all things good and Richard Dean Anderson that I could do the same. I hoped that the sweatshirt I had on would conceal everything well enough to allow me to smuggle them out of the car. I also hoped that I wouldn't have to choke anyone to death.

And that Joey and Tiny didn't open the trunk and put a bullet in my head before I got a chance to do anything, a thought I quickly pushed out of my still-intact brain.

The trunk flew open and I blinked from being in the pitch black. I saw that directly behind Joey's and Tiny's heads was a bright streetlight that flickered on and off. I picked my head up and poked it above the edge of the trunk. We were in a parking lot, alone, just as I'd thought. Behind the two men was the river. Right again. In the distance, I could see a large gazebo, long deserted, and a bunch of benches and dormant barbecue grills dotting the landscape around the water.

The softball was boring into my midsection but I resisted the urge to grimace. "Where are we?" I asked. The place looked vaguely familiar, but my brain was trying to take in the next actions of my kidnappers rather than figure out when I had been there last. The light over our heads flickered out for a few seconds.

"Never mind that," Tiny said, roughly grabbing my arm and lifting me in one fell swoop from the trunk. I stumbled out of the trunk, grabbing my stomach with one hand to hold the softball in place. The light flickered back on. As soon as I was out of the trunk and on my feet, though, I lost my grasp on the softball and it rolled out of my pants and fell to the ground away from me.

Tiny—bless his less than stellar intellect—reacted as one normally would if he weren't charged with overpowering someone smaller and weaker: he bent down to get the ball. I pulled the flashlight out of my pants and, with all of my might, smashed him over the head, nearly vomiting when I heard the sickening sound it made when it connected with his skull.

Joey stood still and looked at Tiny, motionless on the ground, stunned by what I had done.

I started running, tears now coursing down my cheeks, the reality of the situation coupled with my violent act making me scared and hysterical. Joey started running behind me, angrily calling my name. "I'll shoot you, Alison! Stop running!"

I figured that if he had a gun, he would have already shot me, so I sped up and ran the length of the parking lot, noticing that there was a path designed for joggers and bikers adjacent to the river. And beyond that, the lights of a waterfront condominium complex. How ironic, I thought, in my overwrought state. A waterfront condominium complex had gotten me into this mess, and a waterfront condominium complex might just be my way out. I ran as fast as my untoned, out-of-shape legs would take me, Joey's footfalls bearing down on me. I was banking on the fact that he had something besides a gun in his pocket and I prayed that I wasn't wrong, but I couldn't let him get close enough to find out. So I ran like my life depended on it. Which it did, whether it was a pasta spoon, a cheese grater, or a Glock.

Every muscle in my body was screaming in pain and I didn't have an ounce of air left in my lungs when I reached the top of the hill and the end of the running path. To the right was the condo complex and, hopefully, the security checkpoint that many Westchester complexes had. I ran toward the little nautically themed hut that sat in the middle of a circular drive.

A laconic young man sat on a cushy desk chair in the hut, casually examining a bank of cameras, but more concerned with some television program to which his private television was tuned. I banged on the window, scaring him out of his fugue state and nearly knocking him off his chair.

"Help! Please help me!" I screamed. The hut wasn't big enough for two, but I pulled on the locked door, hoping I could get inside and fold myself up small enough to fit. He looked at me and shrank back into his chair. "Please! I need help!" I looked around frantically and didn't see Joey but knew that didn't mean he wasn't there somewhere. "Please call 911!"

He finally snapped to and stood, opening the window. "Are you here to see someone?" He didn't look any older than Frankie and it occurred to me that at least now I knew where teenagers got their pot. The stench coming from inside the booth almost calmed me down. And made me want a brownie. Right away.

"No! I'm being chased! Please call 911!" I said, banging on the glass to make sure he stayed focused.

"Whoa . . . dude . . . I mean, lady . . . calm down." He sat back down in the chair and consulted his chart of residents, the tail of his uniform shirt hanging down over the back of the chair. "Now, who are you going to see?"

I leaned in and grabbed the front of his shirt and brought his face as close to mine as I could. "I'm . . . not . . . seeing . . . anyone. Please . . . call . . . 911." I spoke as slowly as I possibly could to make sure that he understood the message. Under normal circumstances, the look of horror on his face would have made me laugh, but in this instance it just brought me back to consciousness. I let go of his shirt and pulled my head out of the hut. I turned and saw my car idling at the top of the hill, the lights off, Joey at the steering wheel. I leaned in again. "Call 911. Now."

He raised a shaking hand and turned the volume down on the show he was watching just as some B-list actress completed a full split in a flamenco skirt; the show seemed to be some kind of dancing competition. If I had been stoned, I would have been mesmerized, too, but as I was running for my life, I only gave it a quick glance. He punched the numbers into the phone and handed it to me, not sure of what to say.

"My name is Alison Bergeron and I'm being followed by a man. I am . . ." I said, pausing, because it occurred to me that I didn't know where I was. I looked at the kid. "Where am I?"

He looked back at me, his shaggy hair covering his eyes. "Um . . . Croton?"

"Not what town! What's the name of the complex?" I screamed, my hysteria peaking. I resisted the urge to hit him over the head with the phone and settled for kicking the side of the hut a few times to make sure I had his attention.

"Hudson Pointe."

I didn't ask if "point" ended with an *e*. I've come to learn that they all do. "I'm at the Hudson Pointe condominium complex at the guard booth. I'm being followed by a man in 2006 navy blue Volvo sedan." I took a deep breath before giving the dispatcher my license plate number. I looked back up the hill and saw that Joey was gone. "The man driving it was here a minute ago but now he's gone. And I didn't see which way he went," I said, anticipating the dispatcher's next question. The dispatcher assured me that someone would be arriving at Hudson Pointe within minutes.

It must have been a slow night in Croton because three police cars followed by an ambulance and a fire truck, showed up within seconds. Mr. Stoned Security Guy reached down and shoved something into his sock as I was approached by one of the local cops.

I tried to tell him that there was probably another man in the adjacent park with a head wound. I had a feeling that Joey hadn't taken the time to revive Tiny and put him in the car, opting instead to save himself. . . . But maybe I was wrong and there *was* honor among thieves. By then I was gasping for breath. I tried to remain calm, focusing on the cop's neat, blond brush cut, my breath going in and out of my lungs at a rapid clip. When the brush cut turned red and my knees started getting weak, I thought to myself that bringing an ambulance along had been a very good idea.

I hit the ground with what I suppose was an indelicate thud.

Thirty-One

"Is there somewhere other than your home where you can stay tonight?"

I looked at the detective and nodded. My shaking hands were wrapped around a cup of very hot tea, which had been presented to me as soon as I had arrived at the Croton police station after my brief stint in the ambulance. I had been there for more than an hour and with that question, it had finally occurred to me that an ex-con was driving around in my car with my pocketbook, house keys, and all my credit cards.

The detective was a nice guy in his early fifties with a ruddy complexion and giant hands that resembled bear claws. He folded his hands together in front of him. "I think it would be safe to assume that he'll ditch the car, and, hopefully, its contents, in favor of stealing something new. But if we don't get him in the next few hours and if by chance, he keeps some of the contents," I noticed that he avoided using the words "house keys," "then you'll need to be very careful. Change the locks. Cancel your credit cards. Don't travel alone." He stood. "I don't mean to scare you but we have to be realistic."

I took a sip of my tea. I'd rather be unrealistic but that might end up with me being un-alive. "Thank you, Detective Simcock." Thank god Max hadn't arrived yet; she'd never be able to keep a straight face around a guy with that name.

He went to the door. "Your boyfriend is a cop, right?" he asked.

I guess "boyfriend" was going to have to do; I didn't have the energy to go into my thoughts on what an appropriate label would be for Crawford. "Yes. Were you able to get in touch with him?"

"I was. He should be here in the next half hour or so. You can hang out in here, if you'd like."

I didn't know what my other options were—I guessed the teeny tiny lobby was the other—so I decided to stay put. I was in a wood-paneled room sitting at a Formica table inside a building that seemed to house every municipal organization in the village of Croton; when we had arrived at the station earlier, a group from the Croton Seniors Club was gathering in the parking lot to board a bus to the Westchester Dinner Theater to see an off-off-off-Broadway production of *The Bourne Identity*.

Don't ask—I have no idea how they staged that.

A commotion in the hallway signaled Max's arrival. She burst through the door and flew into my arms, even though I was still seated. I grabbed onto the edge of the table to steady myself and to make sure we didn't go over backward. I couldn't take another head injury.

"You're safe!" she proclaimed. I saw Detective Simcock peek in and then close the door quietly.

"What the hell happened to you?" I asked after extricating myself from her and putting her in the chair across from me. "Where did you go?"

She took a deep breath; this was obviously going to take a while. I noticed that the cardigan was ripped in a few places but I wasn't sure if she had rent the garment with anguish at the thought of my demise or if she had scaled a few fences. Turned out the latter was true. "Well, after I ran up and down Route 9 several hundred times, during which nobody stopped," she said, indignant, "I finally went up the next street and through someone's backyard, where I saw that there was a police station. I had to climb a fence." She poked at a hole in the sweater. "Sorry."

No, you're not, I thought.

"But by the time we got back, you were gone. They did a dragnet or something or what's that thing called?" she asked, looking up at the ceiling for inspiration. "An APB?" Max usually knows these things cold so I assumed she was still in shock. Her pale face was a definite sign. She folded her arms on the table and put her head down. After a few seconds, I could see her shoulders going up and down and could hear little hiccupping squeaks coming from inside of her folded arms.

"Max, are you crying?" I got up and went over to her; I put my hand on her back.

She sobbed for a few minutes; it was the saddest sound I had ever heard. I realized I had never seen or heard Max cry. "I thought you were dead," she said, her voice hoarse. "And it was because I couldn't find the police station."

I knelt down and put my arms around her. "I'm not dead." I rubbed her back. "And if I were, it wouldn't be your fault."

She looked up me, her face a mascara-stained mess. "I hate this freaking sweater," she said. She ripped it off and threw it on the floor.

"I know." I reached across her to the credenza behind us and pulled out a few tissues from an almost empty tissue box. "Here."

She blew her nose loudly.

Before we tackled any other emotions, I needed to know one thing. "Max, where's Frankie?"

"He's at the police station by the Lord's Bounty. He was calling his mom to pick him up. He got there around the same time I did."

That was a relief. I couldn't bear to think that anything had happened to him. That kid had seen a lot of things, thanks to me. I made a mental note to drop by Jane's house as soon as I got back to Dobbs Ferry. I handed Max another tissue. "So, did Detective Simcock," I said, accentuating the more perverse portion of his name for her benefit, "tell you about my latest, greatest adventure?"

"No, but that other hottie cop out there did. You could bounce a quarter off his ass. Did you see it?" she asked, wiping her nose. She was back.

I nodded. "I did."

"He stuck you in the trunk?" she asked, grimacing a bit.

I gave her the rundown of my kidnapping. "The worst part is that he's got my pocketbook. . . ."

"Not the Marc Jacobs I gave you for Christmas?" she said, grabbing her chest in horror.

"No, it's the black tote from Target."

"Oh, thank god," she said, breathing a genuine sigh of relief. She thought about the implications of the missing pleather

Target bag for a moment. "That's still not good," she said gravely when she realized that an ex-con with a bag full of money, credit cards, and my house keys was a fate much worse than a missing Marc Jacobs bag.

"Want a roommate?" I asked brightly.

"You're staying with me," a male voice said from behind me. I turned around and saw Crawford; a lovelier sight I had never beheld.

I jumped into his arms and planted kisses all over his face.

"Down, Trixie," he said. He looked at Max, who was slowly decompensating right before our eyes. "She may be in shock," he whispered.

"I think you're right," I said. And I found myself in the unusual position of being the one holding it together. Wow, this is a new one, I thought.

Crawford grabbed my tea and held it out to Max. "Here, Max. Take a few sips of this," he said. She obediently drank from the cup.

Crawford and I took seats on the opposite side of the table and I gave him a quick rundown of the evening's events. I had told the story so many times that the retelling felt rote. "Simcock told me that they picked up Tiny."

Max let out a little giggle at the mention of his name. "Sorry," she said, and covered her mouth.

"He's at the hospital getting stitched up. Then, he's going back to lockup." Crawford looked at me, concerned. "He said you hit him over the head with a flashlight?"

"I did," I said, a little ashamed, but not too much. At that point in the game, it had been either him or me. "I had no choice."

Crawford shook his head. "No, I'm not judging you. I just . . ."

". . . didn't think I had it in me?" I finished the sentence for him. "Me either. But it was my only chance to get away, so I took it.

"Where's Fred?" I mouthed.

Crawford shrugged, a gesture that spoke volumes. But as concerned as I was about the whereabouts of Max's relatively new husband and Max's emotional state, I had a more pressing concern on my mind. I had to get home to my dog.

Thirty-Two

I woke up the next morning sandwiched between the two beings I loved the most: Crawford and Trixie.

I stretched and realized I was pressed up against one hundred pounds of furry dog flesh. I opened my eyes and found myself face-to-face with Trixie, awake, looking hungry and full of energy for a morning walk.

Crawford had been up late, having made several phone calls to make sure the overnight detectives were up on what had happened and my theory that Jose and Joey had been involved in a green card–forging scam. We didn't have any proof that Joey had killed Jose, but based on his reaction to the conversation between me and Max that he had overheard, it was likely he had been involved in some way. Crawford said he was going to take Sunday off and go back in early on Monday to follow up on all the loose ends in the case.

I propped myself up on my elbow and looked over at the other sleeping creature. Crawford, as opposed to my canine friend, didn't look hungry—or capable of taking Trixie for a walk. He had tossed and turned for the better portion of the night. A restless sleeper under the best circumstances, after the events of the previous evening, there was no way that he would sleep straight through.

But like most restless sleepers, he usually fell into a deep slumber an hour or two before he had to wake up. Seeing his peaceful mien and his chest rising and falling in a gentle rhythm, I got out of bed and pointed to the floor, instructing Trixie to quietly get out of bed. We left the bedroom, me tiptoeing across the hardwood floor, Trixie click-clacking along as her too-long nails made contact with the wood.

I pulled the bedroom door closed behind me and stood in the living room, waking up slowly. Max was in a little ball on the couch, her body unmoving under a down comforter that Crawford had stowed in a closet that held so much detritus I feared ever having to open it again. His neat apartment had always concerned me; for a guy who lived alone, it looked like a team of designers and cleaning people made their way through the rooms on a regular basis. But opening the closet the night before and being hit in the head with a tennis racket, snowboard, and telephone book in rapid succession convinced me that he, too, had his housekeeping secrets.

Trixie went over and lovingly licked Max's face, rousing her only slightly. "Not now, honey; I had a very long evening."

Trixie was single-minded in her quest to get Max to wake up, though, and licked her from chin to hairline repeatedly. Max woke up suddenly and bolted from the couch. "You have got to keep that mutt away from my face with her tongue," she said thickly, her voice still not operational after sleeping.

I called Trixie and she came over to my side. "She's not a mutt. And she loves you," I said. I sat on the couch next to Max. "Do you want to go to breakfast?" I asked.

"What about Detective Hot Pants?" she asked, hooking her thumb toward the bedroom and the sound of Crawford's snores coming from inside.

"Let's let him sleep," I said. "I'll walk Trixie and when I come back, we'll go. OK?" I left her entering the bathroom to get cleaned up. I wrote Crawford a hasty note and left it propped up on his counter. Neither Max nor I had clean clothes so we were particularly ripe; I had been in my house only long enough to get Trixie and to get out. Max had called Fred and told him that she was staying at Crawford's for the night. I didn't know where he was and I didn't ask.

We were seated at a diner in Crawford's neighborhood a half hour later, me with a giant plate of pancakes in front of me, and she with her customary Sunday morning cheeseburger. I knew that Max and Fred, like me and Crawford, had their rituals, given the guys' propensity for being gone for long stretches doing overtime; Sunday morning at their neighborhood diner was one of theirs. This diner was only half full and we were tucked into a large booth near the back of the restaurant and had the undivided attention of our waitress, who only had two tables to service. I waited until she had refilled our coffee cups for the third time since we had sat down before asking Max if there was something she wanted to tell me.

She shrugged nonchalantly. "No. Why?"

I put down my fork, my plate almost empty. "Max. We've

just been through the wringer yet you decide it's better to stay with me and Crawford than go home to your husband?" I gave her a look. "Even you have to admit that's pretty suspicious."

She looked down at her fries, moving a few around to form a cross on her plate. "We had a fight."

"I'll say," I said, forking another mouthful of pancake into my mouth so I wouldn't say anything else.

She looked up at me, her blue eyes filled with tears. I couldn't take this; I hadn't seen Max cry in over fifteen years of friendship and now I had seen her cry twice in two days. "Things haven't been going very well," she said.

I left the sarcasm out of my reply. "Tell me what's going on."

"He's got issues," she said, pausing, "with my . . . history?" she said, trying to find the right word.

And what an illustrious history it was. I had spent most of our adult life married, but Max had cut quite a swath through Manhattan's single male population, leaving behind a trail of consenting adults or broken hearts—take your pick. I spent every weekend at home trying to get in the good graces of a philandering husband who had never been attracted to or in love with me, whereas she was out every Friday, Saturday, and Sunday night with either the same or a different man; it depended on the week. So, when she announced that she was marrying Fred after the shortest courtship that I had ever witnessed, I was justifiably dubious. The only things I knew about Fred I had heard from Crawford and, although Crawford thought the world of him, he had no experience with Fred as a spouse. He did protest that being a partner with the guy for five years lent him some insight but I wasn't so sure. Marriage is complicated; Crawford and I both knew that better than anyone.

"Concannon threw him off the case," Max said, referring to Crawford and Fred's lieutenant. They loved working for him, but they knew that "propriety" was his middle name and he didn't tolerate any hint of indiscretion in his squad. That, coupled with the fact that Fred was one of the lead detectives on the case, had led to his decision to reassign Fred until Jose's and Madeleine's cases had been closed. "And he's blaming it on me."

"Why? He knew about you and Richie," I said with the utmost confidence.

A tear rolled down her cheek.

"He didn't?"

She shook her head.

I put my face in my hands. "Oh, Max."

"And someone found the picture."

"The Bungalow 8 picture?" I asked, referring to the infamous leather dress picture.

She nodded solemnly.

"You never told him about Richie?" I asked. When she reconfirmed that was the case, I exhaled loudly. "What were you thinking, Max?"

"I wasn't!" she wailed.

"Is this part of the 'no secrets' kick that Fred's been on?"

"Guess so."

I took a few deep breaths and tried to think of the kind of advice to give her. It was a sticky situation, but not irreparable. I told her as much.

She pushed her plate away, not hungry anymore. The attentive waitress stopped by again and refilled our coffee. I watched her move on to another table and I glanced casually at its occupants. "Oh, shit," I said, and not as under my breath as I had planned.

Max's head swiveled around, happy for the distraction.

"Turn back around, Max," I hissed.

"What's going on?" she asked, wiping her eyes with a coarse napkin.

I dropped my voice even though they knew I was there and there was no need to whisper. "It's those annoying federal agents. Goldenberg and Abreu."

Abreu lifted his coffee cup and nodded at me, smiling. Goldenberg's back was turned and he continued to work on his omelet. I was staring at Abreu and wondering what he looked like with his shirt off when Crawford slid into the booth beside me, pushing me toward the wall separating us from the booth on the other side.

"Push over," he said, taking the opportunity to grab my butt and give it a little squeeze. Too bad it was the side that Louise had hit with her Chevy Cavalier.

"Ow!" I yelled out, getting Goldenberg's attention. He turned and saluted me with a piece of toast.

Crawford rested his arms on the table and looked at me. "They're still following you?"

"Not that you care," I said.

"They don't call you Detective Hot Pants for nothing," Max said, giving me a look that indicated that she didn't want to pursue the conversation about her husband.

"Hey, that's what she says," Crawford said, leaning into me and giving me a kiss on the cheek. He pulled a menu out of the holder on the table. "What's good?" He craned his neck and examined Max's cheeseburger. "A cheeseburger?" he asked, wrinkling his nose.

"That's what I get," she said, the sniffling and hysterical crying recommencing, "every Sunday!" she cried, and exited the booth, running out of the restaurant and down the street.

Crawford picked one of her French fries from her plate and ate it. "What's that about?"

I smacked him and pushed his large frame out of the booth. "Get out. I have to go after her," I said, sliding across the Naugahyde and out of the booth. I passed by Abreu and Goldenberg's table and stopped briefly. "I'll be right back if we need to talk." I ran to the front door and pushed it open in time to see Max climbing into a silver Mercedes. I couldn't see who was driving but I could see the license plate.

BYE-ATHLEET.

Thirty-Three

Despite how stunned and upset I was by the bad spelling on the vanity license plate, I took off down the street after the car, screaming Max's name above the din of honking cabs and exhaust-spewing buses and weaving around the Sunday morning pedestrian traffic. I dodged a Pomeranian-walking matron in a full-length mink heading toward the river.

"Excuse me," I said, jumping over the yipping dog.

"Excuse *me*," she said snottily.

I didn't have time to go back to explain my situation or tell her to buzz off so I kept running, hoping the light at the corner would turn red and I would be able to pull Max from the car. The last thing she needed to do in yesterday's clothes and with her marriage falling apart was spend the day hanging around with the supermodel biathlete. The car sped off through a yellow light—but not before Morag and I locked eyes in her rearview mirror.

Where the hell were they going? And why? Max was certainly a bit off-kilter emotionally but I had no idea what Morag was doing in this neighborhood and why Max would get in her car and go off to parts unknown. I walked dejectedly down the street, passing the same lady with her little dog. "Well, I never," she harrumphed as I passed her again.

"I don't doubt it," I whispered under my breath, giving her a dazzling smile. "Have a nice day!"

I went back to the diner, where I found Crawford in our booth, but now with Abreu and Goldenberg. They were sharing a laugh about something and the sight of the three of them, chuckling away, made me a little suspicious.

I slid into the booth next to Crawford. "I see you've met?" I said, pointing at the men across from us.

"Where's Max?" Crawford asked, still munching on her leftover fries.

"She had to go," I said cryptically. I pinched him, hard, under the table, and he grimaced. I didn't know why, but I didn't want Abreu and Goldenberg to know about Max, lest they get the idea that they needed to question her, too. That was the last thing she needed.

Goldenberg had a fresh cup of coffee in front of him into which he spooned more sugar than one person should consume in a week. He stirred it around in the cup and then took a small, dainty sip. "So, Dr. Bergeron, what's been happening with you since we last saw each other?"

"You mean since the time you called me a Hispanic male?" I asked. Crawford obviously had no idea what I was talking about and looked at me, his brow furrowed. I didn't feel the need to elaborate.

Goldenberg smiled slightly.

"Any further along in finding Madeleine's real killer?" I asked.

Abreu looked down at the table. "Not really. Any ideas?"

"No." I looked at Crawford. "What about Jose Tomasso?"

Goldenberg smiled sadly. "No on that front, too. But that has more to do with your . . ." he paused, ". . . paramour here than the FBI."

"Paramour." Now there was a word I could get used to saying. I looked over at him. "Did you fill them in on my excellent adventure?"

He nodded, eyeing the remainder of Max's cheeseburger. "But they already knew. Feds are smart," he said in a way that neither Goldenberg nor Abreu could tell was with sarcasm.

Goldenberg took another tentative sip of hot coffee. "I'm going to let you in on something, Dr. Bergeron." He stirred some more sugar into the cup. "We do not think that Mr. Tomasso's death is linked to Agent Cranston's."

I waited for more information. When none was forthcoming, I asked, "So?"

"That's it."

"And you came all this way to tell me that?"

Abreu smiled at me. "No. We just like to follow you around."

Goldenberg shot him a look. "I'm actually curious to find out what you think about that."

I had no thoughts and I wasn't sure why they were interested in anything I had to say. Up until a few hours ago, I was sure they had been thinking that I had had something to do with it. "It's no wonder that the federal government has a multitrillion dollar deficit," I said, moving out of the booth. "If this is how you guys spend your money, you need a new accountant." I stood next to the booth and looked at the three of them.

Abreu held my gaze. "Where's Hernan Escalante, Dr. Bergeron?"

I hadn't expected that question and I tried not to let it show on my face. "I don't know," I said, adding an exaggerated shrug for good measure.

Abreu continued to look at me. "You do know that harboring a fugitive is a federal crime?"

"A fugitive?" And was it really harboring if he wasn't actually living with me? I decided not to ask that question.

"Mr. Escalante is being sought in the murder of Federal Agent Cranston," Abreu said in his monotone. "A crime that carries a life sentence."

My pancakes turned to acid in my stomach. "That's interesting."

"I don't want to get into the sentence for harboring a fugitive." Abreu looked at Crawford, who looked like he was in the middle of a bad dream.

"How do you look in orange?" Goldenberg asked. "Jumpsuits?"

"Hey, Goldenberg? Back off," Crawford said testily. "There's no need to go there." He reached across the table and grabbed my hand.

"This is a very serious situation, Detective Crawford," Goldenberg said.

"You don't think I know that?" Crawford asked, sitting up a little straighter.

"Well, your girlfriend seems to think that we're joking around." Goldenberg stirred the coffee a little more. "We're not."

"Trust me," Crawford said, leaning over the table, "she

knows exactly how serious the situation is." He looked at me and the expression on his face said, "Don't you?"

Their little exchange allowed me to regain my composure. I nodded enthusiastically. "If I find out anything about Mr. Escalante, I will be sure to let you know," I said. I realized that I had slumped a little bit so I pulled myself upright again and looked at Crawford. "Coming?"

He looked at me. "I haven't ordered yet," he said pointedly, leading me to believe that he had a few things to discuss with the agents.

I looked at Max's decimated plate; if the remains of her breakfast hadn't satisfied him, I didn't know what would. "OK. I'm going back to the apartment. Can I have the keys?" I asked.

He reached into his pants pocket and pulled them out. "I'll see you back there?" He squeezed my other hand.

I nodded. "I'll be there." I nodded to Abreu and Goldenberg. "And I hope this is good-bye," I said. I got out to the street, pulled my cell phone from my pocket—luckily I'd left it at home last night—and dialed Max's number. She picked up on the first ring. "Where are you?" I asked.

"Heading downtown," she said. "Morag is going to drop me off at my apartment."

"A cab would have sufficed, don't you think?" I said. "What was she doing outside the diner?"

"She lives in the neighborhood."

"She does?" This was the first I was hearing about that little detail. I thought she lived with Richie on the Upper East Side.

"Yep. Right around the corner." I heard another voice, presumably Morag's, in the background, and I heard Max respond with my name. "Listen, I'll call you later, OK?" She hung up.

I stopped in front of Crawford's building, his keys in my hand. I jingled them slightly, noticing the key to his car, the biggest and heftiest on the ring, slapping against my palm. I shoved my cell phone back into my pocket and continued walking past the apartment and toward Ninety-eighth Street, where Crawford had parked his car the night before. Something about Max being with Morag didn't sit right with me and I was going to drive downtown just to make sure that she got home safely. Call it a hunch. In the back of my mind, I wondered if I should call it jealousy—was Max replacing me with a supermodel biathlete?—but I pushed that aside. I was concerned about my friend. If I was wrong and Morag was just providing a shoulder to cry on, I would feel a little foolish but at least I would know that Max was safe. And if Morag was more involved in this whole situation than I originally thought and was now involving Max, then I would need to get to the bottom of it. I pointed the key ring at Crawford's car and unlocked the doors. It wasn't the first time in our relationship that I had appropriated Crawford's car but I told myself that it would be the last.

My cell phone rang as I got the seat into a comfortable position. It was Jimmy Crawford. "Hey! Did you forget about me?" he asked.

Yes. I had forgotten about him, Hernan, and a bunch of other things. That's what happens when you get locked in a trunk for several hours: You forget things. "Oh, Jimmy. Hi. I'm sorry I didn't call you back."

"Not a problem. Did you tell Bobby that I have his will?"

I adjusted the rearview and side-view mirrors in preparation for my trip to Tribeca. "I did. He hasn't called you back?"

"No, but I didn't expect him to. We've got a command performance at Mom's next week so I figured I'd give him the stuff then. I just wanted to make sure that he knows the will is ready."

"I told him but I'll remind him." As I pulled out of the spot and into the sparse, Sunday-morning traffic, Jimmy asked me why I had originally called him. "Oh, that." I explained the situation with Hernan and asked if he knew a good immigration lawyer.

"As a matter of fact, I do. Where's your friend now?"

I hesitated. I thought about federal prison and how I wouldn't enjoy it.

"If you tell me, you'll have to kill me?" he asked.

"Something like that." I merged onto the West Side Highway and headed south.

"Well, I'll need a little more information to go on in order to help you."

I hadn't taken that into account. "Listen, Jimmy. I'll call you when I get home so we can either talk about this in more detail or we can meet and discuss it. How would that be?"

"Sounds good. Hey, the Rangers are doing great this year, huh?"

That brought a smile to my face. "They are. And I'm taking Bobby to a game next Thursday night."

"The good seats?"

"The good seats," I confirmed.

"That oughta make him happy. If not, wanna be my girlfriend?"

I flipped the phone closed and threw it onto the seat next to me. I figured I had another twenty minutes before Crawford realized that I was missing, then another ten before he realized I had his car. I prayed that I would find Max in her apartment, her arms wrapped around that Neanderthal she called her husband.

I called her cell phone one more time but this time it rang about ten times before going to voice mail.

Thirty-Four

I sat outside Max's building waiting to see if she appeared. I had double-parked outside the building and run in to ask the doorman if she was home. She wasn't; I had just missed her. And neither was Fred, but I didn't know that until I saw him walking down the street with a petite redhead alongside him. I slumped down in the seat so that my head wasn't visible over the steering wheel but I always forget: detectives are observant. It was only seconds later that a giant hand was rapping on the driver's side window. I recognized it as Fred's. I looked up and gave him a little wave.

"We don't allow double-parking on this street," he said through the closed window.

I sat up. "I'll be moving along shortly."

He shoved his hands into his pocket. "Where's Crawford?"

"Eating breakfast."

He looked at the car, clearly not mine, and raised his eyebrow at me. "Did you have fun last night?"

I made a face. "What do you think?" He was either completely clueless or the most accomplished asshole I had ever met. I decided to go with the former.

"Where's my wife?"

"I don't know. I was hoping that you did."

He stared back at me and for the first time since I had met him, I saw the traces of emotion on his face. He was worried.

We stared at each other for a few seconds until our inaction was interrupted by my cell phone. I saw Max's number on the caller ID and immediately felt calm flood through my body. "Max! Where are you?"

"I'm on my way to Riviera Pointe. The sales office. I'm buying an apartment."

I looked at Fred but I didn't tell him what she'd said. "Don't do that." I tried to sound forceful without arousing Fred's suspicion. Too late: he was walking around the car and getting into the passenger's seat before I had a chance to think.

"It's over, Alison. It was a huge mistake," she said. In addition to being a fast runner, an infrequent crier, and my best friend, nobody makes a decision as quickly—and with as much finality—as Max. "I got married too fast. You were right."

"No," I said. "Listen, I'm with Fred. We'll come up there. Don't do anything until we get there." She protested slightly but I could tell that her heart wasn't entirely in this acquisition. "Wait for us. We'll be there in twenty minutes. Tops." I closed the phone, for once ending the conversation before she could. I angled out of my awkward double-parked spot and onto the street, heading back toward the West Side Highway, this time to go north to the Bronx.

"What did she say?" he asked.

I didn't respond to the question. "More importantly, who's the redhead?"

"God, you're a pain in the ass."

"I'm a pain in the ass?" I asked, incredulous. "Your wife is ready to call it quits with you and I'm trying to make sure that doesn't happen."

"She is?" He seemed genuinely surprised at that news.

"What did you think when she didn't come home last night? After what had happened to us, don't you think she would have wanted to come home to you?" I asked.

He turned and looked at me, his giant bald head just inches from my face. "She told me that she was going to spend the night at your house and that I shouldn't expect to see her until this afternoon. What happened to the two of you?"

I filled him in on the night's events. He put his face into his hands as I recounted my evening and Max's role in it. "So, to recap, there's an ex-con out there with my car, my house keys, and all my credit cards and cash."

He groaned a little bit. "Who's looking for him?"

"Hopefully the entire state of New York, but for sure, the Westchester County cops are on the case."

"You're not going home, right?"

I looked at him and gave him a look. "I think that's obvious."

"You can stay with us if you wear out your welcome with Bobby," he said.

I was hoping that wasn't a possibility but I thanked him for his hospitality. I didn't want to remind him that he might not be living with Max for very long and that I might be her permanent roommate in the wake of his departure. I looked at him out of the corner of my eye and got the impression that he was considering the same thing. His right elbow was resting on the edge of the window and his forehead was resting in his palm. He stared out the window at the passing cars.

After a few minutes of silence, I asked my initial question again. "Who's the redhead?"

He hesitated, seemingly deciding whether to tell me anything, and if so, how much. He started and then stopped. Finally, he said, "She's the Bronx ME."

I've learned a thing or two in the years since I divorced my late ex-husband. One, where there's smoke, there's fire. And two . . . well, there is no two. Let's just say that I'm really, really paranoid and suspicious as a result of Ray's philandering. "What's the Bronx ME doing in your neighborhood on a Sunday morning?"

He hesitated again and then started talking. And talking. And talking. In the year since I had met Fred, he hadn't said so much. Now he wouldn't shut up. The upshot? They had had a relationship a long time ago. They had even talked marriage. But the relationship had ended badly.

It still didn't explain what she was doing in the neighborhood on a Sunday morning, but it explained Fred's "no secrets" rule. He and Melanie Moscowitz—the infamous Bronx ME who Max was obsessed with—were now working more closely than either had anticipated when they had parted eight years earlier and he was trying to find a way to tell Max. Or not tell her. He couldn't decide what to do. Because based on his reactions to finding out about Max's prodigious dating career prior to her marriage to him, he wasn't sure how she'd react to her finding out about Moscowitz.

"You've really created a problem where none exists," I said, pointing out what I thought was obvious.

"How so?"

"Do you really think that Max is going to care about a relationship that was over eight years ago?"

He shrugged and grunted. "She might."

"But you'll never know until you talk about this like adults," I said. Boy, did I sound reasonable. I had no idea how Max would respond but I had to give her the benefit of the doubt. I had never known Max to be the jealous type, but I had never known Max to be in love, either. It was a crap shoot, but in my heart I knew that this was not an insurmountable problem. Maybe I should open up a relationship counseling center; I seemed to be very good at this kind of thing.

"The relationship ended because I had a one-night stand." He looked out the window. "With her sister."

"OK . . ." I said slowly. Forget the relationship counseling center. I didn't have the stomach for this.

"It was a long time ago," he said. "A long time ago." He turned and looked at me. "I'm not that guy anymore, Alison."

You'd better not be, I thought. I chewed on all this for a few minutes. Strangely enough, I believed him. I wasn't the same woman who had married a serial philanderer, so I knew that people could change. "So why was she down here today?"

"She wanted to clear the air. We're going to be working together and we couldn't have this stuff between us."

We needed to spend more time on this topic, but we had pulled up to Riviera Pointe and had to suspend our discussion, at least temporarily. I pulled into the same spot that I had the first time I had been there but saw no sign of Class of '59, my cranky friend—and I breathed a sigh of relief for that. I didn't think I could take much more of him, given the events and revelations of the last twenty-four hours.

I turned off the car and took off my seat belt. "This is not the best time to get into this with Max, obviously, but you have to tell her, Fred."

He closed his eyes. "I know." I saw tears seep out from under his closed lids. "Now she'll leave me for sure." He swiped a giant hand across his eyes. "I'm not that guy, Alison."

I couldn't dispute his suspicion that she would hit the road over this but I told him to keep the faith. I looked over at the hulking form that was the foundation and framework of Riviera Pointe, the glass-enclosed sales office just a few hundred feet to the north. The parking lot and the front door were on the other side of the building; we had pulled up to a side street that was perpendicular to the back of the sales office. Richie had smartly built the front of the sales office facing the river, with the parking lot in front of it; I couldn't see if Morag's car was there or not.

"I'll go in and get her," I said. "Wait here."

I got out of the car and jogged down the hill toward the sales office, the midday sun glinting off the river. I shielded my eyes while I ran down a path that flanked the side of the sales office. I tried to look into the building, but the bright sun just made me see my own reflection.

I got down to the front door, my hand on the door handle. I looked into the parking lot, which was behind me and fronted the river. I saw Morag's car so I knew they were there.

And then I saw my car.

I knew that whatever plan I had needed to change dramatically.

Thirty-Five

My hand was still on the door when it was pulled inward, me with it. I stumbled onto the polished marble floor of the sales office, skidding along its slippery surface. I came to a stop at Daphne's desk, now unoccupied, bumping my head against the front of her rounded, mahogany work area. I looked up and saw Max standing by the entrance to Richie's office. Morag was standing behind her with a thick sheaf of papers in one hand and her other hand behind her back.

I looked back toward the door and greeted Joey. "If there is one scratch on my car, Joey, I'm going to add that to my list of complaints to your parole officer," I said.

Max looked at me. "Where did he come from?" she said, pointing at Joey.

I gave him an angry look. "You tried to hit me and run me over, didn't you, Joey?" I thought back to the night I had been walking Trixie, back when all of this madness had begun. I had ruined a perfectly good pair of boots that night.

He just stared back at me blankly without answering.

"Spell 'business,'" I said, thinking back to the note that was on my car when the tires got slashed.

"B-i-z-n-e-s," he said.

"Aha!" Max yelled. "There are two s's!" She turned and looked at me, lowering her voice. "Why are we asking him to spell?"

"And you slashed my tires, too?" I asked, disappointed. "Gosh, Joey, what did I ever do to you?"

"It's what you did to me." Morag brushed past Max and came into the hallway. Man, she was tall. I'm tall but she was a giant. She was six two if she was an inch. She had on black leggings tucked into high-heeled boots and a very cute tunic with jewels on the neckline and sleeves. If I didn't want to get away from her so badly at that point, I would have complimented her on her style. It was a vast improvement on the 1940s gun moll look she had been sporting at Jose Tomasso's funeral. And instead of her usual blond do, today she had a jet black bob with bangs. Which did not suit her at all, but I opted not to tell her that, either. "What are you doing here?" she asked. "God, you are so nosy."

I stood up. "I've come to talk some sense into my friend here." I rested my hand on Daphne's desk, which was about chest high on me. "Max, let's go." I decided not to show my hand and reveal that Fred was in the car. I had a feeling that might escalate things faster than I was ready for, both with Morag and with Max. I was trying to remain calm, but I knew that Joey's presence at the sales office signaled that we were in a situation that was rapidly getting out of control.

Max looked at me and I nodded at her. She walked toward me slowly, her eyes not leaving mine the whole time. I drifted away from Daphne's desk and toward the door. I wondered how many blows to the head it was going to take before Max and Crawford put me in an assisted-living facility and fed me applesauce from a baby spoon. I could feel the bruise taking shape as I stood there.

We just might get out of this, I thought as I got closer to the front door. Max was at my side, and I grabbed her hand. "Let's go," I whispered.

I heard a click behind me, and while my original thought was that it was Morag's stiletto heel making contact with the marble, deep in my brain I recognized the sound as that of a safety being released on a revolver. "Stop." She said it once, and she said it politely. "Please."

Joey looked back at Morag and went pale. And this was a guy who had stuffed me into the trunk of my car. I didn't want to turn around and see what had made him blanch, but I had to. And when I saw that we were on the business end of a big gun with a silencer, I did as I was told.

"Max's husband is outside, Morag, and he's waiting for us."

Max looked at me, her eyes filling with tears. I couldn't take much more of the emotional Max; it was throwing me off. "He is?" she said so plaintively that I thought I'd start crying, too.

Yes, I thought, he's out there, but boy, do you have some talking to do. I squeezed her hand. "Yes."

"You'll be dead before he gets here," she said calmly, and an image of her on skis, shooting at targets in the wintry woods of Switzerland floated into my head. That ruled out making a break for it. She could ski and shoot; certainly, she could mow down a tall college professor and her petite friend, even if we were moving targets. She leveled the gun at us and asked us to move back toward Daphne's desk.

"Morag, I don't want any part of this," Joey said, his hand still on the door handle. "I'm already in too deep on this."

"Did you kill Jose, Joey?" I asked as I stood against Daphne's desk.

He threw his hands up. "No!" He pointed at her. "She did!"

And with that, she shot him in the chest.

Max screamed as we watched him clutch his chest, his eyes filled with surprise. He fell to the floor with a sickening thud. She broke away from me and ran over to him, covering his inert body with hers. "Why did you do that?!" she yelled at Morag.

"Get back against the desk, Max," Morag said.

Max disregarded her and I repeated what Morag had asked her to do. "Come on, Max. Do it," I said. From the way his body lay lifeless on the floor, I knew that it was too late to help Joey.

Morag watched her walk back and then turned toward the two of us. "You two couldn't be more annoying," she said in her barely accented English. "This whole thing would have been so much easier if you," she said, pointing the gun at me, "would have stayed out of it. I asked Joey to try to scare you, but you don't scare easily, do you?" she asked, a small, cruel smile playing on her lips. "A possible hit-and-run and a couple of slashed tires weren't enough to get you to back off."

"Is that why we went to dinner, Morag? So you could see how much Alison knew?" Max asked, her face flushed.

Morag didn't answer. I kept my eyes on her to see if I could get any indication of what she would do next. I wondered how long it would take Fred to realize that it had taken far too long for me to bring Max back to the car.

"Why did you kill Jose, Morag?" I asked.

She thought for a moment, not sure how much she wanted to tell us. But considering that she was going to kill us, I guess she decided that she could tell us everything. "Kid was blackmailing me. Wanted more of a cut on each forge than I was prepared to give," she said, shaking her head at the thought. "I wonder who he thought he was dealing with?" she asked, almost to herself.

The front door burst open and Richie came barreling in with Class of '59 in tow. "I have had enough of your crap, O'Laughlin!" Richie shouted, Class of '59 behind him with a briefcase overflowing with papers. "You're not getting an injunction, we're not stopping construction, and, no, your daughter cannot get a fifty-percent discount on an apartment just because you're losing your view! She's also going to lose her job because she may be the dumbest receptionist I have ever met!" Richie, not paying attention to where he was going, tripped over Joey's lifeless body and did as I had done earlier: he skidded headfirst into Daphne's desk. He grabbed at his head, stunned.

Class of '59—O'Laughlin, I presumed, and, weirdly enough, Daphne's father—had stopped inside the door and was fixated on Joey's body, the blood running out of it thick and black and leaving a muddy Rorschach pattern on the floor. He dropped the briefcase next to the body and ran back out the door.

Morag took a shot that shattered the front floor-to-ceiling pane of glass but missed him by a hair. He ran off around the building, screaming. I'll say this for Class of '59: he was a spry little bastard. He could have lettered in track, too.

Morag waved the gun at us and motioned for us to go into Madeleine Cranston's former office. Once inside, she put her fingers to her lips and smiled. "Shh . . ." she said, collecting our cell phones. "I have to think." She stepped out and closed the door.

Richie, ever the businessman, took a seat behind Madeleine's desk, leaving me to sit on the credenza and Max to take the one remaining guest chair in front of the desk. "What the hell is going on?" Richie asked.

"Your girlfriend is a freaking psycho, that's what!" Max screamed, lunging at him across the desk. "If I end up dead because you're dating a serial killer, I will kill you," she said, grabbing at his shirt.

Richie wheeled back in the desk chair and flattened himself against the back wall, leaving Max spread across the empty desktop. Once away from Max's clutches, he looked at me. "Got any ideas, Stretch?" he asked.

"Are you talking to me?" I asked, pointing at my chest.

"Yeah. You're the only one over five five in the room, right?" He bared his discolored little teeth at me.

"What did you ever see in this troll, Max?" I asked, my mind off the murderous Morag for the moment.

She peeled herself off the desk and sat back in her chair. "I've been asking myself that for the last five years," she said, glaring at him.

"All I know is this, Richie: ever since you started this operation, only bad things have happened." I stood up and pressed myself against Madeleine's window, hoping to catch a glimpse of Fred. "First, the nonunion laborers, the illegals, the shoddy construction . . . do you need money that badly that you had to break every possible building code in New York City?"

Richie looked at me. "What are you talking about?"

"This is all news to you?" I asked.

He smiled. "Well, some of it," he said. He held his hands up in protest. "But I don't know anything about illegal aliens. Every guy on this job site has a green card."

I snorted derisively. "Yes, Richie, they all had green cards because the dead guy out there and the first dead guy—Jose

Tomasso—were forging them and bringing them to the job site."

He stared at me. Finally, it dawned on him. "The dead guy was involved?"

"Yes. His name is Joey and he's an ex-con who did a lengthy stint at Sing Sing for forgery."

"He was framed," Max whispered under her breath.

"Morag told me that was her cousin," he said.

"You're a moron," Max said. She turned to me and lowered her voice. "That's not her cousin, right?"

I shook my head. "No." I walked around the office, getting antsy from being locked inside. I prayed that Fred was somewhere outside with the Fighting Sixty-Ninth, but it was eerily quiet. I wasn't even sure that Morag was still out there, but my instincts told me that she was. I felt pretty confident that she was going to kill us as soon as she cleared her head and got her thoughts straight. "All right. How are we going to get out of here? Richie? Any ideas?" I leaned on the desk and got in his face. "Is this place built in as shitty a way as the rest of your buildings? In other words, can we bust out through a cardboard wall or something?"

"What is wrong with you?" he asked. "We scrimp on the foundations. The framing and Sheetrock are top-notch."

"Oh, that's a relief," I said sarcastically. I looked around, settling on an air-conditioning grate in the ceiling. "Where does that go?" I asked.

Richie shrugged. "No idea. I just cash the checks."

At least he was honest. "Help me barricade the door with the credenza," I said. I figured that would buy us some time.

He looked at me, shamefaced. "All the furniture is bolted to the floor."

"What?"

"Why do you think she locked us in here? She knew that there was nowhere for us to go and that we couldn't barricade ourselves in," he said. "I didn't want the cleaning crew walking off with the furniture in the middle of the night."

"Yes, Richie, a fake plastic credenza is just what every New York City apartment needs." I looked at him and shook my head. "What's wrong with you?"

Max ignored the two of us and stood on the desk, reaching toward the ceiling. "Give me a boost," she said.

My luck that I got locked in an office with two of the shortest people I had ever met. I got on the desk and jockeyed around with Max until she was sitting on my shoulders while Richie regarded the two of us with a newfound respect. Or it might have been some kind of weird sexual interest; I couldn't tell. We didn't even have to talk to each other to figure out what the plan was. She pushed at the ceiling grate and I stood up straight, shoving her through the grate and into the ventilation system, her ballet-flatted feet hanging down in my face.

Relief flooded through my body as I saw her disappear into the ceiling of the Riviera Pointe sales office.

At that moment, Morag chose to come back in to get us.

Thirty-Six

Standing on the desk, I was now taller than Morag. I looked down at her.

"Where are you, Max?" she said, firing a shot into the ceiling. I heard Max yelp but it wasn't the yelp of the wounded. Then she scurried overhead and into the airspace over Richie's office. I prayed Morag wouldn't move through each office trying to shoot Max down, but that's precisely what she did. Although the silencer saved our ears, nothing could dampen the odor of gunpowder that flooded the office after Morag left.

Richie had turned into a statue in the corner of the office. "Where is she?" he asked.

I heard the muted sounds of shots being fired into the ceiling and the sound of Morag's pointy boot heels making their way across the marble floor of the lobby.

Richie picked up a desk chair and moved back several feet. When he was across from the desk, he hurled it at the window in back of Madeleine Cranston's desk. A spiderweb pattern grew in the tempered glass, but it didn't shatter.

"If you break the window, Richie, you can go, but I'm not leaving Max here," I said as he attempted to shatter the glass again. The chair bounced off the window and onto the floor, a few of its screws coming out in the process. Obviously, Richie scrimped on his office furniture, too.

I heard a man's voice yelling Morag's name, but the thick door muffled her response. I pressed an ear to the door but all I could hear was a scuffle followed by a thud and then, a shot.

The sound of that shot, louder than the ones that Morag had fired with her silenced revolver, reverberated through the office, and Richie hit the ground, his hands over his head like he was in the midst of an air raid. I stood and listened to the quiet that followed the first report.

After a few minutes, Richie stood again and picked up the chair, holding it aloft. I could hear footsteps; they weren't the sound made by stiletto-heeled boots but by shoes with rubber soles. There was a knock at the door and when it swung open and I saw Fred's face on the other side of it, I burst into tears.

"It's OK," he said and closed the door. "She's not going anywhere."

I presumed, by that comment, that Morag was dead.

"Where's Max?" he asked, his calm delivery belying the terror in his eyes.

I pointed at the ceiling. "Somewhere up there," I said.

He looked crestfallen and it occurred to me that perhaps he had misconstrued what "up there" might mean. "No!" I said. "She's in the ceiling."

Fred lumbered up onto the desk and stuck his head into the air vent. "Max!" he hollered. I'm sure his baritone, coupled with the surround sound of air-conditioning ductwork, played havoc with Max's hearing.

"What?" she called back.

"You can come out!" he responded.

I could hear her scrambling back through the ductwork; finding her way back was not as easy as she expected. "Keep talking so I can find my way back!"

Instead of talking, Fred started singing the words from their wedding song, which was the Bee Gees version of "More Than a Woman." I saw his arms go up into the ceiling and his heels leave the desk as he stood on his toes to get a better look into the shaft.

Richie looked at me and finally put the chair down, convinced that we weren't going to be killed. "Well, I think I'll be going," he said, moving toward the door.

I stood in front of it. "Not so fast, Kraecker."

"It's Kray-ker."

"Whatever." I kept my hand on the doorknob. "You're going to have to tell us what happened here. And why Morag was so intent on killing all of us. And Jose."

"I have no idea," he protested and came closer to me.

I threw my arms across the door. "You had a relationship with this woman and you have no idea what she was thinking?"

He thought for a moment. "Well, she is a bit of a hothead."

That was vastly understated. "That's it? She's a 'bit of a hothead'?" I asked.

Fred bent his knees and crouched on the desk, looking at his watch. Within seconds, I heard the wail of sirens and he shook his head and smiled. "That didn't take long."

I heard a voice coming from the lobby, whiny with a faint Swiss accent. "Is anyone going to help me?"

Fred jumped off the desk, Max dropping from the ceiling behind him. "Shut up!" he yelled after he had opened the door. "I've had enough of you!"

I peeked out and saw Morag handcuffed to the front door, her body inches from Joey. There was blood coming out of the side of one of her boots, but other than that, she looked particularly unscathed by whatever had happened with Fred. I looked at him, my eyes wide. "I thought you killed her."

"Couldn't get a good shot off," he said, back to his economical conversational style. "Besides, we need to find out what happened. With her dead, we wouldn't have any idea."

Richie peeked around me. "Aren't you guys trained to shoot to kill?"

Fred gave him a look that indicated that Richie would be best advised to keep his thoughts on the police department's shooting tactics to himself.

I looked over at Max, who leapt from the desk to the floor. She was covered in dust and grime but obviously happy to see Fred. She jumped on his back and wrapped her arms around his neck, kissing his bald head. "What took you so long?"

"You didn't buy an apartment, did you?" he asked.

Richie pushed past me and went into the lobby, not waiting for Max's answer. I followed close behind him, not wanting him to take off before he could be interrogated. As he pushed through the door, he walked right into a uniformed cop's arms. "Going somewhere, Mr. Kraecker?" the cop asked.

Richie stared back at the cop, not sure whether to play the blustery businessman or the rule-following possible criminal. He decided to play it safe. "No, Officer. Just trying to get some air after the events of the morning."

Carmen Montoya strutted into the lobby, her black leather

pants whispering a samba as she made her way into the center of the room. "Bergeron," she said to me. "You OK?"

I was never so glad to see her or her prodigious behind. "I am. Thanks for coming," I said, stupidly and unnecessarily. "What are you doing working on a Sunday?"

She smirked. "Pulled a double," she said. "I got a kid going to Cornell in the fall."

Enough said.

"What the hell happened here? You guys are really messin' up my Sunday morning." She put her hands on her hips and surveyed the damage. She looked at Joey and blessed herself.

I looked over at him, too, and said a little prayer before telling her what had happened. "He," I said, pointing at his dead body, "said that she," I said, pointing at Morag, still hand-cuffed to the front door, "killed Jose Tomasso."

Morag looked at me. "Which I didn't. What's an ex-con going to say?"

An ambulance pulled up and with it, a bunch of paramedics, who wheeled in a couple of stretchers. They went to work on Morag, seeing instantly that Joey was a lost cause. Carmen looked at me. "And him?"

I pointed at Morag. "Her again."

Carmen knelt down and got in Morag's face; I feared for the seat of her pants. "Two for two, lady."

She shrugged. "Her word against mine." She screamed as one of the paramedics started to cut off her boot. Turns out it wasn't pain that made her exclaim. "Those are Prada! What, are you crazy?"

The paramedic looked at her. "We can leave the bullet in, lady, and you can die of sepsis. Or we can take it out and you can buy a new pair of boots. Your choice."

Put to her that way, she really didn't have an argument. She watched, in horror, as the boot was cut away. I'm sure that even she realized, deluded as she was, that Prada didn't make good jailwear.

I walked outside and made my way through the phalanx of uniformed cops. Montoya called out to me that I shouldn't go far; she wanted to talk to me. I knew the drill; I'd been through stuff like this too many times not to. I scanned the crowd for Crawford and saw him leaning against a cruiser talking to another plainclothes cop, presumably a detective. The two of them looked completely unconcerned by what was going on around them.

If Fred's economy is in his speech, Crawford's is in his movement. He spied me, casually lifted his butt from the fender of the vehicle, and walked toward me at his usual amble, his arms swinging by his sides. I stopped where I was, resisting the urge to run straight to him. He reached me and took me in his arms. "You OK?" he asked in his usual understated way and kissed my head.

I felt my knees buckle and his hands supporting me under my arms. "No."

He put me in the backseat of one of the cruisers and I slid far enough in so that he could sit in there with me. His long legs stuck out the side of the car. "Tell me what happened," he said, putting his hand on my head.

"If I tell you, will I have to tell Montoya again?" I asked. The thought of telling the story a thousand times held no appeal for me.

"Probably," he admitted. "I'm sure every detective I work with is going to want to hear this story."

It *was* quite a story. I told him everything, from start to finish.

Thirty-Seven

Richie helped fill in the blanks, as did a soon-to-be orange-jumpsuited Morag.

"She was a tough one to crack, but eventually she did." Crawford slurped up an oyster. "Crack, that is. Richie, on the other hand, folded like a cheap suitcase. Once he started talking, we couldn't shut him up."

"I love when you talk like Sam Spade," I said, putting my hand to his cheek. We were sitting in our favorite restaurant on City Island and Crawford was putting away oysters like he was eating his last meal. It was two days after the debacle at the sales office and I hadn't seen him since. He had spent almost the entire time dealing with the fallout from Morag taking Max, Richie, and me hostage and murdering Joey. I felt like I had repeated the story to just about every member of the New York City Police Department and the Federal Bureau of Investigation. "Take it easy, there. You don't want a belly full of oyster juice spoiling the rest of the evening."

"Nothing could spoil this evening," he said. I hoped he was right. He leaned in and gave me a briny-tasting kiss. "So do you want to hear what I found out or not?" he asked, tired of my interruptions.

I snuggled in close to him in the booth that we were sitting in. "Shoot." I grabbed a hunk of the restaurant's famous garlic bread and shoved it into my mouth, relishing the taste of salt, garlic, and parsley that dotted the top of the toasted bread. I figured his brine breath would equal my garlic breath in intensity so we would cancel each other out.

"Well, Richie couldn't find his way out of a paper bag, but I guess you knew that. But we're still trying to figure out how Morag hooked up with Joey and Jose—who I presume knew each other from town—to get this green card thing going." He tilted his head back and inhaled another oyster. "I'm leaving that to the Feds and INS, though. I'm more interested in getting her for Jose's and Madeleine Cranston's murders."

"Have you found which building inspectors Richie was paying off?"

Crawford nodded. "Every single one. Richie gave everybody up."

"What happens to them?" I asked, biting off another chunk of garlic bread.

"Well for one, they lose their jobs. There are two, in particular, who are in deep . . ." he paused, thinking of the right word to use and eventually opting for the less offensive one, ". . . trouble."

"What happens to Richie?"

"Riviera Pointe is done, unless Leon can bail him out," he said, referencing Richie's father. "I'm not sure what kind of fines or jail time comes with a bribery conviction, so I don't know. That's all we've got right now. He's not the only developer to employ less than stellar construction practices in New York, so we can't get him there." He finished his beer and motioned to the passing waiter for another one. "Maybe you could ask my brother what the jail time is for a bribery conviction," he said, pointedly raising an eyebrow at me.

I giggled nervously. "That won't be necessary. I don't really care what happens to Richie." I ran my hand along his thigh. "What did Morag say about Madeleine Cranston?"

"Nothing."

"Nothing?"

"She's really pleading innocent on that one. I can't figure it out. She copped to the Joey murder . . ."

"As if she had a choice," I said, reminding him that she had two reliable witnesses on that front.

". . . and the Jose murder," he continued, "but she won't cop to Cranston's murder."

I thought for a moment. "Maybe because it's a capital offense?"

He shrugged. "Maybe."

Another thought crossed my mind. "Maybe because she didn't do it?"

"Maybe," he said more definitively.

I nodded and continued nodding as I stated, "But that's for the Feds to figure out?"

He nodded and continued nodding. "Yes." In other words:

don't give it another thought. He finished off the oysters just as his new beer was delivered.

"What was Madeleine Cranston doing at Riviera Pointe?"

He looked at me as if to say, "Isn't that obvious?"

I nodded. "Looking into the green card thing."

He pointed at me. "Bingo. The Feds were working the case with Immigration and Naturalization." He took a sip of his beer and then changed the subject entirely, startling me. "So, where's Hernan Escalante?" he asked casually.

I had a mouth full of garlic bread and took the opportunity to stay silent. I coughed a bit and then went with an exaggerated shrug.

"God, you are such a bad liar."

My eyes got wide. "Don't know where he is. No idea. Not a clue."

He moved away from me a little bit and looked at the ceiling, thinking. "OK. How about this? Hernan Escalante maybe should go to Twenty-six Federal Plaza"—the FBI headquarters in New York—"and tell them what he knows. Would that work?"

"He doesn't know anything," I blurted out, realizing too late that I had said too much. I shoved another hunk of garlic bread into my mouth.

Crawford looked at me and I was reminded of how intimidating he might be during an interrogation. "Here's what we're going to do: we're going to eat our dinner and then you're going to take me to him." I started to protest and he put his fingers to my lips. "No discussion. Nothing to discuss."

I took his fingers from my lips and squeezed them between my hands. "You have to promise me that nothing will happen to him."

"Ouch," he said, pulling his fingers away. He rubbed them. "I can't do that."

"You have to."

He thought for a moment, looking at the ceiling and exhaling loudly. "I can promise you that whatever happens, I will make sure that he is treated fairly and with respect."

I shook my head. "Not good enough."

"Alison, you know I'll do anything I can to help him."

"Better."

"That's the best I can do."

My fried clams came and I dug in. "After dinner."

"After dinner," he confirmed, finishing the garlic bread.

Bastard. That was mine.

Thirty-Eight

We made our way onto the dark campus, the road lit by the intermittent halogen lamps that cast a green glow over the main drive into the college. Crawford flashed his badge at one of the octogenarian guards and pulled through the narrow opening between the guard booth and the sidewalk. He slowed down and adjusted his rearview mirror.

"Looks like we've got company," he said.

My head swiveled around almost of its own accord. I saw the nondescript black car following at a safe distance.

"Turn back around," he said. "It's Goldenberg and Abreu."

"God, they are so annoying! They're always around. Except when I'm locked in a trunk or being held at gunpoint in the sales office at Riviera Pointe."

Crawford maneuvered into a spot in front of the main building, which housed just about every major office in the college: the president's office, the administrative offices, the professors' offices. It also served as the classroom building. And at the far end, right where we were parked, was the convent. Crawford threw the car into park and turned to me. "How are we going to do this?"

"Well, you can't come in with me," I said.

He threw his thumb over his shoulder, indicating the car in the spot behind us. "They will."

"They can't go into the convent."

He rolled his eyes. "They probably won't see it that way."

I opened the car door. "Then I'll tell them."

Goldenberg and Abreu were standing under the grand portico that fronted the building. "Ready?" Goldenberg asked.

"You can't come into the convent with me," I said, as defiantly as I could.

He held his ground. "If you give me twenty minutes, I can get a federal judge to say that I can."

Abreu looked at me and raised an eyebrow. I appealed to him as a Catholic, which I was convinced he would be, given his Portuguese heritage. He held up his hands. "I'm an atheist."

Great.

Crawford got out of the car and followed me up the steps to the front door of the building; I used my master key to let us all in, Crawford holding the door. We walked down the long hallway and to the bottom of the long, winding staircase that went to the upper floors of the building and the convent. I gave them all one last look. "Come on, guys. Give it a rest."

Goldenberg held his hand out. "Ladies first."

I trudged up the steps, not sure what I would find. Instead of taking the elevator with the three of them, I made them climb all the way up to the fifth floor, where I knew Sister Louise had stashed Hernan. Maybe if I could tire them out, they'd lose a little of the piss and vinegar that they had brought to this adventure.

It was dark on the floor and I felt around on the wall for a light switch. There was none. I looked down the hallway and saw a light coming out from under a door. The sounds of shrieking could be heard all the way down the hallway, reverberating off the marble floor. I saw all three grab for their guns—Crawford from his ankle, Abreu from the back of his pants, and Goldenberg from the holster on his hip. The three of them crept down the darkened hallway, me trailing Crawford and holding on to his belt loop so that I wouldn't lose him.

"Let go," he whispered.

I loosened my grip but kept my index finger in the back loop. We made our way down the hallway, none of us uttering a sound. Crawford and I made it there first and he tapped lightly but firmly on the door. "Detective Crawford, Fiftieth Precinct. Open the door."

There was a scuffle behind the door but it remained closed. Crawford backed up and, with my index finger still in his belt loop, kicked the door down. When it simultaneously splintered and opened, we were treated to the sight of three nuns—Sister Alphonse, Sister Louise, and Sister Catherine—all in their bonnets and bathrobes, and Hernan, seated at a card table.

Playing, it appeared, Texas Hold'em.

A vast mound of pennies sat in the middle of the table, as did a pile of cards. Hernan was frozen in place, his cards fanned out in front of him, his bandaged finger sticking straight out. Sister Alphonse—the Fonz—looked at Crawford.

"That was rather dramatic, dear. Was that necessary?" She took a long swig from her can of Sprite, adjusting her false teeth after taking the can from her lips.

Crawford sputtered a little bit and backed out of the room. I took my finger out of his pants. Nuns scare the crap out of Crawford. I don't know what happened to him as a kid, but he was clearly scarred.

Goldenberg entered the room and gave Hernan a steely look. "Mr. Escalante, I am Agent Goldenberg of the Federal Bureau of Investigation. You are under arrest for the murder of Agent Madeleine Cranston."

Hernan looked at me and paled.

Goldenberg turned to me. "And Dr. Bergeron, you are under arrest for obstruction of justice in the investigation of a murder." He turned to Abreu. "Agent Abreu, would you please take Dr. Bergeron into custody?"

When I had imagined Agent Abreu taking me into custody, the scenario had been a lot different. I was wearing Jean Naté and not much else and he was applying sunscreen to my alabaster shoulders. However, when Abreu took out his handcuffs I almost lost control of my bodily functions. Sister Alphonse stood up—all six feet of her—and stared down Abreu. Crawford was standing by the door, seemingly trying to figure out what to do. He let out a half-hearted, "hey," but that was all. We were definitely going to talk about that later.

The Fonz helped me out. "Put those away, young man." Straightened to her full height, her teeth slightly askew, she bore more than a slight resemblance to Rod Gilbert, my second favorite Ranger of all time. I had never noticed that before.

Abreu looked at her and shrank back a little bit. Atheist, my ass.

The Fonz adjusted her teeth again; they had a habit of slipping and making everything she said sound like a snake hissing. "Mr. Escalante took refuge in this convent because of a threat on his life."

Goldenberg rolled his eyes. "Oh, really?"

"Yes," she said, staring down Goldenberg. "Tell them, Mr. Escalante." She stared at him pointedly and I realized that they had rehearsed this moment during the time that he had been here.

"I came here of my own . . ." he said, searching for the right word. The Fonz mouthed "accord" and he repeated it. ". . . accord. I was looking for safe haven after having been threatened at the job site of Riviera Pointe."

Goldenberg threw his hands up. "So you came to the convent at St. Thomas University? On your own? You expect me to believe this crap?"

Sister Louise stood up. "Excuse you, Agent Goldenstein."

Sister Catherine, Hernan's legally blind floormate, looked around, unseeing. I made a mental note to ask Louise how she played cards if she couldn't see. "What's going on?"

Louise put a hand on her shoulder. "It's OK, Sister." Sister Louise stared at Agent Goldenberg. "So, Agent Goldenstein, Dr. Bergeron had nothing to do with his."

"Goldenberg."

"Goldenberg," she repeated, but I could tell she was thinking "whatever." "I'll have to ask you to leave."

Hernan stood, finally sure of what he needed to say and do. "I do have something to say."

The nuns, the agents, Crawford, and I stood there, staring at him. He knitted his hands together worriedly.

"I saw who murdered Agent Cranston."

Thirty-Nine

Who knew? Turns out that if you scratch the Feds' backs, they'll scratch yours.

But more on that later.

Hernan described a scene that none of us could have imagined: Class of '59 (and Hernan described him perfectly, down to his giant class ring and his letterman's jacket) driving along, talking on a cell phone, pulling into the parking lot of Riviera Point, and, as it turns out, up to no good. I don't think he ever imagined, though, that he would be facing manslaughter charges in the death of a federal agent. He corroborated Hernan's story, telling all, and hoping for leniency.

His goal was simple: to vandalize the building and equipment so much that construction would cease for the short term, until his injunction went before a judge. Hernan had been poking around after dark—amassing some concrete information on the building's code violations—the illuminated sales office just a few hundred feet to the north of where he was. He watched as O'Laughlin approached the office, dressed in black, a tire iron at his side. And then he watched as the man took the tire iron and raised it over his head, his goal to shatter the plate-glass windows that fronted the building—an act of pure vandalism and nothing else. Agent Cranston had come from around the side of the building—Hernan wasn't sure where she had come from or where she had been going—surprising O'Laughlin, whose raised tire iron came down on her head instead of through the plate glass.

Hernan's cry of surprise and horror had stopped O'Laughlin in his tracks, but Madeleine was surely already dead. Hernan said that her head had been bashed in, something that Crawford said had been verified by the medical examiner.

So why hadn't Hernan told me this earlier? He was terrified. O'Laughlin had seen him and chased him for a good number of blocks along the river, which is why Hernan had looked the way he did when he arrived at my house. Eventually, O'Laughlin gave up the chase and had stashed Madeleine in her car, trying to make the whole thing look like a bad car accident, or so Hernan surmised when I filled him in on where she had been found. Still reeling from the threats from the foreman—who knew that Hernan's intentions were not in the foreman's or Richie's best interests—he was now practically paralyzed by what he had just witnessed at the sales office.

He thought he could figure out a way to get this information to the authorities on his own without involving me further. That was kind of him, although he had involved three nuns, all of whom were just raring to take on the federal government if it so much as sneezed in their direction.

Hernan revealed all this to the Feds, who in turn filled in Crawford, who was kind enough to complete the tale for me.

O'Laughlin had spilled the beans as soon as he saw the Feds. He was on the hook for manslaughter and obstruction of justice and he was going to lose his view, just as he had anticipated. This wasn't the first time he had been in trouble, either. He had a domestic battery charge to go with a breaking and entering stemming from a dispute with a neighbor. A choir boy our Reginald O'Laughlin was not. He had severe anger management issues, which Crawford was sure would come up in court. And which his daughter, Daphne—apparently the dumbest receptionist ever to work on a Kraecker project—had confirmed.

I had met Amalia the day before at the coffee shop by the Lord's Bounty church and the relief etched on her face made me so happy that I could almost absolve myself of all the subterfuge I'd engaged in and illegal sleuthing I had done to protect her father. We talked a little bit about her upcoming senior year and how I wanted to introduce her to Sister Louise and the other professors in the nursing department so that she could get a feel for St. Thomas.

"Frankie's in a basketball tournament at the County Center this weekend," she said, blushing a little bit.

"Really?"

"Are you going?"

I thought for a moment. "Maybe I will." I gave her a hug. "I guess I'll see you there?"

She nodded and made her way to the door of the coffee shop, turning back and giving me a dazzling smile.

Crawford and I were on our way to the hockey game, delighted to be in each other's company and happy to put this whole mess behind us. We were on the escalator at the Garden and fortunately, because our seats were so good, we didn't have to go very far. The Garden escalators make me nauseous and Crawford knew it, so he kept a safe distance from me. We exited at our gate and walked down to our seats. Once seated, he told me the best news of all.

"Hernan's got himself instant citizenship, if all goes well and the conviction comes down. So does Alba. Amalia was born here, so that's not an issue," Crawford said.

Hence the back-scratching analogy. My eyes filled with tears. "Are you kidding me?"

"Goldenberg wasn't going to budge, but Abreu is going to make it happen," he said. He pinched me in the side. "Abreu, who, by the way, makes you act like a fourteen-year-old schoolgirl every time he's in the room."

I blushed deep red.

"I knew it," he said, getting a look at my rosy cheeks.

"I call him Agent Rico Suave in my head."

"I bet you do," he said, and flagged down the beer guy. "I didn't know you were into Latin guys."

"He's Portuguese."

"Same difference. Tall, dark, and handsome. That's all you need to know, huh?"

It was all in good fun but I leaned in and gave him an assurance kiss, just to remind him of how I felt. "Just like you, Crawford."

Satisfied, he handed me the two beers he had purchased, shoving the change from his transaction deep into his pockets. I handed him back his beer just in time for the lights to dim and for the ceremony for the '94 team to get under way. We stood, as did the rest of the fans in the Garden.

"You think they'll ever win another Cup?" Crawford asked.

"Only if these guys come out of retirement," I said, pointing to the players on the ice, who were now older than I by at least ten years.

Being at the Garden for this event was more exciting than I imagined. And being with Crawford made it even better. I knew that he was exhausted; he had worked for almost twenty-four hours straight. But instead of going home and directly to bed, he had come from work, picked me up, and driven me to the game. If I got less than eight hours sleep, I was impossible to be around, yet here he was, eight hours perhaps his total for the previous week. And he was with me, happy and totally engaged in what we were doing.

The game got under way and my beloved Rangers scored three goals in the first period, making me quite possibly the happiest woman on the planet. Until I spied Jack McManus out of the corner of my eye, standing in the aisle next to our seats, a stockily built bald man in a very expensive suit beside him.

My knees almost gave out as I realized who he was at the same time as the rest of our section. The collective cry of "Mess-ee-AY, Mess-ee-AY" went out through the Garden.

Jack shook hands with Crawford and leaned in. "We only have a minute, Alison, but I wanted to introduce you to Mark Messier."

I nearly went to my knees and Crawford obviously sensed this because he put his arm around my waist and hoisted me upright. I put my hand out and shook. "Nice to meet you," I said in a shaky voice.

When I replayed the scene in my head and when I relayed it to Max, it was much more dramatic and I think I even told her there was a marriage proposal in the mix, but in actuality, Mark Messier was congenial and gentlemanly before moving on down the stairs. Our time together was brief, but for me, meaningful. Jack turned around and winked at me, knowing that he had left a quivering mass of Jell-O in his wake.

Crawford turned to me. "You OK?"

I looked at him and broke into a huge smile. "I don't even know what to say."

Crawford smiled. "We should invite Mark Messier over more often."

You know what it's like when you meet your idol, your hero? Sometimes it surpasses your wildest dreams; other times, it's a giant disappointment. Mark Messier didn't stick around long enough to have either effect on me, but at the very least, it made for a good story.

After the game I stared out the window as we hurtled along the West Side Highway in Crawford's very clean and very sensible Volkswagen Passat station wagon. A solid car for a solid guy. I watched the different neighborhoods go by, getting grittier and more urban as we went north, getting more suburban and affluent again as we went farther north. We passed through the neighborhood in which St. Thomas resided, then crossed into Westchester, and finally arrived in Dobbs Ferry. I thought about the previous weeks, the night we had just had, the future that I hoped we would enjoy. When we pulled up in front of my house, I turned to Crawford.

He leaned in and gave me a long kiss. When I broke away, I put my hand to his cheek and looked at the bags under his eyes. "You look so tired."

He kissed me again. "Not that tired," he mumbled between kisses.

"You coming in?"

"Is that an invitation?"

"Best you're gonna get," I said and opened my car door. "But you've got to walk Trixie first."

"She's your dog," he whined. "And I'm so damn tired."

I started up the front walk. "OK. If you're going to be a huge baby about it," I said, holding open the door for him. Trixie ran out between my legs and greeted Crawford by jumping on him. "See? She wants to be with you," I said, laughing.

He gave me a look over his shoulder as he walked down the path to the street, Trixie at his heels. "Hey, is the push-up bra clean?"

"You know it."

"What about the Idaho T-shirt?"

"Uh, not so much."

"The thong?"

"Clean as a whistle."

"Excellent," he said, and he started down the street. I detected a little skip in his step as he watched Trixie run across my sleeping neighbors' lawns. "I'll be right back. Don't fall asleep."

There was no way that was going to happen. I went into the house and pulled off my coat.

The living room was dark when I entered, my attempts to program a light timer abandoned long ago. But I made out a little form curled up on one half of the couch. "Max? Is that you?" I asked.

She lifted her head and in the light that was thrown from the hallway, I took in her tearstained face, her tousled hair. "It's over for us," she said, a sob escaping from her throat.

I didn't have to ask and she didn't need to elaborate. Anyone could have seen this coming a mile away. I sat on the couch and she told me her story.

Here is an excerpt from FINAL EXAM — the next Murder 101 mystery from Maggie Barbieri—available soon in hardcover from Minotaur Books!

One

"I'm Mary Magdalene!"

Now that got my attention. I was leaning against a wall in one of the dorm's dining halls, scanning the crowd in a laconic fashion for anyone drinking an illegal substance and hoping I could get in on that action. We're a dry campus. And let me tell you, there are some people who teach here who just need to get lit.

I was bored silly. Until I saw one of my best friends in the world, Father Kevin McManus, school chaplain and all-around nice guy, cutting a rug to some Kanye West song with another chaperone, a member of the sociology department. Nancy Wei-neger was married, a mother of four, and about fifty years old. She favored the peasant-skirt-cum-clog look, and tonight she was also wearing a white cardigan sweater with, curiously, a lacy camisole underneath it. I had always thought of her as more of an Elisabeth, the proud mother of John the Baptist. It never would have crossed my mind that she fancied herself Mary Magdalene, a woman of (ahem) bad character, as the Bible says.

I don't read the Bible and I hardly ever go to church, but what seventeen-year-old, upon learning that the Bible boasted a pros-titute, hasn't sat up and taken notice? I heard it lo those many years ago and it had stuck with me ever since. And oh yes, I had highlighted every passage devoted to her. Because if the Bible has a hooker, well, I'm in.

I stood up a little straighter as Kevin turned in mid-gyration and looked at me, his eyes wide behind his tortoise-framed eye-glasses. Nancy was doing some kind of cross between a clog dance and the chicken dance and getting progressively closer to Kevin as the song built to a rap-flavored crescendo. We were at a post–spring break faculty mixer that has a history of being the most boring event to be held anywhere. Ever. But it's a com-mand performance and you can't just make a quick appearance and then duck out because the president, Mark Etheridge, thinks he's very clever and prepares awards for everyone, which he hands out only after the buffet dinner has been served. So, if you're not there to accept your "Worst Parallel Parker!" award, you'll hear about it. You can't get out of it by using an excuse— not even my old standby (diarrhea) because he's on to that one.

Nancy was working herself into a frenzy, so Kevin danced closer to me.

"Cut in," he said breathlessly.

I cupped a hand to my ear, faking deafness. "What?" I asked. "I can't hear you."

"Cut in," he said a little louder as Nancy grabbed his arm and dragged him back out into the middle of the floor.

I love to dance—in the privacy of my bedroom. There, I perform nightly. It's a one-woman show and the audience consists of my golden retriever, Trixie, and, I just learned, the prepubescent kid across the street. I caught him with binoculars the week before, peering through my second-story bedroom window. When confronted, he claimed to be concerned that I was having a seizure. But Kevin needed help, and being as he's the one who's usually bailing me out, I felt like I needed to repay the favor. I put down my glass of flat Diet Coke and disco-strutted onto the dance floor. I grabbed Kevin around the waist and spun him around because while he's quick and fit thanks to a childhood filled with Irish dancing and boxing lessons, he's also more of a flyweight to my bantamweight. And he's also a good three inches shorter than I am so that when we do dance together at school functions, I always lead. It's the curse of the tall girl. Or the bossy one. I can't decide which is more accurate.

As I prepared to get down to "Gold Digger," the mood, and song, changed abruptly and we found ourselves slow-dancing to "Wind Beneath My Wings," the top of Kevin's head grazing the bottom of my chin. He's one of my two best friends in this world, so nobody thought twice about seeing us in this terpsichorean clinch, yet I suddenly felt suitably uncomfortable and so we beat a hasty retreat from the dance floor—or middle of the dining hall, as the case may be—and into two open chairs at a small round table.

One of the reasons I love Kevin is because he's an inveterate gossip. The minute we sat down, he leaned in conspiratorially. "So, I guess you heard what happened to Wayne Brookwell?"

I shook my head. "Nope." Unless Kevin tells me, I have no idea what goes on on campus. I flagged down a passing student who was a server for the party and probably getting either community service hours or work study credit for her time. I asked her for two Diet Cokes. "But before we get to that, what's with you and Nancy Weineger? Or should I say, 'Mary Magdalene'?"

Kevin shook his head, clearly embarrassed. "She's one of those wacky Catholics who fall in love with priests. I've seen it a thousand times."

He had? This was a new phenomenon to me. I'd heard of "Fr. What-a-Waste"—the handsome priest who devotes himself to Christ rather than a woman—but I didn't see Kevin in that role. My incredibly handsome boyfriend had once confessed to thinking about becoming a priest. Him? He would have been the ultimate Fr. What-a-Waste. Kevin? Not so much. "Explain."

"Nothing to explain," he said, taking a sip of the soda that had been delivered to our table. "The collar turns some people on." He was pretty matter-of-fact, confident that his collar was setting libidos ablaze, so I took him at his word.

"Interesting." I poked him in the ribs with my elbow. "Ever think of taking her up on it?" I asked, only half joking.

He gave me a horrified look. "No!" He smoothed down the front of his black clerical shirt. "I have to be careful with these kinds of situations. You know that."

"I do know that," I said. "Just joking, Kev."

"Besides," he said, "you know the archdiocese isn't my biggest fan."

I knew that, too. Kevin had been sent to St. Thomas after several complaints from parishioners at the church in which he had been installed prior to this job. Something about repeated sermons about the cardinal and his champagne tastes, which was fine, if said cardinal wasn't closing churches and parochial schools with wild abandon due to lack of funds. The archdiocese figured that sticking him at a Catholic college with a small enrollment and a host of blind and deaf nuns was better than having him preach the Gospel at a thriving parish. So far, Kevin had made it work. And he had made my teaching here that much more enjoyable through our delightful, yet unorthodox, friendship.

He looked around and leaned in again. "So, Wayne Brookwell?"

"Remind me who he is again?" I drank my second flat Diet Coke and made a face. "This would be much better with a shot of rum." Unless I broke into the nurse's office and got us all a shot of Robitussin, flat Diet Coke would have to do.

"He was the resident director over at Siena Hall."

I filed through my brain, trying to remember him. "Tall? Gangly? Just misses at handsome?"

Kevin did a finger gun at me. "Bingo." He looked around again, obviously afraid of being overheard. But "Wind Beneath My Wings" was reaching its crescendo and I could barely hear him, never mind the people standing at least five feet behind us. "He's gone. His room's cleaned out, and he didn't let anyone know he was leaving. Dean Merrimack has no idea where he is or why he left."

Merrimack was the director of student housing and a general douche nozzle, a word I had heard one of my students using. I tried it out in my head and kind of liked the way it fit. "Well, I can't imagine that RD is that fulfilling of a job. Maybe he got something else," I said, not really caring what had happened to Wayne Brookwell or why he left so unceremoniously. "Maybe he got deployed?" I said. "Didn't I see him in a uniform?"

"Yes, as a limo driver," Kevin said. "He had a side job driving executives to the airport."

"Are you even allowed to do that?" Maybe moonlighting could solve my problem of funding a vacation to France. I mulled over a second career as a barista until Kevin brought me back to the conversation by waving his hand in front of my face. I refocused.

"What are they going to do about another RD? Once spring break is over, there's only five weeks left for the semester."

Kevin shrugged. "I have no idea. I know that a couple of the guys who live in the dorm drive limos, too, to make extra money." He looked around the room, taking in the styles of our colleagues and commenting on their dance moves. "I think this whole thing with Wayne is extremely suspicious," he said pointedly after he had finished dance-hall reconnaissance, raising an eyebrow at me.

I stared back at him. "Oh, no you don't," I said, finally seeing where he was going with this conversation. "My sleuthing days are over."

"But where did he go? Aren't you the least bit interested?" he asked, working himself up to the point where he had to down his Diet Coke in one swallow to quench his thirst.

"Couldn't care less." The only reason I knew who Wayne Brookwell was that he bore a passing resemblance to my cousin Armand—quite the cheesemaker and cocksman according to my very proud, and very late mother—from Baie Ste. Paul in Quebec. Other than that, I wouldn't have known him from Adam.

Something over my shoulder caught Kevin's eye and he sat up straight. "Pull yourself together. It's Etheridge."

Mark Etheridge, in addition to bring the president of our college, is also not my biggest fan. He's *mezzo mezzo* on Kevin because of Kevin's lackadaisical attitude toward the pomp and circumstance of Catholicism but has a certain amount of respect for him because he's a priest. Me, I'm just a nontenured professor who's been involved in a few too many skirmishes with the law, mostly stemming from my being involved in a few too many murder investigations. See? Nothing serious. I felt Mark's presence behind me and my back straightened instinctively, too.

"Father. Dr. Bergeron," he said by way of a greeting.

I turned in my chair. "Hello, President Etheridge," I said, trying my best to hide my disdain. What president of a school with a mere twelve hundred students insists on being called "President"? Mark Etheridge, that's who. He and I have a tenuous relationship at best; at worst, we're archenemies, just like in a comic book. I'm "Big Tall Girl" and he's "Little Short Man" and we engage in mortal combat every so often. I still don't have tenure and I'm betting he's behind it because even though my direct boss, Sister Mary, isn't really crazy about my off-hours pursuits—basically, murder investigations—she thinks I'm a good teacher. And not for nothing, but my doctoral dissertation was a masterpiece, if I do say so myself. That should count for something. But Etheridge doesn't like the body count and I don't like that he's just not very nice to me. I remained seated so that I wouldn't tower over him.

"When you get a moment, Dr. Bergeron, I'd like to see you in my office," he said, turning on his heel and walking away.

I guessed that meant now.

Kevin watched in wide-eyed amazement. "Wow. That was rude, even for Etheridge." He pushed his chair back and stood. "You'd better go. Do you think this has to do with tenure?"

I took one last sip of liquid courage—flat Diet Coke—and stood. "I doubt it." I smoothed my skirt and headed across the dance floor. I called back to Kevin, "Wish me luck!"

He crossed his fingers and held them in the air. "Good luck!"

I didn't realize just how badly I would need it.

Two

I followed close on Etheridge's heels to his office in the Adminis-
tration Building. When I got there, Sister Mary was there as was
Dean Merrimack, for whom I had decided "douche nozzle" was
way too kind a moniker. Etheridge waved generously toward the
only open seat across from his desk. Sister Mary kept her eyes on
her hands while Merrimack stared at me with his rat eyes as if I
were a piece of cheese. I sat, placing myself as close as I could to
the edge of the chair without falling off. This wasn't about tenure
and that was painfully obvious.

"I guess you're wondering why I asked you here on a Friday evening," Etheridge said, his eyes glinting behind his Teddy Roosevelt–style horn rims. Out the window behind his head, I could see the bones of a new dorm taking shape.

I stared back at him until it became obvious that I was going to remain silent.

He harrumphed a bit and rearranged himself in his chair. "Well, as you may or may not know, Wayne Brookwell, the resident director at Siena dorm, has unceremoniously left his position."

I continued staring back at him, not sure why I was hearing about Wayne Brookwell not once, but twice, in the same evening. I could barely pick the guy out of a lineup but everyone seemed very concerned about his whereabouts. And I suspected that I should probably be more concerned about his disappearance, too.

"And that, Dr. Bergeron, is where you come in," Dean Merrimack said, close to orgasm in his chair.

"Oh, my sleuthing days are over," I said, as much to convince myself as to convince them.

Etheridge gave me a withering look. "We're not interested in your sleuthing skills, Alison."

I slid a little closer to the edge of my chair, close to tipping it over. "Then why am I here?"

Etheridge looked down at the desk calendar that took up most of his desk and counted the number of weeks left in the semester. "We have five weeks left in the semester, Alison, and we need someone to take Resident Director Brookwell's place until school ends."

I looked over at Sister Mary, who continued to stare at her hands. Her complexion flushed pink all the way up to the hairline of her sensible, gray permanent. Panic was starting to take hold and I felt a little short of breath. "No, I can't . . . ," I said, my voice wavering.

"Yes you can. You must." Etheridge pushed back from his desk. "So, that's settled. Shall we go back to the party?"

"No, we should not go back to the party!" I exclaimed, jumping up from my chair, surprising everyone. The force of my ejection sent the chair flying backward and everyone in the room regarded it with horror. "I have a life. I have a dog. My best friend is going through a horrible separation from her husband and living with me. I have a boyfriend," I said, realizing too late how inane that sounded. "I cannot . . . ," I said, grabbing the edge of Etheridge's desk, "move into the Siena dorm."

Etheridge gave me a steely look. "You can. And you will." He came out from behind his desk and stood before his floor-to-ceiling bookcases. I had once made Kevin a bet that the bookcases only housed decorative spines, and not real books. I suddenly had an urge to race over and pull one of the books down just to check, but I suspected that action wouldn't be a big hit. "You can begin to move your things in this weekend."

"No, I can't," I said.

Etheridge moved closer to me and the air got uncomfortably warm in the dark-paneled room. I towered over him by a good four inches. "Dr. Bergeron, your tenure—or lack thereof—here has been marred by your 'sleuthing' as you call it," he said, finger-quoting, "and the people who love this university are not pleased." We were now just a few inches apart, close-talking to one another. "And by the university, I mean the board. And our donors. One dead body was one thing, but the untimely death of your former husband?" I heard Mary mutter a prayer under her breath for my murdered ex. "That was just too much, even though it had nothing to do with you. You spend too much time in pursuits other than those required of an academic. So being on campus full-time should allow you to focus entirely on St. Thomas, your courses, and your students."

"I love this university!" I protested. Just because a dead student had once been found in the trunk of my car and my ex-husband had been dismembered in my kitchen didn't mean that I didn't love St. Thomas. After all, I had graduated from here years before. They could question my judgment, but they couldn't question my loyalty to the school. "And is anyone concerned about what happened to Wayne?" I asked, sounding way more familiar with him than I was.

"We're looking into his disappearance," Merrimack replied.

"I hope so," I said. Still, he didn't sound terribly concerned, which gave me pause. "Did you call the police?"

Etheridge and Merrimack exchanged a look that could only be described as "fraught," but with what, I had no idea.

Etheridge started for the door, not answering my question. "As for your *boyfriend*?" he said, with a sneer. "Detective Crawford, I presume?" His hand was on the knob and Merrimack was right behind him. "He'll just have to wait."

I ran over all of the options in my head and concluded that I didn't have any. I decided to go with the path of least resistance with one minor caveat. "Fine. But the dog's coming with me." I straightened my spine and attempted to sound unyielding. I really didn't have anything to bargain with but I hoped Etheridge had a heart.

Merrimack decided to exert his influence at that moment. "We don't allow animals on campus."

If that were the case, I thought, you'd be out of a job, Rat Boy. I wisely kept my mouth shut and appealed to Etheridge. "Listen, she's a wonderful animal and very docile. I can't leave her at the house."

Etheridge considered this and decided to confine his cruelty merely to making me move in. "The dog can come."

I heard Mary let out a sigh of relief, for what I wasn't sure.

I hadn't pegged her as a dog lover, but you never know. I also knew that she wasn't mute, though she had done nothing to disprove that during this meeting.

Etheridge opened the door and gestured that I should leave. He smiled as I walked past him and into his secretary's area, vacant at this time of day. "I think this will work out very nicely. Consider it extra credit." He chuckled. "Dean Merrimack will give you the Code of Conduct folder and all of the other necessary information you'll need to execute your tasks. We'll expect you to be ensconced in your suite by Monday morning, latest."

"Code of Conduct?" I asked.

Merrimack rubbed his rat hands together. "Yes. For instance, coeducational visitation ends at eleven P.M."

My heart sank. That was going to put a serious crimp in my relationship with Crawford.

"And we're, of course, a dry campus."

I already knew that, obviously, and I didn't want to hear anything else. I did know that I was going to go home and mainline Ketel One like an addict on their way to rehab. I looked impassively at Merrimack and held out my hands. "Keys, please?"

He dropped an ancient-looking set of keys into my palm. "The black key is the front door and the other key is to your suite. The one with the red dot on it is the school master key. It is imperative that you do not lose that one especially."

Got it, chief. Don't lose the master key. It was a wonder they paid me a salary, so handicapped did they consider me. I knew that "suite" was probably a very misleading term to describe my new accommodations, so I didn't get my hopes up. I had seen one of the resident director's quarters once, twenty years earlier when I was a student. I was sure things hadn't changed dramatically since that time.

I walked out into the hallway outside of Etheridge's office cursing a blue streak in my head. I stopped by my office and picked up my bag, papers spilling out and reminding me that my spring break was supposed to have been spent grading. But now I was moving, and with the lack of grading I had done, I was up the creek.

Before I left my office, I clicked on the school intranet and looked up Wayne Brookwell. There was a picture and a bio. He was exactly who I thought he was—skinny, with a square jaw and eyes just a little too closely set. His mouth hung open slightly in the picture, giving me the impression that he was an habitual mouth breather. Just missed at being handsome, as I had reported to Kevin. He was the guy I would have dated in college, while Max, my best friend, would have dated his dumber, yet much better looking, roommate. I read his bio: "Wayne Brookwell graduated from Syracuse University with a degree in art history," I read. That degree made him perfectly suited to a life as a resident director because, God knows, without a master's degree, he wasn't getting a job anywhere outside of the souvenir shop at the Metropolitan Museum of Art. No offense to art history majors. The bio was brief, but to the point. It said that Wayne was twenty-six but didn't make any mention of his moonlighting career as a limousine driver. I stared at his picture. "We've never met, Mr. Brookwell, but you've ruined my life. I hope you're happy."

He stared back at me, in all of his slack-jawed awesomeness.

"Where did you go, Wayne?" I asked, staring at the picture for a few more minutes. When Wayne didn't answer, I printed out his picture and folded it up so that it would fit in the front of my briefcase. I turned off the computer and headed home to give the news to my new roommate, Max, that I was moving out for several weeks.

And to let my dog, Trixie, know that we had a new home.

And to let Crawford know that his level of sexual frustration—at a fever pitch since I had inherited Max as a roommate—was about to increase tenfold.